CHILDREN'S CLASSICS

The Jungle Book

RUDYARD KIPLING

The Jungle Book

PARRAGON

The Jungle Book
A Parragon Classic

This is a Siena Book
Siena is an imprint of Parragon

This edition published in 1999 by
Parragon
13 Whiteladies Road
Clifton
Bristol BS8 1PB

Printed and bound in the UK

PREFACE

The demands made by a work of this nature upon the generosity of specialists are very numerous, and the Editor would be wanting in all title to the generous treatment he has received were he not willing to make the fullest possible acknowledgement of his indebtedness.

His thanks are due in the first place to the scholarly and accomplished Bahadur Shah, baggage elephant 174 on the Indian Register, who, with his amiable sister Pudmini, most courteously supplied the history of "Toomai of the Elephants" and much of the information contained in "Her Majesty's Servants". The adventures of Mowgli were collected at various times and in various places from a multitude of informants, most of whom desire to preserve the strictest anonymity. Yet, at this distance, the Editor feels at liberty to thank a Hindu gentleman of the old rock, an esteemed resident of the upper slopes of Jakko, for his convincing if somewhat caustic estimate of the national characteristics of his caste—the Presbytes. Sahi, a savant of infinite research and industry, a member of the recently disbanded Seeonee Pack, and an artist well known at most of the local fairs of Southern India, where his muzzled dance with his master attracts the youth, beauty, and culture of many villages, have contributed most valuable data on people, manners, and customs. These have been freely drawn upon, in the stories of "Tiger! Tiger!", "Kaa's Hunting", and "Mowgli's Brothers". For the outlines of "Rikki-tikki-tavi" the Editor stands indebted to one of the leading herpetologists of Upper India, a fearless and independent investigator who, resolving "not to live but know", lately sacrificed his life through over-application to the study of our Eastern Thanatophidia. A happy accident of travel enabled the Editor, when a passenger on the *Empress of India,* to be of some slight assistance to a fellow-passenger. How richly his poor services were repaid, readers of "The White Seal" may judge for themselves.

R.K.

CHAPTER 1

MOWGLI'S BROTHERS

Now Chil the Kite brings home the night
  That Mang the Bat sets free—
The herds are shut in byre and hut,
  For loosed till dawn are we.
This is the hour of pride and power,
  Talon and tush and claw.
Oh, dear the call!—Good hunting all
  That keep the Jungle Law!

Night-Song in the Jungle.

It was seven o'clock of a very warm evening in the Seeonee hills when Father Wolf woke up from his day's rest, scratched himself, yawned, and spread out his paws one after the other to get rid of the sleepy feeling in their tips. Mother Wolf lay with her big grey nose dropped across her four tumbling, squealing cubs, and the moon shone into the mouth of the cave where they all lived. "Augrh!" said Father Wolf, "it is time to hunt again;" and he was going to spring downhill when a little shadow with a bushy tail crossed the threshold and whined: "Good luck go with you. O Chief of the Wolves; and good luck and strong white teeth go with the noble children, that they may never forget the hungry in this world."

It was the jackal—Tabaqui, the Dish-licker—and the wolves of India despise Tabaqui because he runs about making mischief, and telling tales, and eating rags and pieces of leather from the village rubbish-heaps. But they are afraid of him too, because Tabaqui, more than anyone else in the Jungle, is apt to go mad, and then he forgets that he was ever afraid of any one, and runs through the forest biting everything in his way. Even the tiger runs and hides when little Tabaqui goes mad, for madness is the most disgraceful thing that can overtake a wild creature. We call it hydro-phobia, but they call it *dewanee*—the madness—and run.

"Enter, then, and look," said Father Wolf stiffly; "but there is no food here."

"For a Wolf, no," said Tabaqui; "but for so mean a person as myself a dry bone is a good feast. Who are we, the *Gidur-log* [the Jackal-People], to pick and choose?" He scuttled to the back of the cave, where he found the bone of a buck with some meat on it, and sat cracking the end merrily.

"All thanks for this good meal," he said, licking his lips. "How beautiful are the noble children! How large are their eyes! And so young too! Indeed, indeed, I might have remembered that the children of Kings are men from the beginning."

Now, Tabaqui knew as well as any one else that there is nothing so unlucky as to compliment children to their faces; and it pleased him to see Mother and Father Wolf look uncomfortable.

Tabaqui sat still, rejoicing in the mischief that he had made: then he said spitefully:

"Shere Khan, the Big One, has shifted his hunting-grounds. He will hunt among these hills for the next moon, so he has told me."

Shere Khan was the tiger who lived near Waingunga River, twenty miles away.

"He has no right!" Father Wolf began angrily—"By the Law of the Jungle he has no right to change his quarters without due warning. He will frighten every head of game within ten miles, and I—I have to kill for two, these days."

"His mother did not call him Lungri [the Lame One] for nothing," said Mother Wolf quietly. "He has been lame in one foot from his birth. That is why he has only killed cattle. Now the villagers of the Waingunga are angry with him, and he has come here to make *our* villagers angry. They will scour the Jungle for him when he is far away, and we and our children must run when the grass is set alight. Indeed, we are very grateful to Shere Khan!"

"Shall I tell him of your gratitude?" said Tabaqui.

"Out!" snapped Father Wolf. "Out and hunt with thy master. Thou hast done harm enough for one night."

"I go," said Tabaqui quietly. "Ye can hear Shere Khan below in the thickets. I might have saved myself the message."

Father Wolf listened, and below in the valley that ran down to a little river, he heard the dry, angry, snarly, singsong whine of a tiger who has caught nothing and does not care if all the Jungle knows it.

"The fool!" said Father Wolf. "To begin a night's work with that noise! Does he think that our buck are like his fat Waingunga bullocks?"

"H'sh! It is neither bullock nor buck he hunts tonight," said Mother Wolf. "It is man." The whine had changed to a sort of humming purr that seemed to come from every quarter of the compass. It was the noise that bewilders woodcutters and gipsies sleeping in the open, and makes them run sometimes into the very mouth of the tiger.

"Man!" said Father Wolf, showing all his white teeth. "Faugh! Are there not enough beetles and frogs in the tanks that he must eat Man, and on our ground too?"

The Law of the Jungle, which never orders anything without a reason, forbids every beast to eat Man except when he is killing to show his children how to kill, and then he must hunt outside the hunting-grounds of his pack or tribe. The real reason for this is that man-killing means, sooner or later, the arrival of white men on elephants, with guns, and hundreds of brown men with gongs and rockets and torches. Then everybody in the Jungle suffers. The reason the beasts give among themselves is that Man is the weakest and most defenceless of all living things, and it is unsportsmanlike to touch him. They say too—and it is true—than man-eaters become mangy, and lose their teeth.

The purr grew louder, and ended in the full-throated "Aarh!" of the tiger's charge.

Then there was a howl—an untigerish howl—from Shere Khan. "He has missed," said Mother Wolf. "What is it?"

Father Wolf ran out a few paces and heard Shere Khan muttering and mumbling savagely, as he tumbled about in the scrub.

"The fool has had no more sense than to jump at a woodcutter's camp-fire, and has burned his feet," said Father Wolf, with a grunt. "Tabaqui is with him."

"Something is coming uphill," said Mother Wolf, twitching one ear. "Get ready."

The bushes rustled a little in the thicket, and Father Wolf dropped with his haunches under him, ready for his leap. Then, if you had been watching, you would have seen the most wonderful thing in the world—the wolf checked in mid-spring. He made his bound before he saw what it was he was jumping at, and then he tried to stop himself. The result was that he shot up straight into the air for four or five feet, landing almost where he left ground.

"Man!" he snapped. "A man's cub. Look!"

Directly in front of him, holding on by a low branch, stood a naked brown baby who could just walk—as soft and as dimpled a little atom as ever came to a wolf's cave at night. He looked up into Father Wolf's face, and laughed.

"Is that a man's cub?" said Mother Wolf. "I have never seen one. Bring it here."

A wolf accustomed to moving his own cubs can, if necessary, mouth an egg without breaking it, and though Father Wolf's jaws closed right on the child's back not a tooth even scratched the skin, as he laid it down among the cubs.

"How little! How naked, and—how bold!" said Mother Wolf softly. The baby was pushing his way between the cubs to get close to the warm hide. "*Ahai!* He is taking his meal with the others. And so this is a man's cub. Now, was there ever a wolf that could boast of a man's cub among her children?"

"I have heard now and again of such a thing, but never in our Pack or in my time," said Father Wolf. "He is altogether without hair, and I could kill him with a touch of my foot. But see, he looks up and is not afraid."

The moonlight was blocked out of the mouth of the cave, for Shere Khan's great square head and shoulders were thrust into the entrance. Tabaqui, behind him, was squeaking: "My lord, my lord, it went in here!"

"Shere Khan does us great honour," said Father Wolf,

but his eyes were very angry. "What does Shere Khan need?"

"My quarry. A man's cub went this way," said Shere Khan. "Its parents have run off. Give it to me."

Shere Khan had jumped at a woodcutter's camp-fire, as Father Wolf had said, and was furious from the pain of his burned feet. But Father Wolf knew that the mouth of the cave was too narrow for a tiger to come in by. Even where he was, Shere Khan's shoulders and forepaws were cramped for want of room, as a man's would be if he tried to fight in a barrel.

"The Wolves are a free people," said Father Wolf. "They take orders from the Head of the Pack, and not from any striped cattle-killer. The man's cub is ours—to kill if we choose."

"Ye choose and ye do not choose! What talk is this of choosing? By the bull that I killed, am I to stand nosing into your dog's den for my fair dues? It is I, Shere Khan, who speak!"

The tiger's roar filled the cave with thunder. Mother Wolf shook herself clear of the cubs and sprang forward, her eyes, like to green moons in the darkness, facing the blazing eyes of Shere Khan.

"And it is I, Raksha [The Demon], who answer. The man's cub is mine, Lungri—mine to me! He shall not be killed. He shall live to run with the Pack and to hunt with the Pack; and in the end, look you, hunter of little naked cubs—frog-eater—fish-killer—he shall hunt *thee*! Now get hence, or by the Sambhur that I killed (*I* eat no starved cattle), back thou goest to thy mother, burned beast of the Jungle, lamer than ever thou camest into the world! Go!"

Father Wolf looked amazed. He had almost forgotten

the days when he won Mother Wolf in fair fight from five other wolves, when she ran in the Pack and was not called The Demon for compliment's sake. Shere Khan might have faced Father Wolf, but he could not stand up against Mother Wolf, for he knew that where he was she had all the advantage of the ground, and would fight to the death. So he backed out of the cave-mouth growling, and when he was clear he shouted:-

"Each dog barks in his own yard! We will see what the Pack will say to this fostering of man-cubs. The cub is mine, and to my teeth he will come in the end, O bush-tailed thieves!"

Mother Wolf threw herself down panting among the cubs, and Father Wolf said to her gravely:-

"Shere Khan speaks this much truth. The cub must be shown to the Pack. Wilt thou still keep him, Mother?"

"Keep him!" she gasped. "He came naked, by night, alone and very hungry; yet he was not afraid! Look, he has pushed one of my babes to one side already. And that lame butcher would have killed him and would have run off to the Waingunga while the villagers here hunted through all our lairs in revenge! Keep him? Assuredly I will keep him. Lie still, little frog. O thou Mowgli—for Mowgli the frog I will call thee—the time will come when thou wilt hunt Shere Khan as he has hunted thee."

"But what will our Pack say?" said Father Wolf.

The Law of the Jungle lays down very clearly that any wolf may, when he marries, withdraw from the Pack he belongs to; but as soon as his cubs are old enough to stand on their feet he must bring them to the Pack Council, which is generally held once a month at full moon, in order that the other wolves may identify them.

After that inspection the cubs are free to run where they please, and until they have killed their first buck no excuse is accepted if a grown wolf of the Pack kills one of them. The punishment is death where the murderer can be found; and if you think for a minute you will see that this must be so.

Father Wolf waited till his cubs could run a little, and then on the night of the Pack Meeting took them and Mowgli and Mother Wolf to the Council Rock—a hilltop covered with stones and boulders where a hundred wolves could hide. Akela, the grey Lone Wolf who led all the Pack by strength and cunning, lay out full length on his rock, and below him sat forty or more wolves of every size and colour, from badger-coloured veterans who could handle a buck alone, to young black three-year-olds who thought they could. The Lone Wolf had led them for a year now. He had fallen twice into a wolf-trap in his youth, and once he had been beaten and left for dead; so he knew the manners and customs of men. There was very little talking at the Rock. The cubs tumbled over each other in the centre of the circle where their mothers and fathers sat, and now and again a senior wolf would go quietly up to a cub, look at him carefully, and return to his place on noiseless feet. Sometimes a mother would push her cub far out into the moonlight, to be sure that he had not been overlooked. Akela from his rock would cry: "Ye know the Law—ye know the Law. Look well, O Wolves!" and the anxious mothers would take up the call: "Look—look well, O Wolves!"

At last—and Mother Wolf's neck-bristles lifted as the time came—Father Wolf pushed 'Mowgli the Frog', as they called him, into the centre, where he sat laughing and playing with some pebbles that glistened in the moonlight.

Akela never raised his head from his paws, but went on with the monotonous cry: "Look well!" A muffled roar came up from the rocks—the voice of Shere Khan crying: "The cub is mine. Give him to me. What have the Free People to do with a man's cub?" Akela never twitched his ears: all he said was: "Look well, O Wolves! What have the Free People to do with the orders of any save the Free People? Look well!"

There was a chorus of deep growls, and a young wolf in his fourth year flung back Shere Khan's question to Akela: "What have the Free People to do with a man's cub?" Now, the Law of the Jungle lays down that if there is any dispute as to the right of a cub to be accepted by the Pack, he must be spoken for by at least two members of the Pack who are not his father and mother.

"Who speaks for this cub?" said Akela. "Among the Free People who speaks?" There was no answer, and Mother Wolf got ready for what she knew would be her last fight, if things came to fighting.

Then the only other creature who is allowed at the Pack Council—Baloo, the sleepy brown bear who teaches the wolf-cubs the Law of the Jungle: old Baloo, who can come and go where he pleases because he eats only nuts and roots and honey—rose up on his hindquarters and grunted.

"The man's cub—the man's cub?" he said. "*I* speak for the man's cub. There is no harm in a man's cub. I have no gift of words, but I speak the truth. Let him run with the Pack, and be entered with the others. I myself will teach him."

"We need yet another," said Akela. "Baloo has

spoken, and he is our teacher for the young cubs. Who speaks besides Baloo?"

A black shadow dropped down into the circle. It was Bagheera the Black Panther, inky black all over, but with the panther markings showing up in certain lights like the pattern of watered silk. Everybody knew Bagheera, and nobody cared to cross his path; for he was as cunning as Tabaqui, as bold as the wild buffalo, and as reckless as the wounded elephant. But he had a voice as soft as wild honey dripping from a tree, and a skin softer than down.

"O Akela, and ye the Free People," he purred, "I have no right in your assembly; but the Law of the Jungle says that if there is a doubt which is not a killing matter in regard to a new cub, the life of that cub may be bought at a price. And the Law does not say who may or may not pay that price. Am I right?"

"Good! good!" said the young wolves, who are always hungry. "Listen to Bagheera. The cub can be bought for a price. It is the Law."

"Knowing that I have no right to speak here, I ask your leave."

"Speak then," cried twenty voices.

"To kill a naked cub is shame. Besides, he may make better sport for you when he is grown. Baloo has spoken on his behalf. Now to Baloo's word I will add one bull, and a fat one, newly killed, not half a mile from here, if ye will accept the man's cub according to the Law. Is it difficult?"

There was a clamour of scores of voices, saying: "What matter? He will die in the winter rains. He will scorch in the sun. What harm can a naked frog do us? Let him run with the Pack. Where is the bull, Bagheera? Let him be accepted." And then came Akela's deep bay, crying: "Look well—look well, O Wolves!"

Mowgli was still deeply interested in the pebbles and he did not notice when the wolves came and looked at him one by one. At last they all went down the hill for the dead bull, and only Akela, Bagheera, Baloo, and Mowgli's own wolves were left. Shere Khan roared still in the night, for he was very angry that Mowgli had not been handed over to him.

"Ay, roar well," said Bagheera, under his whiskers; "for the time comes when this naked thing will make thee roar to another tune, or I know nothing of Man."

"It was well done," said Akela. "Men and their cubs are very wise. He may be a help in time."

"Truly, a help in time of need; for none can hope to lead the Pack for ever," said Bagheera.

Akela said nothing. He was thinking of the time that comes to every leader of every pack when his strength goes from him and he gets feebler and feebler, till at last he is killed by the wolves and a new leader comes up—to be killed in his turn.

"Take him away," he said to Father Wolf, "and train him as befits one of the Free People."

And that is how Mowgli was entered into the Seeonee Wolf-Pack at the price of a bull and Baloo's good word. Now you must be content to skip ten or eleven whole years, and only guess at all the wonderful life that Mowgli led among the wolves, because if it were written out it would fill ever so many books. He grew up with the cubs, though they, of course, were grown wolves almost before he was a child, and Father Wolf taught him his business, and the meaning of things in the Jungle, till every rustle in the grass, every breath of the warm night air, every note of the owls above his head, every scratch of a bat's claws as it roosted for a while in a tree, and every splash of every little fish jumping in a pool, meant just as much to him as the work of his office means to a business man. When he was not learning, he sat out in the sun and slept, and ate and went to sleep again; when he felt dirty or hot he swam in the forest pools; and when he wanted honey (Baloo told him that honey and nuts were just as pleasant to eat as raw meat) he climbed up for it, and that Bagheera showed him how to do. Bagheera would lie out on a branch and call, "Come along, Little Brother," and at first Mowgli would cling like the sloth, but afterwards he would fling himself through the branches almost as boldly as the grey ape. He took his place at the Council Rock, too, when the Pack met, and there he discovered that if he stared hard at any wolf, the wolf would be forced to drop his eyes, and so he used to stare for fun. At other times he would pick the long thorns out of the pads of his friends, for wolves suffer terribly from thorns and burrs in their coats. He would go down the hillside into the cultivated lands by night, and look very curiously at the villagers in their huts, but he had a mistrust of men because Bagheera showed him a square box with a drop-gate so cunningly hidden in the Jungle that he nearly walked into it, and told him that it was a trap. He loved better than anything else to go with Bagheera into the dark warm heart of the forest, to sleep all through the drowsy day, and at night to see how Bagheera did his killing. Bagheera killed right and left as he felt hungry, and so did Mowgli—with one exception. As soon as he was old enough to understand things, Bagheera told him that he must never touch cattle because he had been bought into the Pack at the price of a bull's life. "All the Jungle is thine," said Bagheera, "and thou canst kill everything that thou art strong enough to kill; but for the sake of the bull that bought thee thou must never kill or eat any cattle young or old. That is the Law of the Jungle." Mowgli obeyed faithfully.

And he grew and grew strong as a boy must grow who does not know that he is learning any lessons, and who has nothing in the world to think of except things to eat.

Mother Wolf told him once or twice that Shere Khan was not a creature to be trusted, and that some day he must kill Shere Khan; but though a young wolf would have remembered that advice every hour, Mowgli forgot it because he was only a boy—though he would have called himself a wolf if he had been able to speak in any human tongue.

Shere Khan was always crossing his path in the Jungle, for as Akela grew older and feebler the lame tiger had come to be great friends with the younger wolves of the Pack, who followed him for scraps, a thing that Akela would never have allowed if he had dared to push his authority to the proper bounds. Then Shere Khan would flatter them and wonder that such fine young hunters were content to be led by a dying wolf and a man's cub. "They tell me," Shere Khan would say, "that at Council ye dare not look him between the eyes;" and the young wolves would growl and bristle.

Bagheera, who had eyes and ears everywhere, knew something of this, and once or twice he told Mowgli in so many words that Shere Khan would kill him some day; and Mowgli would laugh and answer: "I have the Pack and I have thee; and Baloo, though he is so lazy, might strike a blow or two for my sake. Why should I be afraid?"

It was one very warm day that a new notion came to

Bagheera—born of something that he had heard. Perhaps Ikki the Porcupine had told him; but he said to Mowgli when they were deep in the Jungle, as the boy lay with his head on Bagheera's beautiful black skin: "Little Brother, how often have I told thee that Shere Khan is thy enemy?"

"As many times as there are nuts on that palm," said Mowgli, who, naturally, could not count. "What of it? I am sleepy, Bagheera, and Shere Khan is all long tail and loud talk—like Mao, the Peacock."

"But this is no time for sleeping. Baloo knows it; I know it; the Pack know it; and even the foolish, foolish deer know. Tabaqui has told thee, too."

"Ho! ho!" said Mowgli. "Tabaqui came to me not long ago with some rude talk that I was a naked man's cub and not fit to dig pig-nuts; but I caught Tabaqui by the tail and swung him twice against a palm-tree to teach him better manners."

"That was foolishness; for though Tabaqui is a mischief-maker, he would not have told thee of something that concerned thee closely. Open those eyes, Little Brother. Shere Khan dare not kill thee in the Jungle; but remember, Akela is very old, and soon the day comes when he cannot kill his buck, and then he will be leader no more. Many of the wolves that looked thee over when thou wast brought to the Council first are old too, and the young wolves believe, as Shere Khan has taught them, that a man-cub has no place with the Pack. In a little thou wilt be a man."

"And what is a man that he should not run with his brothers?" said Mowgli. "I was born in the Jungle. I have obeyed the Law of the Jungle, and there is no wolf of ours from whose paws I have not pulled a thorn. Surely they are brothers!"

Bagheera stretched himself at full length and half shut his eyes. "Little Brother," said he, "feel under my jaw."

Mowgli put up his strong brown hand, and just under Bagheera's silky chin, where the giant rolling muscles were all hid by the glossy hair, he came upon a little bald spot.

"There is no one in the Jungle that knows that I, Bagheera, carry that mark—the mark of the collar; and yet, Little Brother, I was born among men, and it was among men that my mother died—in the cages of the King's Palace at Oodeypore. It was because of this that I paid the price for thee at the Council when thou wast a little naked cub. Yes, I too was born among men. I had never seen the Jungle. They fed me behind bars from an iron pan till one night I felt that I was Bagheera—the Panther—and no man's plaything, and I broke the silly lock with one blow of my paw and came away; and because I had learned the ways of men, I became more terrible in the Jungle than Shere Khan. Is it no so?"

"Yes," said Mowgli; "all the Jungle fear Bagheera—all except Mowgli."

"Oh, *thou* art a man's cub," said the Black Panther, very tenderly; "and even as I returned to my Jungle, so thou must go back to men at last,—to the men who are thy brothers,—if thou are not killed in the Council."

"But why—but why should any wish to kill me?" said Mowgli.

"Look at me," said Bagheera; and Mowgli looked at him steadily between the eyes. The big panther turned his head away in half a minute.

"*That* is why," he said, shifting his paw on the leaves.

"Not even I can look thee between the eyes, and I was born among men, and I love thee, Little Brother. The others they hate thee because their eyes cannot meet thine—because thou art wise—because thou hast pulled out thorns from their feet—because thou art a man."

"I did not know these things," said Mowgli sullenly; and he frowned under his heavy black eyebrows.

"What is the Law of the Jungle? Strike first and then give tongue. By thy very carelessness they know that thou art a man. But be wise. It is in my heart that when Akela misses his next kill,—and at each hunt it costs him more to pin the buck,—the Pack will turn against him and against thee. They will hold a Jungle Council at the Rock, and then—and then—I have it!" said Bagheera, leaping up. "Go thou down quickly to the men's huts in the valley, and take some of the Red Flower which they grow there, so that when the time comes thou mayest have even a stronger friend than I or Baloo or those of the Pack that love thee. Get the Red Flower."

By Red Flower Bagheera meant fire, only no creature in the Jungle will call fire by its proper name. Every beast lives in deadly fear of it, and invents a hundred ways of describing it.

"The Red Flower?" said Mowgli. "That grows outside their huts in the twilight. I will get some."

"There speaks the man's cub," said Bagheera proudly. "Remember that it grows in little pots. Get one swiftly, and keep it by thee for time of need."

"Good!" said Mowgli. "I go. But art thou sure, O my Bagheera"—he slipped his arm round the splendid neck, and looked deep into the big eyes—"art thou sure that all this is Shere Khan's doing?"

"By the Broken Lock that freed me, I am sure, Little Brother."

"Then, by the Bull that bought me, I will pay Shere Khan full tale for this, and it may be a little over," said Mowgli; and he bounded away.

"That is a man. That is all a man," said Bagheera to himself, lying down again. "Oh, Shere Khan, never was a blacker hunting than that frog-hunt of thine ten years ago!"

Mowgli was far and far through the forest, running hard, and his heart was hot in him. He came to the cave as the evening mist rose, and drew breath, and looked down the valley. The cubs were out, but Mother Wolf, at the back of the cave, knew by his breathing that something was troubling her frog.

"What is it, Son?" she said.

"Some bat's chatter of Shere Khan," he called back. "I hunt among the ploughed fields tonight," and he plunged downward through the bushes, to the stream at the bottom of the valley. There he checked, for he heard the yell of the Pack hunting, heard the bellow of a hunted sambhur, and the snort as the buck turned at bay. Then there were wicked, bitter howls from the young wolves: "Akela! Akela! Let the Lone Wolf show his strength. Room for the leader of the Pack! Spring, Akela!"

The Lone Wolf must have sprung and missed his hold, for Mowgli heard the snap of his teeth and then a yelp as the sambhur knocked him over with his forefoot.

He did not wait for anything more, but dashed on; and the yells grew fainter behind him as he ran into the crop-lands where the villagers lived.

"Bagheera spoke truth," he panted, as he nestled

down in some cattle-fodder by the window of a hut. "To-morrow is one day both for Akela and for me."

Then he pressed his face close to the window and watched the fire on the hearth. He saw the husbandman's wife get up and feed it in the night with black lumps; and when the morning came and the mists were all white and cold, he saw the man's child pick up a wicker pot plastered inside with earth, fill it with lumps of red-hot charcoal, put it under his blanket, and go out to tend the cows in the byre.

"Is that all?" said Mowgli. "If a cub can do it, there is nothing to fear;" so he strode round the corner and met the boy, took the pot from his hand, and disappeared into the mist while the boy howled with fear.

"They are very like me," said Mowgli, blowing into the pot, as he had seen the woman do. "This thing will die if I do not give it things to eat;" and he dropped twigs and dried bark on the red stuff. Half-way up the hill he met Bagheera with the morning dew shining like moonstones on his coat.

"Akela has missed," said the Panther. "They would have killed him last night, but they needed thee also. They were looking for thee on the hill."

"I was among the ploughed lands. I am ready. See!" Mowgli held up the fire-pot.

"Good! Now, I have seen men thrust a dry branch into that stuff, and presently the Red Flower blossomed at the end of it. Art thou not afraid?"

"No. Why should I fear? I remember now—if it is not a dream—how, before I was a Wolf, I lay beside the Red Flower, and it was warm and pleasant."

All that day Mowgli sat in the cave tending his fire-pot and dipping dry branches into it to see how they looked. He found a branch that satisfied him, and in the evening when Tabaqui came to the cave and told him rudely enough that he was wanted at the Council Rock, he laughed till Tabaqui ran away. Then Mowgli went to the Council, still laughing.

Akela the Lone Wolf lay by the side of his rock as a sign that the leadership of the Pack was open, and Shere Khan with his following of scrap-fed wolves walked to and fro openly, being flattered. Bagheera lay close to Mowgli, and the fire-pot was between Mowgli's knees. When they were all gathered together, Shere Khan began to speak—a thing he would never have dared to do when Akela was in his prime.

"He has no right," whispered Bagheera. "Say so. He is a dog's son. He will be frightened."

Mowgli sprang to his feet. "Free People," he cried, "does Shere Khan lead the Pack? What has a tiger to do with our leadership?"

"Seeing that the leadership is yet open, and being asked to speak—" Shere Khan began.

"By whom?" said Mowgli. "Are we *all* jackals, to fawn on this cattle-butcher? The leadership of the Pack is with the Pack alone."

There were yells of "Silence, thou man's cub!" "Let him speak. He has kept our Law;" and at last the seniors of the Pack thundered: "Let the Dead Wolf speak." When a leader of the Pack has missed his kill, he is called the Dead Wolf as long as he lives, which is not long, as a rule.

Akela raised his old head wearily:-

"Free People, and ye too, jackals of Shere Khan, for many seasons I have led ye to and from the kill, and in all my time not one had been trapped or maimed. Now

I have missed my kill. Ye know how that plot was made. Ye know how ye brought me up to an untried buck to make my weakness known. It was cleverly done. Your right is to kill me here on the Council Rock now. Therefore, I ask, who comes to make an end of the Lone Wolf? For it is my right, by the Law of the Jungle, that ye come one by one."

There was a long hush, for no single wolf cared to fight Akela to the death. Then Shere Khan roared: "Bah! what have we to do with this toothless fool? He is doomed to die! It is the man-cub who has lived too long. Free People, he was my meat from the first. Give him to me. I am weary of this man-wolf folly. He has troubled the Jungle for ten seasons. Give me the man-cub, or I will hunt here always, and not give you one bone. He is a man, a man's child, and from the marrow of my bones I hate him!"

Then more than half the Pack yelled: "A man! a man! What has a man to do with us? Let him go to his own place."

"And turn all the people of the villages against us?" clamoured Shere Khan. "No; give him to me. He is a man, and none of us can look him between the eyes."

Akela lifted his head again, and said: "He has eaten our food. He has slept with us. He has driven game for us. He has broken no word of the Law of the Jungle."

"Also, I paid for him with a bull when he was accepted. The worth of a bull is little, but Bagheera's honour is something that he will perhaps fight for," said Bagheera, in his gentlest voice.

"A bull paid ten years ago!" the Pack snarled. "What do we care for bones ten years old?"

"Or for a pledge?" said Bagheera, his white teeth bared under his lip. "Well are ye called the Free People!"

"No man's cub can run with the people of the Jungle," howled Shere Khan. "Give him to me!"

"He is our brother in all but blood," Akela went on: "and ye would kill him here! In truth, I have lived too long. Some of ye are eaters of cattle, and of others I have heard that, under Shere Khan's teaching, ye go by dark night and snatch children from the villager's door-steps. Therefore I know ye to be cowards, and it is to cowards I speak. It is certain that I must die, and my life is of no worth, or I would offer that in the Man-cub's place. But for the sake of the Honour of the Pack,—a little matter that by being without a leader ye have forgotten,—I promise that if ye let the Man-cub go to his own place, I will not, when my time comes to die, bare one tooth against ye. I will die without fighting. That will at least save the Pack three lives. More I cannot do; but if ye will, I can save ye the shame that comes of killing a brother against whom there is no fault,—a brother spoken for and bought into the Pack according to the Law of the Jungle."

"He is a man—a man—a man!" snarled the Pack; and most of the wolves began to gather round Shere Khan, whose tail was beginning to switch.

"Now the business is in thy hands," said Bagheera to Mowgli. "*We* can do no more except fight."

Mowgli stood upright—the fire-pot in his hands. Then he stretched out his arms, and yawned in the face of the Council; but he was furious with rage and sorrow, for, wolf-like, the wolves had never told him how they hated him. "Listen, you!" he cried. "There is no need for this dog's jabber. Ye have told me so often tonight that I am a man (and indeed I would have been a wolf with you to my life's end), that I feel your words are true. So I do not call ye my brothers any more, but *sag* [dogs], as a man should. What ye will do, and what ye will not do, is not yours to say. That matter is with *me*; and that we may see the matter more plainly, I, the man, have brought here a little of the Red Flower which ye, dogs, fear."

He flung the fire-pot on the ground, and some of the red coals lit a tuft of dried moss that flared up, as all the Council drew back in terror before the leaping flames.

Mowgli thrust his dead branch into the fire till the twigs lit and crackled, and whirled it above his head among the cowering wolves.

"Thou art the master," said Bagheera, in an undertone. "Save Akela from the death. He was ever thy friend."

Akela, the grim old wolf who had never asked for mercy in his life, gave one piteous look at Mowgli as the boy stood all naked, his long black hair tossing over his shoulders in the light of the blazing branch that made the shadows jump and quiver.

"Good!" said Mowgli, staring round slowly, "I see that ye are dogs. I go from you to my own people—if they be my own people. The Jungle is shut to me, and I must forget your talk and your companionship; but I will be more merciful than ye are. Because I was all but your brother in blood, I promise that when I am a man among men I will not betray ye to men as ye have betrayed me." He kicked the fire with his foot, and the sparks flew up. "There shall be no war between any of us and the Pack. But here is a debt to pay before I go." He strode forward to where Shere Khan sat blinking stupidly at the flames, and caught him by the tuft on his chin. Bagheera followed in case of accidents. "Up, dog!" Mowgli cried. "Up, when a man speaks, or I will set that coat ablaze!"

Shere Khan's ears lay flat back on his head, and he shut his eyes, for the blazing branch was very near.

"This cattle-killer said he would kill me in the Council because he had not killed me when I was a cub. Thus and thus, then, do we beat dogs when we are men. Stir a whisker, Lungri, and I ram the Red Flower down thy gullet!" He beat Shere Khan over the head with the branch, and the tiger whimpered and whined in an agony of fear.

"Pah! Singed jungle-cat—go now! But remember when next I come to the Council Rock, as a man should come, it will be with Shere Khan's hide on my head. For the rest, Akela goes free to live as he pleases. Ye will *not* kill him, because that is not my will. Nor do I think that ye will sit here any longer, lolling out your tongues as though ye were somebodies, instead of dogs whom I drive out—thus! Go!" The fire was burning furiously at the end of the branch, and Mowgli struck right and left round the circle, and the wolves ran howling with the sparks burning their fur. At last there were only Akela, Bagheera, and perhaps ten wolves that had taken Mowgli's part. Then something began to hurt Mowgli inside him, as he had never been hurt in his life before, and he caught his breath and sobbed, and the tears ran down his face.

"What is it? What is it?" he said. "I do not wish to leave the Jungle, and I do not know what this is. Am I dying, Bagheera?"

"No, Little Brother. Those are only tears such as men use," said Bagheera. "Now I know thou art a man, and a man's cub no longer. The Jungle is shut indeed to thee hence-forward. Let them fall, Mowgli. They are only tears." So Mowgli sat and cried as though his heart would break; and he had never cried in all his life before.

"Now," he said, "I will go to men. But first I must say farewell to my mother;" and he went to the cave where she lived with Father Wolf, and he cried on her coat, while the four cubs howled miserably.

"Ye will not forget me?" said Mowgli.

"Never while we can follow a trail," said the cubs. "Come to the foot of the hill when thou art a man, and we will talk to thee; and we will come into the croplands to play with thee by night."

"Come soon!" said Father Wolf. "Oh, wise little frog, come again soon; for we be old, thy mother and I."

"Come soon," said Mother Wolf, "little naked son of mine; for, listen, child of man, I loved thee more than ever I loved my cubs."

"I will surely come," said Mowgli; "and when I come it will be to lay out Shere Khan's hide upon the Council Rock. Do not forget me! Tell them in the Jungle never to forget me!"

The dawn was beginning to break when Mowgli went down the hillside alone, to meet those mysterious things that are called men.

HUNTING-SONG OF THE SEEONEE PACK

As the dawn was breaking the Sambhur belled
  Once, twice and again!
And a doe leaped up, and a doe leaped up
From the pond in the wood where the wild deer sup
This I, scouting alone, beheld
  Once, twice and again!

As the dawn was breaking the Sambhur belled
  Once, twice and again!
And a wolf stole back, and a wolf stole back
To carry the word to the waiting pack,
And we sought and we found and we bayed on his track
  Once, twice and again!

As the dawn was breaking the Wolf-Pack yelled
  Once, twice and again!
Feet in the Jungle that leave no mark!
Eyes that can see in the dark—the dark!
Tongue—give tongue to it! Hark! Oh, hark!
  Once, twice and again!

Chapter 2

KAA'S HUNTING

His spots are the joy of the Leopard:
his horns are the Buffalo's pride.
Be clean, for the strength of the hunter
is known by the gloss of his hide.
If ye find that the bullock can toss you,
or the heavy-browed Sambhur can gore;
Ye need not stop work to inform us:
we knew it ten seasons before.
Oppress not the cubs of the stranger,
but hail them as Sister and Brother,
For though they are little and furry,
it may be the Bear is their mother.
'There is none like to me!' says the Cub
in the pride of his earliest kill;
But the Jungle is large and the Cub he is small.
Let him think and be still.

Maxims of Baloo

All that is told here happened some time before Mowgli was turned out of the Seeonee Wolf-Pack, or revenged himself on Shere Khan the tiger. It was in the days when Baloo was teaching him the Law of the Jungle. The big, serious, old brown bear was delighted to have so quick a pupil, for the young wolves will only learn as much of the Law of the Jungle as applies to their own pack and tribe, and run away as soon as they can repeat the

Hunting Verse:—"Feet that make no noise; eyes that can see in the dark; ears that can hear the winds in their lairs, and sharp white teeth, all of these things are the marks of our brothers except Tabaqui the Jackal and the Hyaena whom we hate." But Mowgli, as a man-cub, had to learn a great deal more than this. Sometimes Bagheera, the Black Panther, would come lounging through the Jungle to see how his pet was getting on, and would purr with his head against a tree while Mowgli recited the day's lesson to Baloo. The boy would climb almost as well as he could swim, and swim almost as well as he could run; so Baloo, the Teacher of the Law, taught him the Wood and Water Laws; how to tell a rotten branch from a sound one; how to speak politely to the wild bees when he came upon a hive of them fifty feet above ground; what to say to Mang the Bat when he disturbed him in the branches at midday; and how to warn the water-snakes in the pools before he splashed down among them. None of the Jungle-People like being disturbed, and all are very ready to fly at an intruder. Then, too, Mowgli was taught the Stranger's Hunting Call, which must be repeated aloud till it is answered, whenever one of the Jungle-People hunts outside his own grounds. It means, translated: "Give me leave to hunt here because I am hungry;" and the answer is: "Hunt then for food, but not for pleasure."

All this will show you how much Mowgli had to learn by heart, and he grew very tired of saying the same thing over a hundred times; but, as Baloo said to Bagheera, one day when Mowgli had been cuffed and run off in a temper: "A Man-cub is a Man-cub, and he must learn *all* the Law of the Jungle."

"But think how small he is," said the Black Panther,

who would have spoiled Mowgli if he had had his own way. "How can his little head carry all thy long talk?"

"Is there anything in the Jungle too little to be killed? No. That is why I teach him these things, and that is why I hit him, very softly, when he forgets."

"Softly! What dost thou know of softness, old Ironfeet?" Bagheera grunted. "His face is all bruised to-day by thy—softness. Ugh!"

"Better he should be bruised from head to foot by me who love him than that he should come to harm through ignorance," Baloo answered very earnestly. "I am now teaching him the Master-Words of the Jungle that shall protect him with the birds and the Snake-People, and all that hunt on four feet, except his own pack. He can now claim protection, if he will only remember the words, from all in the Jungle. Is not that worth a little bruising?"

"Well, look to it then that thou dost not kill the Man-cub. He is no tree-trunk to sharpen thy blunt claws upon. But what are those Master-Words? I am more likely to give him help than to ask it"—Bagheera stretched out one paw and admired the steel-blue, ripping chisel talons at the end of it—"still I should like to know."

"I will call Mowgli and he shall say them—if he will. Come, Little Brother!"

"My head is ringing like a bee-tree," said a sullen little voice over their heads, and Mowgli slid down a tree-trunk very angry and indignant, adding as he reached the ground: "I come for Bagheera and not for *thee*, fat old Baloo!"

"That is all one to me," said Baloo, though he was hurt and grieved. "Tell Bagheera, then, the Master-Words of the Jungle that I have taught thee this day."

"Master-Words for which people?" said Mowgli, delighted to show off. "The Jungle has many tongues. *I* know them all."

"A little thou knowest, but not much. See, O Bagheera, they never thank their teacher. Not one small wolfling has ever came back to thank old Baloo for his teachings. Say the word for the Hunting-People, then—great scholar."

"We be of one blood, ye and I," said Mowgli, giving the words the Bear accent which all the Hunting-People use.

"Good. Now for the birds."

Mowgli repeated, with the Kite's whistle at the end of the sentence.

"Now for the Snake-People," said Bagheera.

The answer was a perfectly indescribable hiss, and Mowgli kicked up his feet behind, clapped his hands together to applaud himself, and jumped on to Bagheera's back, where he sat sideways, drumming with his heels on the glossy skin and making the worst faces he could think of at Baloo.

"There—there! That was worth a little bruise," said the brown bear tenderly. "Some day thou wilt remember me." Then he turned aside to tell Bagheera how he had begged the Master-Words from Hathi the Wild Elephant, who knows all about these things, and how Hathi had taken Mowgli down to a pool to get the Snake Word from a water-snake, because Baloo could not pronounce it, and how Mowgli was now reasonably safe against all accidents in the Jungle, because neither snake, bird, nor beast would hurt him.

"No one, then, is to be feared," Baloo wound up, patting his big furry stomach with pride.

"Except his own tribe," said Bagheera, under his breath;

and then aloud to Mowgli: "Have a care for my ribs, Little Brother! What is all this dancing up and down?"

Mowgli had been trying to make himself heard by pulling at Bagheera's shoulder-fur and kicking hard. When the two listened to him he was shouting at the top of his voice: "And so I shall have a tribe of my own, and lead them through the branches all day long."

"What is this new folly, little dreamer of dreams?" said Bagheera.

"Yes, and throw branches and dirt at old Baloo," Mowgli went on. "They have promised me this. Ah!"

"*Whoof!*" Baloo's big paw scooped Mowgli off Bagheera's back, and as the boy lay between the big fore-paws he could see the Bear was angry.

"Mowgli," said Baloo, "thou hast been talking with the *Bandar-log*—the Monkey-People."

Mowgli looked at Bagheera to see if the Panther was angry too, and Bagheera's eyes were as hard as jade-stones.

"Thou hast been with the Monkey-People—the grey apes—the people without a Law—the eaters of everything. That is great shame."

"When Baloo hurt my head," said Mowgli (he was still on his back), "I went away, and the grey apes came down from the trees and had pity on me. No one else cared." He snuffled a little.

"The pity of the Monkey-People!" Baloo snorted. "The stillness of the mountain stream! The cool of the summer sun! And then, Man-cub?"

"And then, and then, they gave me nuts and pleasant things to eat, and they—they carried me in their arms up to the top of the trees and said I was their blood-brother except that I had no tail, and should be their leader some day."

"They have *no* leader," said Bagheera. "They lie. They have always lied."

"They were very kind and bade me come again. Why have I never been taken among the Monkey-People? They stand on their feet as I do. They do not hit me with sharp paws. They play all day. Let me get up! Bad Baloo, let me up! I will play with them again."

"Listen, Man-cub," said the Bear, and his voice rumbled like thunder on a hot night. "I have taught thee all the Law of the Jungle for all the peoples of the Jungle—except the Monkey-Folk who live in the trees. They have no Law. They are outcasts. They have no speech of their own, but use the stolen words which they overhear when they listen, and peep, and wait up above in the branches. Their way is not our way. They are without leaders. They have no remembrance. They boast and chatter and pretend that they have a great people about to do great affairs in the Jungle, but the falling of a nut turns their minds to laughter and all is forgotten. We of the Jungle have no dealings with them. We do not drink where the monkeys drink; we do not go where the monkeys go; we do not hunt where they hunt; we do not die where they die. Hast thou ever heard me speak of the *Bandar-log,* till to-day?"

"No," said Mowgli in a whisper, for the forest was very still now Baloo had finished.

"The Jungle-People put them out of their mouths and out of their minds. They are very many, evil, dirty, shameless, and they desire, if they have any fixed desire, to be noticed by the Jungle-People. But we do *not* notice them even when they throw nuts and filth on our heads."

He had hardly spoken when a shower of nuts and

twigs spattered down through the branches; and they could hear coughings and howlings and angry jumpings high up in the air among the thin branches.

"The Monkey-People are forbidden," said Baloo, "forbidden to the Jungle-People. Remember."

"Forbidden," said Bagheera; "but I still think Baloo should have warned thee against them."

"I—I? How was I to guess he would play with such dirt? The Monkey-People! Faugh!"

A fresh shower came down on their heads and the two trotted away, taking Mowgli with them. What Baloo had said about the monkeys was perfectly true. They belonged to the tree-tops, and as beasts very seldom look up, there was no occasion for the monkeys and the Jungle-People to cross each other's path. But whenever they found a sick wolf, or a wounded tiger, or bear, the monkeys would torment him, and would throw sticks and nuts at any beast for fun and in the hope of being noticed. Then they would howl and shriek senseless songs, and invite the Jungle-People to climb up their trees and fight them, or would start furious battles over nothing among themselves, and leave the dead monkeys where the Jungle-People could see them. They were always just going to have a leader, and laws and customs of their own, but they never did, because their memories would not hold over from day to day, and so they compromised things by making up a saying: "What the *Bandar-log* think now the Jungle will think later," and that comforted them a great deal. None of the beasts could reach them, but on the other hand none of the beasts would notice them, and that was why they were so pleased when Mowgli came to play with them, and they heard how angry Baloo was.

They never meant to do any more—the *Bandar-log* never mean anything at all; but one of them invented what seemed to him a brilliant idea, and he told all the others that Mowgli would be a useful person to keep in the tribe, because he could weave sticks together for protection from the wind; so, if they caught him, they could make him teach them. Of course, Mowgli, as a woodcutter's child, inherited all sorts of instincts, and used to make little huts of fallen branches without thinking how he came to do it, and the Monkey-People, watching in the trees, considered his play most wonderful. This time, they said, they were really going to have a leader and become the wisest people in the Jungle—so wise that every one else would notice and envy them. Therefore they followed Baloo and Bagheera and Mowgli through the Jungle very quietly till it was time for the midday nap, and Mowgli, who was very much ashamed of himself, slept between the Panther and the Bear, resolving to have no more to do with the Monkey-People.

The next thing he remembered was feeling hands on his legs and arms—hard, strong, little hands—and then a swash of branches in his face, and then he was staring down through the swaying boughs as Baloo woke the Jungle with his deep cries and Bagheera bounded up the trunk with every tooth bared. The *Bandar-log* howled with triumph and scuffled away to the upper branches where Bagheera dared not follow, shouting: "He has noticed us! Bagheera has noticed us. All the Jungle-People admire us for our skill and our cunning." Then they began their flight; and the flight of the Monkey-People through tree-land is one of the things nobody can describe. They have their regular roads and cross-roads, up hills and down hills, all laid out from fifty to seventy or a hundred feet above ground, and by these they can travel even at night if necessary. Two of the strongest monkeys caught Mowgli under the arms and swung off with him through the tree-tops, twenty feet at a bound. Had they been alone they could have gone twice as fast, but the boy's weight held them back. Sick and giddy as Mowgli was he could not help enjoying the wild rush, though the glimpses of earth far down below frightened him, and the terrible check and jerk at the end of the swing over nothing but empty air brought his heart between his teeth. His escort would rush him up a tree till he felt the thinnest topmost branches crackle and bend under them, and then with a cough and a whoop would fling themselves into the air outward and downward, and bring up, hanging by their hands or their feet to the lower limbs of the next tree. Sometimes he could see for miles and miles across the still green Jungle, as a man on the top of a mast can see for miles across the sea, and then the branches and leaves would lash him across the face, and he and his two guards would be almost down to earth again. So, bounding and crashing and whooping and yelling, the whole tribe of *Bandar-log* swept along the tree-roads with Mowgli their prisoner.

For a time he was afraid of being dropped: then he grew angry but knew better than to struggle, and then he began to think. The first thing was to send back word to Baloo and Bagheera, for, at the pace the monkeys were going, he knew his friends would be left far behind. It was useless to look down, for he could only see the top-sides of the branches, so he stared upward and saw, far away in the blue, Chil the Kite balancing and wheeling as he kept watch over the Jungle waiting for things to die. Chil saw that the monkeys were carrying something, and dropped a few hundred yards to find out whether their load was good to eat. He whistled with surprise when he saw Mowgli being dragged up to a tree-top and heard him give the Kite call for—"We be of one blood, thou and I." The waves of the branches closed over the boy, but Chil balanced away to the next tree in time to see the little brown face come up again. "Mark my trail," Mowgli shouted. "Tell Baloo of the Seeonee Pack and Bagheera of the Council Rock."

"In whose name, Brother?" Chil had never seen Mowgli before, though of course he had heard of him.

"Mowgli, the Frog. Man-cub they call me! Mark my tra-il!"

The last words were shrieked as he was being swung through the air, but Chil nodded and rose up till he looked no bigger than a speck of dust, and there he hung, watching with his telescope eyes the swaying of the tree-tops as Mowgli's escort whirled along.

"They never go far," he said with a chuckle. "They never do what they set out to do. Always pecking at new things are the *Bandar-log*. This time, if I have any eyesight, they have pecked down trouble for themselves, for Baloo is no fledgling and Bagheera can, as I know, kill more than goats."

So he rocked on his wings, his feet gathered under him, and waited.

Meantime, Baloo and Bagheera were furious with rage and grief. Bagheera climbed as he had never climbed before, but the thin branches broke beneath his weight, and he slipped down, his claws full of bark.

"Why didst thou not warn the Man-cub?" he roared to poor Baloo, who had set off at a clumsy trot in the hope of overtaking the monkeys. "What was the use of half slaying him with blows if thou didst not warn him?"

"Haste! Oh, haste! We—we may catch them yet!" Baloo panted.

"At that speed! It would not tire a wounded cow. Teacher of the Law—cub-beater—a mile of that rolling to and fro would burst thee open. Sit still and think! Make a plan. This is not time for chasing. They may drop him if we follow too close."

"*Arrula! Whoo!* They may have dropped him already, being tired of carrying him. Who can trust the *Bandar-log*? Put dead bats on my head! Give me black bones to eat! Roll me into the hives of the wild bees that I may be stung to death, and bury me with the Hyaena, for I am the most miserable of bears! *Arrulala! Wahooa!* Oh, Mowgli, Mowgli! why did I not warn thee against the Monkey-Folk instead of breaking thy head? Now perhaps I may have knocked the day's lesson out of his mind, and he will be alone in the Jungle without the Master-Words."

Baloo clasped his paws over his ears and rolled to and fro moaning.

"At least he gave me all the Words correctly a little time ago," said Bagheera impatiently. "Baloo, thou hast neither memory nor respect. What would the Jungle think if I, the Black Panther, curled himself up like Ikki the Porcupine, and howled?"

"What do I care what the Jungle thinks? He may be dead by now."

"Unless and until they drop him from the branches in sport, or kill him out of idleness, I have no fear for the Man-cub. He is wise and well taught, and above all he has the eyes that make the Jungle-People afraid. But (and it is a great evil) he is in the power of the *Bandar-log*, and they, because they live in trees, have no fear of any of our people." Bagheera licked one forepaw thoughtfully.

"Fool that I am! Oh, fat, brown, root-digging fool that I am," said Baloo, uncurling himself with a jerk, "it is true what Hathi the Wild Elephant says: '*To each his own fear*'; and they, the *Bandar-log*, fear Kaa the Rock Snake. He can climb as well as they can. He steals the young monkeys in the night. The whisper of his name makes their wicked tails cold. Let us go to Kaa."

"What will he do for us? He is not of our tribe, being footless—and with most evil eyes," said Bagheera.

"He is very old and very cunning. Above all, he is always hungry," said Baloo hopefully. "Promise him many goats."

"He sleeps for a full month after he has once eaten. He may be asleep now, and even were he awake what if he would rather kill his own goats?" Bagheera, who did not know much about Kaa, was naturally suspicious.

"Then in that case, thou and I together, old hunter, might make him see reason," Here Baloo rubbed his faded brown shoulder against the Panther, and they went off to look for Kaa the Rock Python.

They found him stretched out on a warm ledge in the afternoon sun, admiring his beautiful new coat, for he had been in retirement for the last ten days, changing his skin, and now he was very splendid—darting his big blunt-nosed head along the ground, and twisting the thirty feet of his body into fantastic knots and curves, and licking his lips as he thought of his dinner to come.

"He has not eaten," said Baloo, with a grunt of relief, as soon as he saw the beautifully mottled brown-and-yellow jacket. "Be careful, Bagheera! He is always a little blind after he had changed his skin, and very quick to strike."

Kaa was not a poison-snake—in fact he rather despised the poison-snakes as cowards—but his strength lay in his hug, and when he had once lapped his huge coils round anybody there was no more to be said. "Good hunting!" cried Baloo, sitting up on his haunches. Like all snakes of his breed, Kaa was rather deaf, and did not hear the call at first. Then he curled up ready for any accident, his head lowered.

"Good hunting for us all!" he answered. "Oho, Baloo, what dost thou do here? Good hunting, Bagheera! One of us at least needs food. Is there any news of game afoot? A doe now, or even a young buck? I am as empty as a dried well."

"We are hunting," said Baloo carelessly. He knew that you must not hurry Kaa. He is too big.

"Give me permission to come with you," said Kaa. "A blow more or less is nothing to thee, Bagheera or Baloo, but I—I have to wait and wait for days in a wood-path and climb half a night on the mere chance of a young ape. Pss-haw! The branches are not what they were when I was young. Rotten twigs and dry boughs are they all."

"Maybe thy great weight has something to do with the matter," said Baloo.

"I am a fair length—a fair length," said Kaa, with a little pride. "But for all that, it is the fault of this new-grown timber. I came very near to falling on my last hunt—very near indeed—and the noise of my slipping, for my tail was not tight wrapped round the tree, waked the *Bandar-log*, and they called me most evil names."

"Footless, yellow earth-worm," said Bagheera under his whiskers, as though he were trying to remember something.

"Sssss! Have they ever called me *that*?" said Kaa.

"Something of that kind it was that they shouted to us last moon, but we never noticed them. They will say anything—even that thou hast lost all thy teeth, and wilt not face anything bigger than a kid, because (they are indeed shameless, these *Bandar-log*)—because thou art afraid of the he-goat's horns," Bagheera went on sweetly.

Now a snake, especially a wary old python like Kaa, very seldom shows that he is angry, but Baloo and Bagheera could see the big swallowing-muscles on either side of Kaa's throat ripple and bulge.

"The *Bandar-log* have shifted their grounds," he said quietly. "When I came up into the sun to-day I heard them whooping among the tree-tops."

"It—it is the *Bandar-log* that we follow now," said Baloo; but the words stuck in his throat, for that was the first time in his memory that one of the Jungle-People had owned to being interested in the doings of the monkeys.

"Beyond doubt then it is no small thing that takes two such hunters—leaders in their own Jungle I am certain—on the trail of the *Bandar-log*," Kaa replied courteously, as he swelled with curiosity.

"Indeed," Baloo began, "I am no more than the old and sometimes very foolish Teacher of the Law to the Seeonee wolf-cubs, and Bagheera here—"

"Is Bagheera," said the Black Panther, and his jaws shut with a snap, for he did not believe in being humble. "The trouble is this, Kaa. Those nut-stealers and pickers of palm-leaves have stolen away our Man-cub, of whom thou hast perhaps heard."

"I heard some news from Ikki (his quills make him presumptuous) of a man-thing that was entered into a wolf-pack, but I did not believe him. Ikki is full of stories half heard and very badly told."

"But it is true. He is such a Man-cub as never was," said Baloo. "The best and wisest and boldest of Man-cubs—my own pupil, who shall make the name of Baloo famous through all the jungles; and besides, I—we—love him, Kaa."

"Tss! Tss!" said Kaa, shaking his head to and fro. "I also have known what love is. There are tales I could tell that—"

"That need a clear night when we are all fed to praise properly," said Bagheera quickly. "Our Man-cub is in the hands of the *Bandar-log* now, and we know that of all the Jungle-People they fear Kaa alone."

"They fear me alone. They have good reason," said Kaa. "Chattering, foolish, vain—vain, foolish, and chattering, are the monkeys. But a man-thing in their hands is in no good luck. They grow tired of the nuts they pick, and throw them down. They carry a branch half a day, meaning to do great things with it, and then they snap it in two. That man-thing is not to be envied. They called me also—'yellow fish,' was it not?"

"Worm—worm—earth-worm," said Bagheera, "as well as other things which I cannot now say for shame."

"We must remind them to speak well of their master. Aaa-ssh! We must help their wandering memories. Now, whither went they with the cub?"

"The Jungle alone knows. Toward the sunset, I

believe," said Baloo. "We had thought that thou wouldst know, Kaa."

"I? How? I take them when they come in my way, but I do not hunt the *Bandar-log*, or frogs—or green scum on a waterhole for that matter."

"Up! Up! Up! Up! Hillo! Illo! Illo! Look up, Baloo of the Seeonee Wolf-Pack!"

Baloo looked up to see where the voice came from, and there was Chil the Kite, sweeping down with the sun shining on the upturned flanges of his wings. It was near Chil's bedtime, but he had ranged all over the Jungle looking for the bear and had missed him in the thick foliage.

"What is it?" said Baloo.

"I have seen Mowgli among the *Bandar-log*. He bade me tell you. I watched. The *Bandar-log* have taken him beyond the river to the monkey city—to the Cold Lairs. They may stay there for a night, or ten nights, or an hour. I have told the bats to watch through the dark time. That is my message. Good hunting, all you below!"

"Full gorge and a deep sleep to you, Chil," cried Bagheera. "I will remember thee in my next kill, and put aside the head for thee alone, O best of kites!"

"It is nothing. It is nothing. The boy held the Master-Word. I could have done no less," and Chil circled up again to his roost.

"He has not forgotten to use his tongue," said Baloo, with a chuckle of pride. "To think of one as young remembering the Master-Word for the birds too while he was being pulled across trees!"

"It was most firmly driven into him," said Bagheera. "But I am proud of him, and now we must go to the Cold Lairs."

They all knew where the place was, but few of the Jungle-People ever went there, because what they called the Cold Lairs was an old deserted city, lost and buried in the Jungle, and beasts seldom use a place that men have once used. The wild boar will, but the hunting-tribes do not. Besides, they lived there as much as they could be said to live anywhere, and no self-respecting animal would come within eye-shot of it except in times of drought, when the half-ruined tanks and reservoirs held a little water.

"It is half a night's journey—at full speed," said Bagheera, and Baloo looked very serious. "I will go as fast as I can," he said anxiously.

"We dare not wait for thee. Follow, Baloo. We must go on the quick-foot—Kaa and I."

"Feet or no feet, I can keep abreast of all thy four," said Kaa shortly. Baloo made one effort to hurry, but had to sit down panting, and so they left him to come on later, while Bagheera hurried forward, at the quick panther-canter. Kaa said nothing, but, strive as Bagheera might, the huge Rock Python held level with him. When they came to a hill-stream, Bagheera gained, because he bounded across while Kaa swam, his head and two feet of his neck clearing the water, but on level ground Kaa made up the distance.

"By the Broken Lock that freed me," said Bagheera, when twilight had fallen, "thou art no slow goer!"

"I am hungry," said Kaa. "Besides, they called me speckled frog."

"Worm—earth-worm, and yellow to boot."

"All one. Let us go on," and Kaa seemed to pour himself along the ground, finding the shortest road with his steady eyes, and keeping to it.

In the Cold Lairs the Monkey-People were not thinking of Mowgli's friends at all. They had brought the boy to the Lost City, and were very pleased with themselves for the time. Mowgli had never seen an Indian city before, and though this was almost a heap of ruins it seemed very wonderful and splendid. Some king had built it long ago on a little hill. You could still trace the stone causeways that led up to the ruined gates where the last splinters of wood hung to the worn, rusted hinges. Trees had grown into and out of the walls; the battlements were tumbled down and decayed, and wild creepers hung out of the windows of the towers on the walls in bushy hanging clumps.

A great roofless palace crowned the hill, and the marble of the courtyards and the fountains was split, and stained with red and green, and very cobblestones in the courtyard where the king's elephants used to live had been thrust up and apart by grasses and young trees. From the palace you could see the rows and rows of roofless houses that made up the city looking like empty honeycombs filled with blackness; the shapeless block of stone that had been an idol, in the square where four roads met; the pits and dimples at street-corners where the public wells once stood, and the shattered domes of temples with wild figs sprouting on their sides. The monkeys called the place their city, and pretended to despise the Jungle-People because they lived in the forest. And yet they never knew what the buildings were made for nor how to use them. They would sit in circles on the hall of the king's council chamber, and scratch for fleas and pretend to be men; or they would run in and out of the roofless houses and collect pieces of plaster and old bricks in a corner, and forget where they had hidden them, and fight and cry in scuffling crowds, and then break off to play up and down the terraces of the king's garden, where they would shake the rose-trees and the oranges in sport to see the fruit and flowers fall. They explored all the passages and dark tunnels in the palace and the hundreds of little rooms, but they never remembered what they had seen and what they had not; and so drifted about in ones and twos or crowds telling each other that they were doing as men did. They drank at the tanks and made the water all muddy, and then they fought over it, and then they would all rush together in mobs and shout: "There is no one in the Jungle so wise and good and clever and strong and gentle as the *Bandar-log*." Then all would begin again till they grew tired of the city and went back to the tree-tops, hoping the Jungle-People would notice them.

Mowgli, who had been trained under the Law of the Jungle, did not like or understand this kind of life. The monkeys dragged him into the Cold Lairs late in the afternoon, and instead of going to sleep, as Mowgli would have done after a long journey, they joined hands and danced about and sang their foolish songs. One of the monkeys made a speech and told his companions that Mowgli's capture marked a new thing in the history of the *Bandar-log*, for Mowgli was going to show them how to weave sticks and canes together as a protection against rain and cold. Mowgli picked up some creepers and began to work them in and out, and the monkeys tried to imitate; but in a few minutes they lost interest and began to pull their friends' tails or jump up and down on all fours, coughing.

"I wish to eat," said Mowgli. "I am a stranger in this

part of the Jungle. Bring me food, or give me leave to hunt here."

Twenty or thirty monkeys bounded away to bring him nuts and wild pawpaws; but they fell to fighting on the road, and it was too much trouble to go back with what was left of the fruit. Mowgli was sore and angry as well as hungry, and he roamed through the empty city giving the Stranger's Hunting Call from time to time, but no one answered him, and Mowgli felt that he had reached a very bad place indeed. "All that Baloo has said about the *Bandar-log* is true," he thought to himself. "They have no Law, no Hunting Call, and no leaders—nothing but foolish words and little picking thievish hands. So if I am starved or killed here, it will be all my own fault. But I must try to return to my own Jungle. Baloo will surely beat me, but that is better than chasing silly rose-leaves with the *Bandar log*."

No sooner had he walked to the city wall than the monkeys pulled him back, telling him that he did know how happy he was, and pinching him to make him grateful. He set his teeth and said nothing, but went with the shouting monkeys to a terrace above the red sandstone reservoirs that were half-full of rainwater. There was a ruined summer-house of white marble in the centre of the terrace, built for queens dead a hundred years ago. The domed roof had half fallen in and blocked up the underground passage from the palace by which the queens used to enter; but the walls were made of screens of marble tracery beautiful milk-white fretwork, set with agates and cornelians and jasper and lapis lazuli, and as the moon came up behind the hill it shone through the open-work, casting shadows on the ground like black velvet embroidery. Sore, sleepy, and hungry as he was, Mowgli could not help laughing when the *Bandar-log* began, twenty at a time, to tell him how great and wise and strong and gentle they were, and how foolish he was to wish to leave them. "We are great. We are free. We are wonderful. We are the most wonderful people in all the Jungle! We all say so, and so it must be true," they shouted. "Now, as you are a new listener and can carry our words back to the Jungle-People so that they may notice us in future, we will tell you about our most excellent selves." Mowgli made no objection, and the monkeys gathered by hundreds and hundreds on the terrace to listen to their own speakers singing the praises of the *Bandar-log*, and whenever a speaker stopped for want of breath they would all shout together: "This is true; we all say so." Mowgli nodded and blinked, and said "Yes" when they asked him a question, and his head spun with the noise. "Tabaqui the Jackal must have bitten all these people," he said to himself, "and now they have the madness. Certainly this is *dewanee,* the madness. Do they never go to sleep? Now there is a cloud coming to cover that moon. If it were only a big enough cloud I might try to run away in the darkness. But I am tired."

That same cloud was being watched by two good friends in the ruined ditch below the city wall, for Bagheera and Kaa, knowing well how dangerous the Monkey-People were in large numbers, did not wish to run any risks. The monkeys never fight unless they are a hundred to one, and few in the Jungle care for those odds.

"I will go to the west wall," Kaa whispered, "and come down swiftly with the slope of the ground in my favour. They will not throw themselves upon *my* back in their hundreds, but—"

"I know it," said Bagheera. "Would that Baloo were here; but we must do what we can. When that cloud covers the moon I shall go to the terrace. They hold some sort of council there over the boy."

"Good hunting!" said Kaa grimly, and glided away to the west wall. That happened to be the least ruined of any, and the big snake was delayed a while before he could find a way up the stones. The cloud hid the moon, and as Mowgli wondered what would come next he heard Bagheera's light feet on the terrace. The Black Panther had raced up the slope almost without a sound and was striking—he knew better than to waste time in biting—right and left among the monkeys, who were seated round Mowgli in circles fifty and sixty deep. There was a howl of fright and rage, and then as Bagheera tripped on the rolling, kicking bodies beneath him, a monkey shouted: "There is only one here! Kill him! Kill him!" A scuffling mass of monkeys, biting, scratching, tearing, and pulling, closed over Bagheera, while five or six laid hold of Mowgli, dragged him up the wall of the summer-house and pushed him through the hole of the broken dome. A man-trained boy would have been badly bruised, for the fall was a good fifteen feet, but Mowgli fell as Baloo had taught him to fall, and landed on his feet.

"Stay there," shouted the monkeys, "till we have killed thy friends, and later we will play with thee—if the Poison-People leave thee alive."

"We be of one blood, ye and I," said Mowgli, quickly giving the Snake's Call. He could hear rustling and hissing in the rubbish all round him and gave the Call a second time, to make sure.

"Even ssso! Down hoods all!" said half-a-dozen low

voices (every ruin in India becomes sooner or later a dwelling-place of snakes, and the old summer-house was alive with cobras). "Stand still, Little Brother, for thy feet may do us harm."

Mowgli stood as quietly as he could, peering through the open-work and listening to the furious din of the fight round the Black Panther—the yells and chatterings and scufflings, and Bagheera's deep, hoarse cough as he backed and bucked and twisted and plunged under the heaps of his enemies. For the first time since he was born, Bagheera was fighting for his life.

"Baloo must be at hand; Bagheera would not have come alone," Mowgli thought; and then he called aloud: "To the tank, Bagheera! Roll to the water-tank. Roll and plunge! Get to the water!"

Bagheera heard, and the cry that told him Mowgli was safe gave him new courage. He worked his way desperately, inch by inch, straight for the reservoirs, hitting in silence. Then from the ruined wall nearest the Jungle rose up the rumbling war-shout of Baloo. The old bear had done his best, but he could not come before. "Bagheera," he shouted, "I am here. I climb! I haste! *Ahuwora!* The stones slip under my feet! Wait my coming, O most infamous *Bandar-log*!" He panted up the terrace only to disappear to the head in a wave of monkeys, but he threw himself squarely on his haunches, and, spreading out his fore-paws, hugged as many as he could hold, and then began to hit with a regular *bat-bat-bat*, like the flipping strokes of a paddle-wheel. A crash and a splash told Mowgli that Bagheera had fought his way to the tank where the monkeys would not follow. The panther lay gasping for breath, his head just out of water, while the monkeys stood three deep on the red steps, dancing up and down with rage, ready to spring upon him from all sides if he came out to help Baloo. It was then that Bagheera lifted up his dripping chin, and in despair gave the Snake's Call for protection—"We be of one blood, ye and I"—for he believed that Kaa had turned tail at the last minute. Even Baloo, half smothered under the monkeys on the edge of the terrace, could not help chuckling as he heard the Black Panther asking for help.

Kaa had only just worked his way over the west wall, landing with a wrench that dislodged a coping-stone into the ditch. He had no intention of losing any advantage of the ground, and coiled and uncoiled himself once or twice, to be sure that every foot of his long body was in working order. All that while the fight with Baloo went on, and the monkeys yelled in the tank around Bagheera, and Mang the Bat, flying to and fro, carried the news of the great battle over the Jungle, till even Hathi the Wild Elephant trumpeted, and, far away, scattered bands of the Monkey-Folk woke and came leaping along the tree-roads to help their comrades in the Cold Lairs, and the noise of the fight roused all the day-birds for miles round. Then Kaa came straight, quickly, and anxious to kill. The fighting-strength of a python is in the driving blow of his head backed by all the strength and weight of his body. If you can imagine a lance, or a battering-ram, or a hammer weighing nearly half a ton driven by a cool, quiet mind living in the handle of it, you can roughly imagine what Kaa was like when he fought. A python four or five feet long can knock a man down if he hits him fairly in the chest, and Kaa was thirty feet long, as you know. His first stroke was delivered into the heart of the crowd round Baloo—

was sent home with shut mouth in silence, and there was no need of a second. The monkeys scattered with cries of—"Kaa! It is Kaa! Run! Run!"

Generations of monkeys had been scared into good behaviour by the stories their elders told them of Kaa, the night-thief, who could slip along the branches as quietly as moss grows, and steal away the strongest monkey that ever lived; of old Kaa, who could make himself look so like a dead branch or a rotten stump that the wisest were deceived, till the branch caught them. Kaa was everything that the monkey feared in the Jungle, for none of them knew the limits of his power, none of them could look him in the face, and none had ever come alive out of his hug. And so they ran, stammering with terror, to the walls and the roofs of the houses, and Baloo drew a deep breath of relief. His fur was much thicker than Bagheera's, but he had suffered sorely in the fight. Then Kaa opened his mouth for the first time and spoke one long hissing word, and the far-away monkeys, hurrying to the defence of the Cold Lairs, stayed where they were, cowering, till the loaded branches bent and crackled under them. The monkeys on the walls and the empty houses stopped their cries, and in the stillness that fell upon the city Mowgli heard Bagheera shaking his wet sides as he came up from the tank. Then the clamour broke out again. The monkeys leaped higher up the walls; they clung round the necks of the big stone idols and shrieked as they skipped along the battlements, while Mowgli, dancing in the summer-house, put his eye to the screen-work and hooted owl-fashion between his front teeth, to show his derision and contempt.

"Get the Man-cub out of that trap; I can do no more,"

Bagheera gasped. "Let us take the Man-cub and go. They may attack again."

"They will not move till I order them. Stay you sssso!" Kaa hissed, and the city was silent once more. "I could not come before, Brother, but I *think* I heard thee call"—this was to Bagheera.

"I—I may have cried out in the battle," Bagheera answered. "Baloo, art thou hurt?"

"I am not sure that they have not pulled me into a hundred little bearlings," said Baloo gravely, shaking one leg after the other. "Wow! I am sore. Kaa, we owe thee, I think, our lives—Bagheera and I."

"No matter. Where is the Manling?"

"Here, in a trap. I cannot climb out," cried Mowgli. The curve of the broken dome was above his head.

"Take him away. He dances like Mao the Peacock. He will crush our young," said the cobras inside.

"Hah!" said Kaa, with a chuckle, "he has friends everywhere, this Manling. Stand back, Manling; and hide you, O Poison-People. I break down the wall."

Kaa looked carefully till he found a discoloured crack in the marble tracery showing a weak spot, made two or three light taps with his head to get the distance, and then, lifting up six feet of his body clear of the ground, sent home half-a-dozen full-power, smashing blows, nose-first. The screen-work broke and fell away in a cloud of dust and rubbish, and Mowgli leaped through the opening and flung himself between Baloo and Bagheera—an arm round each big neck.

"Art thou hurt?" said Baloo, hugging him softly.

"I am sore, hungry, and not a little bruised; but, oh, they handled ye grievously, my Brothers! Ye bleed."

"Others also," said Bagheera, licking his lips, and

looking at the monkey-dead on the terrace and round the tank.

"It is nothing, it is nothing, if thou art safe, O my pride of all little frogs!" whimpered Baloo.

"Of that we shall judge later," said Bagheera, in a dry voice that Mowgli did not at all like. "But here is Kaa, to whom we owe the battle and thou owest thy life. Thank him according to our customs, Mowgli."

Mowgli turned and saw the great python's head swaying a foot above his own.

"So this is the Manling," said Kaa. 'Very soft is his skin, and he is not so unlike the *Bandar-log*. Have a care, Manling, that I do not mistake thee for a monkey some twilight when I have newly changed my coat."

"We be of one blood, thou and I," Mowgli answered. "I take my life from thee, to-night. My kill shall be thy kill if ever thou art hungry, O Kaa."

"All thanks, Little Brother," said Kaa, though his eyes twinkled. "And what may so bold a hunter kill? I ask that I may follow when next he goes abroad."

"I kill nothing,—I am too little,—but I drive goats toward such as can use them. When thou art empty come to me and see I speak the truth. I have some kill in these"—he held out his hands—"and if ever thou art in a trap, I may pay the debt which I owe to thee, to Bagheera, and to Baloo, here. Good hunting to ye all, my masters."

"Well said," growled Baloo, for Mowgli had returned thanks very prettily. The python dropped his head lightly for a minute on Mowgli's shoulder. "A brave heart and a courteous tongue," said he. "They shall carry thee far through the Jungle, Manling. But now go hence quickly with thy friends. Go and sleep, for the moon sets, and what follows it is not well that thou shouldst see."

The moon was sinking behind the hills, and the lines of trembling monkeys huddled together on the walls and battlements looked like ragged, shaky fringes of things. Baloo went down to the tank for a drink, and Bagheera began to put his fur in order, as Kaa glided out into the centre of the terrace and brought his jaws together with a ringing snap that drew all the monkeys' eyes upon him.

"The moon sets," he said. "Is there yet light to see?"

From the walls came a moan like the wind in the tree-tops: "We see, O Kaa."

"Good. Begins now the Dance—the Dance of the Hunger of Kaa. Sit still and watch."

He turned twice or thrice in a big circle, weaving his head from right to left. Then he began making loops and figures of eight with his body, and soft, oozy triangles that melted into squares and five-sided figures, and coiled mounds, never resting, never hurrying, and never stopping his low, humming song. It grew darker and darker, till at last the dragging, shifting coils disappeared, but they could hear the rustle of the scales.

Baloo and Bagheera stood still as stones, growling in their throats, their neck-hair bristling, and Mowgli watched and wondered.

"*Bandar-log,*" said the voice of Kaa at last, "can ye stir foot or hand without my order? Speak!"

"Without thy order we cannot stir foot or hand, O Kaa!"

"Good! Come all one pace closer to me."

The lines of the monkeys swayed forward helplessly, and Baloo and Bagheera took one stiff step forward with them.

"Closer!" hissed Kaa, and they all moved again.

Mowgli laid his hands on Baloo and Bagheera to get them away, and the two great beasts started as though they had been waked from a dream.

"Keep thy hand on my shoulder," Bagheera whispered. "Keep it there, or I must go back—must go back to Kaa. *Aah!*"

"It is only old Kaa making circles on the dust," said Mowgli; "let us go;" and the three slipped off through a gap in the walls to the Jungle.

"*Whoof!*" said Baloo, when he stood under the still trees again. "Never more will I make an ally of Kaa," and he shook himself all over.

"He knows more than we," said Bagheera, trembling. "In a little time, had I stayed, I should have walked down his throat."

"Many will walk by that road before the moon rises again," said Baloo. "He will have good hunting—after his own fashion."

"But what was the meaning of it all?" said Mowgli, who did not know anything of a python's powers of fascination. "I saw no more than a big snake making foolish circles till the dark came. And his nose was all sore. Ho! Ho!"

"Mowgli," said Bagheera angrily, "his nose was sore on *thy* account; as my ears and sides and paws and Baloo's neck and shoulders are bitten on *thy* account. Neither Baloo nor Bagheera will be able to hunt with pleasure for many days."

"It is nothing," said Baloo; "we have the Man-cub again."

"True; but he has cost us heavily in time which might have been spent in good hunting, in wounds, in hair—

I am half plucked along my back,—and, last of all, in honour. For, remember, Mowgli, I, who am the Black Panther, was forced to call upon Kaa for protection, and Baloo and I were both made stupid as little birds by the Hunger-Dance. All this, Man-cub, came of thy playing with the *Bandar-log*."

"True; it is true," said Mowgli sorrowfully. "I am an evil Man-cub, and my stomach is sad in me."

"*Mf!* What says the Law of the Jungle, Baloo?"

Baloo did not wish to bring Mowgli into any more trouble, but he could not tamper with the Law, so he mumbled: "Sorrow never stays punishment. But remember, Bagheera, he is very little."

"I will remember; but he has done mischief, and blows must be dealt now. Mowgli, hast thou anything to say?"

"Nothing. I did wrong. Baloo and thou are wounded. It is just."

Bagheera gave him half-a-dozen love-taps; from a panther's point of view they would hardly have waked one of his own cubs, but for a seven-year-old boy they amounted to as severe a beating as you could wish to avoid. When it was all over Mowgli sneezed, and picked himself up without a word.

"Now," said Bagheera, "jump on my back, Little Brother, and we will go home."

One of the beauties of Jungle Law is that punishment settles all scores. There is no nagging afterward.

Mowgli laid his head down on Bagheera's back and slept so deeply that he never waked when he was put down by Mother Wolf's side in the home-cave.

ROAD-SONG OF THE *BANDER-LOG*

Here we go in a flung festoon,
Half-way up to the jealous moon!
Don't you envy our pranceful bands?
Don't you wish you had extra hands?
Wouldn't you like if your tails were *—so—*
Curved in the shape of a Cupid's bow?
  Now you're angry, but—never mind,
  Brother, thy tail hangs down behind!

Here we sit in a branchy row,
Thinking of beautiful things we know;
Dreaming of deeds that we mean to do,
All complete, in a minute or two—
Something noble and grand and good,
Won by merely wishing we could.
  Now we're going to- never mind,
  Brother, thy tail hangs down behind!

All the talk we ever have heard
Uttered by bat or beast or bird—
Hide or fin or scale or feather—
Jabber it quickly and all together!
Excellent! Wonderful! Once again!
Now we are talking just like men.
  Let's pretend we are . . . never mind,
  Brother, thy tail hangs down behind!
  This is the way of the Monkey-kind.

Then join our leaping lines that skirmish through the pines,
That rocket by where, light and high, the wild-grape swings,
By the rubbish in our wake, and the noble noise we make,
Be sure, be sure, we're going to do some splendid things!

CHAPTER 3

"TIGER! TIGER!"

What of the hunting, hunter bold?
  Brother, the watch was long and cold.
What of the quarry ye went to kill?
  Brother, he crops in the Jungle still.
Where is the power that made your pride?
  Brother, it ebbs from my flank and side.
Where is the haste that ye hurry by?
  Brother, I go to my lair—to die!

Now we must go back to the first tales. When Mowgli left the wolf's cave after the fight with the Pack at the Council Rock, he went down to the ploughed lands where the villagers lived, but he would not stop there because it was too near to the Jungle, and he knew that he had made at least one bad enemy at the Council. So he hurried on, keeping to the rough road that ran down the valley, and followed it at a steady jog-trot for nearly twenty miles, till he came to a country that he did not know. The valley opened out into a great plain dotted over with rocks and cut up by ravines. At one end stood a little village, and at the other the thick Jungle came down in a sweep to the grazing-grounds, and stopped there as though it had been cut off with a hoe. All over the plain, cattle and buffaloes were grazing, and when the little boys in charge of the herds saw Mowgli they shouted and ran away, and the yellow pariah dogs that hang about every Indian village barked. Mowgli walked on, for he was feeling hungry, and when he came to the village gate he saw the big thorn-bush that was drawn up before the gate at twilight pushed to one side.

"Umph!" he said, for he had come across more than one such barricade in his night rambles after things to eat. "So men are afraid of the People of the Jungle here also." He sat down by the gate, and when a man came out he stood up, opened his mouth, and pointed down it to show that he wanted food. The man stared, and ran back up the one street of the village shouting for the priest, who was a big, fat man dressed in white, with a red-and-yellow mark on his forehead. The priest came to the gate, and with him at least a hundred people, who stared and talked and shouted and pointed at Mowgli.

"They have no manners, these Men-Folk," said Mowgli to himself. "Only the grey ape would behave as they do." So he threw back his long hair and frowned at the crowd.

"What is there to be afraid of?" said the priest. "Look at the marks on his arms and legs. They are bites of wolves. He is but a wolf-child run away from the Jungle."

Of course, in playing together, the cubs had often nipped Mowgli harder than they intended, and there were white scars all over his arms and legs. But he would have been the last person in the world to call these bites, for he knew what real biting meant.

"*Arré! Arré!*" said two or three women together. "To be bitten by wolves, poor child! He is a handsome boy. He has eyes like red fire. By my honour, Messua, he is not unlike thy boy that was taken by the tiger."

"Let me look," said a woman with heavy copper rings on her wrists and ankles, and she peered at Mowgli under the palm of her hand. "Indeed he is not. He is thinner, but he has the very look of my boy."

The priest was a clever man, and he knew that Messua was wife to the richest villager in the place. So he looked up at the sky for a minute, and said solemnly: "What the Jungle has taken the Jungle has restored. Take the boy into thy house, my sister, and forget not to honour the priest who sees so far into the lives of men."

"By the Bull that bought me," said Mowgli to himself, "but all this talking is like another looking-over by the Pack! Well, if I am a man, a man I must become."

The crowd parted as the woman beckoned Mowgli to her hut, where there was a red-lacquered bedstead, a great earthen grain-chest with curious raised patterns on it, half-a-dozen copper cooking-pots, an image of a Hindu god in a little alcove, and on the wall a real looking-glass, such as they sell at the county fairs.

She gave him a long drink of milk and some bread, and then she laid her hand on his head and looked into his eyes; for she thought that perhaps he might be her real son come back from the Jungle where the tiger had taken him. So she said: "Nathoo, O Nathoo!" Mowgli did not show that he knew the name. "Dost thou not remember the day when I gave thee thy new shoes?" She touched his foot, and it was almost as hard as horn. "No," she said sorrowfully, "those feet have never worn shoes, but thou art very like my Nathoo, and thou shalt be my son."

Mowgli was uneasy, because he had never been under a roof before; but as he looked at the thatch, he saw that he could tear it out any time if he wanted to get away, and that the window had no fastenings. "What is the good of a man," he said to himself at last, "if he does not understand man's talk? Now I am as silly and dumb as a man would be with us in the Jungle. I must learn their talk."

It was not for fun that he had learned while he was with the wolves to imitate the challenge of bucks in the Jungle and the grunt of the little wild pig. So as soon as Messua pronounced a word Mowgli would imitate it almost perfectly, and before dark he had learned the names of many things in the hut.

There was a difficulty at bedtime, because Mowgli would not sleep under anything that looked so like a panther-trap as that hut, and when they shut the door he went through the window. "Give him his will," said Messua's husband. "Remember he can never till now have slept on a bed. If he is indeed sent in the place of our son he will not run away."

So Mowgli stretched himself in some long, clean grass at the edge of the field, but before he had closed his eyes a soft grey nose poked him under the chin.

"Phew!" said Grey Brother (he was the eldest of Mother Wolf's cubs). "This is a poor reward for following thee twenty miles. Thou smellest of woodsmoke and cattle—altogether like a man already. Wake, Little Brother; I bring news."

"Are all well in the Jungle?" said Mowgli, hugging him.

"All except the wolves that were burned with the Red Flower. Now, listen. Shere Khan has gone away to hunt far off till his coat grows again, for he is badly singed. When he returns he swears that he will lay thy bones in the Waingunga."

"There are two words to that. I also have made a little promise. But news is always good. I am tired to-night,—

very tired with new things, Grey Brother,—but bring me the news always."

"Thou wilt not forget that thou art a wolf? Men will not make thee forget?" said Grey Brother anxiously.

"Never. I will always remember that I love thee and all in our cave; but also I will always remember that I have been cast out of the Pack."

"And that thou mayest be cast out of another pack. Men are only men, Little Brother, and their talk is like the talk of frogs in a pond. When I come down here again, I will wait for thee in the bamboos at the edge of the grazing-ground."

For three months after that night Mowgli hardly ever left the village gate, he was so busy learning the ways and customs of men. First he had to wear a cloth round him, which annoyed him horribly; and then he had to learn about money, which he did not in the least understand, and about ploughing, of which he did not see the use. Then the little children in the village made him very angry. Luckily, the Law of the Jungle has taught him to keep his temper, for in the Jungle life and food depend on keeping your temper; but when they made fun of him because he would not play games or fly kites, or because he mispronounced some word, only the knowledge that it was unsportsmanlike to kill little naked cubs kept him from picking them up and breaking them in two.

He did not know his own strength in the least. In the Jungle he knew he was weak compared with the beasts, but in the village people said that he was as strong as a bull.

And Mowgli had not the faintest idea of the difference that caste makes between man and man. When the potter's donkey slipped in the clay-pit, Mowgli hauled it out by the tail, and helped to stack the pots for their journey to the market at Khanhiwara. That was very shocking, too, for the potter is a low-caste man, and his donkey is worse. When the priest scolded him, Mowgli threatened to put him on the donkey, too, and the priest told Messua's husband that Mowgli had better be set to work as soon as possible; and the village head-man told Mowgli that he would have to go out with the buffaloes next day, and herd them while they grazed. No one was more pleased than Mowgli; and that night, because he had been appointed, as it were, a servant of the village, he went off to a circle that met every evening on a masonry platform under a great fig-tree. It was the village club, and the head-man and the watchman and the barber (who knew all the gossip of the village), and old Buldeo, the village hunter, who owned a Tower musket, met and smoked. The monkeys sat and talked in the upper branches, and there was a hole under the platform where a cobra lived, and he had his little platter of milk every night because he was sacred; and the old men sat around the tree and talked, and pulled at the big hookahs [water-pipes], till far into the night. They told wonderful tales of gods and men and ghosts; and Buldeo told even more wonderful ones of the ways of beasts in the Jungle, till the eyes of the children sitting outside the circle bulged out of their heads. Most of the tales were about animals, for the Jungle was always at their door. The deer and the wild pig grubbed up their crops, and now and again the tiger carried off a man at twilight, within sight of the village gates.

Mowgli, who, naturally, knew something about what they were talking of, had to cover his face not to show that he was laughing, while Buldeo, the Tower musket across his knees, climbed on from one wonderful story to another, and Mowgli's shoulders shook.

Buldeo was explaining how the tiger that had carried away Messua's son was a ghost-tiger, and his body was inhabited by the ghost of a wicked old money-lender, who had died some years ago. "And I know that this is true," he said, "because Purun Dass always limped from the blow that he got in a riot when his account-books were burned, and the tiger that I speak of, *he* limps, too, for the tracks of his pads are unequal."

"True, true; that must be the truth," said the greybeards, nodding together.

"Are all these tales such cobwebs and moon-talk?" said Mowgli. "That tiger limps because he was born lame, as every one knows. To talk of the soul of a money-lender in a beast that never had the courage of a jackal is child's talk."

Buldeo was speechless with surprise for a moment, and the head-man stared.

"Oho! It is the Jungle brat, is it?" said Buldeo. "If thou art so wise, better bring his hide to Khanhiwara, for the Government has set a hundred rupees on his life. Better still, do not talk when thy elders speak."

Mowgli rose to go. "All evening I have lain here listening," he called back over his shoulder, "and, except once or twice, Buldeo has not said one word of truth concerning the Jungle, which is at his very doors. How, then, shall I believe the tales of ghosts and gods and goblins which he says he has seen?"

"It is full time that boy went to herding," said the head-man, while Buldeo puffed and snorted at Mowgli's impertinence.

The custom of most Indian villages is for a few boys

to take the cattle and buffaloes out to graze in the early morning, and bring them back at night; and the very cattle that would trample a white man to death allow themselves to be banged and bullied and shouted at by children that hardly come up to their noses. So long as the boys keep with the herds they are safe, for not even the tiger will charge a mob of cattle. But if they straggle to pick flowers or hunt lizards, they are sometimes carried off. Mowgli went through the village street in the dawn, sitting on the back of Rama, the great herd bull; and the slaty-blue buffaloes, with their long, backward-sweeping horns and savage eyes, rose out of their byres, one by one, and followed him, and Mowgli made it very clear to the children with him that he was the master. He beat the buffaloes with a long, polished bamboo, and told Kamya, one of the boys, to graze the cattle by themselves, while he went on with the buffaloes, and to be very careful not to stray away from the herd.

An Indian grazing-ground is all rocks and scrub and tussocks and little ravines, among which the herd scatter and disappear. The buffaloes generally keep to the pools and muddy places, where they lie wallowing or basking in the warm mud for hours. Mowgli drove them on to the edge of the plain where the Waingunga River came out of the Jungle; then he dropped from Rama's neck, trotted off to a bamboo clump, and found Grey Brother. "Ah!" said Grey Brother. "I have waited here for many days. What is the meaning of this cattle-herding work?"

"It is an order," said Mowgli, "I am a village herd for a while. What news of Shere Khan?"

"He has come back to this country, and has waited here a long time for thee. Now he has gone off again, for the game is scarce. But he means to kill thee."

"Very good," said Mowgli. "So long as he is away do thou or one of the four brothers sit on that rock, so that I can see thee as I come out of the village. When he comes back wait for me in the ravine by the *dhâk*-tree in the centre of the plain. We need not walk into Shere Khan's mouth."

Then Mowgli picked out a shady place, and lay down and slept while the buffaloes grazed round him. Herding in India is one of the laziest things in the world. The cattle move and crunch, and lie down, and move on again, and they do not even low. They only grunt, and the buffaloes very seldom say anything, but get down into the muddy pools one after another, and work their way into the mud till only their noses and staring china-blue eyes show above the surface, and there they lie like logs. The sun makes the rocks dance in the heat, and the herd-children hear one kite (never any more) whistling almost out of sight overhead, and they know that if they died, or a cow died, that kite would sweep down, and the next kite miles away would see him drop and would follow, and the next, and the next, and almost before they were dead there would be a score of hungry kites come out of nowhere. Then they sleep and wake and sleep again, and weave little baskets of dried grass and put grasshoppers in them; or catch two praying-mantises and make them fight; or string a necklace of red and black Jungle-nuts; or watch a lizard basking on a rock, or a snake hunting a frog near the wallows. Then they sing long, long songs with odd native quavers at the end of them, and the day seems longer than most people's whole lives, and perhaps they make a mud castle with mud figures of men and horses and buffaloes, and put reeds into the men's hands, and pretend that they are kings and the figures are their armies, or that they are gods to be worshipped. Then evening comes, and the children call, and the buffaloes lumber up out of the sticky mud with noises like gunshots going off one after the other, and they all string across the grey plain back to the twinkling village lights.

Day after day Mowgli would lead the buffaloes out to their wallows, and day after day he would see Grey Brother's back a mile and a half away across the plain (so he knew that Shere Khan had not come back), and day after day he would lie on the grass listening to the noises round him, and dreaming of old days in the Jungle. If Shere Khan had made a false step with his lame paw up in the Jungle by the Waingunga, Mowgli would have heard him in those long, still mornings.

At last a day came when he did not see Grey Brother at the signal-place, and he laughed and headed the buffaloes for the ravine by the *dhâk*-tree, which was all covered with golden-red flowers. There sat Grey Brother, every bristle on his back lifted.

"He has hidden for a month to throw thee off thy guard. He crossed the ranges last night with Tabaqui, hot-foot on thy trail," said the wolf, panting.

Mowgli frowned. "I am not afraid of Shere Khan, but Tabaqui is very cunning."

"Have no fear," said Grey Brother, licking his lips a little. "I met Tabaqui in the dawn. Now he is telling all his wisdom to the kites, but he told *me* everything before I broke his back. Shere Khan's plan is to wait for thee at the village gate this evening—for thee and for no one else. He is lying up now in the big dry ravine of the Waingunga."

"Has he eaten to-day, or does he hunt empty?" said Mowgli, for the answer meant life or death to him.

"He killed at dawn,—a pig,—and he has drunk too. Remember, Shere Khan could never fast, even for the sake of revenge."

"Oh! Fool, fool! What a cub's cub it is! Eaten and drunk too, and he thinks that I shall wait till he has slept! Now, where does he lie up? If there were but ten of us we might pull him down as he lies. These buffaloes will not charge unless they wind him, and I cannot speak their language. Can we get behind his track so that they may smell it?"

"He swam far down the Waingunga to cut that off," said Grey Brother.

"Tabaqui told him that, I know. He would never have thought of it alone." Mowgli stood with his finger in his mouth, thinking. "The big ravine of the Waingunga. That opens out on the plain not half a mile from here. I can take the herd round through the Jungle to the head of the ravine and then sweep down—but he would slink out at the foot. We must block that end. Grey Brother, canst thou cut the herd in two for me?"

"Not I, perhaps—but I have brought a wise helper." Grey Brother trotted off and dropped into a hole. Then there lifted up a huge grey head that Mowgli knew well, and the hot air was filled with the most desolate cry of all the Jungle—the hunting-howl of a wolf at midday.

"Akela! Akela!" said Mowgli, clapping his hands. "I might have known that thou wouldst not forget me. We have a big work in hand. Cut the herd in two, Akela. Keep the cows and calves together, and the bulls and the plough-buffaloes by themselves."

The two wolves ran, ladies'-chain fashion, in and out

of the herd, which snorted and threw up its head, and separated into two clumps. In one the cow-buffaloes stood, with their calves in the centre, and glared and pawed, ready if a wolf would only stay still, to charge down and trample the life out of him. In the other the bulls and the young bulls snorted and stamped; but, though they looked more imposing, they were much less dangerous, for they had no calves to protect. No six men could have divided the herd so neatly.

"What orders?" panted Akela. "They are trying to join again."

Mowgli slipped on to Rama's back. "Drive the bulls away to the left, Akela. Grey Brother, when we are gone, hold the cows together, and drive them into the foot of the ravine."

"How far?" said Grey Brother, panting and snapping.

"Till the sides are higher than Shere Khan can jump," shouted Mowgli. "Keep them there till we come down." The bulls swept off as Akela bayed, and Grey Brother stopped in front of the cows. They charged down on him, and he ran just before them to the foot of the ravine, as Akela drove the bulls far to the left.

"Well done! Another charge and they are fairly started. Careful, now—careful, Akela. A snap too much, and the bulls will charge. *Huyah!* This is wilder work than driving black-duck. Didst thou think these creatures could move so swiftly?" Mowgli called.

"I have—have hunted these too in my time," gasped Akela in the dust. "Shall I turn them into the Jungle?"

"Ay, turn! Swiftly turn them! Rama is mad with rage. Oh, if I could only tell him what I need of him to-day!"

The bulls were turned to the right this time, and crashed into the standing thicket. The other herd-children, watching with the cattle half a mile away, hurried to the village as fast as their legs could carry them, crying that the buffaloes had gone mad and run away.

But Mowgli's plan was simple enough. All he wanted to do was to make a big circle uphill and get at the head of the ravine, and then take the bulls down it and catch Shere Khan between the bulls and the cows; for he knew that after a meal and a full drink Shere Khan would not be in any condition to fight or to clamber up the sides of the ravine. He was soothing the buffaloes now by voice, and Akela had dropped far to the rear, only whimpering once or twice to hurry the rear-guard. It was a long, long circle, for they did not wish to get too near the ravine and give Shere Khan warning. At last Mowgli rounded up the bewildered herd at the head of the ravine on a grassy patch that sloped steeply down to the ravine itself. From that height you could see across the tops of the trees down to the plain below; but what Mowgli looked at was the sides of the ravine, and he saw with a great deal of satisfaction that they ran nearly straight up and down, while the vines and creepers that hung over them would give no foothold to a tiger who wanted to get out.

"Let them breathe, Akela," he said, holding up his hand. "They have not winded him yet. Let them breathe. I must tell Shere Khan who comes. We have him in the trap."

He put his hands to his mouth and shouted down the ravine,—it was almost like shouting down a tunnel,—and the echoes jumped from rock to rock.

After a long time there came back the drawling, sleepy snarl of a full-fed tiger just wakened.

"Who calls?" said Shere Khan, and a splendid peacock fluttered up out of the ravine screeching.

"I, Mowgli. Cattle thief, it is time to come to the Council Rock! Down—hurry them down, Akela! Down, Rama, down!"

The herd paused for an instant at the edge of the slope, but Akela gave tongue in the full hunting-yell, and they pitched over one after the other, just as steamers shoot rapids, the sand and stones spurting up round them. Once started, there was no chance of stopping, and before they were fairly in the bed of the ravine Rama winded Shere Khan and bellowed.

"Ha! Ha!" said Mowgli, on his back. "Now thou knowest!" and the torrent of black horns, foaming muzzles, and staring eyes whirled down the ravine like boulders in flood-time; the weaker buffaloes being shouldered out to the sides of the ravine, where they tore through the creepers. They knew what the business was before them—the terrible charge of the buffalo-herd, against which no tiger can hope to stand. Shere Khan heard the thunder of their hoofs, picked himself up, and lumbered down the ravine, looking from side to side for some way of escape; but the walls of the ravine were straight, and he had to keep on, heavy with his dinner and his drink, willing to do anything rather than fight. The herd splashed through the pool he had just left, bellowing till the narrow cut rang. Mowgli heard an answering bellow from the foot of the ravine, saw Shere Khan turn (the tiger knew if the worst came to the worst it was better to meet the bulls than the cows with their calves), and then Rama tripped, stumbled, and went on again over something soft, and, with the bulls at his heels, crashed full into the other herd, while the weaker buffaloes were lifted clean off their feet by the shock of the meeting. That charge carried both herds out into the plain, goring and stamping and snorting. Mowgli watched his time, and slipped off Rama's neck, laying about him right and left with his stick.

"Quick, Akela! Break them up. Scatter them, or they will be fighting one another. Drive them away, Akela. *Hai,* Rama! *Hai! hai! Hai!* my children. Softly now, softly! It is all over."

Akela and Grey Brother ran to and fro nipping the buffaloes' legs, and though the herd wheeled once to charge up the ravine again, Mowgli managed to turn Rama, and the others followed him to the wallows.

Shere Khan needed no more trampling. He was dead, and the kites were coming for him already.

"Brothers, that was a dog's death," said Mowgli, feeling for the knife he always carried in a sheath round his neck now that he lived with men. "But he would have never shown fight. His hide will look well on the Council Rock. We must get to work swiftly."

A boy trained among men would never have dreamed of skinning a ten-foot tiger alone, but Mowgli knew better than any one else how an animal's skin is fitted on, and how it can be taken off. But it was hard work, and Mowgli slashed and tore and grunted for an hour, while the wolves lolled out their tongues, or came forward and tugged as he ordered them.

Presently a hand fell on his shoulder, and looking up he saw Buldeo with the Tower musket. The children had told the village about the buffalo stampede, and Buldeo went out angrily, only too anxious to correct Mowgli for not taking better care of the herd. The wolves dropped out of sight as soon as they saw the man coming.

"What is this folly?" said Buldeo angrily. "To think that thou canst skin a tiger! Where did the buffaloes kill him? It is the Lame Tiger, too, and there is a hundred rupees on his head. Well, well, we will overlook thy letting the herd run off, and perhaps I will give thee one of the rupees of the reward when I have taken the skin to Khanhiwara." He fumbled in his waist-cloth for flint and steel, and stooped down to singe Shere Khan's whiskers. Most native hunters singe a tiger's whiskers to prevent his ghost haunting them.

"Hum!" said Mowgli, half to himself as he ripped back the skin of a fore-paw. "So thou wilt take the hide to Khanhiwara for the reward, and perhaps give me one rupee? Now it is in my mind that I need the skin for my own use. Heh! old man, take away that fire!"

"What talk is this to the chief hunter of the village? Thy luck and the stupidity of thy buffaloes have helped thee to this kill. The tiger has just fed, or he would have gone twenty miles by this time. Thou canst not even skin him properly, little beggar-brat, and forsooth I, Buldeo, must be told not to singe his whiskers. Mowgli, I will not give thee one anna of the reward, but only a very big beating. Leave the carcass!"

"By the Bull that bought me," said Mowgli, who was trying to get at the shoulder, "must I stay babbling to an old ape all noon? Here, Akela, this man plagues me."

Buldeo, who was stooping over Shere Khan's head, found himself sprawling on the grass, with a grey wolf standing over him, while Mowgli went on skinning as though he were alone in all India.

"Ye-es," he said, between his teeth. "Thou art

altogether right, Buldeo. Thou wilt never give me one anna of the reward. There is an old war between the lame tiger and myself—a very old war, and—I have won."

To do Buldeo justice, if he had been ten years younger he would have taken his chance with Akela had he met the wolf in the woods; but a wolf who obeyed the orders of this boy who had private wars with man-eating tigers was not a common animal. It was sorcery, magic of the worst kind, thought Buldeo, and he wondered whether the amulet round his neck would protect him. He lay as still as still, expecting every minute to see Mowgli turn into a tiger, too.

"Maharaj! Great King!" he said at last, in a husky whisper.

"Yes," said Mowgli, without turning his head, chuckling a little.

"I am an old man. I did not know that thou wast anything more than a herd-boy. May I rise up and go away, or will thy servant tear me to pieces?"

"Go, and peace go with thee. Only, another time do not thou meddle with my game. Let him go, Akela."

Buldeo hobbled away to the village as fast as he could, looking back over his shoulder in case Mowgli should change into something terrible. When he got to the village he told a tale of magic and entrancement and sorcery that made the priest look very grave.

Mowgli went on with his work, but it was nearly twilight before he and the wolves had drawn the great gay skin clear of the body.

"Now we must hide this and take the buffaloes home! Help me to herd them, Akela."

The herd rounded up in the misty twilight, and when

they got near the village Mowgli saw lights, and heard the conches and bells blowing and banging. Half the village seemed to be waiting for him by the gate. "That is because I have killed Shere Khan," he said to himself; but a shower of stones whistled about his ears, and the villagers shouted: "Sorcerer! Wolf's brat! Jungle-demon! Go away! Get hence quickly, or the priest will turn thee into a wolf again. Shoot, Buldeo, shoot!"

The old Tower musket went off with a bang, and a young buffalo bellowed in pain.

"More sorcery!" shouted the villagers. "He can turn bullets. Buldeo, that was *thy* buffalo."

"Now what is this?" said Mowgli, bewildered, as the stones flew thicker.

"They are not unlike the Pack, these brothers of thine," said Akela, sitting down composedly. "It is in my head that, if bullets mean anything, they would cast thee out."

"Wolf! Wolf's cub! Go away!" shouted the priest, waving a sprig of the sacred *tulsi* plant.

"Again! Last time it was because I was a man. This time it is because I am a wolf. Let us go, Akela."

A woman—it was Messua—ran across to the herd, and cried: "Oh, my son, my son! They say thou art a sorcerer who can turn himself into a beast at will. I do not believe, but go away or they will kill thee. Buldeo says thou art a wizard, but I know thou hast avenged Nathoo's death."

"Come back, Messua!" shouted the crowd. "Come back, or we will stone thee."

Mowgli laughed a little short ugly laugh, for a stone had hit him in the mouth. "Run back, Messua. This is one of the foolish tales they tell under the big tree at dusk. I have at least paid for thy son's life. Farewell; and run quickly, for I shall send the herd in more swiftly than their brickbats. I am no wizard, Messua. Farewell!"

"Now, once more, Akela," he cried. "Bring the herd in."

The buffaloes were anxious enough to get to the village. They hardly needed Akela's yell, but charged through the gate like a whirlwind, scattering the crowd right and left.

"Keep count!" shouted Mowgli scornfully. "It may be that I have stolen one of them. Keep count, for I will do your herding no more. Fare you well, children of men, and thank Messua that I do not come in with my wolves and hunt you up and down your street."

He turned on his heel and walked away with the Lone Wolf; and as he looked up at the stars he felt happy. "No more sleeping in traps for me, Akela. Let us get Shere Khan's skin and go away. No; we will not hurt the village, for Messua was kind to me."

When the moon rose over the plain, making it look all milky, the horrified villagers saw Mowgli, with two wolves at his heels and a bundle on his head, trotting across at the steady wolf's trot that eats up the long miles like fire. Then they banged the temple bells and blew the conches louder than ever; and Messua cried, and Buldeo embroidered the story of his adventure in the Jungle, till he ended by saying that Akela stood up on his hind legs and talked like a man.

The moon was just going down when Mowgli and the two wolves came to the hill of the Council Rock, and they stopped at Mother Wolf's cave.

"They have cast me out from the Man-Pack, Mother," shouted Mowgli, "but I come with the hide of Shere Khan to keep my word." Mother Wolf walked stiffly from the cave with the cubs behind her, and her eyes glowed as she saw the skin.

"I told him on that day, when he crammed his head and shoulders into this cave, hunting for thy life, Little Frog—I told him that the hunter would be hunted. It is well done."

"Little Brother, it is well done," said a deep voice in the thicket. "We were lonely in the Jungle without thee," and Bagheera came running to Mowgli's bare feet. They clambered up the Council Rock together, and Mowgli spread the skin out on the flat stone where Akela used to sit, and pegged it down with four slivers of bamboo, and Akela lay down upon it, and called the old call to the Council, "Look—look well, O Wolves!" exactly as had called when Mowgli was first brought there.

Ever since Akela had been deposed, the Pack had been without a leader, hunting and fighting at their own pleasure. But they answered the call from habit, and some of them were lame from the traps they had fallen into, and some limped from shot-wounds, and some were mangy from eating bad food, and many were missing; but they came to the Council Rock, all that were left of them, and saw Shere Khan's striped hide on the rock, and the huge claws dangling at the end of the empty, dangling feet. It was then that Mowgli made up a song without any rhymes, a song that came up into his throat all by itself, and he shouted it aloud, leaping up and down on the rattling skin, and beating time with his heels till he had no more breath left, while Grey Brother and Akela howled between the verses.

"Look well, O Wolves! Have I kept my word?" said Mowgli when he had finished; and the wolves bayed, "Yes," and one tattered wolf howled:-

"Lead us again, O Akela. Lead us again, O Man-cub, for we be sick of this lawlessness, and we would be the Free People once more."

"Nay," purred Bagheera, "that may not be. When ye are full-fed, the madness may come upon ye again. Not for nothing are ye called the Free People. Ye fought for freedom, and it is yours. Eat it, O Wolves."

"Man-Pack and Wolf-Pack have cast me out," said Mowgli. "Now I will hunt alone in the Jungle."

"And we will hunt with thee," said the four cubs.

So Mowgli went away and hunted with the four cubs in the Jungle from that day on. But he was not always alone, because years afterwards he became a man and married.

But that is a story for grown-ups.

MOWGLI'S SONG

THAT HE SANG AT THE COUNCIL ROCK WHEN HE DANCED ON SHERE KHAN'S HIDE

The Song of Mowgli—I, Mowgli, am singing. Let the Jungle listen to the things I have done.
Shere Khan said he would kill—would kill! At the gates in the twilight he would kill Mowgli, the Frog!
He ate and he drank. Drink deep, Shere Khan, for when wilt thou drink again? Sleep and dream of the kill.
I am alone on the grazing-grounds. Grey Brother, come to me! Come to me, Lone Wolf, for there is big game afoot.
Bring up the great bull-buffaloes, the blue-skinned herd-bulls with the angry eyes. Drive them to and fro as I order.
Sleepest thou still, Shere Khan? Wake, oh, wake! Here come I, and the bulls are behind.
Rama, the King of the Buffaloes, stamped with his foot. Waters of the Waingunga, whither went Shere Khan?
He is not Ikki to dig holes, nor Mao, the Peacock, that he should fly. He is not Mang, the Bat, to hang in the branches. Little bamboos that creak together, tell me where he ran.
Ow! He is there. *Ahoo!* He is there. Under the feet of Rama lies the Lame One! Up, Shere Khan! Up and Kill! Here is meat; break the necks of the bulls!
Hsh! He is asleep. We will not wake him, for his strength

is very great. The kites have come down to see it. The black ants have come up to know it. There is a great assembly in his honour.

Alala! I have no cloth to wrap me. The kites will see that I am naked. I am ashamed to meet all these people.

Lend me thy coat, Shere Khan. Lend me thy gay striped coat that I may go to the Council Rock.

By the Bull that bought me, I have made a promise—a little promise. Only thy coat is lacking before I keep my word.

With the knife—with the knife that men use—with the knife of the hunter, the man, I will stoop down for my gift.

Waters of the Waingunga, bear witness that Shere Khan gives me his coat for the love that he bears me. Pull, Grey Brother! Pull, Akela! Heavy is the hide of Shere Khan.

The Man-Pack are angry. They throw stones and talk child's talk. My mouth is bleeding. Let us run away.

Through the night, through the hot night, run swiftly with me, my brothers. We will leave the lights of the village and go to the low moon.

Waters of the Waingunga, the Man-Pack have cast me out. I did them no harm, but they were afraid of me. Why?

Wolf-Pack, ye have cast me out too. The Jungle is shut to me and the village gates are shut. Why?

As Mang flies between the beasts and the birds, so fly I between the village and the Jungle. Why?

I dance on the hide of Shere Khan, but my heart is very heavy. My mouth is cut and wounded with the stones from the village, but my heart is very light because I have come back to the Jungle. Why?

These two things fight together in me as the snakes fight in the spring.
The water comes out of my eyes; yet I laugh while it falls. Why?
I am two Mowglis, but the hide of Shere Khan is under my feet.
All the Jungle knows that I have killed Shere Khan.
Look—look well, O Wolves!
Ahae! My heart is heavy with the things that I do not understand.

CHAPTER 4

THE WHITE SEAL

Oh! hush thee, my baby, the night is behind us,
And black are the waters that sparkled so green.
The moon, o'er the combers, looks downward to find us
At rest in the hollows that rustle between.
Where billow meets billow, there soft be thy pillow;
Ah, weary wee flipperling, curl at thy ease!
The storm shall not wake thee, nor shark overtake thee,
Asleep in the arms of the slow-swinging seas.

Seal Lullaby

All these things happened several years ago at a place called Novastoshnah, or North-East Point, on the Island of St. Paul, away and away in the Bering Sea. Limmershin, the Winter Wren, told me the tale when he was blown on to the rigging of a steamer going to Japan, and I took him down into my cabin and warmed and fed him for a couple of days till he was fit to fly back to St. Paul's again. Limmershin is a very odd little bird, but he knows how to tell the truth.

Nobody comes to Novastoshnah except on business, and the only people who have regular business there are the seals. They come in the summer months by hundreds and hundreds of thousands out of the cold grey sea; for Novastoshnah Beach has the finest accommodation for seals of any place in all the world.

Sea Catch knew that, and every spring would swim from whatever place he happened to be in—would swim like a torpedo-boat straight for Novastoshnah, and spend a month fighting with his companions for a good place on the rocks as close to the sea as possible. Sea Catch was fifteen years old, a huge grey fur-seal with almost a mane on his shoulders, and long, wicked dog-teeth. When he heaved himself up on his front flippers he stood more than four feet clear of the ground, and his weight, if any one had been bold enough to weigh him, was nearly seven hundred pounds. He was scarred all over with the marks of savage fights, but he was always ready for just one fight more. He would put his head on one side, as though he was afraid to look his enemy in the face; then he would shoot it out like lightning, and when the big teeth were firmly fixed on the other seal's neck, the other seal might get away if he could, but Sea Catch would not help him.

Yet Sea Catch never chased a beaten seal, for that was against the Rules of the Beach. He only wanted room by the sea for his nursery; but as there were forty or fifty thousand other seals hunting for the same thing each spring, the whistling, bellowing, roaring, and blowing on the beach were something frightful.

From a little hill called Hutchinson's Hill you could look over three and a half miles of ground covered with fighting seals; and the surf was dotted all over with the heads of seals hurrying to land and begin their share of the fighting. They fought in the breakers, they fought in the sand, and they fought on the smooth-worn basalt rocks of the nurseries; for they were just as stupid and unaccommodating as men. Their wives never came to the island until late May or early in June, for they did not care to be torn to pieces; and the young two-, three-, and four-year-old seals who had not begun housekeeping went inland about half a mile through the ranks of the fighters and played about on the sand-dunes in droves and legions, and rubbed off every single green thing that grew. They were called the holluschickie,—the bachelors,—and there were perhaps two or three hundred thousand of them at Novastoshnah alone.

Sea Catch had just finished his forty-fifth fight one spring when Matkah, his soft, sleek, gentle-eyed wife, came up out of the sea, and he caught her by the scruff of the neck and dumped her down on his reservation, saying gruffly: "Late, as usual. Where *have* you been?"

It was not the fashion for Sea Catch to eat anything during the four months he stayed on the beaches, and so his temper was generally bad. Matkah knew better than to answer back. She looked round and cooed: "How thoughtful of you! You've taken the old place again,"

"I should think I had," said Sea Catch. "Look at me!"

He was scratched and bleeding in twenty places; one eye was almost blind, and his sides were torn to ribbons.

"Oh, you men, you men!" Matkah said, fanning herself with her hind flipper. "Why can't you be sensible and settle your places quietly? You look as though you had been fighting with the Killer Whale."

"I haven't been doing anything *but* fight since the middle of May. The beach is disgracefully crowded this season. I've met at least a hundred seals from Lukannon Beach, house-hunting. Why can't people stay where they belong?"

"I've often thought we should be much happier if we hauled out at Otter Island instead of this crowded place," said Matkah.

"Bah! Only the holluschickie go to Otter Island. If we went there they would say we were afraid. We must preserve appearances, my dear."

Sea Catch sunk his head proudly between his fat shoulders and pretended to go to sleep for a few minutes, but all the time he was keeping a sharp lookout for a fight. Now that all the seals and their wives were on the land, you could hear their clamour miles out to sea above the loudest gales. At the lowest counting there were over a million seals on the beach,—old seals, mother seals, tiny babies, and holluschickie, fighting, scuffling, bleating, crawling, and playing together,—going down to the sea and coming up from it in gangs and regiments, lying over every foot of ground as far as the eye could reach, and skirmishing about in brigades through the fog. It is nearly always foggy at Novastoshnah, except when the sun comes out and make everything look all pearly and rainbow-coloured for a little while.

Kotick, Matkah's baby, was born in the middle of that confusion, and he was all head and shoulders, with pale, watery-blue eyes, as tiny seals must be; but there was something about his coat that made his mother look at him very closely.

"Sea Catch," she said at last, "our baby's going to be white!"

"Empty clam-shells and dry seaweed!" snorted Sea

Catch. "There never has been such a thing in the world as a white seal."

"I can't help that," said Matkah; "there's going to be now;" and she sang the low, crooning seal-song that all the mother seals sing to their babies:-

> You mustn't swim till you're six weeks old,
> Or your head will be sunk by your heels;
> And summer gales and Killer Whales
> Are bad for baby seals.
>
> Are bad for baby seals, dear rat,
> As bad as bad can be;
> But splash and grow strong,
> And you can't be wrong,
> Child of the Open Sea!

Of course the little fellow did not understand the words at first. He paddled and scrambled about by his mother's side, and learned to scuffle out of the way when his father was fighting with another seal, and the two rolled and roared up and down the slippery rocks. Matkah used to go to sea to get things to eat, and the baby was fed only once in two days; but then he ate all he could, and throve upon it.

The first thing he did was to crawl inland, and there he met tens of thousands of babies of his own age, and they played together like puppies, went to sleep on the clean sand, and played again. The old people in the nurseries took no notice of them, and the holluschickie kept to their own grounds, so the babies had a beautiful playtime.

When Matkah came back from her deep-sea fishing

she would go straight to their playground and call as a sheep calls for a lamb, and wait until she heard Kotick bleat. Then she would take the straightest of straight lines in his direction, striking out with her fore flipper and knocking the youngsters head over heels right and left. There were always a few hundred mothers hunting for their children through the playgrounds, and the babies were kept lively; but, as Matkah told Kotick, "So long as you don't lie in muddy water and get mange, or rub the hard sand into a cut or scratch, and so long as you never go swimming when there is a heavy sea, nothing will hurt you here."

Little seals can no more swim than little children, but they are unhappy till they learn. The first time that Kotick went down to the sea a wave carried him out beyond his depth, and his big head sank and his little hind flippers flew up exactly as his mother had told him in the song, and if the next wave had not thrown him back again he would have drowned.

After that he learned to lie in a beach-pool and let the wash of the waves just cover him and lift him up while he paddled, but he always kept his eyes open for big waves that might hurt. He was two weeks learning to use his flippers; and all that while he floundered in and out of the water, and coughed and grunted and crawled up the beach and took cat-naps on the sand, and went back again, until at last he found that he truly belonged to the water.

Then you can imagine the times that he had with his companions, ducking under the rollers; or coming in on top of a comber and landing with a swash and a splutter as the big wave went whirling far up the beach; or standing up on his tail and scratching his head as the old people did; or playing "I'm the King of the Castle" on slippery, weedy rocks that just stuck out of the wash. Now and then he would see a thin fin, like a big shark's fin, drifting along close to shore, and he knew that that was the Killer Whale, the Grampus, who eats young seals when he can get them; and Kotick would head for the beach like an arrow, and the fin would jig off slowly, as if it were looking for nothing at all.

Late in October the seals began to leave St. Paul's for the deep sea, by families and tribes, and there was no more fighting over the nurseries, and the holluschickie played anywhere they liked. "Next year," said Matkah to Kotick, "you will be a holluschickie; but this year you must learn how to catch fish."

They set out together across the Pacific, and Matkah showed Kotick how to sleep on his back with his flippers tucked down by his side and his little nose just out of the water. No cradle is so comfortable as the long, rocking swell of the Pacific. When Kotick felt his skin tingle all over, Matkah told him he was learning the "feel of the water", and that tingly, prickly feelings meant bad weather coming, and he must swim hard to get away.

"In a little time," she said, "you'll know where to swim to, but just now we'll follow Sea Pig, the Porpoise, for he is very wise." A school of porpoises were ducking and tearing through the water, and little Kotick followed them as fast as he could. "How do you know where to go to?" he panted. The leader of the school rolled his white eyes, and ducked under. "My tail tingles, youngster," he said. "That means there's a gale behind me. Come along! When you're south of the Sticky Water [he meant the Equator], and your tail tingles, that means there's a gale in front of you and you must head north. Come along! The water feels bad here."

This was one of the many things that Kotick learned, and he was always learning. Matkah taught him to follow the cod and the halibut along the undersea banks, and wrench the rockling out of his hole among the weeds; how to skirt the wrecks lying a hundred fathoms below water, and dart like a rifle-bullet in at one port hole and out at another as the fishes ran; how to dance on the top of the waves when the lightning was racing all over the sky, and wave his flipper politely to the stumpy-tailed Albatross and the Man-of-war Hawk as they went down the wind; how to jump three or four feet clear of the water, like a dolphin, flippers close to the side and tail curved; to leave the flying-fish alone because they are all bony; to take the shoulder-piece out of a cod at full speed ten fathoms deep; and never to stop and look at a boat or a ship, but particularly a row-boat. At the end of six months, what Kotick did not know about deep-sea fishing was not worth the knowing, and all that time he never set a flipper on dry ground.

One day, however, as he was lying half asleep in the warm water somewhere off the Island of Juan Fernandez, he felt faint and lazy all over, just as human people do when the spring is in their legs, and he remembered the good firm beaches of Novastoshnah seven thousand miles away, the games his companions played, the smell of the seaweed, the seal roar, and the fighting. That very minute he turned north, swimming steadily, and as he went on he met scores of his mates, all bound for the same place, and they said: "Greeting, Kotick! This year we are all holluschickie, and we can dance the Fire-dance in the breakers off Lukannon and play on the new grass. But where did you get that coat?"

Kotick's fur was almost pure white now, and though he felt very proud of it, he only said: "Swim quickly! My bones are aching for the land." And so they all came to the beaches where they had been born, and heard the old seals, their fathers, fighting in the rolling mist.

That night Kotick danced the Fire-dance with the yearling seals. The sea is full of fire on summer nights all the way down from Novastoshnah to Lukannon, and each seal leaves a wake like burning oil behind him, and a flaming flash when he jumps, and the waves break in great phosphorescent streaks and swirls. Then they went inland to the holluschickie grounds, and rolled up and down in the new wild wheat, and told stories of what they had done while they had been at sea. They talked about the Pacific as boys would talk about a wood that they had been hunting in, and if any one had understood them, he could have gone away and made such a chart of that ocean as never was. The three- and four-year-old holluschickie romped down from Hutchinson's Hill, crying: "Out of the way, youngsters! The sea is deep, and you don't know all that's in it yet. Wait till you've rounded the Horn. Hi, you yearling, where did you get that white coat?"

"I didn't get it," said Kotick; "it grew." And just as he was going to roll the speaker over, a couple of black-haired men with flat red faces came from behind a sand-dune, and Kotick, who had never seen a man before, coughed and lowered his head. The holluschickie just bundled off a few yards and sat staring stupidly. The men were no less than Kerick Booterin, the chief of the seal-hunters on the island, and Patalamon, his son. They came from the little village not half a mile from the seal-nurseries, and they were deciding what seals they would drive up to the killing-pens (for the seals were driven just like sheep), to be turned into sealskin jackets later on.

"Ho!" said Patalamon. "Look! There's a white seal!"

Kerick Booterin turned nearly white under his oil and smoke, for he was an Aleut, and Aleuts are not clean people. Then he begun to mutter a prayer. "Don't touch him, Patalamon. There has never been a white seal since—since I was born. Perhaps it is old Zaharrof's ghost. He was lost last year in the big gale."

"I'm not going near him," said Patalamon. "He's unlucky. Do you really think he is old Zaharrof come back? I owe him for some gulls' eggs."

"Don't look at him," said Kerick. "Head off that drove of four-year-olds. The men ought to skin two hundred to-day, but it's the beginning of the season, and they are new to the work. A hundred will do. Quick!"

Patalamon rattled a pair of seal's shoulder-bones in front of a herd of holluschickie, and they stopped dead, puffing and blowing. Then he stepped near, and the seals began to move, and Kerick headed them inland, and they never tried to get back to their companions. Hundreds and hundreds of thousands of seals watched them being driven, but they went on playing just the same. Kotick was the only one who asked questions, and none of his companions could tell him anything, except that the men always drove seals in that way for six weeks or two months of every year.

"I am going to follow," he said, and his eyes nearly popped out of his head as he shuffled along in the wake of the herd.

"The white seal is coming after us," cried Patalamon. "That's the first time a seal has ever come to the killing-grounds alone."

"Hsh! Don't look behind you," said Kerick. "It *is* Zaharrof's ghost! I must speak to the priest about this."

The distance to the killing-grounds was only half a mile, but it took an hour to cover, because if the seals went too fast Kerick knew that they would get heated and then their fur would come off in patches when they were skinned. So they went on very slowly, past Sea-Lion's Neck, past Webster House, till they came to the Salt House just beyond the sight of the seals on the beach. Kotick followed, panting and wondering. He thought that he was at the world's end, but the roar of the seal-nurseries behind him sounded as loud as the roar of a train in a tunnel. Then Kerick sat down on the moss and pulled out a heavy pewter watch and let the drove cool off for thirty minutes, and Kotick could hear the fog-dew dripping from the brim of his cap. Then ten or twelve men, each with an iron-bound club three or four feet long, came up, and Kerick pointed out one or two of the drove that were bitten by their companions or were too hot, and the men kicked those aside with their heavy boots made of the skin of a walrus's throat, and then Kerick said: "Let's go!" and then the men clubbed the seals on the head as fast as they could.

Ten minutes later little Kotick did not recognize his friends any more, for their skins were ripped off from the nose to the hind flippers—whipped off and thrown down on the ground in a pile.

That was enough for Kotick. He turned and galloped (a seal can gallop very swiftly for a short time) back to the sea, his little new moustache bristling with horror.

At Sea-Lion's Neck, where the great sea-lions sit on the edge of the surf, he flung himself flipper over head into the cool water, and rocked there, gasping miserably.

"What's here?" said a sea-lion gruffly; for as a rule the sea-lions keep themselves to themselves.

"Scoochnie! Ochen Scoochnie! [I'm lonesome, very lonesome!]" said Kotick. "They're killing all the holluschickie on *all* the beaches!"

The sea-lion turned his head inshore. "Nonsense!" he said; "your friends are making as much noise as ever. You must have seen old Kerick polishing off a drove. He's done that for thirty years."

"It's horrible," said Kotick, backing water as a wave went over him, and steadying himself with a screw-stroke of his flippers that brought him up all standing within three inches of a jagged edge of rock.

"Well done for a yearling!" said the sea-lion, who could appreciate good swimming. "I suppose it *is* rather awful from your way of looking at it; but if you seals will come here year after year, of course the men get to know of it, and unless you can find an island where no men ever come, you will always be driven."

"Isn't there any such island?" began Kotick.

"I've followed the *poltoos* [the halibut] for twenty years, and I can't say I've found it yet. But look here—you seem to have a fondness for talking to your betters; suppose you go to Walrus Islet and talk to Sea Vitch. He may know something. Don't flounce off like that. It's a six-mile swim, and I were you, I should haul out and take a nap first, little one."

Kotick thought that that was good advice, so he swam round to his own beach, hauled out, and slept for half an hour, twitching all over, as seals will. Then he headed straight for Walrus Islet, a little low sheet of rocky island almost due north-east from Novastoshnah, all ledges of rocks and gulls' nests, where the walrus herded by themselves.

He landed close to old Sea Vitch—the big, ugly, bloated, pimpled, fat-necked, long-tusked walrus of the North Pacific, who has no manners except when he is asleep—as he was then, with his hind flippers half in and half out of the surf.

"Wake up!" barked Kotick, for the gulls were making a great noise.

"Hah! Ho! Hmph! What's that?" said Sea Vitch, and he struck the next walrus a blow with his tusks and waked him up, and the next struck the next, and so on till they were all awake and staring in every direction but the right one.

"Hi! It's me," said Kotick, bobbing in the surf and looking like a little white slug.

"Well! May I be—skinned!" said Sea Vitch, and they all looked at Kotick as you can fancy a club full of drowsy old gentlemen would look at a little boy. Kotick did not care to hear any more about skinning just then; he had seen enough of it; so he called out: "Isn't there any place for seals to go where men don't ever come?"

"Go and find out," said Sea Vitch, shutting his eyes. "Run away. We're busy here."

Kotick made his dolphin-jump in the air and shouted as loud as he could: "Clam-eater! Clam-eater!" He knew that Sea Vitch never caught a fish in his life, but always rooted for clams and seaweeds, though he pretended to be a very terrible person. Naturally the Chickies and the Gooverooskies and the Epatkas, the Burgomaster Gulls and the Kittiwakes and the Puffins, who are always looking for a chance to be rude, took up the cry, and—so Limmershin told me—for nearly five minutes you could not have heard a gun fired on Walrus Islet. All the population was yelling and screaming: "Clam-eater! *Stareek!* [old man!]" while Sea Vitch rolled from side to side grunting and coughing.

"*Now* will you tell?" said Kotick, all out of breath.

"Go and ask Sea Cow," said Sea Vitch. "If he is living still, he'll be able to tell you."

"How shall I know Sea Cow when I meet him?" said Kotick, sheering off.

"He's the only thing in the sea uglier than Sea Vitch," screamed a Burgomaster Gull, wheeling under Sea Vitch's nose. "Uglier, and with worse manners! *Stareek!*"

Kotick swam back to Novastoshnah, leaving the gulls to scream. There he found that no one sympathized with him in his little attempts to discover a quiet place for the seals. They told him that men had always driven the holluschickie—it was part of the day's work—and that if he did not like to see ugly things he should not have gone to the killing-grounds. But none of the other seals had seen the killing, and that made the difference between him and his friends. Besides, Kotick was a white seal.

"What you must do," said old Sea Catch, after he had heard his son's adventures, "is to grow up and be a big seal like your father, and have a nursery on the beach, and then they will leave you alone. In another five years you ought to be able to fight for yourself." Even gentle Matkah, his mother, said: "You will never be able to stop the killing. Go and play in the sea, Kotick." And Kotick went off and danced the Fire-dance with a very heavy little heart.

That autumn he left the beach as soon as he could, and set off alone because of a notion in his bullet-head. He was going to find Sea Cow, if there was such a person in the sea, and he was going to find a quiet island with good firm beaches for seals to live on, where men could not get at them. So he explored and explored by himself from the North to the South Pacific, swimming as much as three hundred miles in a day and a night. He met with more adventures than can be told, and narrowly escaped being caught by the Basking Shark, and the Spotted Shark, and the Hammerhead, and he met all the untrustworthy ruffians that loaf up and down the seas, and the heavy polite fish, and the scarlet-spotted scallops that are moored in one place for hundreds of years, and grow very proud of it; but he never met Sea Cow, and he never found an island that he could fancy.

If the beach was good and hard, with a slope behind it for seals to play on, there was always the smoke of a whaler on the horizon, boiling down blubber, and Kotick knew what *that* meant. Or else he could see that seals had once visited the island and been killed off, and Kotick knew that where men had come once they would come again.

He picked up with an old stumpy-tailed albatross, who told him that Kerguelen Island was the very place for peace and quiet, and when Kotick went down there he was all but smashed to pieces against some wicked black cliffs in a heavy sleet-storm with lightning and thunder. Yet as he pulled out against the gale he could see that even there had once been a seal-nursery. And so it was in all the other islands that he visited.

Limmershin gave a long list of them, for he said that Kotick spent five seasons exploring, with a four months' rest each year at Novastoshnah, when the holluschickie used to make fun of him and his imaginery islands. He went to the Galapagos, a horrid dry place on the Equator, where he was nearly baked to death; he went on to the Georgia Islands, the South Orkneys, Emerald Island, Little Nightingale Island, Gough's Island, Bouvet's Island, the Crossets, and even to a little speck of an island south of the Cape of Good Hope. But everywhere the People of the Sea told him the same things. Seal had come to those islands once upon a time, but men had killed them all off. Even when he swam thousands of miles out in the Pacific, and got to a place called Cape Corrientes (that was when he was coming back from Gough's Island), he found a few hundred mangy seals on a rock, and they told him that men came there too.

That nearly broke his heart, and he headed round the Horn back to his own beaches; and on his way north he hauled out on an island full of green trees, where he found an old, old seal who was dying, and Kotick caught fish for him, and told him all his sorrows. "Now," said Kotick, "I am going back to Novastoshnah, and if I am driven to the killing-pens with the holluschickie I shall not care."

The old seal said: "Try once more. I am the last of the Lost Rookery of Masafuera, and in the days when men killed us by the hundred thousand there was a story on the beaches that some day a white seal would come out of the north and lead the seal people to a quiet place. I am old and I shall never live to see that day, but others will. Try once more."

And Kotick curled up his moustache (it was a beauty), and said: "I am the only white seal that has ever been born on the beaches, and I am the only seal, black or white, who ever thought of looking for new islands."

That cheered him immensely; and when he came back to Novastoshnah that summer, Matkah, his mother, begged him to marry and settle down, for he was no longer a holluschickie, but a full-grown sea-catch, with a curly white mane on his shoulders, as heavy, as big, and as fierce as his father. "Give me another reason," he said. "Remember, mother, it is always the seventh wave that goes farthest up the beach."

Curiously enough, there was another seal who thought that she would put off marrying till the next year, and Kotick dance the Fire-dance with her all down Lukannon Beach the night before he set off on his last exploration.

This time he went westward, because he had fallen on the trail of a great shoal of halibut, and he needed at least one hundred pounds of fish a day to keep him in good condition. He chased them till he was tired, and then he curled himself up and went to sleep on the hollows of the groundswell that sets in to Copper Island. He knew the coast perfectly well, so about midnight, when he felt himself gently bumped on a weed-bed, he said, "Hm, tides running strong tonight," and turning over under water opened his eyes slowly and stretched. Then he jumped like a cat, for he saw huge things nosing about in the shoal water and browsing on the heavy fringes of the weeds.

"By the Great Combers of Magellan!" he said, beneath his moustache. "Who in the Deep Sea are these people?"

They were like no walrus, sea-lion, seal bear, whale, shark, fish, squid, or scallop that Kotick had ever seen before. They were between twenty and thirty feet long, and they had no hind flippers, but a shovel-like tail that looked as if it had been whittled out of wet leather. Their heads were the most foolish-looking things you ever saw, and they balanced on the ends of the tails in deep water when they weren't grazing, bowing solemnly to one another and waving their front flippers as a fat man waves his arm.

"Ahem!" said Kotick. "Good sport, gentlemen?" The big things answered by bowing and waving their flippers like the Frog-Footman. When they began feeding again Kotick saw that their upper lip was split into two pieces that they could twitch apart about a foot and bring together again with a whole bushel of seaweed between the splits. They tucked the stuff into their mouths and chumped solemnly.

"Messy style of feeding, that," said Kotick. They bowed again, and Kotick began to lose his temper. "Very good," he said. "If you do happen to have en extra joint in your front flipper you needn't show off so. I see you bow gracefully, but I should like to know your names." The split lips moved and twitched, and the glassy green eyes stared; but they did not speak.

"Well!" said Kotick. "You're the only people I've ever met uglier than Sea Vitch—and with worse manners."

Then he remembered in a flash what the Burgomaster Gull had screamed to him when he was a little yearling at Walrus Islet, and he tumbled backward in the water, for he knew that he had found Sea Cow at last.

The sea cows went on schlooping and grazing and chumping in the weed, and Kotick asked them questions in every language that he had picked up in his travels: and the Sea People talk nearly as many languages as human beings. But the Sea Cow did not answer, because Sea Cow cannot talk. He has only six bones in his neck where he ought to have seven, and they say under the sea that that prevents him from speaking even to his companions; but, as you know, he has an extra joint in his fore flipper, and by waving it up and down and about he makes a sort of clumsy telegraphic code.

By daylight Kotick's mane was standing on end and his temper was gone where the dead crabs go. Then the Sea Cow began to travel northward very slowly, stopping to hold absurd bowing councils from time to time, and Kotick followed them, saying to himself: "People who are such idiots as these are would have been killed long ago if they hadn't found out some safe island; and what is good enough for the Sea Cow is good enough for the Sea Catch. All the same, I wish they'd hurry."

It was weary work for Kotick. The herd never went more than forty or fifty miles a day, and stopped to feed at night, and kept close to the shore all the time; while Kotick swam round them, and over them, and under them, but he could not hurry them on one half-mile. As they went farther north they had a bowing council every few hours, and Kotick nearly bit off his moustache with impatience till he saw that they were following up a warm current of water, and then he respected them more.

One night they sank through the shiny water—sank like stones—and, for the first time since he had known them, began to swim quickly. Kotick followed, and the pace astonished him, for he had never dreamed that Sea Cow was anything of a swimmer. They headed for a cliff by the shore—a cliff that ran down into deep water, and plunged into a dark hole at the foot of it, twenty fathoms under the sea. It was a long, long swim, and Kotick badly wanted fresh air before he was out of the dark tunnel that they had led him through.

"My wig!" he said, when he rose, gasping and puffing, into open water at the farther end. "it was a long dive, but it was worth it."

The sea cows had separated, and were browsing lazily along the edges of the finest beaches that Kotick had ever seen. There were long stretches of smooth-worn rock running for miles, exactly fitted to make seal-nurseries, and there were playgrounds of hard sand sloping inland behind them, and there were rollers for seals to dance in, and long grass to roll in, and sand-dunes to climb up and down; and, best of all, Kotick knew by the feel of the water, which never deceives a true sea catch, that no men had ever come there.

The first thing he did was to assure himself that the fishing was good, and then he swam along the beaches and counted up the delightful low sandy islands half hidden in the beautiful rolling fog. Away to the north-ward out to sea ran a line of bars and shoals and rocks that would never let a ship come within six miles of the beach; and between the islands and the mainland was a stretch of deep water that ran up to the perpendicular cliffs, and somewhere below the cliffs was the mouth of the tunnel.

"It's Novastoshnah over again, but ten times better," said Kotick. "Sea Cow must be wiser than I thought. Men can't come down the cliffs, even if there were any men; and the shoals to seaward would knock a ship to splinters. If any place in the sea is safe, this is it."

He began to think of the seal he had left behind him,

but though he was in a hurry to go back to Novastoshnah, he thoroughly explored the new country, so that he would be able to answer all questions.

Then he dived and made sure of the mouth of the tunnel, and raced through to the southward. No one but a sea cow or a seal would have dreamed of there being such a place, and when he looked back at the cliffs even Kotick could hardly believe that he had been under them.

He was six days going home, though he was not swimming slowly; and when he hauled out just above Sea-Lion's Neck the first person he met was the seal who had been waiting for him, and she saw by the look in his eyes that he had found his island at last.

But the holluschickie and Sea Catch, his father, and all the other seals, laughed at him when he told them what he had discovered, and a young seal about his own age said: "This is all very well, Kotick, but you can't come from no one knows where and order us off like this. Remember we've been fighting for our nurseries, and that's a thing you never did. You preferred prowling about in the sea."

The other seals laughed at this, and the young seal began twisting his head from side to side. He had just married that year, and was making a great fuss about it.

"I've no nursery to fight for," said Kotick. "I want only to show you all a place where you will be safe. What's the use of fighting?"

"Oh, if you're trying to back out, of course I've no more to say," said the young seal, with an ugly chuckle.

"Will you come with me if I win?" said Kotick; and a green light came into his eyes, for he was very angry at having to fight at all.

"Very good," said the young seal carelessly. "*If* you win, I'll come."

He had no time to change his mind, for Kotick's head darted out and his teeth sank in the blubber of the young seal's neck. Then he threw himself back on his haunches and hauled his enemy down the beach, shook him, and knocked him over. Then Kotick roared to the seals: "I've done my best for you these five seasons past. I've found you the island where you'll be safe, but unless your heads are dragged off your silly necks you won't believe. I'm going to teach you now. Look out for yourselves!"

Limmershin told me that never in his life—and Limmershin sees ten thousand big seals fighting every year—never in all his life did he see anything like Kotick's charge into the nurseries. He flung himself at the biggest sea catch he could find, caught him by the throat, choked him and bumped him and dragged him till he grunted for mercy, and then threw him aside and attacked the next. You see, Kotick had never fasted for four months as the big seals did every year, and his deep-sea swimming-trips kept him in perfect condition, and, best of all, he had never fought before. His curly white mane stood up with rage, and his eyes flamed, and his big dog-teeth glistened, and he was splendid to look at.

Old Sea Catch, his father, saw him tearing past, hauling the grizzled old seals about as though they had been halibut, and upsetting the young bachelors in all directions; and Sea Catch gave one roar and shouted: "He may be a fool, but he is the best fighter on the Beaches. Don't tackle your father, my son! He's with you!"

Kotick roared in answer, and old Sea Catch waddled

in, his moustache on end, blowing like a locomotive, while Matkah and the seal that was going to marry Kotick cowered down and admired their men-folk. It was a gorgeous fight, for the two fought as long as there was a seal that dared lift up his head, and then they paraded grandly up and down the beach side by side, bellowing.

At night, just as the Northern Lights were winking and flashing through the fog, Kotick climbed a bare rock and looked down on the scattered nurseries and the torn and bleeding seals. "Now," he said, "I've taught you your lesson."

"My wig!" said old Sea Catch, boosting himself up stiffly, for he was fearfully mauled. "The Killer Whale himself could not have cut them up worse. Son, I'm proud of you, and what's more, *I'll* come with you to your island—if there is such a place."

"Here you, fat pigs of the sea! Who comes with me to the Sea Cow's tunnel? Answer, or I shall teach you again," roared Kotick.

There was a murmur like the ripple of the tide all up and down the beaches. "We will come," said thousands of tired voices. "We will follow Kotick, the White Seal."

Then Kotick dropped his head between his shoulders and shut his eyes proudly. He was not a white seal any more, but red from head to tail. All the same, he would have scorned to look at or touch one of his wounds.

A week later he and his army (nearly ten thousand holluschickie and old seals) went away north to the Sea Cow's tunnel, Kotick leading them, and the seals that stayed at Novastoshnah called them idiots. But next spring, when they all met off the fishing-banks of the Pacific, Kotick's seals told such tales of the new beaches beyond Sea Cow's tunnel that more and more seals left Novastoshnah.

Of course it was not all done at once, for the seals need a long time to turn things over in their minds, but year by year more seals went away from Novastoshnah, and Lukannon, and other nurseries, to the quiet, sheltered beaches where Kotick sits all the summer through, getting bigger and fatter and stronger each year, while the holluschickie play round him, in that sea where no man comes.

LUKANNON

[This is the great deep-sea song that all the St. Paul seals sing when they are heading back to their beaches in the summer. It is a sort of very sad seal National Anthem.]

I met my mates in the morning (and oh, but I am old!)
Where roaring on the ledges the summer ground-swell rolled;
I heard them lift the chorus that drowned the breaker's song—
The Beaches of Lukannon—two million voices strong!

The song of pleasant stations beside the salt lagoons,
The song of blowing squadrons that shuffled down the dunes,
The song of midnight dances that churned the sea to flame—
The Beaches of Lukannon—before the sealers came!

I met my mates in the morning (I'll never meet them more!);
They came and went in legions that darkened all the shore.

And through the foam-flecked offing as far as voice could reach
We hailed the landing-parties and we sang them up the beach.

The Beaches of Lukannon—the winter-wheat so tall—
The dripping, crinkled lichens, and the sea-fog drenching all!
The platforms of our playground, all shining smooth and worn!
The Beaches of Lukannon—the home where we were born!

I meet my mates in the morning, a broken, scattered band.
Men shoot us in the water and club us on the land;
Men drive us to the Salt House like silly sheep and tame,
And still we sing Lukannon—before the sealers came.

Wheel down, wheel down to southward! Oh! Gooverooska, go!
And tell the Deep-Sea Viceroys the story of our woe;
Ere, empty as the shark's egg the temptest flings ashore,
The Beaches of Lukannon shall know their sons no more!

CHAPTER 5

"RIKKI-TIKKI-TAVI"

At the hole where he went in
Red-Eye called to Wrinkle-Skin.
Hear what little Red-Eye saith:
"Nag, come up and dance with death!"

Eye to eye and head to head,
  (*Keep the measure, Nag.*)
This shall end when one is dead;
  (*At thy pleasure, Nag.*)
Turn for turn and twist for twist—
  (*Run and hide thee, Nag.*)
Hah! The hooded Death has missed!
  (*Woe betide thee, Nag!*)

This is the story of the great war that Rikki-tikki-tavi fought single-handed, through the bathrooms of the big bungalow in Segowlee cantonment. Darzee, the tailor-bird, helped him, and Chuchundra, the musk-rat, who never comes out into the middle of the floor, but always creeps round by the wall, gave him advice; but Rikki-tikki-tavi did the real fighting.

He was a mongoose, rather like a little cat in his fur and his tail, but quite like a weasel in his head and his habits. His eyes and the end of his restless nose were pink; he could scratch himself anywhere he pleased, with any leg, front or back, that he chose to use; he could fluff up his tail till it looked like a bottle-brush, and his war-cry, as he scuttled through the long grass, was: "*Rikk-tikk-tikki-tikki-tchk!*

One day, a high summer flood washed him out of the burrow, where he lived with his father and mother, and carried him, kicking and clucking, down a roadside ditch. He found a little wisp of grass floating there, and clung to it till he lost his senses. When he revived, he was lying in the hot sun on the middle of a garden path, very draggled indeed, and a small boy was saying: "Here's a dead mongoose. Let's have a funeral."

"No," said his mother; "let's take him in and dry him. Perhaps he isn't really dead."

They took him into the house, and a big man picked him up between his finger and thumb, and said he was not dead but half choked; so they wrapped him in cotton-wool, and warmed him, and he opened his eyes and sneezed.

"Now," said the big man (he was an Englishman who had just moved into the bungalow); "don't frighten him, and we'll see what he'll do."

It is the hardest thing in the world to frighten a mongoose, because he is eaten up from nose to tail with curiosity. The motto of all the mongoose family is, "Run and find out"; and Rikki-tikki was a true mongoose. He looked at the cotton-wool, decided that it was not good to eat, ran all round the table, sat up and put his fur in order, scratched himself, and jumped on the small boy's shoulder.

"Don't be frightened, Teddy," said his father. "That's his way of making friends."

"Ouch! He's tickling under my chin," said Teddy.

Rikki-tikki looked down between the boy's collar and neck, snuffed at his ear, and climbed down to the floor, where he sat rubbing his nose.

"Good gracious," said Teddy's mother, "and that's a wild creature! I suppose he's so tame because we've been kind to him."

"All mongooses are like that," said her husband. "If Teddy doesn't pick him up by the tail, or try to put him in a cage, he'll run in and out of the house all day long. Let's give him something to eat."

They gave him a little piece of raw meat. Rikki-tikki liked it immensely, and when it was finished he went out into the veranda and sat in the sunshine and fluffed up his fur to make it dry to the roots. Then he felt better.

"There are more things to find out about in this house," he said to himself, "than all my family could find out in all their lives. I shall certainly stay and find out."

He spent all that day roaming over the house. He nearly drowned himself in the bath-tubs, put his nose into the ink on a writing-table, and burnt it on the end of the big man's cigar, for he climbed up in the big man's lap to see how writing was done. At nightfall he ran into Teddy's nursery to watch how kerosene-lamps were lighted, and when Teddy went to bed Rikki-tikki climbed up too; but he was a restless companion, because he had to get up and attend to every noise all through the night, and find out what made it. Teddy's mother and father came in, the last thing, to look at their boy, and Rikki-tikki was awake on the pillow. "I don't like that," said Teddy's mother; "he may bite the child." "He'll do no such thing," said the father. "Teddy's safer with that little beast than if he had a bloodhound to watch him. If a snake came into the nursery now—"

But Teddy's mother wouldn't think of anything so awful.

Early in the morning Rikki-tikki came to early breakfast in the veranda riding on Teddy's shoulder, and they gave him banana and some boiled egg; and he sat on all their laps one after the other, because every well-brought-up mongoose always hopes to be a house-mongoose some day and have rooms to run about in, and Rikki-tikki's mother (she used to live in the General's house at Segowlee) had carefully told Rikki what to do if he ever came across white men.

Then Rikki-tikki went out into the garden to see what was to be seen. It was a large garden, only half-cultivated, with bushes as big as summer-houses of Marshal Niel roses, lime and orange trees, slumps of bamboos, and thickets of high grass. Rikki-tikki licked his lips. "This is a splendid hunting-ground," he said, and his tail grew bottle-brushy at the thought of it, and he scuttled up and down the garden, snuffing here and there till he heard very sorrowful voices in a thornbush.

It was Darzee, the tailor-bird, and his wife. They had made a beautiful nest by pulling two big leaves together and stitching them up the edges with fibres, and had filled the hollow with cotton and downy fluff. The nest swayed to and fro, as they sat on the rim and cried.

"What is the matter?" asked Rikki-tikki.

"We are very miserable," said Darzee. "One of our babies fell out of the nest yesterday, and Nag ate him."

"H'm!" said Rikki-tikki, "that is very sad—but I am a stranger here. Who is Nag?"

Darzee and his wife only cowered down in the nest without answering, for from the thick grass at the foot of the bush there came a low hiss—a horrid cold sound that made Rikki-tikki jump back two clear feet. Then inch by inch out of the grass rose up the head and spread hood of Nag, the big black cobra, and he was five feet long from tongue to tail. When he had lifted one-third of himself clear of the ground, he stayed balancing to and fro exactly as a dandelion-tuft balances in the wind, and he looked at Rikki-tikki with the wicked snake's eyes that never change their expression, whatever the snake may be thinking of.

"Who is Nag?" said he. "*I* am Nag. The great god Brahm put his mark upon all our people when the first cobra spread his hood to keep the sun off Brahm as he slept. Look, and be afraid!"

He spread out his hood more than ever, and Rikki-tikki saw the spectacle-mark on the back of it that looks exactly like the eye part of a hook-and-eye fastening. He was afraid for the minute; but it is impossible for a mongoose to stay frightened for any length of time, and though Rikki-tikki had never met a live cobra before, his mother has fed him on dead ones, and he knew that all a grown mongoose's business in life was to fight and eat snakes. Nag knew that too, and at the bottom of his cold heart he was afraid.

"Well," said Rikki-tikki, and his tail began to fluff up again, "marks or no marks, do you think it is right for you to eat fledglings out of a nest?"

Nag was thinking to himself, and watching the least little movement in the grass behind Rikki-tikki. He knew that mongooses in the garden meant death sooner or later for him and his family, but he wanted to get Rikki-tikki off his guard. So he dropped his head a little, and put it on one side.

"Let us talk," he said. "You eat eggs. Why should not I eat birds?"

"Behind you! Look behind you!" sang Darzee.

Rikki-tikki knew better than to waste time in staring. He jumped up in the air as high as he could go, and just under him whizzed by the head of Nagaina, Nag's wicked wife. She had crept up behind him as he was talking, to make an end of him; and he heard her savage hiss as the stroke missed. He came down almost across her back, and if he had been an old mongoose he would have known that then was the time to break her back with one bite; but he was afraid of the terrible lashing return-stroke of the cobra. He bit, indeed, but did not bite long enough, and jumped clear of the whisking tail, leaving Nagaina torn and angry.

"Wicked, wicked Darzee!" said Nag, lashing up as high as he could reach toward the nest in the thornbush; but Darzee had built it out of reach of snakes, and it only swayed to and fro.

Rikki-tikki felt his eyes growing red and hot (when a mongoose's eyes grow red, he is angry), and he sat back on his tail and hind legs like a kangaroo, and looked all round him, and chattered with rage. But Nag and Nagaina had disappeared into the grass. When a snake misses its stroke, it never says anything or gives any sign of what it means to do next. Rikki-tikki did not care to follow them, for he did not feel sure that he could manage two snakes at once. So he trotted off to the gravel path near the house, and sat down to think. It was a serious matter for him.

If you read the old books of natural history, you will find they say that when the mongoose fights the snake and happens to get bitten, he runs off and eats some herb that cures him. That is not true. The victory is only a matter of quickness of eye and quickness of foot,—

snake's blow against mongoose's jump,—and as no eye can follow the motion of a snake's head when it strikes, that makes things much more wonderful than any magic herb. Rikki-tikki knew he was a young mongoose, and it made him all the more pleased to think that he had managed to escape a blow from behind. It gave him confidence in himself, and when Teddy came running down the path, Rikki-tikki was ready to be petted.

But just as Teddy was stooping, something flinched a little in the dust, and a tiny voice said: "Be careful. I am death!" it was Karait, the dusty brown snakeling that lies for choice on the dusty earth; and his bite is as dangerous as the cobra's. But he is so small that nobody thinks of him, and so he does the more harm to people.

Rikki-tikki's eyes grew red again, and he danced up to Karait with the peculiar rocking, swaying motion that he had inherited from his family. It looks very funny, but it is so perfectly balanced a gait that you can fly off from it at any angle you please; and in dealing with snakes this is an advantage. If Rikki-tikki had only known, he was doing a much more dangerous thing than fighting Nag, for Karait is so small, and can turn so quickly, that unless Rikki bit him close to the back of the head; he would get the return-stroke in his eye or lip. But Rikki did not know; his eyes were all red, and he rocked back and forth, looking for a good place to hold. Karait struck out. Rikki jumped sideways and tried to run in, but the wicked little dusty grey head lashed within a fraction of his shoulder, and he had to jump over the body, and the head followed his heels close.

Teddy shouted to the house: "Oh, look here! Our mongoose is killing a snake"; and Rikki-tikki heard a scream from Teddy's mother. His father ran out with a stick, but by the time he came up, Karait had lunged out once too far, and Rikki-tikki had sprung, jumped on the snake's back, dropped his head far between his fore-legs, bitten as high up the back as he could get hold, and rolled away. That bite paralysed Karait, and Rikki-tikki was just going to eat him up from the tail, after the custom of his family at dinner, when he remembered that a full meal makes a slow mongoose, and if he wanted all his strength and quickness ready, he must keep himself thin.

He went away for a dust-bath under the castor-oil bushes, while Teddy's father beat the dead Karait. "What is the use of that?" thought Rikki-tikki. 'I have settled it all;" and then Teddy's mother picked him up from the dust and hugged him, crying that he had saved Teddy from death, and Teddy's father said that he was a providence, and Teddy looked on with big scared eyes. Rikki-tikki was rather amused at all the fuss, which, of course, he did not understand. Teddy's mother might just as well have petted Teddy for playing in the dust. Rikki was thoroughly enjoying himself.

That night, at dinner, walking to and fro among the wine-glasses on the table, he could have stuffed himself three times over with nice things; but he remembered Nag and Nagaina, and though it was very pleasant to be patted and petted by Teddy's mother, and to sit on Teddy's shoulder, his eyes would get red from time to time, and he would go off into his long war-cry of "*Rikk-tikk-tikki-tikki-tchk!*"

Teddy carried him off to bed, and insisted on Rikki-tikki sleeping under his chin. Rikki-tikki was to well-bred to bite or scratch, but as soon as Teddy was asleep he went off for his nightly walk round the house, and in the dark he ran up against Chuchundra, the musk-rat, creeping round by the wall. Chuchundra is a broken-hearted little beast. He whimpers and cheeps all the night, trying to make up his mind to run into the middle of the room, but he never gets there.

"Don't kill me," said Chuchundra, almost weeping. "Rikki-tikki, don't kill me."

"Do you think a snake-killer kills musk-rats?" said Rikki-tikki scornfully.

"Those who kill snakes get killed by snakes," said Chuchundra, more sorrowfully than ever. "And how am I to be sure that Nag won't mistake me for you some dark night?"

"There's not the least danger," said Rikki-tikki; "but Nag is in the garden, and I know you don't go there."

"My cousin Chua, the rat, told me—" said Chuchundra, and then he stopped.

"Told you what?"

"H'sh! Nag is everywhere, Rikki-tikki. You should have talked to Chua in the garden."

"I didn't—so you must tell me. Quick, Chuchundra, or I'll bite you!"

Chuchundra sat down and cried till the tears rolled off his whiskers. "I am a very poor man," he sobbed. "I never had spirit enough to run out into the middle of the room. H'sh! I mustn't tell you anything. Can't you *hear*, Rikki-tikki?"

Rikki-tikki listened. The house was as still as still, but he thought he could just catch the faintest *scratch-scratch* in the world,—a noise as faint as that of a wasp walking on a window-pane,—the dry scratch of a snake's scales on brickwork.

"That's Nag or Nagaina," he said to himself; "and he is crawling into the bath-room sluice. You're right, Chuchundra; I should have talked to Chua."

He stole off to Teddy's bath-room, but there was nothing there, and then to Teddy's mother's bath-room. At the bottom of the smooth plaster wall there was a brick pulled out to make a sluice for the bath-water, and as Rikki-tikki stole in by the masonry curb where the bath is put, he heard Nag and Nagaina whispering together outside in the moonlight.

"When the house is emptied of people," said Nagaina to her husband, "*he* will have to go away, and then the garden will be our own again. Go in quietly, and remember that the big man who killed Karait is the first one to bite. Then come out and tell me, and we will hunt for Rikki-tikki together."

"But are you sure that there is anything to be gained by killing the people?" said Nag.

"Everything. When there were no people in the bungalow, did we have any mongoose in the garden? So long as the bungalow is empty, we are king and queen of the garden; and remember that as soon as our eggs in the melon-bed hatch (as they may to-morrow), our children will need room and quiet."

"I had not thought of that," said Nag. "I will go, but there is no need that we should hunt for Rikki-tikki afterward. I will kill the big man and his wife, and the child if I can, and come away quietly. Then the bungalow will be empty, and Rikki-tikki will go."

Rikki-tikki tingled all over with rage and hatred at this, and then Nag's head came through the sluice, and his five feet of cold body followed it. Angry as he was, Rikki-tikki was very frightened as he saw the size of the big cobra. Nag coiled himself up, raised his head, and looked into the bath-room in the dark, and Rikki could see his eyes glitter.

"Now, if I kill him here, Nagaina will know; and if I fight him on the open floor, the odds are in his favour. What am I to do?" said Rikki-tikki-tavi.

Nag waved to and fro, and then Rikki-tikki heard him drinking from the biggest water-jug that was used to fill the bath. "That is good," said the snake. "Now, when Karait was killed, the big man had a stick. He may have that stick still, but when he comes in to bathe in the morning he will not have a stick. I shall wait here till he comes. Nagaina—do you hear me?—I shall wait here in the cool till daytime."

There was no answer from outside, so Rikki-tikki knew Nagaina had gone away. Nag coiled himself down, coil by coil, round the bulge at the bottom of the water-jug, and Rikki-tikki stayed still as death. After an hour, he began to move, muscle by muscle, toward the jar. Nag was asleep, and Rikki-tikki looked at his big back, wondering which would be the best place for a good hold. "if I don't break his back at the first jump," said Rikki, "he can still fight; and if he fights—oh, Rikki!" He looked at the thickness of the neck below the hood, but that was too much for him; and a bite near the tail would only make Nag savage.

"It must be the head;" he said at last; "the head above the hood; and when I am once there, I must not let go."

Then he jumped. The head was lying a little clear of the water-jar, under the curve of it; and, as his teeth met, Rikki braced his back against the bulge of the red earthenware to hold down the head. This gave him just one second's purchase, and he made the most of it. Then he was battered to and fro as a rat is shaken by a dog—to and fro on the floor, up and down, and round in great circles; but his eyes were red, and he held on as the body cart-whipped over the floor, upsetting the tin dipper and the soap-dish and the flesh-brush, and banged against the tin side of the bath. As he held he closed his jaws tighter and tighter, for he made sure he would be banged to death, and, for the honour of his family, he preferred to be found with his teeth locked. He was dizzy, aching, and felt shaken to pieces when something went off like a thunderclap just behind him; a hot wind knocked him senseless, and red fire singed his fur. The big man had been wakened by the noise, and had fired both barrels of a shotgun into Nag just behind the hood.

Rikki-tikki held on with his eyes shut, for now he was quite sure he was dead; but the head did not move, and the big man picked him up and said: "It's the mongoose again, Alice; the little chap has saved *our* lives now." Then Teddy's mother came in with a very white face, and saw what was left of Nag, and Rikki-tikki dragged himself to Teddy's bedroom and spent half the rest of the night shaking himself tenderly to find out whether he really was broken into forty pieces, as he fancied.

When morning came he was very stiff, but well pleased with his doings. "Now I have Nagaina to settle with, and she will be worse than five Nags, and there's no knowing when the eggs she spoke of will hatch. Goodness! I must go and see Darzee," he said.

Without waiting for breakfast, Rikki-tikki ran to the thornbush where Darzee was singing a song of triumph at the top of his voice. The news of Nag's death was all over the garden, for the sweeper had thrown the body on the rubbish-heap.

"Oh, you stupid tuft of feathers!" said Rikki-tikki angrily. "Is this the time to sing?"

"Nag is dead—is dead—is dead!" sang Darzee. "The valiant Rikki-tikki caught him by the head and held fast. The big man brought the bang-stick, and Nag fell into two pieces! He will never eat my babies again."

"All that's true enough; but where's Nagaina?" said Rikki-tikki, looking carefully round him.

"Nagaina came to the bath-room sluice and called for Nag," Darzee went on; "and Nag came out on the end of a stick—the sweeper picked him up on the end of a stick and threw him upon the rubbish-heap. Let us sing about the great, the red-eyed Rikki-tikki!" and Darzee filled his throat and sang.

"If I could get up to your nest, I'd roll all your babies out!" said Rikki-tikki. "You don't know when to do the right thing at the right time. You're safe enough in your nest there, but it's war for me down here. Stop singing a minute, Darzee."

"For the great, the beautiful Rikki-tikki's sake I will stop," said Darzee. "What is it, O killer of the terrible Nag?"

"Where is Nagaina, for the third time?"

"On the rubbish-heap by the stables, mourning for Nag. Great is Rikki-tikki with the white teeth."

"Bother ny white teeth! Have you ever heard where she keeps her eggs?"

"In the melon-bed, on the end nearest the wall, where the sun strikes nearly all day. She hid them there weeks ago."

"And you never thought it worth while to tell me? The end nearest the wall, you said?"

"Rikki-tikki, you are not going to eat her eggs?"

"Not eat exactly; no. Darzee, if you have a grain of sense you will fly off to the stables and pretend that your wing is broken, and let Nagaina chase you away to this bush. I must get to the melon-bed, and if I went there now she'd see me."

Darzee was a feather-brain little fellow who could never hold more than one idea at a time in his head; and just because he knew that Nagaina's children were born in eggs like his own, he didn't think at first that it was fair to kill them. But his wife was a sensible bird, and she knew that cobra's eggs meant young cobras later on; so she flew off from the nest, and left Darzee to keep the babies warm, and continue his song about the death of Nag. Darzee was very like a man in some ways.

She fluttered in front of Nagaina by the rubbish-heap, and cried out: "Oh, my wing is broken! The boy in the house threw a stone at me and broke it." Then she fluttered more desperately than ever.

Nagaina lifted her head and hissed: "You warned Rikki-tikki when I would have killed him. Indeed and truly you've chosen a bad place to be lame in." And she moved toward Darzee's wife, slipping along the dust.

"The boy broke it with a stone!" shrieked Darzee's wife.

"Well, it may be some consolation to you when you're dead to know that I shall settle accounts with the boy. My husband lies on the rubbish-heap this morning, but before the night the boy in the house will lie very still. What is the use of running away? I am sure to catch you. Little fool, look at me!"

Darzee's wife knew better than to do *that*, for a bird who looks at a snake's eyes gets too frightened that she cannot move. Darzee's wife fluttered on, piping sorrowfully, and never leaving the ground, and Nagaina quickened her pace.

Rikki-tikki heard them going up the path from the stables, and he raced for the end of the melon-patch near the wall. There, in the warm litter about the melons, very cunningly hidden, he found twenty-five eggs, about the size of a bantam's eggs, but with whitish skin instead of shell.

"I was not a day too soon," he said; for he could see the baby cobras curled up inside the skin, and he knew that the minute they were hatched they could kill a man or a mongoose. He bit off the tops of the eggs as fast as he could, taking care to crush the young cobras, and turned over the litter from time to time to see whether he had missed any. At last there were only three eggs left, and Rikki-tikki began to chuckle to himself, when he heard Darzee's wife screaming:

"Rikki-tikki, I led Nagaina toward the house, and she has gone into the veranda, and—oh, come quickly—she means killing!"

Rikki-tikki smashed two eggs, and tumbled backward down the melon-bed with the third egg in his mouth, and scuttled to the veranda as hard as he could put foot to the ground. Teddy and his mother and father were there at early breakfast; but Rikki-tikki saw that they were not eating anything. They sat stone-still, and their faces were white. Nagaina was coiled up on the matting by Teddy's chair, within easy striking distance of Teddy's bare leg, and she was swaying to and fro singing a song of triumph.

"Son of the big man that killed Nag," she hissed, "stay still. I am not ready yet. Wait a little. Keep very still, all you three. If you move I strike, and if you do not move I strike. Oh, foolish people, who killed my Nag!"

Teddy's eyes were fixed on his father, and all his father could do was to whisper: "Sit still, Teddy. You mustn't move. Teddy, keep still."

Then Rikki-tikki came up and cried: "Turn round, Nagaina; turn and fight!"

"All in good time," said she, without moving her eyes. "I will settle my account with *you* presently. Look at your friends, Rikki-tikki. They are still and white; they are afraid. They dare not move, and if you come a step nearer I strike."

"Look at your eggs," said Rikki-tikki, " in the melon-bed near the wall. Go and look, Nagaina."

The big snake turned half round, and saw the egg on the veranda. "Ah-h! Give it to me," she said.

Rikki-tikki put his paws one on each side of the egg, and his eyes were blood-red. "What price for a snake's egg? For a young cobra? For a young king-cobra? For the last—the very last of the brood? The ants are eating the others down by the melon-bed."

Nagaina spun clear round, forgetting everything for the sake of the one egg; and Rikki-tikki saw Teddy's father shoot out a big hand, catch Teddy by the shoulder, and drag him across the little table with the tea-cups, safe and out of reach of Nagaina.

"Tricked! Tricked! Tricked! *Rikk-tck-tck!*" chuckled Rikki-tikki. "The boy is safe, and it was I—I—I that caught Nag by the hood last night in the bath-room." Then he began to jump up and down, all four feet together, his head close to the floor. "He threw me to and fro, but he could not shake me off. He was dead before the big man blew him in two. I did it. *Rikki-tikki-tck-tck!* Come then, Nagaina. Come and fight with me You shall not be a widow long."

Nagaina saw that she had lost her chance of killing Teddy, and the egg lay between Rikki-tikki's paws. "Give me the egg, Rikki-tikki. Give me the last of my eggs, and I will go away and never come back," she said, lowering her hood.

"Yes you will go away, and you will never come back; for you will go to the rubbish-heap with Nag. Fight, widow! The big man has gone for his gun! Fight!"

Rikki-tikki was bounding all round Nagaina, keeping just out of reach of her stroke, his little eyes like hot coals. Nagaina gathered herself together, and flung out at him. Rikki-tikki jumped up and backward. Again and again and again she struck, and each time her head came with a whack on the matting of the veranda, and she gathered herself together like a watch-spring. Then Rikki-tikki danced in a circle to get behind her, and Nagaina spun round to keep her head to his head, so that the rustle of her tail on the matting sounded like dry leaves blown along by the wind.

He had forgotten the egg. It still lay on the veranda, and Nagaina came nearer and nearer to it, till at last, while Rikki-tikki was drawing breath, she caught it in her mouth, turned to the veranda steps, and flew like an arrow down the path, with Rikki-tikki behind her. When the cobra runs for her life, she goes like a whiplash flicked across a horse's neck.

Rikki-tikki knew that he must catch her, or all the trouble would begin again. She headed straight for the long grass by the thorn-bush, and as he was running Rikki-tikki heard Darzee still singing his foolish little song of triumph. But Darzee's wife was wiser. She flew off her nest as Nagaina came along, and flapped her wings about Nagaina's head. If Darzee had helped they might have turned her; but Nagaina only lowered her hood and went on. Still, the instant's delay brought Rikki-tikki up to her, and as she plunged into the rat-hole where she and Nag used to live, his little white teeth were clenched on her tail, and he went down with her—and very few mongooses, however wise and old they may be, care to follow a cobra into its hole. It was dark in the hole; and Rikki-tikki never knew when it might open out and give Nagaina room to turn and strike him. He held on savagely, and stuck out his feet to act as brakes on the dark slope of the hot, moist earth.

Then the grass by the mouth of the hole stopped waving, and Darzee said: "It is all over with Rikki-tikki! We must sing his death-song. Valiant Rikki-tikki is dead! For Nagaina will surely kill him underground."

So he sang a very mournful song that he made up on the spur of the minute, and just as he got to the most touching part the grass quivered again, and Rikki-tikki, covered with dirt, dragged himself out of the hole leg by leg, licking his whiskers. Darzee stopped with a little shout. Rikki-tikki shook some of the dust out of his fur and sneezed. "It is all over," he said. "The widow will never come out again." And the red ants that live between the grass-stems heard him, and began to troop down one after another to see if he had spoken the truth.

Rikki-tikki curled himself up in the grass and slept where he was—slept and slept till it was late in the afternoon, for he had done a hard day's work.

"Now," he said, when he awoke, "I will go back to the house. Tell the Coppersmith, Darzee, and he will tell the garden that Nagaina is dead."

The Coppersmith is a bird who makes a noise exactly like the beating of a little hammer on a copper pot; and the reason he is always making it is because he is the town-crier to every Indian garden, and tells all the news to everybody who cares to listen. As Rikki-tikki went up the path, he heard his "attention" notes like a tiny dinner-gong; and then the steady *"Ding-dong-tock!* Nag is dead—*dong!* Nagaina is dead! *Ding-dong-tock!"* That set all the birds in the garden singing, and the frogs croaking; for Nag and Nagaina used to eat frogs as well as little birds.

When Rikki got to the house, Teddy and Teddy's mother (she still looked very white, for she had been fainting) and Teddy's father came out and almost cried over him; and that night he ate all that was given him till he could eat no more, and went to bed on Teddy's shoulder, where Teddy's mother saw him when she came to look late at night.

"He saved our lives and Teddy's life," she said to her husband. "Just think, he saved all our lives!"

Rikki-tikki woke up with a jump, for all the mongooses are light sleepers.

"Oh, it's you," said he. "What are you bothering for? All the cobras are dead; and if they weren't, I'm here."

Rikki-tikki had a right to be proud of himself; but he did not grow too proud, and he kept that garden as a mongoose should keep it, with tooth and jump and spring and bite, till never a cobra dared showed its head inside the walls.

DARZEE'S CHAUNT

(SUNG IN HONOUR OF RIKKI-TIKKI-TAVI)

Singer and tailor am I—
Double the joys that I know—
Proud of my lilt through the sky,
Proud of the house that I sew—
Over and under, so weave I my music—so weave I the house that I sew.

Sing to your fledglings again,
Mother, oh, lift up your head!
Evil that plagues us is slain,
Death in the garden lies dead.
Terror that his in the roses is impotent—flung on the dung-hill and dead!

Who hath delivered us, who?
Tell me his nest and his name.
Rikki, the valiant, the true,
Tikki, with eyeballs of flame,
Rik-tikki-tikki, the ivory-fangèd, the hunter with eyeballs of flame.

Give him the Thanks of the Birds,
Blowing with tail-feathers spread!
Praise him with nightingale-words—
Nay, I will praise him instead.
Hear! I will sing you the praise of the bottle-tailed Rikki, with eyeballs of red!

(Here Rikki-tikki interrupted, and the rest of the song is lost.)

CHAPTER 6

TOOMAI OF THE ELEPHANTS

I will remember what I was. I am sick of rope and chain.
I will remember my old strength and all my forest affairs.
I will not sell my back to man for a bundle of sugar-cane,
I will go out to my own kind, and the wood-folk in their lairs.

I will go out until the day, until the morning break,
Out to the winds' untainted kiss, the waters' clean caress:
I will forget my ankle-ring and snap my picket-stake.
I will revisit my lost loves, and playmates masterless!

Kala Nag, which means Black Snake, had served the Indian Government in every way that an elephant could serve it for forty-seven years, and as he was fully twenty years old when he was caught, that makes him nearly seventy—a ripe age for an elephant. He remembered pushing, with a big leather pad on his forehead, at a gun stuck in deep mud, and that was before the Afghan War of 1842, and he had not then come to his full strength. His mother, Radha Pyari,—Radha the darling,—who had been caught in the same drive with Kala Nag, told him, before his little milk-tusks had dropped out, that elephants who were afraid always got hurt; and Kala Nag knew that that advice was good, for the first time that he saw a shell burst he backed, screaming, into a stand of piled rifles, and the bayonets pricked him in all his softest places. So before he was twenty-five he gave up being afraid, and so he was the best-loved and the best-looked-after elephant in the service of the Government of India. He had carried tents, twelve hundred pounds' weight of tents, on the march in Upper India; he had been hoisted into a ship at the end of a steam-crane and taken for days across the water, and made to carry a mortar on his back in a strange and rocky country very far from India, and had seen the Emperor Theodore lying dead in Magdala, and had come back again in the steamer; entitled, so the soldiers said, to the Abyssinian War medal. He had seen his fellow-elephants die of cold and epilepsy and starvation and sunstroke up at a place called Ali Musjid, ten years later; and afterwards he had been sent down thousands of miles south to haul and pile big baulks of teak in the timber-yards at Moulmein. There he had half killed an insubordinate young elephant who was shirking his fair share of the work.

After that he was taken off timber-hauling, and employed with a few score other elephants who were trained to the business, in helping to catch wild elephants among the Garo hills. Elephants are very strictly preserved by the Indian Government. There is one whole department which does nothing else but hunt them, and catch them, and break them in, and send them up and down the country as they are needed for work.

Kala Nag stood ten fair feet at the shoulders, and his tusks had been cut off short at five feet, and bound round the ends, to prevent them splitting, with bands of copper; but he could do more with those stumps than any untrained elephant could do with the real sharpened ones.

When, after weeks and weeks of cautious driving of scattered elephants across the hills, the forty or fifty wild monsters were driven into the last stockade, and the big drop-gate, made of tree-trunks lashed together, jarred down behind them, Kala Nag, at the word of command, would go into that flaring, trumpeting pandemonium (generally at night, when the flicker of the torches made it difficult to judge distances), and, picking out the biggest and wildest tusker of the mob, would hammer him and hustle him into quiet while the men on the backs of the other elephants roped and tied the smaller ones.

There was nothing in the way of fighting that Kala Nag, the old wise Black Snake, did not know, for he had stood up more than once in his time to the charge of the wounded tiger, and, curling up his soft trunk to be out of harm's way, had knocked the springing brute sideways in mid-air with a quick sickle-cut of his head, that he had invented all by himself; had knocked him over, and kneeled upon him with his huge knees till the life went out with a gasp and a howl, and there was only a fluffy striped thing on the ground for Kala Nag to pull by the tail.

"Yes," said Big Toomai, his driver, the son of Black Toomai who had taken him to Abyssinia, the grand-son of Toomai of the Elephants who had seen him caught, "there is nothing that the Black Snake fears except me.

He has seen three generations of us feed him and groom him, and he will live to see four."

"He is afraid of *me* also," said Little Toomai, standing up to his full height of four feet, with only one rag upon him. He was ten years old, the eldest son of Big Toomai, and, according to custom, he would take his father's place on Kala Nag's neck when he grew up, and would handle the heavy iron ankus, the elephant-goad that had been worn smooth by his father, and his grandfather and his great-grandfather. He knew what he was talking of; for he had been born under Kala Nag's shadow, had played with the end of his trunk before he could walk, had taken him down to water as soon as he could walk, and Kala Nag would no more have dreamed of disobeying his shrill little orders than he would have dreamed of killing him on that day when Big Toomai carried the little brown baby under Kala Nag's tusks, and told him to salute his master that was to be.

"Yes," said Little Toomai, "he is afraid of *me*," and he took long strides up to Kala Nag, called him a fat old pig, and made him lift up his feet one after the other.

"Wah!" said Little Toomai, "thou art a big elephant," and he wagged his fluffy head, quoting his father. "The Government may pay for elephants, but they belong to us mahouts. When thou art old, Kala Nag, there will come some rich Rajah, and he will buy thee from the Government, on account of thy size and thy manners, and then thou wilt have nothing to do but to carry gold earings in thy ears, and a gold howdah on thy back, and a red cloth covered with gold on thy sides, and walk at the head of the processions of the King. Then I shall sit on thy neck. O Kala Nag, with a silver ankus, and men will run before us with golden sticks, crying, 'Room for the King's elephant!' That will be good, Kala Nag, but not so good as this hunting in the jungles."

"Umph!" said Big Toomai, "Thou art a boy, and as wild as a buffalo-calf. This running up and down among the hills is not the best Government service. I am getting old, and I do not love wild elephants. Give me brick elephant-lines, one stall to each elephant, and big stumps to tie them to safely, and flat, broad roads to exercise upon, instead of this come-and-go camping. Aha, the Cawnpore barracks were good. There was a bazaar close by, and only three hours' work a day."

Little Toomai remembered the Cawnpore elephant-lines and said nothing. He very much preferred the camp life, and hated those broad, flat roads, with the daily grubbing for grass in the forage-reserve, and the long hours when there was nothing to do except to watch Kala Nag fidgeting in his pickets.

What Little Toomai liked was the scramble up bridle-paths that only an elephant could take; the dip into the valley below; the glimpse of the wild elephants browsing miles away; the rush of the frightened pig and peacock under Kala Nag's feet; the blinding warm rains, when all the hills and valleys smoked; the beautiful misty mornings when nobody knew where they would camp that night; the steady, cautious drive of the wild elephants, and the mad rush and blaze and hullabaloo of the last night's drive, when the elephants poured into the stockade like boulders in a landslide, found that they could not get out, and flung themselves at the heavy posts only to be driven back by yells and flaring torches and volleys of blank cartridge.

Even a little boy could be of use there, and Toomai was as useful as three boys. He would get his torch and wave it, and yell with the best. But the really good time came when the driving out began, and the Keddah—that is, the stockade—looked like a picture of the end of the world, and men had to make signs to one another, because they could not hear themselves speak. Then Little Toomai would climb up to the top of one of the quivering stockade-posts, his sun-bleached brown hair flying all over his shoulders, and he looking like a goblin in the torch-light; and as soon as there was a lull you could hear his high-pitched yells of encouragement to Kala Nag, above the trumpeting and crashing, and snapping of ropes, and groans of the tethered elephants. "*Maîl, maîl, Kala Nag!* [Go on, go on, Black Snake!] *Dant do!* [Give him the tusk!] *Somalo! Somalo!* [Careful, careful!] *Maro! Mar!* [Hit him, hit him!] Mind the post! *Arrê! Arrê! Hai! Yai! Kya-a-ah!*" he would shout, and the big fight between Kala Nag and the wild elephant would sway to and fro across the Keddah, and the old elephant-catchers would wipe the sweat out of their eyes, and find time to nod to Little Toomai wriggling with joy on the top of the posts.

He did more than wriggle. One night he slid down from the post and slipped in between the elephants, and threw up the loose end of a rope, which had dropped, to a driver who was trying to get a purchase on the leg of a kicking young calf (calves always give more trouble than grown-up animals). Kala Nag saw him, caught him in his trunk, and handed him up to Big Toomai, who slapped him then and there, and put him back on the post.

Next morning he gave him a scolding, and said: "Are not good brick elephant-lines and a little tent-carrying enough, that thou must needs go elephant-catching on thy own account, little worthless? Now those foolish hunters, whose pay is less than my pay, have spoken to Petersen Sahib of the matter." Little Toomai was frightened. He did not know much of white men, but Petersen Sahib was the greatest white man in the world to him. He was the head of all the Keddah operations—the man who caught all the elephants for the Government of India, and who knew more about the ways of elephants than any living man.

"What—what will happen?" said Little Toomai.

"Happen! the worst that can happen. Petersen Sahib is a madman. Else why should he go hunting these wild devils? He may even require thee to be an elephant-catcher, to sleep anywhere in these fever-filled jungles, and at last to be trampled to death in the Keddah. It is well that this nonsense ends safely. Next week the catching is over, and we of the plains are sent back to our stations. Then we will march on smooth roads, and forget all this hunting. But, son, I am angry that thou shouldst meddle in the business that belongs to these dirty Assamese jungle-folk. Kala Nag will obey none but me, so I must go with him into the Keddah; but he is only a fighting elephant, and he does not help to rope them. So I sit at my ease, as befits a mahout,—not a mere hunter,—a mahout, I say, and a man who gets a pension at the end of his service. Is the family of Toomai of the Elephants to be trodden underfoot in the dirt of a Keddah? Bad one! Wicked one! Worthless son! Go and wash Kala Nag and attend to his ears, and see that there are no thorns in his feet; or else Petersen Sahib will surely catch thee and make thee a wild hunter—a follower of elephants' foot-tracks, a jungle-bear. Bah! Shame! Go!"

Little Toomai went off without saying a word, but he told Kala Nag all his grievances while he was examining his feet. "No matter," said Little Toomai, turning up the fringe of Kala Nag's huge right ear. "They have said my name to Petersen Sahib, and perhaps—and perhaps—and perhaps—who knows? Hai! That is a big thorn that I have pulled out!"

The next few days were spent in getting the elephants together, in walking the newly caught wild elephants up and down between a couple of tame ones, to prevent them from giving too much trouble on the downward march to the plains, and in taking stock of the blankets ropes and things that had been worn out or lost in the forest.

Petersen Sahib came in on his clever she-elephant Pudmini. He had been paying off other camps among the hills, for the season was coming to an end, and there was a native clerk sitting at a table under a tree to pay the driver their wages. As each man was paid he went back to his elephant, and joined the line that stood ready to start. The catchers, and hunters, and beaters, the men of the regular Keddah, who stayed in the jungle year in and year out, sat on the backs of the elephants that belonged to Petersen Sahib's permanent force, or leaned against the trees with their guns across their arms, and made fun of the drivers who were going away, and laughed when the newly caught elephants broke the line and ran about.

Big Toomai went up to the clerk with Little Toomai behind him, and Machua Appa, the head-tracker, said in an undertone to a friend of his, "There goes one piece of good elephant-stuff at least. 'Tis a pity to send that young jungle-cock to moult in the plains."

Now Petersen Sahib had ears all over him, as a man must have who listens to the most silent of all living things—the wild elephant. He turned where he was lying all along on Pudmini's back, and said, "What is that? I did not know of a man among the plains-drivers who had wit enough to rope even a dead elephant."

"This is not a man, but a boy. He went into the Keddah at the last drive, and threw Barmao there the rope when we were trying to get that young calf with the blotch on his shoulder away from his mother."

Machua Appa pointed at Little Toomai, and Petersen Sahib looked, and Little Toomai bowed to the earth.

"He throw a rope? He is smaller than a picket-pin. Little one, what is thy name?" said Petersen Sahib.

Little Toomai was too frightened to speak, but Kala Nag was behind him, and Toomai made a sign with his hand, and the elephant caught him up in his trunk and held him level with Pudmini's forehead, in front of the great Petersen Sahib. Then Little Toomai covered his face with his hands, for he was only a child, and except where elephants were concerned, he was just as bashful as a child could be.

"Oho!" said Petersen Sahib, smiling underneath his moustache, "and why didst thou teach thy elephant *that* trick? Was it to help thee steal green corn from the roofs of the houses when the ears are put out to dry?"

"Not green corn, Protector of the Poor,—melons," said Little Toomai, and all the men sitting about broke into a roar of laughter. Most of them had taught their elephants that trick when they were boys. Little Toomai was hanging eight feet up in the air, and he wished very much that he were eight feet underground.

"He is Toomai, my son, Sahib," said Big Toomai,

scowling. "He is a very bad boy, and he will end in a jail, Sahib."

"Of that I have my doubts," said Petersen Sahib. "A boy who can face a full Keddah at his age does not end in jails. See, little one, here are four annas to spend in sweetmeats because thou hast a little head under that great thatch of hair. In time thou mayest become a hunter too." Big Toomai scowled more than ever. "Remember, though, that Keddahs are not good for children to play in," Petersen Sahib went on.

"Must I never go there, Sahib?" asked Little Toomai, with a big gasp.

"Yes." Petersen Sahib smiled again. "When thou hast seen the elephants dance. That is the proper time. Come to me when thou hast seen the elephants dance, and then I will let thee go into all the Keddahs."

There was another roar of laughter, for that is an old joke among elephant-catchers, and it means just never. There are great cleared flat places hidden away in the forests that are called elephants' ball-rooms, but even these are only found by accident, and no man has ever seen the elephants dance. When a driver boasts of his skill and bravery the other drivers say, "And when didst *thou* see the elephants dance?"

Kala Nag put Little Toomai down, and he bowed to the earth again and went away with his father, and gave the silver four-anna piece to his mother, who was nursing his baby brother, and they all were put on Kala Nag's back, and the line of grunting, squealing elephants rolled down the hill-path to the plains. It was a very lively march on account of the new elephants, who gave trouble at every ford, and who needed coaxing or beating every other minute.

Big Toomai prodded Kala Nag spitefully, for he was very angry, but Little Toomai was too happy to speak. Petersen Sahib had noticed him, and given him money, so he felt as a private soldier would feel if he had been called out of the ranks and praised by his commander-in-chief.

"What did Petersen Sahib mean by the elephant-dance?" he said, at last, softly to his mother.

Big Toomai heard him and grunted. "That thou shouldst never be one of these hill-buffaloes of trackers. *That* was what he meant. Oh, you in front, what is blocking the way?"

An Assamese driver, two or three elephants ahead, turned round angrily, crying: "Bring up Kala Nag, and knock this youngster of mine into good behaviour. Why should Petersen Sahib have chosen *me* to go down with you donkeys of the rice-fields? Lay your beast alongside, Toomai, and let him prod with his tusks. By all the gods of the Hills, these new elephants are possessed, or else they can smell their companions in the jungle."

Kala Nag hit the new elephant in the ribs and knocked the wind out of him, as Big Toomai said, "We have swept the hills of wild elephants at the last catch. It is only your carelessness in driving. Must I keep order along the whole line?"

"Hear him!" said the other driver. "We have swept the hills! Ho! ho! You are very wise, you plains-people. Anyone but a mud-head who never saw the jungle would know that *they* know that the drives are ended for the season. Therefore all the wild elephants to-night will—but why should I waste wisdom on a river-turtle?"

"What will they do?" Little Toomai called out.

"*Ohé*, little one. Art thou there? Well, I will tell thee,

for thou hast a cool head. They will dance, and it behoves thy father, who has swept *all* the hills of *all* the elephants, to double-chain his pickets to-night."

"What talk is this?" said Big Toomai. "For forty years, father and son, we have tended elephants, and we have never heard such moonshine about dances."

"Yes; but a plains-man who, lives in a hut knows only the four walls of his hut. Well, leave thy elephants unshackled to-night and see what comes; as for their dancing, I have seen the place where—*Bapree-Bap!* how many windings has the Dihang River? Here is another ford, and we must swim the calves. Stop still, you behind there."

And in this way, talking and wrangling and splashing through the rivers, they made their first march to a sort of receiving-camp for the new elephants; but they lost their tempers long before they got there.

Then the elephants were chained by their hind legs to their big stumps of pickets, and extra ropes were fitted to the new elephants, and the fodder was piled before them, and the hill-drivers went back to Petersen Sahib through the afternoon light, telling the plains-drivers to be extra careful that night, and laughing when the plains-drivers asked the reason.

Little Toomai attended to Kala Nag's supper, and as evening fell wandered through the camp, unspeakably happy, in search of a tom-tom. When an Indian child's heart is full, he does not run about and make a noise in an irregular fashion. He sits down to a sort of revel all by himself. And Little Toomai had been spoken to by Petersen Sahib! If he had not found what he wanted, I believe he would have burst. But the sweetmeat-seller in the camp lent him a little tom-tom—a drum beaten with the flat of the hand—and he sat down, cross-legged, before Kala Nag as the stars began to come out, the tom-tom in his lap, and he thumped and he thumped and he thumped, and the more he thought of the great honour that had been done to him, the more he thumped, all alone among the elephant-fodder. There was no tune and no words, but the thumping made him happy.

The new elephants strained at their ropes, and squealed and trumpeted from time to time, and he could hear his mother in the camp hut putting his small brother to sleep with an old, old song about the great God Shiv, who once told all the animals what they should eat. It is a very soothing lullaby, and the first verse says:-

Shiv, who poured the harvest and made the winds to blow,
Sitting at the doorways of a day of long ago,
Gave to each his portion, food and toil and fate,
From the king upon the *guddee* to the Beggar at the gate.
    All things made he—Shiva the Preserver.
    Mahadeo! Mahadeo! He made all,—
    Thorn for the camel, fodder for the kine,
    And mother's heart for sleepy head, O little son of mine!

Little Toomai came in with a joyous *tunk-a-tunk* at the end of each verse, till he felt sleepy and stretched himself on the fodder at Kala Nag's side.

At last the elephants began to lie down one after another, as is their custom, till only Kala Nag at the right of the line was left standing up; and he rocked slowly from side to side, his ears put forward to listen to the night wind as it blew very slowly across the hills. The air was full of all the night noises that, taken together, make one big silence—the click of one bamboo-stem against the other, the rustle of something alive in the undergrowth, the scratch and squawk of a half-waked bird (birds are awake in the night much more often than we imagine), and the fall of water ever so far away. Little Toomai slept for some time, and when he waked it was brilliant moonlight, and Kala Nag was still standing up with his ears cocked. Little Toomai turned, rustling in the fodder, and watched the curve of his big back against half the stars in heaven; and while he watched he heard, so far away that it sounded no more than a pinhole of noise pricked through the stillness, the "hoot-toot" of a wild elephant.

All the elephants in the lines jumped up as if they had been shot, and their grunts at last waked the sleeping mahouts, and they came out and drove in the picket-pegs with big mallets, and tightened this rope and knotted that till all was quiet. One new elephant had nearly grubbed up his picket, and Big Toomai took off Kala Nag's leg-chain and shackled that elephant fore-foot to hind-foot, but slipped a loop of grass-string round Kala Nag's leg, and told him to remember that he was tied fast. He knew that he and his father and his grandfather had done the very same thing hundreds of times before. Kala Nag did not answer to the order by gurgling, as he usually did. He stood still, looking out across the moonlight, his head a little raised, and his ears spread like fans, up to the great folds of the Garo hills.

"Look to him if he grows restless in the night." said Big Toomai to Little Toomai, and he went into the hut and slept. Little Toomai was just going to sleep, too, when he heard the coir string snap with a little "tang," and Kala Nag rolled out of his pickets as slowly and as silently as a cloud rolls out of the mouth of a valley. Little Toomai pattered after him, barefooted, down the road in the moonlight, calling under his breath, "Kala Nag! Kala Nag! Take me with you, O Kala Nag!" The elephant turned without a sound, took three strides back to the boy in the moonlight, put down his trunk, swung him up to his neck, and almost before Little Toomai had settled his knees slipped into the forest.

There was one blast of furious trumpeting from the lines, and then the silence shut down on everything, and Kala Nag began to move. Sometimes a tuft of high grass washed along his sides as a wave washes along the side of a ship, and sometimes a cluster of wild pepper vines would scrape along his back, or a bamboo would creak where his shoulder touched it; but between those times he moved absolutely without any sound, drifting through the thick Garo forest as though it had been smoke. He was going uphill, but though Little Toomai watched the stars in the rifts of the trees, he could not tell in what direction.

Then Kala Nag reached the crest of the ascent and stopped for a minute, and Little Toomai could see the tops of the trees lying all speckled and furry under the moonlight for miles and miles, and the blue-white mist over the river in the hollow. Toomai leaned forward and looked, and he felt that the forest was awake below him—awake and alive and crowded. A big brown fruit-eating bat brushed past his ear; a porcupine's quills rattled in the thicket; and in the darkness between the tree-stems he heard a hog-bear digging hard in the moist, warm earth, and snuffing as it digged.

Then the branches closed over his head again, and Kala Nag began to go slowly down into the valley—not quietly this time, but as a runaway gun goes down a steep bank—in one rush. The huge limbs moved as steadily as pistons, eight feet to each stride, and the wrinkled skin of the elbow-points rustled. The undergrowth on either side of him ripped with a noise like torn canvas, and the saplings that he heaved away right and left with his shoulders sprang back again, and banged him on the flank, and great trails of creepers, all matted together, hung from his tusks as he threw his head from side to side and ploughed out his pathway. Then Little Toomai laid himself down close to the great neck, lest a swinging bough should sweep him to the ground, and he wished that he were back in the lines again.

The grass began to get squashy, and Kala Nag's feet sucked and squelched as he put them down, and the night mist at the bottom of the valley chilled Little Toomai. There was a splash and a trample, and the rush of running water, and Kala Nag strode through the bed of river, feeling his way at each step. Above the noise of the water, as it swirled round the elephant's legs, Little Toomai could hear more splashing and some trumpeting both up stream and down—great grunts and angry snorting, and all the mist about him seemed to be full of rolling, wavy shadows.

"*Ai!*" he said, half aloud, his teeth chattering. "The elephant-folk are out to-night. It *is* the dance, then."

Kala Nag swashed out of the water, blew his trunk clear, and began another climb; but this time he was not alone, and he had not to make his path. That was made already, six feet wide, in front of him, where the bent jungle-grass was trying to recover itself and stand up. many elephants must have gone that way only a few minutes before. Little Toomai looked back, and behind him a great wild tusker, with his little pig's eyes glowing like hot coals, was just lifting himself out of the misty river. Then the trees closed up again, and they went on and up, with trumpetings and crashings, and the sound of breaking branches on every side of them.

At last Kala Nag stood still between two tree-trunks at the very top of the hill. They were part of a circle of trees that grew round an irregular space of some three or four acres, and in all that space, as Little Toomai could see, the ground had been trampled down as hard as a brick floor. Some trees grew in the centre of the clearing, but their bark was rubbed away, and the white wood beneath showed all shiny and polished in the patches of moonlight. There were creepers hanging from the upper branches, and the bells of the flowers of the creepers, great waxy white things like convolvuluses, hung down fast asleep; but within the limits of the clearing there was not a single blade of green—nothing but the trampled earth.

The moonlight showed it all iron-grey, except where some elephants stood upon it, and their shadows were inky black. Little Toomai looked, holding his breath, with his eyes starting out of his head, and as he looked, more and more and more elephants swung out into the open from between the tree-trunks. Little Toomai could count only up to ten, and he counted again and again on his fingers till he lost count of the tens, and his head began to swim. Outside the clearing he could hear them crashing in the undergrowth as they worked their way up the hillside; but as soon as they were within the circle of the tree-trunk they moved like ghosts.

There were white-tusked wild males, with fallen leaves and nuts and twigs lying in the wrinkles of their necks and the folds of their ears; fat, slow-footed she-elephants, with restless little pinky-black calves only three or four feet high running under their stomachs; young elephants with their tusks just beginning to show, and very proud of them; lanky, scraggy old-maid elephants, with their hollow, anxious faces, and trunks like rough bark; savage old bull-elephants, scarred from shoulder to flank with great weals and cuts of bygone fights, and the caked dirt of their solitary mud-baths dropping from their shoulders; and there was one with a broken tusk and the marks of the full-stroke, the terrible drawing scrape, of a tiger's claws on his side.

They were standing head to head, or walking to and fro across the ground in couples, or rocking and swaying all by themselves—scores and scores of elephants.

Toomai knew that, so long as he lay still on Kala Nag's neck, nothing would happen to him; for even in the rush and scramble of a Keddah-drive a wild elephant does not reach up with his trunk and drag a man off the neck of a tame elephant; and these elephants were not thinking of men that night. Once they started and put their ears forward when they heard the chinking of a leg-iron in the forest, but it was Pudmini, Petersen Sahib's pet elephant, her chain snapped short off, grunting, snuffling up the hillside. She must have broken her pickets, and come straight from Petersen Sahib's camp; and Little Toomai saw another elephant, one that he did not know, with deep rope-galls on his back and breast.

He, too, must have run away from some camp in the hills about.

At last there was no sound of any more elephants moving in the forest, and Kala Nag rolled out from his station between the trees and went into the middle of the crowd, clucking and gurgling, and all the elephants began to talk in their own tongue, and to move about.

Still lying down, Little Toomai looked down upon scores and scores of broad backs, and wagging ears, and tossing trunks, and little rolling eyes. He heard the click of tusks as they crossed other tusks by accident, and the dry rustle of trunks twined together, and the chafing of enormous sides and shoulder in the crowd, and the incessant flick and *hissh* of the great tails. Then a cloud came over the moon, and he sat in black darkness; but the quiet, steady hustling and pushing and gurgling went on just the same. He knew that there were elephants all round Kala Nag, and that there was no chance of backing him out of the assembly; so he set his teeth and shivered. In a Keddah at least there was torch-light and shouting, but here he was all alone in the dark, and once a trunk came up and touched him on the knee.

Then an elephant trumpeted, and they all took it up for five or ten terrible seconds. The dew from the trees above spattered down like rain on the unseen backs, and a dull booming noise began, not very loud at first, and Little Toomai could not tell what is was; but it grew and grew, and Kala Nag lifted up one fore-foot and then the other, and brought them down on the ground—one-two, one-two, as steadily as trip-hammers. The elephants were stamping all together now, and it sounded like a war-drum beaten at the mouth of a cave. The dew fell from the trees till there was no more left to fall, and the booming went on, and the ground rocked and shivered, and Little Toomai put his hands up to his ears to shut out the sound. But is was all one gigantic jar that ran through him—this stamp of hundreds of heavy feet on the raw earth. Once or twice he could feel Kala Nag and all the others surge forward a few strides, and the trumpeting would change to the crushing sound of juicy green things being bruised, but in a minute or two the boom of feet on hard earth began again. A tree was creaking and groaning somewhere near him. He put out his arm and felt the bark, but Kala Nag moved forward, still tramping, and he could not tell where he was in the clearing. There was no sound from the elephants, except one, when two or three little calves squeaked together. Then he heard a thump and a shuffle and the booming went on. It must have lasted fully two hours, and Little Toomai ached in every nerve; but he knew by the smell of the night air that the dawn was coming.

The morning broke in one sheet of pale yellow behind the green hills, and the booming stopped with the first ray, as though the light had been an order. Before Little Toomai had got the ringing out of his head, before even he had shifted his position, there was not an elephant in sight except Kala Nag, Pudmini, and the elephant with the rope-galls, and there was neither sign nor rustle nor whisper down the hillsides to show where the others had gone.

Little Toomai stared again and again. The clearing, as he remembered it, had grown in the night. More trees stood in the middle of it, but the undergrowth and the jungle-grass at the sides had been rolled back. Little Toomai stared once more. Now he understood the trampling. The elephants had stamped out more room—

had stamped the thick grass and juicy cane to trash, the trash into slivers, the slivers into tiny fibres, and the fibres into hard earth.

"Wah!" said Little Toomai, and his eyes were very heavy. "Kala Nag, my lord, let us keep by Pudmini and go to Petersen Sahib's camp, or I shall drop from thy neck."

The third elephant watched the two go away, snorted, wheeled round, and took his own path. He may have belonged to some little native king's establishment, fifty or sixty or a hundred miles away.

Two hours later, as Petersen Sahib was eating early breakfast, the elephants, who had been double-chained that night, began to trumpet, and Pudmini, mired to the shoulders, with Kala Nag, very foot-sore, shambled into the camp.

Little Toomai's face was grey and pinched, and his hair was full of leaves and drenched with dew; but he tried to salute Petersen Sahib, and cried faintly: "The dance—the elephant-dance! I have seen it, and—I die!" As Kala Nag sat down, he slid off his neck in a dead faint.

But, since native children have no nerves worth speaking of, in two hours he was lying very contently in Petersen Sahib's hammock with Petersen Sahib's shooting-coat under his head, and a glass of warm milk, a little brandy, with a dash of quinine inside of him; and while the old hairy, scarred hunters of the jungles sat three-deep before him, looking at him as though he were a spirit, he told his tale in short words, as a child will, and wound up with:-

"Now, if I lie in one word, send men to see, and they will find that the elephant-folk have trampled down more room in their dance-room, and they will find ten and ten, and many times ten, tracks leading to that dance-room. They made more room with their feet. I have seen it. Kala Nag took me, and I saw, Also Kala Nag is very leg-weary!"

Little Toomai lay back and slept all through the long afternoon and into the twilight, and while he slept Petersen Sahib and Machua Appa followed the track of the two elephants for fifteen miles across the hills. Petersen Sahib had spent eighteen years in catching elephants, and he had only once before found such a dance-place. Machua Appa had no need to look twice at the clearing to see what had been done there, or to scratch with his toe in the packed, rammed earth.

"The child speaks truth," said he. "All this was done last night, and I have counted seventy tracks crossing the river. See, Sahib, where Pudmini's leg-iron cut the bark off that tree! Yes; she was there too."

They looked at each other, and up and down, and they wondered; for the ways of elephants are beyond the wit of any man, black or white, to fathom.

"Forty years and five," said Machua Appa, "have I followed my lord the elephant, but never have I heard that any child of man had seen what this child has seen. By all the Gods of the Hills, it is—what can we say?" and he shook his head.

When they got back to camp it was time for the evening meal. Petersen Sahib ate alone in his tent, but he gave orders that the camp should have two sheep and some fowl, as well as a double ration of flour and rice and salt, for he knew that there would be a feast.

Big Toomai had come up hot-foot from the camp in the plains to search for his son and his elephant, and now that he had found them he looked at them as though he were afraid of them both. And there was a feast by the blazing camp-fires in front of the lines of picketed elephants, and Little Toomai was the hero of it all; and the big brown elephant-catchers, the trackers and drivers and ropers, and the men who know all the secrets of breaking the wildest elephants, passed him from one to the other, and they marked his forehead with blood from the beast of a newly killed jungle-cock, to show that he was a forester, initiated and free of all the jungles.

And at last, when the flames died down, and the red light of the logs made the elephants look as though they had been dipped in blood too, Machua Appa, the head of all the drivers of all the Keddahs,—Machua Appa, Petersen Sahib's other self, who had never seen a made road in forty years: Machua Appa, who was so great that he had no other name than Machua Appa,—leaped to his feet, with Little Toomai held high in the air above his head, and shouted: "Listen, my brothers. Listen, too, you my lords in the lines there, for I, Machua Appa, am speaking! This little one shall no more be called Little Toomai, but Toomai of the Elephants, as his great-grandfather was called before him. What never man has seen he has seen through the long night, and the favour of the elephant-folk and of the Gods of the Jungles is with him. He shall become a great tracker; he shall become greater than I, even I—Machua Appa! He shall follow the new trail, and the stale trail, and the mixed trail, with a clear eye! He shall take no harm in the Keddah when he runs under their bellies to rope the wild tuskers; and if he slips before the feet of the charging bull-elephant, that bull-elephant shall know who he is and shall not crush him. *Aihai!* my lords in the chains,"—he whirled up the line of pickets,—"here is the little one that has seen your dances, in your hidden places—the sight that never man saw! Give him honour, my lords! *Salaam karo,* my children! Make your salute to Toomai of the Elephants! Gunga Pershad, ahaa! Hira Guj, Birchi Guj, Kuttar Guj, ahaa! Pudmini—thou hast seen him at the dance, and thou too, Kala Nag, my pearl among elephants!—ahaa! Together! To Toomai of the Elephants. *Barrao!*"

And at that last wild yell the whole line flung up their trunks till the tips touched their foreheads, and broke out into the full salute, the crashing trumpet-peal that only the Viceroy of India hears—the Salaam-ut of the Keddah.

But it was all for the sake of Little Toomai, who had seen what never man had seen before—the dance of the elephants at night and alone in the heart of the Garo hills!

SHIV AND THE GRASSHOPPER

(THE SONG THAT TOOMAI'S MOTHER SANG TO THE BABY)

Shiv, who poured the harvest and made the winds to blow,
Sitting at the doorways of a day of long ago,
Gave to each his portion, food and toil and fate,
From the King upon the *guddee* to the Beggar at the gate.
All things made he—Shiva the Preserver.
Mahadeo! Mahadeo! He made all,—
Thorn for the camel, fodder for the kine,
And mother's heart for sleepy head, O little son of mine!

Wheat he gave to rich folk, millet to the poor,
Broken scraps for holy men that beg from door to door;
Cattle to the tiger, carrion to the kite,
And rags and bones to wicked wolves without the wall at night.
Naught he found too lofty, none he saw too low—
Parbati beside him watched them come and go;
Thought to cheat her husband, turning Shiv to jest—
Stole the little grasshopper and hid it in her breast.
So she tricked him, Shiva the Preserver.
Mahadeo! Mahadeo! turn and see.
Tall are the camels, heavy are the kite,
But this was least of little things, O little son of mine!

When the dole was ended, laughingly she said,
"Master, of a million mouths is not one unfed?"
Laughing, Shiv made answer, "All have had their part,
Even he, the little one, hidden next thy heart."
From her breast she plucked it, Parbati the thief,
Saw the Least of Little Things gnawed a new-grown leaf!
Saw and feared and wondered, making prayer to Shiv,
Who hath surely given meat to all that live.
All things made he—Shiva the Preserver.
Mahadeo! Mahadeo! He made all,—
Thorn for the camel, fodder for the kine,
And mother's heart for sleepy head, O little son of mine!

CHAPTER 7

HER MAJESTY'S SERVANTS

You can work it out by Fractions or by simple
Rule of Three,
But the way of Tweedle-dum is not the way
of Tweedle-dee.
You can twist it, you can turn it, you can plait
it till you drop,
But they way of Pilly-Winky's not the way of
Winkie-Pop!

It had been raining heavily for one whole month—raining on a camp of thirty thousand men, thousands of camels, elephants, horses, bullocks, and mules, all gathered together at a place called Rawalpindi, to be reviewed by the Viceroy of India. He was receiving a visit from the Amir of Afghanistan—a wild king of a very wild country; and the Amir had brought with him for a bodyguard eight hundred men and horses who had never seen a camp or a locomotive before in their lives—savage men and savage horses from somewhere at the back of Central Asia. Every night a mob of these horses would be sure to break their heel-ropes, and stampede up and down the camp through the mud in the dark, or the camels would break loose and run about and fall over the ropes of the tents, and you can imagine how pleasant that was for men trying to go to sleep. My tent lay far away from the camel-lines, and I thought it was safe; but one night a man popped his head in and shouted, "Get out, quick! They're coming! My tent's gone!"

I knew who "they" were; so I put on my boots and waterproof and scuttled out into the slush. Little Vixen, my fox-terrier, went out through the other side; and then there was a roaring and a grunting and bubbling, and I saw the tent cave in, as the pole snapped, and begin to dance about like a mad ghost. A camel had blundered into it, and wet and angry as I was, I could not help laughing. Then I ran on, because I did not know how many camels might have got loose, and before long I was out of sight of the camp, ploughing my way through the mud.

At last I fell over the tail-end of a gun, and by that knew I was somewhere near the Artillery lines where the cannon were stacked at night. As I did not want to plowter about any more in the drizzle and the dark, I put my waterproof over the muzzle of one gun, and made a sort of wig-wam with two or three rammers that I found, and lay along the tail of another gun, wondering where Vixen had got to, and where I might be.

Just as I was getting ready to sleep I heard a jingle of harness and a grunt, and a mule passed me shaking his wet ears. He belonged to a screw-gun battery, for I could hear the rattle of the straps and rings and chains and things on his saddle-pad. The screw-guns are tiny little cannon made in two pieces that are screwed together when the time come to use them. They are taken up mountains, anywhere that a mule can find a road, and they are useful for fighting in rocky country.

Behind the mule there was a camel, with his big soft feet squelching and slipping in the mud, and his neck bobbing to and fro like a strayed hen's. Luckily, I knew enough of beast language—not wild-beast language, but camp-beast language, of course—from the natives to know what he was saying.

He must have been the one that flapped into my tent, for he called to the mule, "What shall I do? Where shall I go? I have fought with a white thing that waved, and it took a stick and hit me on the neck." (That was my broken tent-pole, and I was very glad to know it.) "Shall we run on?"

"Oh, it was you," said the mule, "you and your friends, that have been disturbing the camp? All right. You'll be beaten for this in the morning; but I may as well give you something on account now."

I heard the harness jingle as the mule backed and caught the camel two kicks in the ribs that rang like a drum. "Another time," he said, "you'll know better than to run through a mule-battery at night, shouting 'Thieves and fire!' Sit down, and keep your silly neck quiet."

The camel doubled up camel-fashion, like a two-foot rule, and sat down whimpering. There was a regular beat of hoofs in the darkness, and a big troop-horse cantered up as steadily as though he were on parade, jumped a gun-tail, and landed close to the mule.

"It's disgraceful," he said, blowing out his nostrils. "Those camels have racketed through our lines again—the third time this week. How's a horse to keep his condition if he isn't allowed to sleep. Who's here?"

"I'm the breech-piece mule of Number Two gun of the First Screw Battery," said the mule, "and the other's one of your friends. He's waked me up too. Who are you?"

"Number Fifteen, E troop, Ninth Lancers—Dick Cuncliffe's horse. Stand over a little, there."

"Oh, beg your pardon," said the mule. "It's too dark to see much. Aren't these camels too sickening for anything? I walked out of my lines to get a little peace and quiet here."

"My lords," said the camel humbly, "we dreamed bad dreams in the night, and we were very much afraid. I am only a baggage-camel of the 39th Native Infantry, and I am not so brave as you are, my lords."

"Then why the pickets didn't you stay and carry baggage for the 39th Native Infantry, instead of running all round the camp?" said the mule.

"They were such very bad dreams," said the camel. "I am sorry. Listen! What is that? Shall we run on again?"

"Sit down," said the mule, "or you'll snap your long legs between the guns." He cocked one ear and listened. "Bullocks!" he said. "Gun-bullocks. On my word, you and your friends have waked the camp very thoroughly. It takes a good deal of prodding to put up a gun-bullock."

I heard a chain dragging along the ground, and a yoke of the great sulky white bullocks that drag the heavy siege-guns when the elephants won't go any nearer to the firing, came shouldering along together; and almost stepping on the chain was another battery-mule, calling wildly for "Billy."

"That's one of our recruits," said the old mule to the troop-horse. "He's calling for me. Here, youngster, stop squealing. The dark never hurt anybody yet."

The gun-bullocks lay down together and began chewing the cud, but the young mule huddled close to Billy.

"Things!" he said. "Fearful and horrible things, Billy! They came into our lines while we were asleep. D'you think they'll kill us?"

"I've a great mind to give you a number-one kicking," said Billy. "The idea of a fourteen-hand mule with your training disgracing the battery before this gentleman!"

"Gently, gently!" said the troop-horse. "Remember they are always like this to begin with. The first time I ever saw a man (it was in Australia when I was a three-year-old) I ran for half a day, and if I'd seen a camel I should have been running still."

Nearly all our horses for the English cavalry are brought to India from Australia, and are broken in by the troopers themselves.

"True enough," said Billy. "Stop shaking, youngster. The first time they put the full harness with all its chains on my back, I stood on my forelegs and kicked every bit of it off. I hadn't learned the real science of kicking then, but the battery said they had never seen anything like it."

"But this wasn't harness or anything that jingled," said the young mule. "You know I don't mind that now, Billy. It was Things like trees, and they fell up and down the lines and bubbled; and my head-rope broke, and I couldn't find my driver, and I couldn't find you, Billy, so I ran off with—with these gentlemen."

"H'm!" said Billy. "As soon as I heard the camels were loose I came away on my own account, quietly. When a battery—a screw-gun mule calls gun-bullocks gentlemen, he must be very badly shaken up. Who are you fellows on the ground there?"

The gun-bullocks rolled their cuds, and answered both together: "The seventh yoke of the first gun of the Big Gun Battery. We were asleep when the camels came, but when we were trampled on we got up and walked away. It is better to lie quiet in the mud than to be disturbed on good bedding. We told your friend here that there was nothing to be afraid of, but he knew so much that he thought otherwise. Wah!"

They went on chewing.

"That comes of being afraid," said Billy. "You get laughed at by gun-bullocks. I hope you like it, young 'un."

The young mule's teeth snapped, and I heard him say something about not being afraid of any beefy old bullock in the world; but the bullocks only clicked their horns together and went on chewing.

"Now, don't be angry *after* you've been afraid. That's the worst kind of cowardice," said the troop-horse. "Anybody can be forgiven for being scared in the night, *I* think, if they see things they don't understand. We've broken out of our pickets, again and again, four hundred and fifty of us, just because a new recruit got to telling tales of whip-snakes at home in Australia till we were scared to death of the loose ends of our head-ropes."

"That's all very well in camp," said Billy; "I'm not above stampeding myself, for the fun of the thing, when I haven't been out for a day or two; but what do you do on active service?"

"Oh, that's quite another set of new shoes," said the troop-horse. "Dick Cuncliffe's on my back then, and drives his knees into me, and all I have to do is to watch where I am putting my feet and to keep my hind legs well under me, and be bridle-wise."

"What's bridle-wise?" said the young mule.

"By the Blue Gums of the Back Blocks." snorted the troop-horse, "do you mean to say you aren't taught to be bridle-wise in your business? How can you do anything, unless you can spin round at once when the rein is pressed on your neck? It means life or death to your man, and of course that's life or death to you. Get round with your hind legs under you the instant you feel the rein on your neck. If you haven't room to swing round, rear up a little and come round on your hind legs. That's being bridle-wise."

"We aren't taught that way," said Billy the mule stiffly. "We're taught to obey the man at our head; step off when he says so, and step in when he says so. I suppose it comes to the same thing. Now, with all this fine fancy business a-rearing, which must be very bad for your hocks, what do you *do*?"

"That depends," said the troop-horse. "Generally I have to go in among a lot of yelling, hairy men with knives,—long shiny knives, worse than the farrier's knives,— and I have to take care that Dick's boot is just touching the next man's boot without crushing it. I can see Dick's lance to the right of my right eye, and I know that I am safe. I shouldn't care to be the man or horse that stood up to Dick and me when we're in a hurry."

"Don't the knives hurt?" said the young mule.

"Well, I got one cut across the chest once, but that wasn't Dick's fault—"

"A lot I should have cared whose fault it was, if it hurt!" said the young mule.

"You must," said the troop-horse. "If you don't trust your man, you may as well run away at once. That's what some of out horses do, and I don't blame them. As I was saying, it wasn't Dick's fault. The man was lying on the ground, and I stretched myself not to tread on him, and he slashed up at me. Next time I have to go over a man lying down I shall step on him—hard."

"H'm!" said Billy; "it sounds very foolish. Knives are dirty things at any time. The proper thing to do is to climb up a mountain with a well-balanced saddle, hang on by all four feet and your ear too, and creep and crawl and wriggle along, till you come out hundreds of feet above any one else, on a ledge where there's just room enough for your hoofs. Then you stand still and keep quiet,—never ask a man to hold your head, young un,—keep quiet while the guns are being put together, and then you watch the little poppy shells drop down into the tree-tops ever so far below."

"Don't you ever trip?" said the troop-horse.

"They say that when a mule trips you can split a hen's ear," said Billy. "Now and again *per-haps* a badly packed saddle will upset a mule, but it's very seldom. I wish I could show you our business. It's beautiful. Why, it took me three years to find out what the men were driving at. The science of the thing is never to show up against the skyline, because, if you do, you may get fired at. Remember that, young un. Always keep hidden as much as possible, even if you have to go a mile out of your way. I lead the battery when it comes to that sort of climbing."

"Fired at without the chance of running into the people who are firing!" said the troop-horse, thinking hard. "I couldn't stand that. I should want to charge, with Dick."

"Oh no, you wouldn't; you know that as soon as the guns are in position *they'll* do all the charging. That's scientific and neat; but knives—pah!"

The baggage-camel had been bobbing his head to and fro for some time past, anxious to get a word in edgeways. Then I heard him say, as he cleared his throat, nervously:-

"I—I—I have fought a little, but not in that climbing way or running way."

"No. Now that you mention it," said Billy, "you don't look as though you were made for climbing or running—much. Well, how was it, old Hay-bales?"

"The proper way," said the camel. "We all sat down—"

"Oh, my cropper and breastplate!" said the troop-horse under his breath. "Sat down?"

"We sat down—a hundred of us," the camel went on, "in a big square, and the men piled our packs and saddles outside the square, and they fired over our backs, the men did, on all sides of the square."

"What sort of men? Any men that came along?" said the troop-horse. "They teach us in riding-school to lie down and let our masters fire across us, but Dick Cuncliffe is the only man I'd trust to do that. It tickles my girths, and, besides, I can't see with my head on the ground."

"What does it matter who fires across you?" said the camel. "There are plenty of men and plenty of other camels close by, and a great many clouds of smoke. I am not frightened then. I sit still and wait."

"And yet," said Billy, "you dream bad dreams and upset the camp at night. Well! Well! Before I'd lie down, not to speak of sitting down, and let a man fire across me, my heels and his head would have something to say to each other. Did you ever hear anything so awful as that?"

There was a long silence, and then one of the gun-bullocks lifted up his big head and said, "This is very foolish indeed. There is only one way of fighting."

"Oh, go on," said Billy. "*Please* don't mind me. I suppose you fellows fight standing on your tails?"

"Only one way," said the two together. (They must have been twins.) "This is that way. To put all twenty yoke of us to the big gun as soon as Two Tails trumpets." ("Two Tails" is camp slang for the elephant.)

"What does Two Tails trumpet for?" said the young mule.

"To show that he is not going any nearer to the smoke on the other side. Two Tails is a great coward. Then we tug the big gun all together—*Heya—Hullah! Heeyah! Hullah! We* do not climb like cats nor run like calves. We go across the level plain, twenty yoke of us, till we are unyoked again, and we graze while the big guns talk across the plain to some town with mud walls, and pieces of the wall fall out, and the dust goes up as though many cattle were coming home."

"Oh! And you choose that time for grazing, do you?" said the young mule.

"That time or any other. Eating is always good. We eat till we are yoked up again and tug the gun back to where Two Tails is waiting for it. Sometimes there are big guns in the city that speak back, and some of us are killed, and then there is all the more grazing for those that are left. This is Fate—nothing but Fate. None the less, Two Tails is a great coward. That is the proper way to fight. We are brothers from Hapur. Our father was a sacred bull of Shiva. We have spoken."

"Well, I've certainly learned something to-night," said the troop-horse. "Do you gentlemen of the screw-gun battery feel inclined to eat when you are being fired at with big guns, and Two Tails is behind you?"

"About as much as we feel inclined to sit down and let men sprawl all over us, or run into people with knives. I never heard such stuff. A mountain-ledge, a well-balanced load, a driver you can trust to let you pick your own way, and I'm your mule; but the other things—no!" said Billy, with a stamp of his foot.

"Of course," said the troop-horse, "every one is not made in the same way, and I can quite see that your family, on your father's side, would fail to understand a great many things."

"Never you mind my family on my father's side," said Billy angrily, for every mule hates to be reminded that his father was a donkey. "My father was a Southern gentleman, and he could pull down and bite and kick into rags every horse he came across. Remember that, you big brown Brumby!"

Brumby means wild horse without any breeding. Imagine the feelings of Sunol if a car-horse called her a "skate," and you can imagine how the Australian horse felt. I saw the white of his eyes glitter in the dark.

"See here, you son of an imported Malaga jackass," he said between his teeth. "I'd have you know that I'm related on my mother's side to Carbine, winner of the Melbourne Cup; and where *I* come from we aren't accustomed to being ridden over roughshod by any parrot-mouthed, pig-headed mule in a pop-gun pea-shooter battery. Are you ready?"

"On your hind legs!" squealed Billy. They both reared up facing each other, and I was expecting a furious fight, when a gurgly, rumbly voice called out of the darkness to the right: "Children, what are you fighting about there? Be quiet."

Both beasts dropped down with a snort of disgust, for neither horse nor mule can bear to listen to an elephant's voice.

"It's Two Tails!" said the troop-horse. "I can't stand him. A tail at each end isn't fair!"

"My feelings exactly," said Billy, crowding into the troop-horse for company. "We're very alike in some things."

"I suppose we've inherited them from our mothers," said the troop-horse. "It's not worth quarreling about. Hi! Two Tails, are you tied up?"

"Yes," said Two Tails, with a laugh all up his trunk. "I'm picketed for the night. I've heard what you fellows have been saying. But don't be afraid. I'm not coming over."

The bullocks and the camel said, half aloud: "Afraid of Two Tails—what nonsense!" And the bullocks went on: "We are sorry that you heard, but it is true. Two Tails, why are you afraid of the guns when they fire?"

"Well," said Two Tails, rubbing one hind leg against the other, exactly like a little boy saying poetry, "I don't quite know whether you'd understand."

"We don't, but we have to pull the guns," said the bullocks.

"I know it, and I know you are a good dealer braver than you think you are. But it's difficult with me. My battery captain called me a Pachydermatous Anachronism the other day."

"That's another way of fighting, I suppose?" said Billy, who was recovering his spirits.

"*You* don't know what that means, of course, but I do. It means betwixt and between, and that is just where I am. I can see inside my head what will happen when a shell bursts; and you bullocks can't."

"I can," said the troop-horse. "At least a little bit. I try not to think about it."

"I can see more than you, and I *do* think about it. I know there's a great deal of me to take care of, and I know that nobody knows how to cure me when I'm sick. All they can do is to stop my driver's pay till I get well, and I can't trust my driver."

"Ah!" said the troop-horse. "That explains it. I can trust Dick."

"You could put a whole regiment of Dicks on my back without making me feel any better. I know just enough to be uncomfortable, and not enough to go on in spite of it."

"We do not understand," said the bullocks.

"I know you don't. I'm not talking to you. You don't know what blood is."

"We do," said the bullocks. "It is red stuff that soaks into the ground and smells."

The troop-horse gave a kick and a bound and a snort.

"Don't talk of it," he said. "I can smell it now, just thinking of it. It makes me want to run—when I haven't Dick on my back."

"But it is not here," said the camel and the bullocks. "Why are you so stupid?"

"It's vile stuff," said Billy. "I don't want to run, but I don't want to talk about it."

"There you are!" said Two Tails, waving his tail to explain.

"Surely. Yes, we have been here all night," said the bullocks.

Two Tails stamped his foot till the iron ring on it jingled. "Oh, I'm not talking to *you*. You can't see inside your heads."

"No. We see out of our four eyes," said the bullocks. "We see straight in front of us."

"If I could do that and nothing else you wouldn't be

needed to pull the big guns at all. If I was like my captain—he can see things inside his head before the firing begins, and he shakes all over, but he knows too much to run away—if I was like him I could pull the guns. But if I were as wise as all that I should never be here. I should be a king in the forest, as I used to be, sleeping half the day and bathing when I liked. I haven't had a good bath for a month."

"That's all very fine," said Billy; "but giving a thing a long name doesn't make it any better."

"H'sh!" said the troop-horse. "I think I understand what Two Tails means."

"You'll understand better in a minute," said Two Tails angrily. "Now, just you explain to me why you don't like *this*!"

He began trumpeting furiously at the top of his trumpet.

"Stop that!" said Billy and the troop-horse together, and I could hear them stamp and shiver. An elephant's trumpeting is always nasty, especially on a dark night.

"I shan't stop," said Two Tails. "Won't you explain that, please? *Hhrrmph! Rrt! Rrrmph! Rrhha!*" Then he stopped suddenly, and I heard a little whimper in the dark, and knew that Vixen had found me at last. She knew as well as I did that if there is one thing in the world the elephant is more afraid of than another, it is a little barking dog; so she stopped to bully Two Tails in his pickets, and yapped round his big feet. Two Tails shuffled and squeaked. "Go away, little dog!" he said. "Don't snuff at my ankles, or I'll kick at you. Good little dog—nice little doggie, then! Go home, you yelping little beast! Oh, why doesn't someone take her away? She'll bite me in a minute."

"Seems to me," said Billy to the troop-horse, "that our friend Two Tails is afraid of most things. Now, if I had a full meal for every dog I've kicked across the parade-ground, I should be nearly as fat as Two Tails."

I whistled, and Vixen ran up to me, muddy all over, and licked my nose, and told me a long tale about hunting for me all through the camp. I never let her know that I understood beast talk, or she would have taken all sorts of liberties. So I buttoned her into the breast of my overcoat, and Two Tails shuffled and stamped and growled to himself.

"Extraordinary! Most Extraordinary!" he said. "It runs in our family. Now, where has that nasty little beast gone to?"

I heard him feeling about with his trunk.

"We all seem to be affected in various ways," he went on, blowing his nose. "Now, you gentlemen were alarmed, I believe, when I trumpeted."

"Not alarmed, exactly," said the troop-horse, "but it made me feel as though I had hornets where my saddle ought to be. Don't begin again."

"I'm frightened of a little dog, and the camel here is frightened by bad dreams in the night."

"It is very lucky for us that we haven't all got to fight in the same way," said the troop-horse.

"What I want to know," said the young mule, who had been quiet for a long time—"what *I* want to know is, why we have to fight at all."

"Because we're told to," said the troop-horse, with a snort of contempt.

"Orders," said Billy the mule; and his teeth snapped.

"*Hukm hai!* [It is an order]," said the camel with a gurgle; and Two Tails and the bullocks repeated, "*Hukm hai!*"

"Yes, but who gives the orders?" said the recruit-mule.

"The man who walks at your head—Or sits on your back—Or holds your nose-rope—Or twists your tail," said Billy and the troop-horse and the camel and the bullocks one after the other.

"But who gives them the orders?"

"Now you want to know too much, young un," said Billy, "and that is the way of getting kicked. All you have to do is to obey the man at your head and ask no questions."

"He's quite right," said Two Tails. "I can't always obey, because I'm betwixt and between; but Billy's right Obey the man next to you who gives the order, or you'll stop all the battery, besides getting a thrashing."

The gun-bullocks got up to go. "Morning is coming," they said. "We will go back to our lines. It is true that we see only out of our eyes, and we are not very clever; but still, we are the only people to-night who have not been afraid. Good night, you brave people."

Nobody answered, and the troop-horse said, to change the conversation, "Where's that little dog? A dog means a man somewhere about."

"Here I am," yapped Vixen, "under the gun-tail with my man. You big, blundering beast of a camel, you upset our tent. My man's very angry."

"Phew!" said the bullocks. "He must be white!"

"Of course he is," said Vixen. "Do you suppose I'm looked after by a black bullock-driver?"

"Huah! Ouach! Ugh!" said the bullocks. "Let us get away quickly."

They plunged forward in the mud, and managed somehow to run their yoke on the pole of an ammunition-wagon, where it jammed.

"Now you *have* done it," said Billy calmly. "Don't struggle. You're hung up till daylight. What on earth's the matter?"

The bullocks went off into the long, hissing snorts that Indian cattle give, and pushed and crowded and slued and stamped and slipped and nearly fell down in the mud, grunting savagely.

"You'll break your necks in a minute," said the troop-horse. "What's the matter with white men? I live with 'em."

"They—eat—us! Pull!" said the near bullock: the yoke snapped with a twang, and they lumbered off together.

I never knew before what made Indian Cattle so scared of Englishmen. We eat beef—a thing that no cattle-driver touches—and of course the cattle do not like it.

"May I be flogged with my own pad-chains! Who'd have thought of two big lumps like those losing their heads?" said Billy.

"Never mind. I'm going to look at this man. Most of the white men, I know, have things in their pockets," said the troop-horse.

"I'll leave you, then. I can't say I'm over-fond of 'em myself. Besides, white men who haven't a place to sleep in are more than likely to be thieves, and I've a good deal of Government property on my back. Come along, young un, and we'll go back to our lines. Good night, Australia! See you on parade to-morrow, I suppose. Good night old Hay-bales!—try to control your feelings, won't you? Good night, Two Tails! If you pass us on the ground to-morrow, don't trumpet. It spoils our formation."

Billy the mule stumped off with the swaggering limp of an old campaigner, as the troop-horse's head came nuzzling into my breast, and I gave him biscuits; while

Vixen, who is a most conceited little dog, told him fibs about scores of horses that she and I kept.

"I'm coming to the parade to-morrow in my dog-cart," she said. "Where will you be?"

"On the left hand of the second squadron. I set the time for all my troop, little lady," he said politely. "Now I must go back to Dick. My tail's all muddy, and he'll have two hours' hard work dressing me for parade."

The big parade of all the thirty thousand men was held that afternoon, and Vixen and I had a good place close to the Viceroy and the Amir of Afghanistan, with his high, big black hat of astrakhan wool and the great diamond star in the centre. The first part of the review was all sunshine, and the regiments went by in wave upon wave of legs all moving together, and guns all in a line, till our eyes grew dizzy. Then the cavalry came up, to the beautiful cavalry canter of "Bonnie Dundee," and Vixen cocked her ear where she sat on the dog-cart. The second squadron of the Lancers shot by, and there was the troop-horse, with his tail like spun silk, his head pulled into his breast, one ear forward and one back, setting the time for all his squadron, his legs going as smoothly as waltz-music. Then the big guns came by, and I saw Two Tails and two other elephants harnessed in line to a forty-pounder siege-gun, while twenty yoke oxen walked behind. The seventh pair had a new yoke, and they looked rather stiff and tired. Last came the screw-guns, and Billy the mule carried himself as though he commanded all the troops, and his harness was oiled and polished till it winked. I gave a cheer all by myself for Billy the mule, but he never looked right or left.

The rain began to fall again, and for a while it was too misty to see what the troops were doing. They had made a big half-circle across the plain, and were spreading out in a line. That line grew and grew and grew till it was three-quarters of a mile long from wing to wing—one solid wall of men, horses and guns. Then it came on straight toward the Viceroy and the Amir, as it got nearer the ground began to shake, like the deck of a steamer when the engines are going fast.

Unless you have been there you cannot imagine what a frightening effect this steady come-down of troops has on the spectators, even when they know it is only a review. I looked at the Amir. Up till then he had not shown the shadow of a sign of astonishment or anything else; but now his eyes began to get bigger and bigger, and he picked up the reins on his horse's neck and looked behind him. For a minute it seemed as though he were going to draw his sword and slash his way out through the English men and women in the carriages at the back. Then the advance stopped dead, the ground stood still, the whole line saluted, and thirty bands began to play all together. That was the end of the review, and the regiments went off to their camps in the rain; and an infantry band struck up:-

The animals went in two by two,
  Hurrah!
The animals went in two by two,
The elephant and the battery mul',
and they all got into the Ark
  For to get out of the rain!

Then I heard an old grizzled, long-haired Central Asian chief, who had come down with the Amir, asking questions of a native officer.

"Now," said he, "in what manner was this wonderful thing done?"

And the officer answered, "There was an order, and they obeyed."

"But are the beasts as wise as the men?" said the chief.

"They obey, as the men do. Mule, horse, elephant, or bullock, he obeys his driver, and the driver his sergeant, and the sergeant his lieutenant, and the lieutenant his captain, and the captain his major, and the major his colonel, and the colonel his brigadier commanding three regiments, and the brigadier his general, who obeys the Viceroy, who is the servant of the Empress. Thus is it done."

"Would it were so in Afghanistan!" said the chief; "for there we obey only our own wills."

"And for that reason," said the native officer, twirling his moustache, "your Amir whom you do not obey must come here and take orders from our Viceroy."

PARADE-SONG OF THE CAMP-ANIMALS

ELEPHANTS OF THE GUN-TEAMS

We lent to Alexander the strength of Hercules,
The wisdom of our foreheads, the cunning of our knees;
We bowed our necks to service; they ne'er were loosed again,—
Make way there, way for the ten-foot teams
Of the Forty-Pounder train!

GUN-BULLOCKS

Those heroes in their harnesses avoid a cannon-ball,
And what they know of powder upsets them one and all;
Then we come into action and tug the guns again,—
Make way there, way for the twenty yoke
Of the Forty-Pounder train!

CAVALRY HORSES

By the brand on my withers, the finest of tunes
Is played by the Lancers, Hussars, and Dragoons,
And it's sweeter than "Stables" or "Water" to me,
The Cavalry Canter of "Bonnie Dundee!"
Then feed us and break us and handle and groom,
And give us good riders and plenty of room,
And launch us in column of squadron and see
The way of the war-horse to "Bonnie Dundee"!

SCREW-GUN MULES

As me and my companions were scrambling up a hill,
The path was lost in rolling stones, but we went forward still;
For we can wriggle and climb, my lads, and turn up everywhere,
And it's our delight on a mountain height, with a leg or two to spare!

Good luck to every sergeant, then, that lets us pick our road!
Bad luck to all the driver-men that cannot pack a load!
For we can wriggle and climb, my lads, and turn up everywhere,
And it's our delight on a mountain height, with a leg or two to spare!

COMMISSARIAT CAMELS

We haven't a camelty tune of our own
To help us trollop along,
But every neck is a hair-trombone
(*Rtt-ta-ta-ta!* is a hair-trombone!)
And this is our marching-song:
Can't! Don't! Shan't! Won't!
Pass it along the line!
Somebody's pack has slid from his back,
'Wish it were only mine!
Somebody's load has tipped off in the road—
Cheer for a halt and a row!
Urr! Yarrh! Grr! Arrh!
Somebody's catching it now!

ALL THE BEASTS TOGETHER

Children of the Camp are we,
Serving each in his degree;
Children of the yoke and goad,
Pack and harness, pad and load.
See our line across the plain,
Like a heel-rope bent again,
Reaching, writhing, rolling far,
Sweeping all away to war!
While the men that walk beside,
Dusty, silent, heavy-eyed,
Cannot tell why we or they
March and suffer day by day.
Children of the Camp are we,
Serving each in his degree,
Children of the yoke and goad,
Pack and harness, pad and load.

CHILDREN'S CLASSICS

Gulliver's Travels

JONATHAN SWIFT

Gulliver's Travels

PARRAGON

Gulliver's Travels
A Parragon Classic

This is a Siena Book
Siena is an imprint of Parragon

First published in 1726

This edition published in 1999 by
Parragon
13 Whiteladies Road
Clifton
Bristol BS8 1PB

Printed and bound in the UK

PART ONE

A VOYAGE TO LILLIPUT

CHAPTER 1

My father had a small estate in Nottinghamshire; I was the third of five sons. He sent me to Emanuel College in Cambridge at fourteen years old, where I resided three years, and applied myself close to my studies: but the charge of maintaining me (although I had a very scanty allowance) being too great for a narrow fortune, I was bound apprentice to Mr. James Bates, an eminent surgeon in London, with whom I continued four years: my father now and then sent me small sums of money, which I spent in learning navigation, and other parts of the mathematics, useful to those who intend to travel, as I always believed it would be some time or other my fortune to do. When I left Mr. Bates, I went down to my father; where, by the assistance of him and my uncle John, and some other relations, I got forty pounds, and a promise of thirty pounds a year to maintain me at Leyden. There I studied physic two years and seven months, knowing it would be useful in long voyages.

Soon after my return from Leyden, I was recommended, by my good master Mr. Bates, to be surgeon to the *Swallow*, Captain Abraham Pannell commander; with whom I continued three years and a half, making a voyage or two into the Levant, and some other parts. When I came back, I resolved to settle in London, to which Mr. Bates, my master, encouraged me, and by him I was recommended to several patients. I took part of a small house in the Old Jury, and being advised to alter my condition, I married Mrs. Mary Burton, second daughter to Mr. Edmund Burton hosier in Newgate-street, with whom I received four hundred pounds for a portion.

But, my good master Bates died two years later, and I having few friends, my business began to fail, for my conscience would not suffer me to imitate the bad practice of too many among my brethen. Having therefore consulted with my wife, and some of my acquaintance, I determined to go to sea again. I was surgeon successively in two ships, and made several voyages, for six years, to the East and West-Indies, by which I got some addition to my fortune. My hours of leisure I spent reading the best authors, ancient and modern, being always provided with a good number of books; and when I was ashore, in observing the manners and dispositions of the people, as well as learning their language, wherein I had a great facility by the strength of my memory.

The last of these voyages not proving very fortunate, I grew weary of the sea, and intended to stay at home with my wife and family. I removed from the Old Jury to Fetter-Lane, and from thence to Wapping, hoping to get business among the sailors, but it would not turn to account. After three years expectation that things would mend, I accepted an advantageous offer from Captain William Prichard, master of the *Antelope,* who was making a voyage to the South-Sea. We set sail from Bristol May 4, 1699, and our voyage at first was very prosperous.

It would not be proper, for some reasons, to trouble the reader with the particulars of our adventures in those seas: let it suffice to inform him, that in our passage from thence to the East-Indies, we were driven by a violent storm to the north-west of Van Diemen's Land. By an observation, we found ourselves in the latitude of 30 degrees 2 minutes south. Twelve of our crew were dead by immoderate labour and ill food, and the rest were in a very weak condition. On the fifth of November, which was the beginning of summer in those parts, the weather being very hazy, the seamen spied a rock, within half a cable's length of the ship; but the wind was so strong, that we were driven directly upon it, and immediately split. Six of the crew, of whom I was one, having let down the boat into the sea, made a shift to get clear of the ship, and the rock. We rowed by my computation about three leagues, till we were able to work no longer, being already spent with labour while we were in the ship. We therefore trusted ourselves to the mercy of the waves, and in about half an hour the boat was overset by a sudden flurry from the north. What became of my companions in the boat, as well as of those who escaped on the rock, or were left in the vessel, I cannot tell, but conclude they were all lost. For my own part, I swam as fortune directed me, and was pushed forward by wind and tide. I often let my legs drop, and could feel no bottom, but when I was almost gone, and able to struggle no longer, I found myself within my depth; and by this time the storm was much abated. The declivity was so small, that I walked nearly a mile before I got to the shore, which I conjectured was about eight o'clock in the evening. I then advanced forward near half a mile, but could not discover any sign of houses or inhabitants, or at least I was in so weak a condition, that I did not observe them. I was extremely tired, and with that, and the heat of the weather, and about half a pint of brandy that I drank as I left the ship, I found myself much inclined to sleep. I lay down on the grass, which was very short and soft, where I slept sounder than ever I remember to have done in my life, and, as I reckoned, above nine hours, for when I awaked, it was just daylight. I attempted to rise, but was not able to stir, for, as I happened to lie on my back, I found my arms and legs were strongly fastened on each side to the ground, and my hair, which was long and thick, tied down in the same manner. I likewise felt several slender ligature across my body, from my arm-pits to my thighs. I could only look upwards; the sun began to grow hot, and the light offended my eyes. I heard a confused noise about me, but in the posture I lay, could see nothing except the sky. In a little time I felt something alive moving on my left leg, which advancing gently forward over my breast, came almost up to my chin, and on bending my eyes downwards as much as I could, I perceived it to be a human creature not six inches high, with a bow and arrow in his hands, and a quiver at his back. In the meantime, I felt at least forty more of the same kind (as I conjectured) following the first. I was in the utmost astonishment, and roared so loud, that they all ran back in a fright, and some of them, as I was afterwards told, were hurt with the falls they got by leaping from my sides upon the ground. However, they soon returned, and one of them, who ventured so far as to get a full sight of my face, lifting up his hands and eyes by way of admiration, cried out in a shrill but distinct voice, *Hekinah degul:* the others repeated the same words several times, but I knew not what they meant. I lay all this while, as the readers may believe, in great uneasiness, and at length, struggling to get loose, I had the fortune to break the strings and wrench out the pegs that fastened my left arm to the ground; for, by lifting it up to my face, I discovered the methods they had taken to bind me. At the same time, with a violent pull, which gave me excessive pain, I a little loosened the strings that tied down my hair on the left side, so that I was just able to turn my head about two inches. But the creatures ran off a second time, before I could seize them, whereupon there was a great shout in a very shrill accent, and after it ceased, I heard one of them cry aloud, *Tolgo phonac;* when in an instant I felt above an hundred arrows discharged on my left hand, which pricked me like so many needles; and besides they shot another flight into the air, as we do bombs in Europe, whereof many, I suppose, fell on my body (though I felt them not) and some on my face, which I immediately covered with my left hand. When this shower of arrows was over, I fell a groaning with grief and pain, and then striving again to get loose, whereupon they discharged another volley larger than the first, and some of them attempted with spears to stick me in the sides. By good luck, I had on me a buff jerkin, which they could not pierce, but I thought it the most prudent method to lie still, and my design was to continue so till night, when, my left hand being already loose, I could easily free myself. As for the inhabitants, I had reason to believe I might be a match for the greatest armies they could bring against me, if they were all of the same size with him that I saw. But fortune disposed otherwise of me. When the people observed I was quiet, they discharged no more arrows, but, by the noise I heard, I knew their numbers increased. About four yards from me, over against my right ear, I heard a knocking for above an hour, like that of people at work, and when turning my head that way, as well as the pegs and strings would permit me, I saw a stage erected, about a foot and a half from the ground, capable of holding four of the inhabitants, with two or three ladders to mount it: from whence one of them, who seemed to be a person of quality, made a long speech, whereof I understood not one syllable. But I should have mentioned that before the principal person began his oration, he cried out three times, *Langro dehul san* (these words and the former were afterwards repeated and explained to me.) Whereupon immediately about fifty of the inhabitants came, and cut the strings that fastened the left side of my head, which gave me the liberty of turning it to the right, and of observing the person and gesture of him that was to speak. He appeared to be of a middle age, and taller than any of the other three who attended him, whereof one was a page that held up his train, and seemed to be somewhat longer than my middle finger; the other two stood one on each side to support him. He acted every part of an orator, and I could observe many periods of threatenings, and others of promises, pity, and kindness. I answered in a few words, but in the most submissive manner, lifting up my left hand and both my eyes to the sun, as calling him for a witness. Being almost famished with hunger, having not eaten a morsel for some hours before I left the ship, I found the demands of nature so strong upon me, that I could not forbear showing my impatience (perhaps against the strict rules of decency) by putting my finger frequently on my mouth, to signify that I wanted food. The *Hurgo* (for so they call a great lord, as I afterwards learnt) understood me very well. He descended from the stage, and commanded that several ladders should be applied to my sides, on which above an hundred of the inhabitants mounted, and walked towards my mouth, laden with baskets full of meat, which had been provided and sent thither by the King's orders, upon the first intelligence he received of me. I observed there was the flesh of several animals, but could not distinguish them by the taste. There were shoulder, legs, and loins, shaped like those of mutton, and very well dressed, but smaller than the wings of a lark. I ate them by two or three at a mouthful, and took three loaves at a time, about the bigness of musket bullets. They supplied me as they could, showing a thousand marks of wonder and astonishment at my bulk and appetite. I then made another sign that I wanted a drink. They found by me eating that a small quantity would not suffice me, and being a most ingenious people, they slung up with great dexterity one of their largest hogheads, then rolled it towards my hand, and beat out the top; I drank it off at a draught, which I might well do, for it did not hold half a pint, and tasted like a small wine of Burgundy, but much more delicious. They brought me a second hoghead, which I drank in the same manner, and made signs for more, but they had none to give me. When I had performed these wonders, they shouted for joy, and danced upon my breast, repeating several times as they did at first, *Hekinah degul.* They made me a sign that I should throw down the two hogheads, but first warning the people below to stand out of the way, crying aloud, *Borach mivola,* and when they saw the vessels in the air, there was an universal shout of *Hekinah degul.* I confess I was often tempted, while they were passing backwards and forwards on my body, to seize forty or fifty of the first that came in my reach, and dash them against the ground. But the remembrance of what I had felt, which probably might not be the worst they could do, and the promise of honour I made them, for so I interpreted my submissive behaviour, soon drove out these imaginations. Besides, I now considered myself as bound by the laws of hospitality to a people who had treated me with so much expense and magnificence. However, in my thoughts I could not sufficiently wonder at the intrepidity of these diminutive mortals, who durst venture to mount and walk upon my body, while one of my hands was at liberty, without trembling at the very sight of so prodigious a creature as I must appear to them. After some time, when they observed that I made no more demands for meat, there appeared before me a person of high rank from his Imperial Majesty. His Excellency, having mounted on the small of my right leg, advanced forwards up to my face, with about a dozen of his retinue. And producing his credentials under the Signet Royal, which he applied close to my eyes, spoke about ten minutes, without any signs of anger, but with a kind of determinate resolution, often pointing forwards, which, as I afterwards found, was towards the capital city, about half a mile distant, whither it was agreed by his Majesty in council that I must be conveyed. I answered in few words, but to no purpose, and made a sign with my hand that was loose, putting it to the other (but over his Excellency's head, for fear of hurting him or his train) and then to my own head and body, to signify that I desired my liberty. It appeared that he understood me well enough, for he shook his head by way of disapprobation, and held his hand in a posture to show that I must be carried as a prisoner. However, he made other signs to let me understand that I should have meat and drink enough, and very good treatment. Whereupon I once more thought of attempting to break my bonds, but again, when I felt the smart of their arrows upon my face and hands, which were all in blisters, and many of the darts still sticking in them, and observing likewise that the number of my enemies increased, I gave tokens to let them know that they might do with me what they pleased. Upon this the *Hurgo* and his train withdrew with much civility and cheerful countenances. Soon after I heard a general shout, with frequent repetitions of the words, *Peplom selan*, and I felt great numbers of the people on my left side relaxing the cords to such a degree, that I was able to turn upon my right. But before this, they had daubed my face and both my hands with a sort of ointment very pleasant to the smell, which in a few minutes removed all the smart of their arrows. These circumstances, added to the refreshment I had received by their victuals and drink, which were very nourishing, disposed me to sleep. I slept about eight hours, as I was afterwards assured, and no wonder, for the physicians, by the Emperor's order, had mingled a sleepy potion in the hogheads of wine.

It seems that upon the first moment I was discovered sleeping on the ground after my landing, the Emperor had early notice of it by an express, and determined in council that I should be tied in the manner I have related (which was done in the night while I slept), that plenty of meat and drink should be sent me, and a machine prepared to carry me to the capital city.

This resolution perhaps may appear very bold and dangerous, and I am confident would not be imitated by any prince in Europe on the like occasion; however, in my opinion, it was extremely prudent, as well as dangerous. For supposing these people had endeavoured to kill me with their spears and arrows while I was asleep, I should certainly have awaked with the first sense of smart, which might so far have roused my rage and strength, as to have enabled me to break the strings wherewith I was tied; after which, as they were not able to make resistance, they could have expected no mercy.

These people are most excellent mathematicians, and arrived to a great perfection in mechanics by the countenance and encouragement of the Emperor, who is a renowned patron of learning. This prince hath several machines fixed on wheels for the carriage of trees and other weights. He often builds his largest men of war, whereof some are nine foot long, in the woods where the timber grows, and has them carried on these engines three or four hundred yards to the sea. Five hundred carpenters and engineers were immediately set at work to prepare the greatest engine they had. It was a frame of wood raised three inches from the ground, about seven foot long and four wide, moving upon twenty-two wheels. The shout I heard was upon the arrival of this engine, which it seems set out in four hours after my landing. It was brought parallel to me as I lay. But the principal difficulty was to raise and place me in this vehicle. Eighty poles, each of one foot high, were erected for this purpose, and very strong cords the size of packthread were fastened by hooks to many bandages, which the workmen had girt round my neck, my ähands, my body, and my legs. Nine hundred of the strongest men were employed to draw up these cords by many pulleys fastened on the poles, and thus, in less than three hours, I was raised and slung into the engine, and there tied fast. All this I was told, for while the whole operation was performing, I lay in a profound sleep, by the force of that soporiferous medicine infused into my liquor. Fifteen hundred of the Emperor's largest horses, each about four inches and a half high, were employed to draw me towards the metropolis, which, as I said, was half a mile distant.

About four hours after we began our journey, I awaked by a very ridiculous accident. The carriage had stopped a while to adjust something that was out of order, and two or three of the young natives had the curiosity to see how I looked when I was asleep. They climbed up into the engine, and advancing very softly to my face, one of them, an officer in the Guards, put the sharp end of his half-pike a good way up into my left nostril, which tickled my nose like a straw, and made me sneeze violently, whereupon they stole off unperceived, and it was three weeks before I knew the cause of my awaking so suddenly. We made a long march the remaining part of that day, and rested at night with five hundred guards on each side of me, half with torches, and half with bows and arrows, ready to shoot me if I should offer to stir. The next morning at sunrise we continued our march, and arrived within two hundred yards of the city gates about noon. The Emperor and all his court came out to meet us, but his great officers would by no means suffer his Majesty to endanger his person by mounting on my body.

At the place where the carriage stopped, there stood an ancient temple, esteemed to be the largest in the whole kingdom, which having been polluted some years before by an unnatural murder, was, according to the zeal of those people, looked on as profane, and therefore had been applied to common uses, and all the ornaments and furniture carried away. In this edifice it was determined I should lodge. The great gate fronting to the north was about four foot high, and almost two foot wide, through which I could easily creep. On each side of the gate was a small window not above six inches from the ground: into that on the left side, the King's smiths conveyed fourscore and eleven chains, like those that hang to a lady's watch in Europe, and almost as large, which were locked to my left leg with six and thirty padlocks. Over against this temple, on t'other side of the great highway, at twenty foot distant, there was a turret at least five foot high. Here the Emperor ascended with many principal lords of his court, to have an opportunity of viewing me, as I was told, for I could not see them. It was reckoned that above an hundred thousand habitants came out of the town upon the same errand, and in spite of my guards, I believe there could not be fewer than ten thousand, at several times, who mounted upon my body by the help of ladders. But a proclamation was soon issued to forbid it upon pain of death. When the workmen found it was impossible for me to break loose, they cut all the strings that bound me, whereupon I rose up with as melancholy a disposition as ever I had in my life. But the noise and astonishment of the people at seeing me rise and walk, are not to be expressed. The chains that held my left leg were about two yards long, and gave me not only the liberty of walking backwards and forwards in a semicircle, but allowed me to creep in, and lie at my full length in the temple.

CHAPTER 2

When I found myself on my feet, I looked about me, and must confess I never beheld a more entertaining prospect. The country round appeared like a continued garden, and the enclosed fields, which were generally forty foot square, resembled so many beds of flowers. These fields were intermingled with woods of half a stang, and the tallest trees, as I could judge, appeared to be seven foot high. I viewed the town on my left hand, which looked like the painted scene of a city in a theatre.

The Emperor had already descended from the tower, and was advancing on horseback towards me, which almost cost him dear, for the beast, though very well trained, yet wholly unused to such a sight, which appeared as if a mountain moved before him, reared up on his hinder feet: but that prince, who is an excellent horseman, kept his seat, till his attendant ran in and held the bridle while his master had time to dismount. When he alighted, he surveyed me round with great admiration, but kept without the length of my chain. He ordered his cooks and butlers, who were already prepared, to give me victuals and drink, which they pushed forward in a sort of vehicles upon wheels till I could reach them. I took these vehicles, and soon emptied them all. Twenty of them were filled with meat, and ten with liquor; each of the former afforded me two or three good mouthfuls, and I emptied the liquor of ten vessels, which was contained in earthen vials, into one vehicle, drinking it off at a draught; and so I did with the rest. The Empress, and young Princes of the blood, of both sexes, attended by many ladies, sat at some distance in their chairs, but upon the accident that happened to the Emperor's horse, they alighted, and came near his person, which I am now going to describe. He is taller by almost the breadth of my nail than any of his court, which alone is enough to strike an awe into the beholders. His features are strong and masculine, with an Austrian lip and arched nose, his complexion olive, his countenance erect, his body and limbs well proportioned, all his motions graceful, and his deportment majestic. He was then past his prime, being twenty-eight years and three quarters old, of which he had reigned about seven, in great felicity, and generally victorious. For the better convenience of beholding him, I lay on my side, so that my face was parallel to his, and he stood but three yards off. However, I have had him since many times in my hand, and therefore cannot be deceived in the description. His dress was very plain and simple, and the fashion of it between the Asiatic and the European; but he had on his head a light helmet of gold, adorned with jewels, and a plume on the crest. He held his sword drawn in his hand, to defend himself, if I should happen to break loose. It was almost three inches long, the hilt and scabbard were gold enriched with diamonds. His voice was shrill, but very clear and articulate, and I could distinctly hear it when I stood up. The ladies and courtiers were all most magnificently clad, so that the spot they stood upon seemed to resemble a petticoat spread on the ground, embroidered with figures of gold and silver: His Imperial Majesty spoke often to me, and I returned answers, but neither of us could understand a syllable. There were several of his priest and lawyers present (as I conjectured by their habits) who were commanded to address themselves to me, and I spoke to them in as many languages as I had the least smattering of, which were High and Low Dutch, Latin, French, Spanish,

Italian, and Lingua Franca; but all to no purpose. After about two hours the court retired, and I was left with a strong guard, to prevent the impertinence, and probably the malice of the rabble, who were very impatient to crowd about me as near as they durst, and some of them had the impudence to shoot their arrows at me as I sat on the ground by the door of my house, whereof one very narrowly missed my left eye. But the colonel ordered six of the ringleaders to be seized, and thought no punishment so proper as to deliver them bound into my hands, which some of his soldiers accordingly did, pushing them forwards with the butt-ends of their pikes into my reach. I took them all in my right hand, put five of them into my coat-pocket, and as to the sixth, I made a countenance as if I would eat them alive. The poor man squalled terribly, and the colonel and his officers were in much pain, especially when they saw me take out my penknife: but I soon put them out of fear, for, looking mildly, and immediately cutting the strings he was bound with, I set him gently on the ground, and away he ran. I treated the rest in the same manner, taking them one by one out of my pocket, and I observed both the soldiers and people were highly obliged at this mark of my clemency, which was represented very much to my advantage at court.

Towards night I got with some difficulty into my house, where I lay on the ground, and continued to do so about a fortnight, during which time the Emperor gave orders to have a bed prepared for me. Six hundred beds of the common measure were brought in carriages, and worked up in my house. An hundred and fifty of their beds sewn together made up the breadth and length, and these were four double, which however kept me but very indifferently from the hardness of the floor, which was of smooth stone.

By the same computation they provided me with sheets, blankets, and coverlets, tolerable enough for one who had been so long inured to hardships as I.

As the news of my arrival spread through the kingdom, it brought prodigious numbers of rich, idle, and curious people to see me, so that the villages were almost emptied, and great neglect of tillage and household affairs must have ensued, if his Imperial Majesty had not provided, by several proclamations and orders of state, against this inconveniency. He directed that those who had already beheld me should return home, and not presume to come with fifty yards of my house without licence from court.

In the mean time, the Emperor held frequent councils to debate what course should be taken with me, and I was afterwards assured by a particular friend, a person of great quality, who was looked upon to be as much in the secret as any, that the court was under many difficulties concerning me. They apprehended my breaking loose, that my diet would be very expensive, and might cause a famine. Sometimes they determined to starve me, or at least to shoot me in the face and hands with poisoned arrows, which would soon dispatch me: but again they considered, that the stench of so large a carcass might produce a plaque in the metropolis, and probably spread through the whole kingdom. In the midst of these consultations, several officers of the army went to the door of the great council-chamber, and two of them being admitted, gave an account of my behaviour to the six criminals above-mentioned, which made so favourable an impression in the breast of his Majesty and the whole board in my behalf, that an Imperial Commission was issued out, obliging all the villages nine hundred yards round the city, to deliver in every morning six beeves, forty sheep, and other victuals for my sustenance; together with a proportional quantity of bread, and wine, and other liquors; for the due payment of which his Majesty gave assignments upon his treasury. For this prince lives chiefly upon his own demesnes, seldom, except upon great occasions, raising any subsidies upon his subjects, who are bound to attend him in his wars at their own expense. An establishment was also made of six hundred persons to be my domestics, who had board-wages allowed for their maintenance, and tents built for them very conveniently on each side of my door. It was likewise ordered, that three hundred tailors should make me a suit of clothes after the fashion of the country: that six of his Majesty's greatest scholars should be employed to instruct me in their language: and, lastly, that the Emperor's horses, and those of nobility, and troops of guards, should be frequently exercised in my sight, to accustom themselves to me. All these orders were duly put in execution, and in about three weeks I made a great progress in learning their language, during which time the Emperor frequently honoured me with his visits, and was pleased to assist my masters in teaching me. We began already to converse together in some sort, and the first words I learnt were to express my desire that he would please to give me my liberty, which I every day repeated on my knees. His answers, as I could apprehend it, was, that this must be a work of time, not to be thought on without the advice of his council, and that first I must *Lumos kelmin pesso desmar lon emposo;* that is, swear a peace with him and his kingdom. However, I should be used with all kindness, and he advised me to acquire, by my patience and discrete behaviour, the good opinion of himself and his subjects. He desired I would not take it ill if he gave orders to certain officers to search me, for probably I might carry about me several weapons, which must needs be dangerous things, if they answered the bulk of so prodigious a person. I said, his Majesty should be satisfied, for I was ready to strip myself, and turn up my pockets before him. This I delivered part in words, and part in signs. He replied, that by the laws of the kingdom I must be searched by two of his officers, that he knew this could not be done without my consent and assistance, that he had so good an opinion of my generosity and justice as to trust their persons in my hands, and that whatever they took from me should be returned when I left the country, or paid for at the rate which I would set upon them. I took up the two officers in my hands, put them first into my coat-pockets, and then into every other pocket about me, except my two fobs, and another secret pocket I had no mind should be searched, wherein I had some little necessaries that were of no consequence to any but myself. In one of my fobs there was a silver watch, and in the other a small quantity of gold in a purse. These gentlemen, having pen, ink, and paper about them, made an exact inventory of everything they saw; and when they had done, desired I would set them down, that they might deliver it to the Emperor. This inventory I afterwards translated into English, and is word for word as follows.

Imprimis, In the right coat-pocket of the Great Man-Mountain (for so I interpret the words *Quinbus Flestrin*) after the strictest search, we found only one great piece of coarse cloth, large enough to be a foot-cloth for your Majesty's chief room of state. In the left pocket we saw a huge silver chest, with a cover of the same metal, which we the searchers were not able to lift. We desired it should be opened, and one of us stepping into it, found himself up to the mid leg in a sort of dust, some part whereof flying up to our faces, set us both a sneezing for several times together. In his right waistcoat-pocket we found a prodigious bundle of white thin substances, folded one over another, about the bigness of three men, tied with a strong cable, and marked with black figures, which we humbly conceive to be writings, every letter almost half as large as the palm of our hands. In the left there was a sort of engine, from the back of which were extended twenty long poles, resembling the palisados before your Majesty's court, wherewith we conjecture the Man-Mountain combs his head, for we did not always trouble him with questions, because we found it a great difficulty to make him understand us. In the large pocket on the right side of his middle cover (so I translated the word *ranfu-lo,* by which they meant my breeches) we saw a hollow pillar of iron, about the length of a man, fastened to a strong piece of timber, larger than the pillar; and upon one side of the pillar were huge pieces of iron sticking out, cut into strange figures, which we know not what to make of. In the left pocket was another engine of the same kind. In the smaller pocket on the right side, were several round flat pieces of white and red metal, of different bulk; some of the white, which seemed to be silver, were so large and heavy, that my comrade and I could hardly lift them. In the left pocket were two black pillars irregularly shaped. We could not, without difficulty, reach the top of them as we stood at the bottom of his pocket. One of them was covered, and seemed all of a piece, but at the upper end of the other, there appeared a white round substance, about twice the bigness of our heads. Within each of these was enclosed a prodigious plate of steel which, by our orders, we obliged him to show us, because we apprehended they might be dangerous engines. He took them out of their cases, and told us, that in his own country his practice was to shave his beard with one of these, and to cut his meat with the other. There were two pockets which we could not enter, and these he called his fobs; they were two large slits cut into the top of his middle cover, but squeezed close by the presence of his belly. Out of the right fob hung a great silver chain, with a wonderful kind of engine at the bottom. We directed him to draw out whatever was fastened to that chain, which appeared to be a globe, half silver, and half of transparent metal. On the transparent side we saw certain strange figures circularly drawn, and thought we could touch them, till we found our fingers stopped by that lucid substance. He put this engine to our ears, and it made an incessant noise like that of a watermill. We conjecture it is either some unknown animal, or the god that he worships, but we are more inclined to the latter opinion, because he assures us, (if we understood him right, for he expressed himself very imperfectly) that he seldom did any thing without consulting it: he called it his oracle, and said it pointed out the time for every action of his life. From the left fob he took out a net almost large enough for a fisherman, but contrived to open and shut like a purse, and served him for the same use: we found therein several massy pieces of yellow metal, which, if they are real gold, must be of immense value.

Having thus, in obedience to your Majesty's commands, diligently searched all his pockets, we observed a girdle about his waist made of the hide of some prodigious animal, from which, on the left side, hung a sword of the length of five men; and on the right, a bag or pouch divided into two cells, each cell capable of holding three of your Majesty's subjects. In one of these cells were several globes or balls of a most ponderous metal, about the size of our heads, and requiring a strong hand to lift them. The other cell contained a heap of certain black grains, but of no great bulk or weight, for we could hold above fifty of them in the palms of our hands.

This is an exact inventory of what we found about the body of the Man-Mountain, who used us with great civility, and due respect to your Majesty's commission. Signed and sealed on the fourth day of the eighty-ninth moon of your Majesty's auspicious reign.

CLEFREN FRELOCK, MARSI FRELOCK.

When this inventory was read over to the Emperor, he directed me, although in very gentle terms, to deliver up the several particulars. He first called for my scimitar, which I took out, scabbard and all. In the meantime he ordered three thousand of his choicest troops (who then attended him) to surround me at a distance, with their bows and arrows just ready to discharge, but I did not observe it, for my eyes were wholly fixed upon his Majesty. He then desired me to draw my scimitar, which, although it had got some rust by the sea-water, was in most parts exceeding bright. I did so, and immediately all the troops gave a shout between terror and surprise, for the sun shone clear, and the reflection dazzled their eyes as I waved the scimitar to and fro in my hand. His Majesty, who is a most magnanimous prince, was less daunted than I could expect. He ordered me to return it into the scabbard, and cast it on the ground as gently as I could, about six foot from the end of my chain. The next thing he demanded was one of the hollow iron pillars, by which he meant my pocketpistols. I drew it out, and at his desire, as well as I could, expressed to him the use of it, and charging it only with powder, which by the closeness of pouch happened to escape wetting in the sea (as inconvenience against which all prudent mariners take special care to provide) I first cautioned the Emperor not to be afraid, and then I let it off in the air. The astonishment here was much greater than at the sight of my scimitar. Hundreds fell down as if they had been struck dead, and even the Emperor, although he stood his ground, could not recover himself for some time. I delivered up both my pistol in the same manner as I had dome my scimitar, and then my pouch of powder and bullets, begging him that the former might be kept from the fire, for it would kindle with the smallest spark, and blow up his imperial palace into the air. I likewise delivered up my watch, which the Emperor was very curious to see, and commanded two of his tallest yeoman of the guards to bear it on a pole upon their shoulders, as draymen in England do a barrel of ale. He was amazed at the continual noise it made, and the motion of the minute-hand, which he could easily discern for their sight is much more acute than ours, and asked the opinions of his learned men about him, which were various and remote, as the reader may well imagine, without my repeating, although äindeed I could not very perfectly understand them. I then gave up my silver and copper money, my purse with nine large pieces of gold, and some smaller ones, my knife and razor, my comb and silver snuff-box, my handkerchief and journal-book. My scimitar, pistols, and pouch, were conveyed in carriages to his Majesty's stores, but the rest of my goods were returned me.

I had, as I before observed, one private pocket which escaped their search, wherein there was a pair of spectacles (which I sometimes use for the weakness of my eyes), a pocket perspective, and several other little conveniences, which, being of no consequence to the Emperor, I did not think myself bound in honour to discover, and I apprehended they might be lost or spoiled if I ventured them out of my possession.

CHAPTER 3

My gentleness and good behaviour had gained so far on the Emperor and his court, and indeed upon the army and people in general, that I began to conceive hopes of getting my liberty in a short time. I took all possible methods to cultivate this favourable disposition. The natives came by degrees to be less apprehensive of any danger from me. I would sometimes lie down, and let five or six of them dance on my hand. And at last the boys and girls would venture to come and play at hide and seek in my hair. I had now made a good progress in understanding and speaking their language. The Emperor had a mind one day to entertain me with several of the country shows, wherein they exceed all nations I have known, both for dexerity and magnificence. I was diverted with none so much as that of the rope-dancers, performed upon a slender white thread, extended about two foot and twelve inches from the ground, and upon which I shall desire liberty, with the reader's patience, to enlarge a little.

This diversion is only practised by those persons who are candidates for great employments and high favour at court. They are trained in this art from their youth, and are not always of noble birth, or liberal education. When a great office is vacant either by death or disgrace (which often happens) five or six of those candidates petition the Emperor to entertain his Majesty and the court with a dance on the rope, and whoever jumps the highest without falling, succeeds in the office. Very often the chief ministers themselves are commanded to show their skill, and to convince the Emperor that they have not lost their faculty.

Flimnap, the Treasurer, is allowed to cut a caper on the straight rope, at least an inch higher than any other lord in the whole empire. I have seen him do the somersault several times together upon a trencher fixed on the rope, which is no thicker than a common pack-thread in England. My friend Reldresal, principal Secretary for Private Affairs, is, in my opinion, if I am not partial, the second after the Treasurer, and the rest of the great officers are much upon a par.

These diversions are often attended with fatal accidents, whereof great numbers are on record. I myself have seen two or three candidates break a limb. But the danger is much greater when the ministers themselves are commanded to show their dexerity, for by contending to excel themselves and their fellows, they strain so far that there is hardly one of them who hath not received a fall, and some of them two or three. I was assured that a year or two before my arrival, Flimnap would definitely have broken his neck, if one of the King's cushions, that accidentally lay on the ground, had not weakened the force of his fall.

There is likewise another diversion, which is only shown before the Emperor and Empress, and first minister, upon particular occasions. The Emperor lays on the table three fine silken threads of six inches long. One is blue, the other red, and the third green. These threads are proposed as prizes for those persons whom the Emperor hath a mind to distinguish by a peculiar mark of his favour. The ceremony is performed in his Majesty's great chamber of state, where the candidates are to undergo a trial of dexerity very different from the former, and such as I have not observed the least resemblance of in any other country of the old or the new world. The Emperor holds a stick in his hands, both ends parallel to the horizon, while the candidates, advancing one by one, sometimes leap over the stick, sometimes creep under it backwards and forwards several times, according as the stick is advanced or depressed. Sometimes the Emperor holds one end of the stick, and his first minister the other, sometimes the minister has it entirely to himself. Whoever performs his part with most agility, and holds out the longest in leaping and creeping, is rewarded with the blue-coloured silk; the red is given to the next, and the green to the third, which they all wear girt twice round about the middle. You see few great persons about this court who are not adorned with one of these girdles.

The horses of the army, and those of the royal stables, having been daily fed before me, were no longer shy, but would come up to my very feet without starting. The riders would leap them over my hand as I held it on the ground, and one of the Emperor's huntsmen, upon a large courser, took my foot, shoe and all which was indeed a prodigious leap. I had the good fortune to divert the Emperor one day in a very extraordinary manner. I desired he would order several sticks of two foot high, and the thickness of an ordinary cane, to be brought to me, whereupon his Majesty commanded the master of his woods to give directions accordingly, and the next morning six woodmen arrived with as many carriages, drawn by eight horses to each. I took nine of these sticks, and fixing them firmly in the ground in a quadrangular figure, two foot and a half square, I took four other sticks, and tied them parallel at each corner, about two foot from the ground. Then I fastened my handkerchief to the nine sticks that stood erect, and extended it on all sides till it was as tight as the top of a drum, and the four parallel sticks rising about five inches higher than the handkerchief served as ledges on each side.

When I had finished my work, I desired the Emperor to let a troop of his best horse, twenty-four in number, come and exercise upon this plain. His Majesty approved of the proposal, and I took them up one by one in my hands, ready mounted and armed, with the proper officers to exercise them. As soon as they got into order they divided into two parties, performed mock skirmishes, discharged blunt arrows, drew their swords, fled and pursued, attacked and retired, and in short showed the best military discipline I ever beheld. The parallel sticks secured them and their horses from falling over the stage, and the Emperor was so much delighted, that he ordered this entertainment to be repeated several days, and once was pleased to be lifted and give the word of command; and, with great difficulty, persuaded even the Empress herself to let me hold her in her close chair within two yards of the stage, from whence she was able to take a full view of the whole performance. It was my good fortune that no ill accident happened in these entertainments, only once a fiery horse that belonged to one of the captains pawing with his hoof struck a hole in my handkerchief, and his foot slipping, he overthrew his rider and himself, but I immediately relieved them both, and covering the hole with one hand, I set down the troop with the other, in the same manner as I took them up. The horse that fell was strained in the left shoulder, but the rider got no hurt, and I repaired my handkerchief as well as I could: however, I would not trust to the strength of it any more in such dangerous enterprises.

About two or three days before I was set at liberty, as I was entertaining the court with these kind of feats, there arrived an express to inform his Majesty that some of his subjects riding near the place where I was taken up, had seen a great black substance lying on the ground, very oddly shaped, extending its edges round as wide as his Majesty's bedchamber, and rising up in the middle as high as a man. It was no living creature, as they at first apprehended, for it lay on the grass without motion, and some of them had walked round it several times. By mounting upon each other's shoulders, they had got to the top, which was flat and even, and stamping upon it they found it was hollow within, and they humbly conceived it might be something belonging to the Man-Mountain, and if his Majesty pleased, they would undertake to bring it with only five horses. I presently knew what they meant, and was glad at heart to receive this intelligence. It seems upon my first reaching the shore after our shipwreck, I was in such confusion, that before I came to the place where I went to sleep, my hat, which I had fastened with a string to my head while I was rowing, and which had stuck on all the time I was swimming, fell off after I came to land, the string, as I conjecture, breaking by some accident when I never observed, but thought my hat had been lost at sea. I entreated his Imperial Majesty to give orders it might be brought to me as soon as possible, describing to him the use and the nature of it, and the next day the waggoners arrived with it, but not in a very good condition. They had bored two holes in the brim, within an inch and half of the edge, and fastened two hooks in the holes. These hooks were tied by a long cord to the harness, and thus my hat was dragged along half an English mile: but the ground in that country being extremely smooth and level, it received less damage than I expected.

Two days after this adventure, the Emperor having ordered that part of his army which quarters in and about his metropolis to be in a readiness, took a fancy of diverting himself in a very singular manner. He desired I would stand like a Colossus, with my legs as far apart as I conveniently could. He then commanded his General (who was an old experienced leader, and a great patron of mine) to draw up the troops in close order, and march them under me, the foot by twenty-four in a breast, and the horse by sixteen, with drums beating, colours flying, and pikes advanced. This body consisted of three thousand foot, and a thousand horse.

I had sent so many memorials and petitions for my liberty, that his Majesty at length mentioned the matter, first in the cabinet, and then in a full council; where it was opposed by none, except Skyresh Bolgolam, who was pleased, without any provocation, to be my mortal enemy. But it was carried against him by the whole board, and confirmed by the Emperor. That minister was *Galbet*, or Admiral of the Realm, very much in his master's confidence, and a person well versed in affairs but of a morose and sour complexion. However, he was at length persuaded to comply, but prevailed that the articles and conditions upon which I should be set free, and to which I must swear, should be drawn up by himself. These articles were brought to me by Skyresh Bolgolam in person, attended by two under-secretaries, and several persons of distinction. After they were read, I was demanded to swear to the performance of them; first in the manner of my own country, and afterwards in the method prescribed by their laws, which was to hold my right foot in my left hand, to place the middle finger of my right hand on the crown of my head, and my thumb on the tip of my right ear. But because the reader may perhaps be curious to have some idea of the style and manner of expression peculiar to that people, as well as to know the articles upon which I recovered my liberty, I have made a translation of the whole document word for word, as near as I was able, which I here offer to the public.

GOLBASTO MOMAREN EVLAME GURDILO SHEFIN MULLY ULLY GUE, most mighty Emperor of Lilliput, delight and terror of the universe, whose dominions extend five thousand *blustrugs* (about twelve miles in circumference) to the extremities of the globe; monarch of all monarchs, taller than the sons of men; whose feet press down to the centre, and whose head strikes against the sun; at whose nod the princes of the earth shake their knees; pleasant as the spring, comfortable as the summer, fruitful as autumn, dreadful as winter. His most sublime Majesty proposeth to the Man-Mountain, lately arrived to our celestial dominions, the following articles, which by a solemn oath he shall be obliged to perform.

First, The Man-Mountain shall not depart from our dominions, without our licence under our great seal.

2nd, He shall not presume to come into our metropolis, without our express order; at which time the inhabitants shall have two hours warning to keep within their doors.

3rd, The said Man-Mountain shall confine his walks to our principal high roads, and not offer to walk or lie down in a meadow or field of corn.

4th, As he walks the said roads, he shall take the utmost care not to trample upon the bodies of any of our loving subjects, their horses, or carriages, nor take any of our said subjects into his hands, without their own consent.

5th, If an express requires extraordinary dispatch, the Man-Mountain shall be obliged to carry in his pocket the messenger and horse a six days journey once in every moon, and return the said messenger back (if so required) safe to our Imperial Presence.

6th, He shall be our ally against our enemies in the Island of Blefuscu, and do his utmost to destroy their fleet, which is now preparing to invade us.

7th, That the said Man-Mountain shall, at his times of leisure, be aiding and assisting to our workmen, in helping to raise certain great stones, towards covering the wall of the principal park, and other royal buildings.

8th, That the said Man-Mountain shall, in two moons' time, deliver in an exact survey of the circumference of our dominions by a computation of his own paces round the coast.

Lastly, That upon his solemn oath to observe all the above articles, the said Man-Mountain shall a daily allowance of meat and drink sufficient for the support of 1728 of our subjects, with free access to our Royal Person, and other marks of our favour. Given at our Palace at Belfaborac the twelfth day of the ninety-first moon of our reign.

I swore and subscribed to these articles with great cheerfulness and content, although some of them were not so honourable as I could have wished thanks to the malice of Skyresh Bolgolam the High Admiral: whereupon my chains were immediately unlocked, and I was at full liberty. The Emperor himself in person did me the honour to be by at the whole ceremony. I made my acknowledgements by prostrating myself at his Majesty's feet, but he commanded me to rise, and after many gracious expressions, which, to avoid the censure of vanity, I shall not repeat, he added that he hoped I should prove a useful servant, and well deserve all the favours he had already conferred upon me, or might do for the future.

The reader may please to observe, that in the last article for the recovery of my liberty the Emperor stipulates to allow me quantity of meat and drink sufficient for the support of 1728 Lilliputians. Some time after, asking a friend at court how they came to fix on that determinate number, he told me that his Majesty's mathematicians, having taken the height of my body by the help of a quadrant, and finding it to exceed theirs in the proportion of twelve to one, they concluded from the similarity of their bodies, that mine must contain at least 1728 of theirs, and consequently would require as much food as was necessary to support that of Lilliputians. By which the reader may conceive an idea of the ingenuity of that people, as well as the prudent and exact economy of so great a prince.

CHAPTER 4

The first request I made after I had obtained my liberty, was that I might have licence to see Mildendo, the metropolis. This the Emperor easily granted me, but with a special charge to do not hurt either to the inhabitants or their houses. The people had notice by proclamation of my design to visit the town. The wall which encompassed it is two foot and an half high, and at least eleven inches broad, so that a coach and horses may be driven very safely round it; and it is flanked with strong towers at ten foot distance. I stepped over the great Western Gate, and passed very gently and carefully through the two principal streets, only in my short waistcoat, for fear of damaging the roofs and eaves of the houses with the skirts of my coat. I walked with the utmost circumspection, to avoid treading on any stragglers that might remain in the streets, although the orders were very strict, that all people should keep in their houses at their own peril. The garret windows and tops of houses were so crowded with spectators, that I thought in all my travels I had not seen a more populous place. The city is an exact square, each side of the wall being five hundred foot long. The two great streets, which run cross and divide it into four quarters, are five foot wide. The lanes and alleys, which I could not enter, but only viewed them as I passed, are from twelve to eighteen inches. The town is capable of holding five hundred thousand souls. The houses are from three to five stories. The shops and markets well provided.

The Emperor's palace is in the centre of the city, where the two great streets meet. It is enclosed by a wall of two foot high, and twenty foot distant from the buildings. I had his Majesty's permission to step over this wall, and the space being so wide between that and the palace, I could easily view it on every side. The outward court is a square of forty foot, and includes two other courts. In the inmost are the royal apartments, which I was very desirous to see, but found it extremely difficult, for the great gates, from one square into another, were but eighteen inches high and seven inches wide. Now the buildings of the outer court were at least five foot high, and it was impossible for me to stride over them without infinite damage to the pile, though the walls were strongly built of hewn stone, and four inches thick. At the same time the Emperor had a great desire that I should see the magnificence of his palace, but this I was not able to do till three days after, which I spent in cutting down with my knife some of the largest trees in the royal park, about an hundred yards distant from the city. Of these trees I made two stools, each about three foot high, and strong enough to bear my weight. The people having received notice a second time, I went again through the city to the palace, with my two stools in my hands. When I came to the side of the outer court, I stood upon one stool, and took the other in my hand: this I lifted over the roof, and gently set it down on the space between the first and second court, which was eight foot wide. I then stepped over the buildings very conveniently from one stool to the other, and drew up the first after me with a hooked stick. By this contrivance I got into the inmost court, and lying down upon my side, I applied my face to the windows of the middle stories, which were left open on purpose, and discovered the most splendid apartments that can be imagined. There I saw the Empress and the young Princes, in their several lodgings, with their chief attendants about them. Her Imperial Majesty was pleased to smile very graciously upon me, and gave me out of the window her hand to kiss.

But I shall not anticipate the reader with farther descriptions of this kind, because I reserve them for a greater work, which is now almost ready for the press, containing a general description of this empire, from its first erection, through a long series of princes, with a particular account of their wars and politics, laws, learning, and religion, their plants and animals, their peculiar manners and customs, with other matters very curious and useful; my chief design at present being only to relate such events and transactions as happened to the public, or to myself, during a residence of about nine months in that empire.

One morning, about a fortnight after I had obtained my liberty, Reldresal, principal Secretary (as they style him) of Private Affairs, came to my house attended only by one servant. He ordered his coach to wait at a distance, and desired I would give him an hour's audience, which I readily consented to, on account of his quality and personal merits, as well as the many good offices he had done my during my solicitations at court. I offered to lie down, that he might the more conveniently reach my ear, but he chose rather to let me hold him in my hand during our conversation. He began with compliments on my liberty, saying he might pretend to some merit in it, but, however, added, that if it had not been for the present situation of things at court, perhaps I might not have obtained it so soon.

For, said he, as flourishing a condition as we may appear to be in to foreigners, we labour under two mighty evils; a violent faction at home, and the danger of an invasion by a most potent enemy from abroad. As to the first, you are to understand, that for above seventy moons past there have been two struggling parties in this empire, under the names of *Tramecksan* and *Slamecksan*, from the high and low heels of their shoes, by which they distinguish themselves. It is alleged indeed, that the high heels are most agreeable to our ancient constitution: but however this be, his Majesty hath determined to make use of only low heels in the administration of the government, and all office in the gift of the Crown, as you cannot but observe; and particularly, that his Majesty's Imperial heels are lower at least by a *drurr* than any of his court (*drurr* is a measure about the fourteenth part of an inch). The animosities between these two parties run so high, that they will neither eat nor drink, nor talk with each other. We compute the *Tramecksan*, or High-Heels, to exceed us in number; but the power is wholly on our side. We apprehend his Imperial Highness, the Heir to the Crown, to have some tendency towards the High-Heels, at least we can plainly discover one of his heels higher than the other, which gives him a hobble in his gait. Now, in the midst of these internal disquiets, we are threatened with an invasion from the Island of Blefuscu, which is the other great empire of the universe, almost as large and powerful as this of his Majesty. For as to what we have heard you affirm, that there are other kingdoms and states in the world inhabited by human creatures ar large as yourself, our philosophers are in much doubt, and would rather conjecture that you dropped from the moon, or one of the stars; because it is certain, that an hundred mortals of your bulk would, in a short time, destroy all the fruits and cattle of his Majesty's dominions. Besides, our histories of six thousand moons make no mention of any other regions, than the two great empires of Lilliput and Blefuscu. Which two mighty powers have, as I was going to tell you, been engaged in a most obstinate war for six and thirty moons past. It began upon the following occasion. It is allowed on all hands, that the primitive way of breaking eggs before we eat them, was at the larger end, but his present Majesty's grandfather, while he was a boy, going to eat an egg, and breaking it according to the ancient practice, happened to cut one of his fingers. Whereupon the Emperor his father published an edict, commanding all his subjects, upon great penalties, to break the smaller end of their eggs. The people so highly resented this law, that our histories tell us there have been six rebellions raised on that account, wherein one Emperor lost his life, and another his crown. These civil commotions were constantly fomented by the monarchs of Blefuscu, and when they were quelled, the exiles always fled for refuge to that empire. It is computed, that eleven thousand persons have, at several times, suffered death, rather than submit to break their eggs at the smaller end. Many hundred large volumes have been published upon this controversy: but the books of the Big-Endians have been long forbidden, and the whole party rendered incapable by law of holding employments. During the course of these troubles, the Emperors of Blefuscu did frequently expostulate by their ambassadors, accusing us of making a schism in religion, by offending against a fundamental doctrine of our great prophet Lustrog, in the fifty-fourth chapter of the *Brundecral* (which is their Alcoran). This, however, is thought to be a mere strain upon the text, for the words are these; *That all true believers shall break their eggs at the convenient end*: and which is the convenient end, seems, in my humble opinion, to be left to every man's conscience, or at least in the power of the chief magistrate to determine. Now the Big-Endian exiles have found so much credit in the Emperor of Blefuscu's court, and so much private assistance and encouragement from their party here at home, that a bloody war hath been carried on between the two empires for six and thirty moons with various success, during which time we have lost forty capital ships, and a much greater number of smaller vessels, together with thirty thousand of our best seamen and soldiers. The damage received by the enemy is reckoned to be somewhat greater then ours. However, they have now equipped a large fleet, and are just preparing to make a descent upon us; and his Imperial Majesty, placing great confidence in your valour and strength, hath commanded me to lay this account of his affairs before you.

I desired the Secretary to present my humble duty to the Emperor, and to let him know that I thought it would not become me, who was a foreigner, to interfere with parties; but I was ready, with the hazard of my life, to defend his person and state against all invaders.

CHAPTER 5

The Empire of Blefuscu is an island situated to the north-north-east side of Lilliput, from whence it is parted only by a channel of eight hundred yards wide. I had not yet seen it, and upon this notice of an intended invasion, I avoided appearing on that side of the coast, for fear of being discovered by some of the enemy's ships. They had received no intelligence of me, all intercourse between the two empires having been strictly forbidden during the war, upon pain of death, and an embargo laid by our Emperor upon all vessels whatsoever. I communicated to his Majesty a project I had formed of seizing the enemy's whole fleet, which, as our scouts assured us, lay at anchor in the harbour ready to sail with the first fair wind. I consulted the most experienced seamen about the depth of the channel, which they had often plumbed, and they told me that in the middle at high-water it was seventy *glumgluffs* deep, which is about six foot of European measures; and the rest of it fifty *glumgluffs* at most. I walked towards the north-east coast over against Blefuscu; and lying down behind a hillock, took out my small pocket perspective-glass, and viewed the enemy's fleet at anchor, consisting of about fifty men of war, and a great number of transports. I then came back to my house, and gave order (for which I had a warrant) for a great quantity of the strongest cable and bars of iron. The cable was about as thick as packthread, and the bars of the length and size of a knitting-needle. I trebled the cable to make it stronger, and for the same reason I twisted three of the iron bars together, binding the extremities into a hook. Having thus fixed fifty hooks to as many cables, I went back to the north-east coast, and putting off my coat, shoes, and stockings, walked into the sea in my leathern jerkin, about half an hour before high water. I waded with what haste I could, and swam in the middle about thirty yards till I felt ground and I arrived at the fleet in less than half an hour. The enemy was so frightened when they saw me, that they leaped out of their ships, and swam to shore, where there could not be fewer than thirty thousand souls. I then took my tackling, and fastening a hook to the hole at the prow of each ship, I tied all the cords together at the end. While I was thus employed, the enemy discharged several thousand arrows, many of which stuck in my hands and face, and besides the excessive smarting, gave me much disturbance in my work. My greatest apprehension was for my eyes, which I should have lost if I had not suddenly thought of an expedient. I kept among other little necessaries a pair of spectacles in a private pocket, which, as I observed before, had escaped the Emperor's searchers. These I took out and fastened as strongly as I could upon my nose, and thus armed went on boldly with my work in spite of the enemy's arrows, many of which struck against the glasses of my spectacles, but without any other effect than unsettling them a little. I had now fastened all the hooks, and taking the knot in my hand, began to pull; but not a ship would stir, for they were held fast by their anchors, so that the boldest part of my enterprise remained. I therefore let go the cord, and leaving the hooks fixed to the ships, I resolutely cut with my knife the cables that fastened the anchors, receiving above two hundred shots in my face and hands; then I took up the knotted end of the cables to which my hooks were tied, and with great ease drew fifty of the enemy's largest men-of-war after me.

The Blefuscudians, who had not the least imagination of what I intended, were at first confounded with astonishment. They had seen me cut the cables, and thought my design was only to let the ships run a-drift, or fall foul on each other: but when they perceived the whole fleet moving in order, and saw me pulling at the end, they set up such a scream of grief and despair, that it is almost impossible to describe or conceive. When I had got out of danger, I stopped awhile to pick out the arrows that stuck in my hands and face, and rubbed on some of the same ointment that was given me at my first arrival, as I have formerly mentioned. I then took off my spectacles, and waiting about an hour, till the tide was a little fallen, I waded through the middle with my cargo, and arrived safe at the royal port of Lilliput.

The Emperor and his whole court stood on the shore expecting the issue of this great adventure. They saw the ships move forward in a large half-moon, but could not discern me, who was up to my breast in water. When I advanced to the middle of the channel, they were yet in more pain, because I was under water to my neck. The Emperor concluded me to be drowned, and that the enemy's fleet was approaching in a hostile manner, but he was soon eased of his fears, for the channel growing shallower every step I made, I came in a short time within hearing, and holding up the end of the cable by which the fleet was fastened, I cried in a loud voice, *Long live the most puissant Emperor of Lilliput!* This great prince received me at my landing with all possible praise, and created me a *Nardac* upon the spot, which is the highest title of honour among them.

His Majesty desired I would take some other opportunity of bringing all the rest of his enemy's ships into his port.

finished, wherein I did them several good offices by the credit I now had, or at least appeared to have at court, their Excellencies, who were privately told how much I had been their friend, made a formal visit. They began with many compliments upon my valour and generosity, invited me to that kingdom in the Emperor their master's name, and desired me to show them some proofs of my prodigious strength, of which they heard so many wonders; wherein I readily obliged them, but shall not trouble the reader with the particulars.

When I had for some time entertained their Excellencies, to their infinite satisfaction and surprise, I desired they would do me the honour to present my most humble respects to the Emperor their master, the renown of whose virtues had so justly filled the whole world with admiration, and whose royal person I resolved to attend before I returned to my own country. Accordingly, the next time I had the honour to see our Emperor, I desired his general licence to wait on the Blefuscudian monarch, which he granted me, as I could plainly perceive, in a very cold manner, but I could not guess the reason, till I had a whisper from a certain person, that Flimnap and Bolgolam had represented my intercourse with those ambassadors as a mark of disaffection, from which I am sure my heart was wholly free. This was the first time I began to conceive some imperfect idea of courts and ministers.

It is to be observed, that these ambassadors spoke to me by an interpreter, the languages of both empires differing as much from each other as any two in Europe, and each nation priding itself upon the antiquity, beauty, and energy of their own tongues, with an avowed contempt for that of their neighbour; yet our Emperor, standing upon the advantage he had got from the seizure of their fleet, obliged

And so unmeasureable is the ambition of princes, that he seemed to think of nothing less than reducing the whole empire of Blefuscu into a province, and governing it by a Viceroy; of destroying the Big-Endian exiles, and compelling that people to break the smaller end of their eggs, by which he would remain the sole monarch of the whole world. But I endeavoured to divert him from this design by many arguments drawn from the topics of policy as well as justice, and I plainly protested, that I would never be an instrument of bringing a free and brave people into slavery. And when the matter was debated in council, the wisest part of the ministry were of my opinion.

This open bold declaration of mine was so opposite to the schemes and politics of his Imperial majesty, that he could never forgive it. He mentioned it in a very artful manner at council, where I was told that some of the wisest appeared, at least by their silence, to be of my opinion; but others, who were my secret enemies, could not forbear some expressions, which by a side-wind reflected on me. And from this time began an intrigue between his Majesty and a junto of ministers maliciously bent against me, which broke out in less than two months, and could have ended in my utter destruction. Of so little weight are the greatest services to princes, when put into the balance with a refusal to gratify their passions.

About three weeks after this exploit, there arrived a solemn embassy from Blefuscu, with humble offers of a peace, which was soon concluded upon conditions very advantageous to our Emperor, wherewith I shall not trouble the reader. There were six ambassadors with a train of about five hundred persons, and their entry was very magnificent, suitable to the grandeur of their master, and the importance of their business. When their treaty was them to deliver their credentials, and make their speech in the Lilliputian tongue. And it must be confessed, that from the great intercourse of trade and commerce between both realms, from the continual reception of exiles, which is mutual among them, and as it is the custom in each empire to send their young nobility and richer gentry to the other, in order to polish themselves by seeing the world and understanding men and manners, there are few persons of distinction, or merchants, or seamen, who dwell in the maritime parts, who cannot hold conversations in both tongues, as I found some weeks after when I went to pay my respects to the Emperor of Blefuscu. In the midst of great misfortunes, caused by the malice of my enemies, this visit proved a very happy adventure to me, as I shall relate in its proper place.

The reader may remember that when I signed those articles upon which I recovered my liberty, there were some which I disliked upon account of their being too servile, neither could anything but an extreme necessity have forced me to submit. But being now a *Nardac*, of the highest rank in that empire, such offices were looked upon as below my dignity, and the Emperor (to do him justice) never once mentioned them to me.

CHAPTER 6

Although I intend to leave the description of this empire to a particular treatise, yet in the meantime I am content to gratify the curious reader with some general ideas. As the common size of the natives is somewhat under six inches high, so there is an exact proportion in all other animals, as well as plants and trees. For instance, the tallest horses and oxen are between four and five inches in height, the sheep an inch and a half, more or less, their geese about the size of a sparrow, and so the several gradations downwards till you come to the smallest, which, to my sight, were almost invisible, but nature had adapted the eyes of the Lilliputians to all objects proper for their view: they see with great exactness, but at no great distance. To show the sharpness of their sight towards objects that are near, I have been much pleased with observing a cook pulling a lark, which was not so large as a common fly; and a young girl threading an invisible needle with invisable silk. Their tallest trees are about seven foot high; I mean some of those in the great royal park, the tops whereof I could just reach with my fist clenched. The other vegetables are in the same proportion, but this I leave to the reader's imagination.

I shall say but little at present of their learning, which for many ages has flourished in all its branches among them: but their manners of writing is very peculiar, being neither from the left to right, like the Europeans, nor from the right to left, like the Arabians, nor from up to down, like the Chinese, nor from down to up, like the Cascagians, but aslant from one corner of the paper to the other, like ladies in England.

They bury their dead with their heads directly downwards, because they hold an opinion, that in eleven thousand moons they are all to rise again, in which period the earth (which they conceive to be flat) will turn upside down, and by this means they shall, at their resurrection, be found ready standing on their feet. The learned among them confess the absurdity of this doctrine, but the practice still continues, in compliance to the vulgar.

There are some very peculiar laws and customs in this empire and if they were not so directly contrary to those of my own dear country, I should be tempted to say a little in their justification. It is only to be wished that they were as well executed. The first I shall mention related to informers. All crimes against the state are punished here with the utmost severity, but if the person accused makes his innocence plain at his trial, the accuser is immediately put to an ignominious death, and out of his goods or lands, the innocent person is quadruply recompensed for the loss of his time, for the danger he underwent, for the hardship of his imprisonment, and for all the charges he incurred making his defence. Or, if that fund be deficient, it is largely supplied by the Crown. The Emperor does also confer on him some public mark of his favour, and proclamation is made of his innocence through the whole city.

They look upon fraud as a greater crime than theft, and therefore seldom fail to punish it with death; for they allege, that care and vigilance, with a very common understanding, may preserve a man's goods from thieves, but honesty has no fence against superior cunning.

Thus since it is necessary that there should be a perpetual intercourse of buying and selling, and dealing upon credit, where fraud is permitted and connived at, or has no law to punish it, the honest dealer is always undone, and the knave gets the advantage. I remember I was once interceding with the King for a criminal who had wronged his master of a great sum of money which he had received by order, and ran away with. I happened to tell his Majesty, by way of extenuation, that it was only a breach of trust, and the Emperor thought it monstrous in me to offer, as a defence, the greatest aggravation of the crime: and truly I had little to say in return, farther than the common answer that different nations had different customs; for, I confess, I was heartily ashamed.

Although we usually reward and punishment the two hinges upon which all governments turns, yet I could never observe this maxim to be put in practice by any nation except that of Lilliput. Whoever can bring sufficient proof there that he hath strictly observed the laws of his country for seventy three moons, has a claim to certain privileges, according to his quality and condition of life, with a proportionable sum of money out of a fund appropriate for that us: he likewise acquires the title of *Snilpall*, or Legal, which is added to his name, but does not descend to his posterity. And these people thought it a prodigious defect of policy among us, when I told them that our laws were enforced only by penalties without any mention of reward. It is upon this account that the image of Justice, in their courts of judicature, is formed with six eyes, two before, as many behind, and on each side one, to signify circumspection, and with a bag of gold open in her right hand, and a sword sheathed in her left, to show she is more disposed to reward him than to punish.

In choosing persons for all employments, they have more regard to good morals than to great abilities, for, since government is necessary to mankind, they believe that the common size of human understandings is fitted to some station or other, and that Providence never intended to make the management of public affairs a mystery to be comprehended only by a few persons of sublime genius, of which there are seldom are three born in an age. They suppose truth, justice, temperance and the like, to be in every man's power, the practice of which virtues, assisted by experience and a good intention, would qualify any man for the service of his country, except where a course of study is required. But they thought the want of moral virtues was so far from being supplied by superior endowments of the mind, that employments could never be put into such dangerous hands as those of persons so qualified; and at least, that the mistakes committed by ignorance in a virtuous disposition, would never be of such fatal consequence to the public weal as the practices of a man whose inclinations led him to by corrupt, and had great abilities to manage, and multiply, and defend his corruptions.

In like manner, the disbelief of a Divine Providence renders a man incapable of holding any public station, for, since kings avow themselves to be the deputies of Providence, the Lilliputians think nothing can be more absurd than for a prince to employ such men as disown the authority under which he acts.

In relating these and the following laws, I would only be understood to mean the original institutions, and not the most scandalous corruptions into which these people are fallen by the degenerate nature of man. For as to that infamous practice of acquiring great employments by dancing on the ropes, or badges of favour and distinction by leaping over sticks and creeping under them, the reader is to observe, that they were first introduced by the grandfather of the Emperor now reigning, and grew to the present height by the gradual increase of party and faction.

Ingratitude is among them a capital crime, as we read it to have been in some other countries. They reason thus, that whoever makes ill returns to his benefactor, must needs be a common enemy to the rest of mankind, from whom he hath received no obligation, and therefore such a man is not fit to live.

Their notions relating to the duties of parents and children differ extremely from ours. Their opinion is that parents are the last of all others to be trusted with the education of their own children, and therefore they have in every town public nurseries, where all parents, except cottagers and labourers, are obliged to send their infants of both sexes to be reared and educated when they come to the age of twenty moons, at which time they are supposed to have some rudiments of docility. These schools are of several kinds, suited to different qualities, and to both sexes. They have certain professors well skilled in preparing children for such a condition of life as befits the rank of their parents, and their own capacities as well as inclinations. I shall first say something of the male nurseries, and then of the female.

The nurseries of males of noble or eminent birth, are provided with grave and learned professors, and their several deputies. The clothes and food of the children are plain and simple. They are bred up in the principles of honour, justice, courage, modesty, clemency, religion, and love of their country; they are always employed in some business, except in the times of eating and sleeping, which are very short, and two hours for diversions, consisting of bodily exercises. They are dressed by men till four years of age, and then are obliged to dress themselves, although their quality be ever so great; and the women attendants, who are aged proportionably to ours at fifty, perform only the most menial offices. They are never suffered to converse with servants, but go together in small or greater numbers to take their diversions, and always in the presence of a professor, or one of his deputies, so they avoid those early bad impressions of folly and vice to which our children are subject. Their parents are suffered to see them only twice a year, and the visit is to last but an hour. They are allowed to kiss the child at meeting and parting, but a professor, who always stands by on these occasions, will not suffer them to whimper, or use any fondling expressions, or bring any presents of toys, sweetmeats, and the like.

The pension from each family for the education and entertainment of a child, upon failure of due payment, is levied by the Emperor's officers.

The nurseries of children of ordinary gentlemen, merchants, traders, and handicrafts, are managed proportionably after the same manner; only those designed for trades are put out apprentices at eleven years old, whereas those of persons of quality continue in their exercises till fifteen, which answers to one and twenty with us, but the confinement is gradually lessened for the last three years.

In the female nurseries, the young girls of quality are educated much like the males, only they are dressed by orderly servants of their own sexes, and always in the presence of a professor or deputy till they come to dress themselves, which is at five years old. And if it be found that these nurses ever presume to entertain the girls with frightful or foolish stories, or the common follies practised by chambermaids among us, they are publicly whipped thrice about the city, imprisoned for a year, and banished for life to the most desolate part of the country. Thus the young ladies there are as much ashamed of being cowards and fools as the men, and despite all personal ornaments beyond decency and cleanliness: neither did I perceive any difference in their education, made by their difference of sex, only that the exercise of the females were not altogether so robust, and that some rules were given them relating to domestic life, and a smaller compass of learning was enjoined them: for their maxim is, that among people of quality a wife should always a reasonable and agreeable companion, because she cannot always be young. When the girls are twelve years old, which among them is the marriageable age, their parents or guardians take them home, with great expressions of gratitude to the professors, and seldom without tears from the young lady and her companions.

In the nurseries of females of the meaner sort, the children are instructed in all kinds of works proper for their sex, and their several degrees: those intended for apprentices are dismissed at nine years old, the rest are kept to thirteen.

The meaner families who have children at these nurseries, are obliged, besides their annual pension, which is as low as possible, to return to the steward of the nursery a small monthly share of their gettings, to be a portion for the child; and therefore all parents are limited in their expenses by the law. For the Lilliputians think nothing can be more unjust than for people to bring children into the world and leave the burden of supporting them on the public. As to persons of quality, they give security to appropriate a certain sum for each child, suitable to their condition; and these funds are always managed with good husbandry, and the most exact justice.

The cottagers and labourers keep their children at home, their business being only to till and cultivate the earth, and therefore their education is of little consequence to the public, but the old and diseased among them are supported by hospitals, for begging is a trade unknown in this kingdom.

And here it may perhaps divert the curious reader, to give some account of my domestics, and my manner of living in this country, during a residence of nine months and thirteen days. Having a head mechanically turned, and being likewise forced by necessity, I had made for myself a table and chair convenient enough, out of the largest trees in the royal park. Two hundred sempstresses were employed to make me shirts, and linen for my bed and table, all of the strongest and coarsest kind they could get, which, however, they were forced to quilt together in several folds, for the thickest was some degrees finer than lawn. Their linen is usually three inches wide, and three foot make a piece. The sempstresses took my measure as I lay on the ground, one standing at my neck, and another at my mid-leg, with a strong cord extended, that each held by the end, while the third measured the length of the cord with a rule of an inch long. Then they measured my right thumb, and desired no more; for by a mathematical computation that twice round the thumb is once round the wrist, and so on to the neck and the waist, and by the help of my old shirt, which I displayed on the ground before them for a pattern, they fitted me exactly. Three hundred tailors were employed in the same manner to make me clothes; but they had another contrivance for taking my measure. I kneeled down, and they raised a ladder from the ground to my neck. Upon this ladder one of them mounted, and let fall a plumb-line from my collar to the floor, which just answered the length of my coat; but my waist and arms I measured myself. When my clothes were finished, which was done in my house (for the largest of theirs would not have been able to hold them) they looked like the patch-work made by the ladies in England, only that mine were all of a colour.

I had three hundred cooks to dress my victuals, in little convenient huts built about my house, where they and their families lived, and prepared me two dishes apiece. I took up twenty waiters in my hand, and placed them on the table; an hundred more attended below on the ground, some with dishes of meat, and some with barrels of wine, and other liquors, slung on their shoulders, all of which the waiters above drew up as I wanted, in a very ingenious manner, by certain cords, as we draw the bucket up a well in Europe. A dish of their meat was a good mouthful, and a barrel of their liquor a reasonable draught. Their mutton yields to ours, but their beef is excellent. I have had a sirloin so large, that I have been forced to make three bits of it; but this rare. My servants are astonished to see me eat bones and all, as in our country we do the leg of a lark. Their geese and turkeys I usually ate at a mouthful, and I must confess they far exceed ours. Of their smaller fowl I could take up twenty or thirty at the end of my knife.

One day his Imperial majesty, being informed of my way of living, desired that himself and his Royal Consort, with the young Princes of the blood of both sexes, might have the happiness (as he was pleased to call it) of dining with me. They came accordingly, and I placed them upon chairs of state on my table, just over against me, with their guards about them. Flimnap, the Lord High Treasurer, attended there likewise with his white staff, and I observed he often looked on me with a sour countenance, which I pretended not to notice, but ate more than usual, in honour to my dear country, as well as to fill the court with admiration. I have some private reasons to believe, that this visit from his

Majesty gave Flimnap an opportunity of doing me ill offices to his master. That minister had always been my secret enemy, though he outwardly caressed me more than was usual to the moroseness of his nature. He represented to the Emperor the low condition of his treasury; that he was forced to take up money at great discount; that exchequer bills would not be circulate under nine per cent, below par; that in short I had cost his Majesty above a million and a half of *sprugs* (their greatest gold coins, about the bigness of a spangle); and upon the whole, that it would be advisable in the Emperor to take the first occasion of dismissing me.

I am here obliged to vindicate the reputation of an excellent lady, who was an innocent sufferer upon my account. The Treasurer took a fancy to be jealous of his wife, from the malice of some evil tongues, who informed him that her Grace had taken a violent affection for my person; and the court-scandal ran for some time, that she once came privately to my lodgings. This I solemnly declare to be a most infamous falsehood, without any grounds, farther than that her Grace was pleased to treat me with all innocent marks of freedom and friendship. I own she came often to my house, but always publicly, nor ever without three more in the coach, who were usually her sister and young daughter, and some particular acquaintance; but this was common to many other ladies of the court. And I still appeal to my servants round, whether they at any time saw a coach at my door without knowing what persons were in it. On those occasions, when a servant had given me notice, my custom was to go immediately to the door, and, after paying my respects, to take up the coach and two horses very carefully in my hands (for if there were six horses, the postillion always unharnessed four) and place them on a table where I had fixed a moveable rim five inches high, to prevent accidents. And I have often had four coaches and horses at once on my table full of company, while I sat in my chair leaning my face towards them, and when I was engaged with one set, the coachmen would gently drive the others round my table. I have passed many an afternoon very agreeably in these conversations. But I defy the Treasurer, or his two informers (I will name them, and let 'em make their best of it) Clustril and Drunlo, to prove that any person ever came to me *incognito*, except the secretary Reldresal, who was sent by express command of his Imperial Majesty, as I have before related. I should not have dwelt so long upon this particular, if it had not been a point wherein the reputation of a great lady is so nearly concerned, to say nothing of my own; though I then had the honour to be a *Nardac*, which the Treasurer himself is not, for all the world knows he is only a *Clum-glum*, a title inferior by one degree, as that of a Marquis is to a Duke in England, although I allow he preceded me in right of his post. These false informations, which I afterwards came to know of by an accident not proper to mention, made Flimnap the Treasurer show his lady for some time an ill countenance, and me a worse. Although he was at last undeceived and reconciled to her, yet I lost all credit with him, and found my interest decline very fast with the Emperor himself, who was indeed too much governed by that favourite.

CHAPTER 7

Before I proceed to give an account of my leaving this kingdom, it may be proper to inform the reader of a private intrigue which had been for two months forming against me.

I had been hitherto all my life a stranger to courts, for which I was unqualified by my humble background. I had indeed heard and read enough of the dispositions of great princes and ministers, but never expected to have found such terrible effects of them in so remote a country, governed, as I thought by very different maxims from those in Europe.

When I was just preparing to pay my attendance on the Emperor of Blefuscu, a considerable person at court (to whom I had been very serviceable at a time when he lay under the highest displeasure of his Imperial Majesty) came to my house very privately at night in a close chair, and without sending his name, desired admittance. The chair-men were dismissed, I put the chair, with his Lordship in it, into my coat-pocket, and giving orders to a trusty servant to say I was indisposed and gone to sleep, I fastened the door of my house, placed the chair on the table, according to my usual custom, and sat down by it. After the common salutations were over, I observed his Lordship's countenance was full of concern, and enquired into the reason. He desired I would hear him with patience in a matter that highly concerned my honour and my life. His speech was to the following effect, for I took notes of it as soon as he left me.

You are to know, said he, that several Committees of Council have been lately called in the most private manner on your account, and it is but two days since his Majesty came to a full resolution.

You are very sensible that Skyresh Bolgolam (*Galbet*, or High Admiral) hath been your mortal enemy almost ever since your arrival. His original reasons I know not, but his hatred is much increased since your great success against Blefuscu, by which his glory as Admiral is obscured. This Lord, in conjunction with Flimnap the High Treasurer, whose enmity against you is notorious on account of his lady, Limtoc the General, Lalcon the Chamberlain, and Balmuff the Grand Justiciary, have prepared articles of impeachment against you, for treason, and other capital crimes.

This preface made me so impatient, being conscious of my own merits and innocence, that I was going to interrupt, but he entreated me to be silent, and thus proceeded.

Out of gratitude for the favours you have done me, I procured information of the whole proceedings, and a copy of the articles, wherein I venture my head for your service.

Articles of Impeachment against Quinbus Flestrin
(the Man-Mountain)

ARTICLE I

That the said Quinbus Flestrin having brought the imperial fleet of Blefuscu into the royal port, and being afterwards commanded by his Imperial majesty to seize all the other ships of the said empire of Blefuscu, and reduce that empire to a province to be governed by a Viceroy from hence, and to destroy and put to death not only all the Big-Endian exiles, but likewise all the people of that empire, who would not immediately forsake the Big-Endian heresy: He, the said Flestrin, like a false traitor against his most Auspicious, Serene, Imperial Majesty, did petition to be excused from the said service, upon pretence of unwillingness to force the consciences, or destroy the liberties and lives of an innocent people.

Article II

That, whereas certain ambassadors arrived from the court of Blefuscu, to sue for peace in his Majesty's court: He, the said Flestrin, did, like a false traitor, aid, abet, comfort, and divert the said ambassadors, although he knew them to be servants to a Prince who was lately an open enemy to his Imperial Majesty, and in open war against his said Majesty.

Article III

That the said Quinbus Flestrin, contrary to the duty of a faithful subject, is now preparing to make a voyage to the court and empire of Blefuscu, for which he hath received only verbal licence from his Imperial Majesty; and under colour of the said licence, doth falsely and traitorously intend to take the said voyage, and thereby to aid, comfort, and abet the Emperor of Blefuscu, so late an enemy, and in open war with his Imperial Majesty aforesaid.

There are some other articles, but these are the most important, of which I have read you an summary.

In the several debates upon this impeachment, it must ne confessed that his Majesty gave many marks of his great lenity, often urging the services you had done him, and endeavouring to extenuate your crimes. The Treasurer and Admiral insisted that you should be put to the most painful and ignominious death, by setting fire on your house at night, and the General was to attend with twenty thousand men armed with poisoned arrows to shoot you on the face and hands. Some of your servants were to have private orders to strew a poisonous juice on your shirts, which would soon make you tear your own flesh, and die in the utmost torture. The General came into the same opinion, so that for a long time there was a majority against you. But his Majesty resolving, if possible, to spare your life, at last brought off the Chamberlain.

Upon this incident, Reldresal, principal Secretary for Private Affairs, who always approved himself your true friend, was commanded by the Emperor to deliver his opinion, which he accordingly did; and therein justified the good thoughts you have of him. He allowed your crimes to be great, but that was still room for mercy, the most commendable virtue in a prince, and for which his majesty was so justly celebrated. He said the friendship between you and him was so well known to the world, that perhaps the most honourable board might think him partial: however, in obedience to the command he had received, he would freely offer his sentiments. That if his Majesty, in consideration of your services, and pursuant to his own merciful disposition, would please to spare your life, and only give order to put out both your eyes, he humbly conceived that by this expedient justice might in some measure be satisfied, and all the world would applaud the lenity of the Emperor, as well as the fair and generous proceedings of those who have the honour to be his counsellors. That the loss of your eyes would be no impediment to your bodily strength, by which you might still be useful to his Majesty. That blindness is an addition to courage, by concealing dangers from us; that the fear you had for your eyes was the greatest difficulty in bringing over the enemy's fleet, and it would be sufficient for you to see by the eyes of the ministers, since the greatest princes do no more.

This proposal was received with the utmost disapprobation by the whole board. Bolgolam, the Admiral, could not preserve his temper, but rising up in fury said he wondered how the Secretary durst presume to give his opinion for preserving the life of a traitor. He said the services you had performed, were, by all true reasons of state, the great aggravation of your crimes: that the same strength which enables you to bring over the enemy's fleet, might serve, upon the first discontent, to carry it back: that he had good reasons to think you were a Big-Endian in your heart, and as treason begins in the heart, before it appears in overt acts, so he accused you as a traitor on that account, and therefore insisted you should be put to death.

The Treasurer was of the same opinion. He showed to what straits his Majesty's revenue was reduced by the charge of maintaining you, which would soon grow insupportable: that the Secretary's expedient of putting out your eyes was so far from being a remedy against this evil, it would probably increase it, as it is manifest from the common practice of blinding some kind of fowl, after which they fed the faster, and grew sooner fat: that his sacred Majesty and the Council, who are your judges, were in their own consciences fully convinced of your guilt, which was a sufficient argument to condemn you to death, without the formal proofs required by the strict letter of the law.

But his Imperial Majesty, fully determined against capital punishment, was graciously pleased to say that since the Council thought the loss of your eyes too easy a censure, some other may be inflicted hereafter. And your friend the

Secretary humbly desiring to be heard again, in answer to what the Treasurer had objected concerning the great charge his Majesty was at in maintaining you, said that his Excellency, who had the sole disposal of the Emperor's revenue, might easily provide against that evil, by gradually lessening your establishment; by which, for want of sufficient food, you would grow weak and faint, and lose your appetite, and consequently decay in a few months; neither would the stench of your carcass be then so dangerous, as it would be more than half diminished; and immediately upon your death, five or six thousand of his Majesty's subjects might, in two or three days, cut your flesh from your bones, take it away by cart-loads, and bury it in distant parts to prevent infection, leaving the skeleton as a monument of admiration to posterity.

Thus by the great friendship of the Secretary, the whole affair was compromised. It was strictly enjoined that the project of starving you by degrees should be kept a secret, but the sentence of putting out your eyes was entered on the books, none dissenting except Bolgolam the Admiral, who, being a creature of the Empress, was perpetually instigated by her Majesty to insist upon your death, she having borne perpetual malice against you.

In three days your friend the Secretary will be directed to come to your house, and read before you the articles of impeachment; and then to signify the great lenity and favour of his Majesty and Council, whereby you are only condemned to the loss of your eyes, which his Majesty doth not question you will gratefully and humbly submit to. Twenty of his Majesty's surgeons will attend, in order to see the operation well performed, by discharging very sharp-pointed arrows into the balls of your eyes, as you lie on the ground.

I leave to your prudence what measures you will take, and to avoid suspicion, I must immediately return in as private a manner as I came.

His Lordship did so, and I remained alone, under many doubts and perplexities of mind.

It was a custom introduced by this prince and his ministry (very different, as I have been assured, from the practices of former times) that after the court had decreed any cruel execution, either to gratify the monarch's resentment, or the malice of a favourite, the Emperor always made a speech to his whole Council, expressing his great lenity and tenderness, as qualities known and confessed by all the world. This speech was immediately published through the kingdom; nor did anything terrify the people so much as those encomiums on his Majesty's mercy, because it was observed that the more these praises were enlarged and insisted on, the more inhuman was the punishment, and the sufferer more innocent. And so to myself, I must confess, having never been designed for a courtier either by my birth or education, I was so ill a judge of things, that I could not discover the lenity and favour of this sentence, but conceived it (perhaps erroneously) rather to be rigorous than gentle. I sometimes thought of standing my trial, for although I could not deny the facts alleged in the several articles, yet I hoped they would admit of some extenuations. But having in my life perused many state trials, which I ever observed to terminate as the judges thought fit to direct, I durst not rely on so dangerous a decision, in so critical a juncture, and against such powerful enemies. Once I was strongly bent upon resistance, for while I had liberty, the whole strength of the empire could hardly subdue me, and I might easily with stones pelt the metropolis to pieces; but I soon rejected that project with horror, by remembering the oath I had made to the Emperor, the favours I received from him, and the high title of *Nardac* he conferred upon me. Neither had I so soon learned the gratitude of courtiers, to persuade myself that his Majesty's present severities quitted me of all past obligations.

At last I fixed upon a resolution, for which it is probable I may incur some censure, and not unjustly, for I confess I owe the preserving my eyes, and consequently my liberty, to my own great rashness and want of experience. If I had then known the nature of princes and ministers, which I have since observed in many other courts, and their methods of treating criminals less obnoxious than myself, I should with great alacrity and readiness have submitted to so easy a punishment. But hurried on by the precipitancy of youth, and having his Imperial Majesty's licence to pay my attendance upon the Emperor of Blefuscu, I took this opportunity, before the three days were elapsed, to send a letter to my friend the Secretary, signifying my resolution of setting out that morning for Blefuscu according to the leave I had got, and without waiting for an answer I went to that side of the island where our fleet lay. I seized a large man of war, tied a cable to the prow, and, lifting up the anchors, I stripped myself, put my clothes (together with my coverlet, which I brought under my arm) into the vessel, and drawing it after me between wading and swimming, arrived at the royal port of Blefuscu, where the people had long expected me. They lent me two guides to direct me to the capital city, which is of the same name. I held them in my hands till I came within two hundred yards of the gate, and desired them to signify my arrival to one of the secretaries, and let him know I there waited his Majesty's commands. I had an answer in about an hour, that his Majesty, attended by the Royal Family and great officers of the court, was coming out to receive me. I advanced an hundred yards. The Emperor and his train alighted from their horses, the Empress and ladies from their coaches, and I did not perceive they were in any fright or concern. I lay on the ground to kiss his Majesty's and the Empress's hand. I told his Majesty that I was come according to my promise, and with the licence of the Emperor my master, to have the honour of seeing so mighty a monarch, and to offer him any service in my power, consistent with my duty to my own prince; not mentioning a word of my disgrace, because I had hitherto no regular information of it, and might suppose myself wholly ignorant of any such design; neither could I reasonably conceive that the Emperor would discover the secret while I was out his power: wherein, however, it soon appeared I was deceived.

I shall not trouble the reader with the particular account of my reception at this court, which was suitable to the generosity of so great a prince; nor of the difficulties I was in for want of a house and bed, being forced to lie on the ground, wrapped up in my coverlet.

CHAPTER 8

Three days after my arrival, walking out of curiosity to the north-east coast of the island, I observed, about half a league off in the sea, something that looked like a boat overturned. I pulled off my shoes and stockings, and wading two or three hundred yards, I found the object to approach nearer by force of the tide; and then plainly saw it to be a real boat, which I supposed might, be some tempest, have been driven from a ship. I returned immediately towards the city, and desired his Imperial Majesty to lend me twenty of the tallest vessels he had left after the loss of his fleet, and three thousand seamen under the command of his Vice-Admiral. This fleet sailed round, while I went back the shortest way to the coast where I first discovered the boat; I found the tide had driven it still nearer. The seamen were all provided with cordage, which I had beforehand twisted to a sufficient strength. When the ships came up, I stripped myself, and waded till I came within an hundred yards of the boat, after which I was forced to swim till I got up to it. The seamen threw me the end of the cord, which I fastened to a hole in the fore-part of the boat, and the other end to a man of war; but I found all my labour to little purpose; for being out of my depth, I was not able to work. In this necessity, I was forced to swim behind, and push the boat forwards as often as I could, with one of my hands; and the tide favouring me, I advanced so far, that I could just hold up my chin and feel the ground. I rested two or three minutes, and then gave the boat another shove, and so on till the sea was no higher than my arm-pits. Now the most laborious part being over,

I took out my other cables, which were stowed in one of the ships, and fastened them first to the boat, and then to nine of the vessels which attended me; the wind being favourable, the seamen towed, and I shoved till we arrived within forty yards of the shore, and waiting till the tide was out, I made a shift to turn it on its bottom, and found it was but little damaged.

I shall not trouble the reader with the difficulties I was under by the help of certain paddles, which cost me ten days making, to get my boat to the royal port of Blefuscu, where a might concourse of people appeared upon my arrival, full of wonder at the sight of so prodigious a vessel. I told the Emperor that my good fortune had thrown this boat in my way, to carry me to some place from whence I might return into my native country, and begged his Majesty's orders for getting materials to fit it up, together with his licence to depart; which, after some kind expostulations, he was pleased to grant.

I did very much wonder, in all this time, not to have heard of any express relating to me from our Emperor to the court of Blefuscu. But I was afterwards given privately to understand, that his Imperial Majesty, never imaging I had the least notice of his designs, believed I was only gone to Blefuscu in performance of my promise, according to the licence he had given me, which was well known at our court, and would return in a few days when that ceremony was ended. But he was at last in pain at my long absence, and after consulting with the Treasurer and the rest of that cabal, a person of quality was dispatched with the copy of the articles against me. This envoy had instructions to represent the monarch of Blefuscu the great lenity of his master, who was content to punish me no farther than with the loss of my eyes; that I had fled from justice, and if I did not return in two hours, I should be deprived of my title of *Nardac*, and declared a traitor. The envoy further added, that in order to maintain the peace and amity between both empires, his master expected that his brother of Blefuscu would give orders to have me sent back to Lilliput, bound hand and foot, to be punished as a traitor.

The Emperor of Blefuscu having taken three days to consult, returned an answer consisting of many civilities and excuses. He said that as for sending me bound, his brother knew it was impossible and that although I had deprived him of his fleet, yet he owed great obligations to me for many good offices I had done him in making the peace. That however both their Majesties would soon be made easy, for I had found a prodigious vessel on the shore, able to carry me on the sea, which he had given order to fit up with my own assistance and direction, and he hoped in a few weeks both empires would be freed from so insupportable an incumbrance.

With this answer the envoy returned to Lilliput, and the monarch of Blefuscu related to me all that had passed, offering me at the same time (but under the strictest confidence) his gracious protection, if I would continue in his service: wherein although I believed him sincere, yet I resolved never more to put any confidence in princes or ministers where I could possible avoid it, and therefore, with all due acknowledgements for his favourable intentions, I humbly begged to be excused. I told him that since fortune, whether good or evil, had thrown a vessel in my way, I was resolved to venture myself in the ocean, rather than be an occasion of difference between two such might monarchs. Neither did I find the Emperor at all displeased, and I discovered by a certain accident, that he was very glad of my resolution, and so were most of his ministers.

These considerations moved me to hasten my departure somewhat sooner than I intended, to which the court, impatient to have me gone, very readily contributed. Five hundred workmen were employed to make two sails to my boat, according to my directions, by quilting thirteen fold of their strongest linen together. I was at the pains of making ropes and cables, by twisting ten, twenty or thirty of the thickest and strongest of theirs. A great stone that I happened to find, after a long search by the sea-shore, served me for an anchor. I had the tallow of three hundred cows for greasing my boat, and other uses. I was at incredible pains in cutting down some of the largest timber-trees for oars and masts, wherein I was, however, much assisted by his Majesty's ship-carpenters, who helped me in smoothing them, after I had done the rough work.

In about a month, when all was prepared, I sent to receive his Majesty's commands, and to take my leave. The Emperor and Royal Family came out of the palace; I lay down on my face to kiss his hand, which he very graciously gave me, as did the Empress and young Princes of the blood. His Majesty presented me with fifty purses of two hundred *sprugs* a-piece, together with his picture at full length, which I put immediately into one of my gloves, to keep it from being hurt. The ceremonies at my departure were too many to trouble the reader with at this time.

I stored the boat with the carcass of an hundred oxen, and three hundred sheep, with bread and drink proportionable, and as much meat ready dressed as four hundred cooks could provide. I took with me six cows and two bulls alive, with as many ewes and rams, intending to carry them into my own country, and propagate the breed. And to feed them on board, I had a good bundle of hay, and a bag of corn. I would gladly have taken a dozen of the natives, but this was a thing the Emperor would by no means permit; and besides a diligent search into my pockets, his Majesty engaged my honour not to carry away any of his subjects, even with their own consent and desire.

Having thus prepared all things as well as I was able, I set sail on the twenty-fourth day of September 1701, at six in the morning, and when I had gone about four leagues to the northward, the wind being at southeast, at six in the evening I desired a small island about half a league to the north-west. I advanced forward, and cast anchor on the lee-side of the island, which seemed to be uninhabited. I then took some refreshment, and went to my rest. I slept well, and I conjecture at least six hours, for I found the day broke in two hours after I awaked. It was a clear night. I ate my breakfast before the sun was up, and heaving anchor, the wind being favourable, I steered the same course that I had done the day before, wherein I was directed by my pocket-compass. My intention was to reach, if possible, one of those islands, which I had reason to believe lay to the north-east of Van Dieman's Land. I discovered nothing all that day, but upon the next, about three in the afternoon, when I had by my computation made twenty-four leagues from Blefuscu, I descried a sail steering to the south-east; my course was due east. I hailed her, but could get no answer, yet I found I gained upon her, for the wind slackened. I made all the sail I could, and in half an hour she spied me, then hung out her ensign, and discharged a gun. It is not easy to express the joy I was in upon the unexpected hope of once more seeing my beloved country, and the dear pledges I had left in it. The ship slackened he sails, and I came up with her between five and six in the evening, September 26; but my heart leapt within me to see her English colours. I put my cows and sheep into my coat-pockets and got on board with all my little cargo of provisions. The vessel was an English merchantman, returning from Japan by the North and South Seas, and the Captain, Mr. John Biddle of Deptford, a very civil man, and an excellent sailor. We were now in the latitude of 30 degrees south. There were about fifty men in the ship, and here I met an old comrade of mine, one Peter Williams, who gave me a good character to the Captain. This gentleman treated me with kindness, and desired I would let him know what place I came from last, and whither I was bound, which I did in few words, but he thought I was raving, and that the dangers I underwent had disturbed my head; whereupon I took my black cattle and sheep out of my pocket, which, after great astonishment, clearly convinced him of my veracity. I then showed him the gold given me by the Emperor of Blefuscu, together with his Majesty's picture at full length, and some other rarities of that country. I gave him two purses of two hundred *sprugs* each, and promised, when we arrived in England, to make him a present of a cow and a sheep.

I shall not trouble the reader with a particular account of this voyage, which was very prosperous for the most part. We arrived in the Downs on the 13th of April, 1702. I had only one misfortune, that the rats on board carried away one of my sheep. I found her bones in a hole, picked clean from the flesh. The rest of my cattle I got safe on shore, and set them a grazing in a bowling-green at Greenwich, where the fineness of the grass made them feed very heartily, though I always feared the contrary: neither could I possibly have preserved them in so long a voyage, if the Captain had not allowed me some of his best biscuit, which, rubbed to powder, and mingled with water, was their constant food. The short time I continued in England, I made a considerable profit by showing my cattle to many persons of quality, and others, and before I began my second voyage, I sold them for six hundred pounds. Since my last return, I find the breed is considerably increased, especially the sheep, which I hope will prove much to the advantage of the wollen manufacture, by the fineness of the fleeces.

I stayed but two months with my wife and family, for my insatiable desire of seeing foreign countries would suffer me to continue no longer. I left fifteen hundred pounds with my wife, and fixed her in a good house at Redriff. My remaining stock I carried with me, part in money, and part in goods, in hopes to improve my fortunes. My eldest uncle John had left me en estate in land, near Epping, of about thirty pounds a year, and I had a long lease of the Black Bull in Fetter Lane, which yielded me as much more, so that I was not in any danger of leaving my family upon the parish. My son Johnny, named so after his uncle, was at the Grammar School, and a promising child. My daughter Betty (who is now well married, and has children) was then at her needlework. I took leave of my wife, and boy and girl, with tears on both sides, and went on board the *Adventure*, a merchant-ship of three hundred tons, bound for Surat, Captain John Nicholas of Liverpool Commander. But my account of this voyage must be referred to the second part of my Travels.

PART TWO

A VOYAGE TO BROBDINGNAG

CHAPTER 1

Having been condemned by nature and fortune to an active and restless life, in two months after my return I again left my native country, and took shipping in the Downs on the 20th day of June, 1702, in the *Adventure*, Captain John Nicholas, a Cornish man, Commander, bound for Surat. We had a very prosperous wind till we arrived at the Cape of Good Hope, where we landed for fresh water, but discovering a leak we unshipped our goods and wintered there, and as the Captain feel sick of an ague, we could not leave the Cape till the end of March. We then set sail, and had a good voyage till we passed the Straits of Madagascar, but having got northward of that island, and to about five degrees south latitude, the winds, which in those seas are observed to blow a constant equal gale between the north and east from the beginning of December to the beginning of May, on the 19th of April began to blow with much greater violence, and more westerly than usual, continuing so for twenty days together, during which time we were driven a little to the east of the Molucca Islands, and about three degrees northward of the Line, as our Captain found by an observation he took the 2nd of May, at which time the wind ceased, and it was perfectly calm, whereat I was not a little rejoiced. But he, being a man well experienced in the navigation of those seas, bid us all prepare against a storm, which accordingly happened the following day, for a southern wind, called the southern monsoon, began to set in.

Finding it was likely to overblow, we took in our sprit-sail, and stood by to hand the fore-sail; but making foul weather, we looked the guns were all fast, and handed the mizen. The ship lay very broad off, so we thought it better spooning before the sea, than trying or hulling. We reefed the fore-sail and set him, and we hauled aft the fore-sheet; the helm was hard a weather. The ship wore bravely. We belayed the fore-down haul, but the sail was split, and we hauled down the yard, and got the sail into the ship, and unbound all the things clear of it. It was a very fierce storm. The sea broke strange and dangerous. We hauled off upon the lanyard of the whipstaff, and helped the man at helm. We would not get down out top-mast, but let all stand, because she scubbed before the sea very well, and we knew that the top-mast being aloft, the ship was the wholesomer, and made better way through the sea, seeing we had searoom. When the storm was over, we set fore-sail and main-sail, and brought the ship to: then we set the mizen, main-top-sail, and the fore-top-sail. Our course was east-north-east, the wind was at south-west. We got the starboard tacks aboard, we cast off our weather-braces and lifts set in the lee-braces, and hauled forward by the weather-bowlings, and hauled them tight, and belayed them, and hauled over the mizen tack to windward, and kept her full and by as near as she would lie.

During this storm, which was followed by a strong wind west-south-west, we were carried by my computation about five hundred leagues to the east, so that the oldest sailor on board could not tell in what part of the world we were. Our provisions held out well, our ship was staunch, and our crew all in good health, but we lay in the utmost distress for water. We thought it best to hold on the same course, rather than turn more northerly, which might have brought us to the north-west parts of Great Tartary, and into the frozen sea.

On the 16th day of June, 1703, a boy on the top-mast discovered land. On the 17th we came in full view of a great island or continent (for we knew not whether) on the south side whereof was a small neck of land jutting out into the sea, and a creek too shallow to hold a ship above one hundred tons. We cast anchor within a league of this creek, and our Captain sent a dozen of his men well armed in the long-boat, with vessels for water if any could be found. I desired his leave to go with them, that I might see the country, and make what discoveries I could. When we came to land we saw no river or spring, nor any signs of inhabitants. Our men therefore wandered on the shore to find out some fresh water near the sea, and I walked alone about a mile on the other side, where I observed the country all barren and rocky. I now began to be weary, and seeing nothing to entertain my curiosity, I returned gently down towards the creek; and the sea being full in my view, I saw our men already got into the boat, and rowing for life to the ship. I was going to shout after them, although it had been to little purpose, when I observed a huge creature walking after them in the sea, as fast as he could: he waded not much deeper than his knees, and took prodigious strides: but our men had the start of him half a league, and the sea thereabouts being full of sharp-pointed rocks, the monster was not able to overtake the boat. This I was afterwards told, for I durst not stay to see the issue of that adventure; but ran as fast as I could the way I first went, and then climbed up a steep hill, which gave me some prospect of the country. I found it fully cultivated; but that which first surprised me was the length of the grass, which in those grounds that seemed to be kept for hay, was about twenty foot high.

I fell into a high road, for so I took it to be, though it served to the inhabitants only as a footpath through a field of barley. Here I walked on for some time, but could see little on either side, it being now near harvest, and the corn rising at least forty foot. I was an hour walking to the end of this field, which was fenced in with a hedge of at least one hundred and twenty foot high, and the trees so lofty that I could make no computation of their altitude. There was a stile to pass from this field into the next. It had four steps, and a stone to cross over when you came to the uppermost. It was impossible for me to climb this stile, because every step was six foot high, and the upper stone above twenty. I was endeavouring to find some gap in the hedge, when I discovered one of the inhabitants in the next field, advancing towards the stile, of the same size with him whom I saw in the sea pursuing our boat. He appeared as tall as an ordinary spire-steeple, and took about ten yards at every stride, as near as I could guess. I was struck with the utmost fear and astonishment, and ran to hide myself in the corn, from whence I saw him at the top of the stile, looking back into the next field on the right hand, and heard him call in a voice many degrees louder than a speaking-trumpet, but the noise was so high in the air, that at first I certainly thought it was thunder. Whereupon seven monsters like himself came towards him with reaping-hooks in their hands, each hook about the largeness of six scythes. These people were not so well clad as the first, whose servants or labourers they seemed to be, for upon some words he spoke, they went to reap the corn in the field where I lay. I kept from them at as great a distance as I could, but was forced to move with extreme difficulty, for the stalks of the corn were sometimes not above a foot distant, so that I could hardly squeeze my body betwixt them. However, I made a shift to go forward till I came to a part of the field where the corn had been laid by the rain and wind. Here it was impossible for me to advance a step; for the stalks were so interwoven that I could not creep through, and the beards of the fallen ears so strong and pointed that they pierced through my clothes into my flesh. At the same time I heard the reapers not above an hundred yards behind me. Being quite dispirited with toil, and wholly overcome by grief and despair, I lay down between two ridges, and heartily wished I might there end my days. I bemoaned my desolate widow, and fatherless children. I lamented my own folly and wilfulness in attempting a second voyage against the advice of all my friends and relations. In this terrible agitation of mind I could not forbear thinking of Lilliput, whose inhabitants looked upon me as the greatest prodigy that ever appeared in the world and where I was able to draw an Imperial Fleet in my hand, and perform those other actions which will be recorded for ever in the chronicles of that empire, while posterity shall hardly believe them, although attested by millions. I reflected what a mortification it must prove to me to appear as inconsiderable in this nation as one single Lilliputian would be among us. But this I conceived was to be the least of my misfortunes, for as human creatures are observed to be more savage and cruel in proportion to their bulk, what could I expect but to be a morsel in the mouth of the first among these enormous barbarians that should happen to seize me? Undoubtedly philosophers are in the right when they tell us, that nothing is great or little otherwise than by comparison. It might have pleased fortune to let the Lilliputians find some nation, where the people were as diminutive with respect to them, as they were to me. And who knows but that even this prodigious race of mortals might be equally overmatched in some distant part of the world, whereof we have yet no discovery?

Scared and confounded as I was, I could not forbear going on with these reflections, when one of the reapers approaching within ten yards of the ridge where I lay, made me apprehend that with the next step I should be squashed to death under his foot, or cut in two with his reaping-hook. And therefore when he was again about to move, I screamed as loud as fear could make me. Whereupon the huge creature trod short, and looking round about under him for some time, as last espied me as I lay on the ground. He considered a while with the caution of one who endeavours to lay hold on a small dangerous animal in such a manner that it shall not be able either to scratch or to bite him, as I myself have sometimes done with a weasel in England. At length he ventured to take me up behind by the middle between his forefinger and thumb, and brought me within three yards of his eyes, that he might behold my shape more perfectly. I guessed his meaning, and my good fortune gave me so much presence of mind, that I resolved not to struggle in the least as he held me in the air about sixty foot from the ground, although he grievously pinched my sides, for fear I should slip through his fingers. All I ventured was to raise my eyes towards the sun, and place my hands together in a supplicating posture, and to speak some words in an humble melancholy tone, suitable to the condition I then was in. For I apprehended every moment that he would dash me against the ground, as we usually do any little hateful animal which we have a mind to destroy. But my good star would have it that he appeared pleased with my voice and gestures, and began to look upon me as a curiosity, much wondering to hear me pronounce articulate words, although he could not understand them. In the mean time I was not able to forbear groaning and shedding tears, and turning my head towards my sides, letting him know, as well as I could, how cruelly I was hurt by the pressure of his thumb and finger. He seemed to apprehend my meaning; for, lifting up the flap of his pocket, he put me gently into it, and immediately ran along with me to his master, who was a substantial farmer, and the same person I had first seen in the field.

The farmer having (as I supposed by their talk) received such an account of me as his servant could give him, took a piece of a small straw, about the size of a walking staff, and therewith lifted up my coat, which it seems he thought to be some kind of covering that nature had given me. He blew my hairs aside to take a better view of my face. He called his hinds about him, and asked them (as I afterwards learned) whether they had ever seen in the fields any little creature that resembled me. He then placed me softly on the ground upon all four, but I got immediately up, and walked slowly backwards and forwards, to let these people see I had no intent to run away. They all sat down in a circle about me, the better to observe my motions. I pulled off my hat, and made a low bow towards the farmer. I fell on my knees, and lifted up my hands and eyes, and spoke several words as loud as I could, and I took a purse of gold out of my pocket, and humbly presented it to him. He received it on the palm of his hand, then applied it close to his eyes, to see what it was, and afterwards turned it several times with the point of a pin (which he took out of his sleeve), but could make nothing of it. Whereupon I made a sign that he should place his hand on the ground. I took the purse, and opening it, poured all the gold into his palm. There were six Spanish pieces of four pistoles each, beside twenty or thirty smaller coins. I saw him wet the tip of his little finger upon his tongue, and take up one of my largest pieces, and then another, but he seemed to be wholly ignorant what they were. He made a sign to put them again into my purse, and the purse again into my pocket, and after offering it to him several times, I thought it best to do.

The farmer by this time was convinced I must be a rational creature. He spoke often to me, but the sound of his voice pierced my ears like that of a water-mill, yet his words were articulate enough. I answered as loud as I could, in several languages, and he often laid his ear within two yards of me, but all in vain, for we were wholly unintelligible to each other. He then sent his servants to their work, and taking his handkerchief out of his pocket, he doubled and spread it on his left hand, which he placed flat on the ground, with the palm upwards, making me a sign to step into it, as I could easily do, for it was not above a foot in thickness. I thought it my part to obey, and for fear of falling, laid myself at length upon the handkerchief, with the remainder of which he lapped me up to the head for further security, and in this manner carried me home to his house. There he called his wife, and showed me to her, but she screamed and ran back, as women in England do at the sight of a toad or a spider. However, when she had a while seen my behaviour, and how well I observed the signs her husband made, she was soon reconciled, and by degrees grew extremely fond of me.

It was about twelve at noon, and a servant brought in dinner. It was only one substantial dish of meat (fit for the plain condition of an husbandman) in a dish of about four-and-twenty foot diameter. The company were the farmer and his wife, three children, and an old grandmother.

When they were sat down, the farmer placed me at some distance from him on the table, which was thirty foot high from the floor. I was in a terrible fright, and kept as far as I could from the edge for fear of falling. The wife minced a bit of meat, then crumbled some bread on a trencher, and placed it before me. I made her a low bow, took out my knife and fork, and fell to eat, which gave them exceeding delight. The mistress sent her maid for small dram cup, which held about three gallons, and filled it with drink; I took up the vessel with much difficulty in both hands, and in a most respectful manner drank to her ladyship's health, expressing the words as loud as I could in English, which made the company laugh so heartily, that I was almost deafened with the noise. This liquor tasted like a small cyder, and was not unpleasant. Then the master made a sign to come to his trencher side, but as I walked on the table, being in great surprise all the time, as the indulgent reader will easily conceive and excuse, I happened to stumble against a crust and fell flat on my face, but received no hurt. I got up immediately, and observing the good people to be in much concern I took my hat (which I held under my arm out of good manners) and waving it over my head, made three huzzas, to show I had got no mischief by my fall. But advancing forwards my master (as I shall henceforth call him) his youngest son who sat next him, an arch boy of about ten years old, took me up by the legs, and held me so high in the air, that I trembled every limb; but his father snatched me from him, and at the same time gave him a box on the left ear, as would have felled an European troop of horse to the earth, ordering him to be taken from the table. But being afraid the boy might owe me a spite, and well remembering how mischievous all children among us naturally are to sparrows, rabbits, young kittens, and puppy dogs, I fell on my knees, and pointing to the boy, made my master to understand, as well as I could, that I desired his son might be pardoned. The father complied, and the lad took his seat again, whereupon I went to him and kissed has hand, which my master took, and made him stroke me gently with it.

In the midst of dinner, my mistress's favourite cat leapt into her lap. I heard a noise behind me like that of a dozen stocking-weavers at work, and turning my head, I found it proceeded from the purring of this animal, who seemed to be three times larger than an ox, as I computed by the view of her head, and one of her paws, while her mistress was feeding and stroking her. The fierceness of this creature's countenance altogether discomposed me, though I stood at the farther end of the table, above fifty foot off, äand although my mistress held her fast for fear she might give a spring and seize me in her talons. But it happened there was no danger, for the cat took not the least notice of me when my master placed me within three yards of her. And as I have always been told, and found true by experience in my travels, that flying, or discovering fear before a fierce animal, is a certain way to make it pursue or attack you, so I resolved in this dangerous juncture to show no manner of concern. I walked with intrepidity five or six times before the very head of the cat, and came within half a yard of her, whereupon she drew herself back, as if she was more afraid of me. I had less apprehension concerning the dogs, whereof three or four came into the room, as it is usual in farmer's houses. One was a mastiff, equal in bulk to four elephants, and a greyhound, somewhat taller than the mastiff, but no so large.

When dinner was almost done, the nurse came in with a child of a year old in her arms, who immediately spied me, and began a squall that you might have heard from London Bridge to Chelsea, after the usual oratory of infants, to get me for a plaything. The mother out of pure indulgence took me up, and put me towards the child, who presently seized me by the middle, and got my head in his mouth, where I roared so loud that the urchin was frighted, and let me drop, and I should infallibly have broke my neck if the mother had not held her apron under me.

When dinner was done, my master went out to his labourers, and as I could discover by his voice and gesture, gave his wife a strict charge to take care of me. I was very much tired, and disposed to sleep, which my mistress noticed, and she put me on her own bed, and covered me with a clean white handkerchief, but larger and coarser than the mainsail of a man of war.

I slept about two hours, and dreamed I was at home with my wife and children, which aggravated my sorrows when I awaked and found myself alone in a vast room, between two and three hundred foot wide, and above two hundred high, lying in a bed twenty yards wide. My mistress was gone about her household affairs, and had locked me in. The bed was eight yards from the floor. While I was under these circumstances, two rats crept up the curtains, and ran smelling backwards and forwards on the bed. One of them came up almost to my face, whereupon I rose in a fright, and drew out my short sword to defend myself. These horrible animals had the boldness to attack me on both sides, and one of them held his fore-feet at my collar, but I had the good fortune to rip up his belly before he could do me any mischief. He fell down at my feet, and the other seeing the fate of his comrade, made his escape, but not without one good wound on the back, which I gave him as he fled, and made the blood run trickling from him. After this exploit, I walked gently to and fro on the bed, to recover my breath and loss of spirits. These creatures were of the size of a large mastiff, but infinitely more nimble and fierce, so that if I had not taken off my belt before I went to sleep, I would have been torn to pieces and devoured. I measured the tail of the dead rat, and found it to be two yards long, but for an inch, but it went against my stomach to drag the carcass off the bed, where it lay still bleeding. I observed it had yet some life, but with a strong slash cross the neck, I thoroughly dispatched it.

Soon after my mistress came into the room, and seeing me all bloody, ran and took me up in her hands. I pointed to the dead rat, smiling and making other signs to show I was not hurt, whereat she was extremely rejoiced, calling the maid to take up the dead rat with a pair of tongs, and throw it out of the window. Then she set me on a table, where I showed her my short sword, all bloody, and wiping it on my coat, returned it to the scabbard.

I hope the gentle reader will excuse me for dwelling on these and the like particulars, which however insignificant they may appear to grovelling vulgar minds, yet will certainly help a philosopher to enlarge his thoughts and imagination, and apply them to the benefit of public as well as private life, which was my sole design in presenting this and other accounts of my travels to the world. I have been chiefly studious of truth, without affecting any ornaments of learning or of style, but the whole scene of this voyage made so strong an impression on my mind, and is so deeply fixed in my memory, that in committing it to paper I did not omit one material circumstance: although upon a strict review, I blotted out several passages of less moment which were in my first copy, for fear of being censured as tedious and trifling, whereof travellers are often, perhaps not without justice, accused.

CHAPTER 2

My mistress had a daughter of nine years old, a forward child for her age, very dexterous at her needle, and skilful in dressing her baby. Her mother and she contrived to fit up the baby's cradle for me at night: the cradle was put into a small drawer of a cabinet, and the drawer placed upon a hanging shelf for fear of the rats. This was my bed all the time I stayed with these people, though made more convenient by degrees, as I began to learn their language, and make my wants known. This young girl was so handy, that after I had once or twice pulled off my clothes before her, she was able to dress and undress me, though I never gave her that trouble when she would let me do either myself. She made me seven shirts, and some other linen, of as fine cloth as could be got, which indeed was coarser than sackcloth; and these she constantly washed for me with her own hands. She was likewise my school-mistress to teach me the language. When I pointed to anything, she told me the name of it in her own tongue, so that in a few days I was able to call for whatever I had a mind to. She was very goodnatured, and not above forty foot high, being little for her age. She gave me the name *Grildrig*, which the family took up, and afterwards the whole kingdom. The words imports what the Latins call *nanunculus*, the Italians *homunceletino*, and the English *mannikin*. To her I chiefly owe my preservation in that country: we never parted while I was there. I called her my *Glumdalclitch*, or little nurse, and I should be guilty of great ingratitude if I ommitted this honourable mention of her care and affection towards me, which I heartily wish it lay in my power to requite as she deserves, instead of being the innocent but unhappy instrument of her disgrace, as I have too much reason to fear.

It now began to be known and talked of in the neighbourhood, that my master had found a strange animal in the field, about the bigness of a *splacknuck,* but exactly shaped in every part like a human creature; which it likewise imitated in all its actions. It seemed to speak in a little language of its own, had already learned several words of theirs, went erect upon two legs, was tame and gentle, would come when it was called, do whatever it was bid, had the finest limbs in the world, and a complexion fairer than a nobleman's daughter of three years old. Another farmer who lived hard by, and was a particular friend of my master, came on a visit on purpose to enquire into the truth of this story. I was immediately produced, and placed upon a table, where I walked as I was commanded, drew my short sword, put it up again, made ny reverence to my master's guest, asked him in his own language how he did, and told him he was welcome, just as my little nurse had instructed me. This man, who was old and dim-sighted, put on his spectacles to behold me better, at which I could not forbear laughing very heartily, for his eyes appeared like the full moon shining into a chamber at two windows. Our people, who discovered the cause of my mirth, bore me company in laughing, at which the old fellow was fool enough to be angry and out of countenance. He had the character of a great miser, and to my misfortune he well deserved it, by the cursed advice he gave my master to show me as a sight upon a market-day in the next town, which was an hour's riding, about two and twenty miles from our house. I guessed there was some mischief contriving when I observed my master and his friend whispering long together, sometimes pointing at me, and my fears made me fancy that I overheard and understood some of their words. But the next morning Glumdalclitch my little nurse told me the whole matter, which she had cunningly picked out from her mother. The poor girl laid me on her besom, and fell a weeping with shame and grief. She apprehended some mischief would happen to me from rude vulgar folks, who might squeeze me to death, or break one of my limbs by taking me in their hands. She had also observed how modest I was in my nature, how nicely I regarded my honour, and what an indignity I should conceive it to be exposed for money as a public spectacle to the meanest of the people. She said her papa and mamma had promised that Grildrig should be hers, but now she found they meant to serve her as they did last year, when they pretended to give her a lamb, and yet, as soon as it was fat, sold it to a butcher. For my own part, I may truly affirm that I was less concerned than my nurse. I had a strong hope which never left me, that I should one day recover my liberty, and as to the ignominy of being carried about for a monster, I considered myself to be a perfect stranger in the country, and that such a misfortune could never be charged upon me as a reproach if ever I should return to England, since the King of Great Britain himself, in my condition, must have undergone the same distress.

My master, according to the advice of his friend, carried me in a box the next market-day to the neighbouring town, and took along with him his little daughter my nurse upon a pillon behind him. The box was close on every side, with a little door for me to go in and out, and a few gimlet-holes to let in air. The girl had been so careful to put the quilt of her baby's bed into it, for me to lie down on. However, I was terribly shaken and discomposed in this journey, though it lasted only half an hour, for the horse went about forty foot at every step, and trotted so high, that the agitation was equal to the rising and falling of a ship in a great storm, but much more frequent. Our journey was somewhat further than from London to St. Albans. My master alighted at an inn which he used to frequent, and after consulting a while with the inn-keeper, and making some necessary preparations, he hired the *Grultrud*, or crier, to give notice through the town of a strange creature to be seen at the Sign of the Green Eagle, not so big as a *splacknuck* (an animal in that country very finely shaped, about six foot long) and in every part of the body resembling an human creature, could speak several words, and perform an hundred diverting tricks.

I was placed upon a table in the largest room of the inn, which might be near three hundred foot square. My little nurse stood on a low stool close to the table, to take care of me, and direct what I should do. My master, to avoid a crowd, would suffer only thirty people at a time to see me. I walked about on the table as the girl commanded: she asked me questions as far as she knew my understanding of the language reached, and I answered them as loud as I could. I turned about several times to the company, paid my humble respects, said they were welcome, and used some other speeches I had been taught. I took up a thimble filled with liquor, which Glumdalclitch had given me for a cup, and drank their health. I drew out my short sword, and flourished with if after the manner of fencers in England. My nurse gave me part of a straw, which I exercised as a pike, having learned the art in my youth. I was that day shown to twelve sets of company, and as often forced to go over again with the same performance, till I was half dead with weariness and vexation. For those who had seen me made such wonderful reports, that the people were ready to break down the doors to come in. My master for his own interest would not suffer any one to touch me except my nurse; and, to prevent danger, benches were set round the table at such a distance as put me out of every body's reach. However, an unlucky school-boy aimed a hazel nut directly at my head, which very narrowly missed me; otherwise, it came with so much violence, that it would have infallibly knocked out my brains, for it was almost as large as a small pumpkin: but I had the satisfaction to see the young rogue well beaten, and turned out of the room.

My master gave public notice that he would show me again the next market-day, and in the meantime he prepared a more convenient vehicle for me, which he had reason enough to do; for I was so tired with my first journey, and with entertaining company for eight hours together, that I could hardly stand upon my legs or speak a word. It was at least three days before I recovered my strength, and that I might have no rest at home, all the neighbouring gentlemen from an hundred miles round, hearing of my fame, came to see me at my master's own home. There could not be fewer than thirty persons with their wives and children (for the country is very populous); and my master demanded the rate of a full room whenever he showed me at home, even if it were only to a single family; so that for some time I had but little ease every day of the week (except Wednesday, which is their Sabbath) although I was not carried to the town.

My master finding how profitable I was likely to be, resolved to carry me to the most considerable cities of the kingdom. Having therefore provided himself with all things necessary for a long journey, and settled his affairs at home, he took leave of his wife, and upon the 17th of August, 1703, about two months after my arrival, we set out for the metropolis, situated near the middle of that empire, and about three thousand miles distance from our house. My master made his daughter Glumdalclitch ride behind him. She carried me on her lap in a box tied about her waist. The girl had lined it on all sides with the softest cloth she could get, well quilted underneath, furnished it with her baby's bed, provided me with linen and other necessaries, and made everything as convenient as she could. We had no other company but a boy of the house, who rode after us with the luggage.

My master's design was to show me in all the towns by the way, and to step out of the road for fifty or an hundred miles, to any village or person of quality's house where he might expect custom. We made easy journeys of not above seven or eight score miles a day: for Glumdalclitch, on purpose to spare me, complained she was tired with the trotting of the horse. She often took me out of my box at my own desire, to give me air and show me the country, but always held me fast by a leading-string. We passed over five or six rivers many degrees broader and deeper than the Nile or the Ganges; and there was hardly a rivulet so small as the Thames at London bridge. We were ten weeks in our journey, and I was shown in eighteen large towns besides many villages and private families.

On the 20th day of October, we arrived at the metropolis, called in their language *Lorbrulgrud*, or Pride of the Universe. My master took a lodging in the principal street of the city, not far from the royal palace, and put out bills in the usual form, containing an exact description of my person and parts. He hired a large room between three and four hundred foot wide. He provided a table sixty foot in diameter, upon which I was to act my part, and palisaded it round three foot from the edge, and as many high, to prevent my falling over. I was shown ten times a day to the wonder and satisfaction of all people. I could now speak the language tolerably well, and perfectly understood every word that was spoken to me. Besides, I had learnt their alphabet, and could make a shift to explain a sentence here and there; for Glumdalclitch had been my instructor while we were at home, and at leisure hours during our journey. She carried a little book in her pocket, not much larger than a Sanson's Atlas; it was a common treatise for the use of young girls, giving a short account of their religion: out of this she taught me my letters, and interpreted the words.

CHAPTER 3

The frequent labours I underwent every day made in a few weeks a very considerable change in my health: the more my master got by me, the more insatiable he grew. I had quite lost my stomach, and was almost reduced to a skeleton. The farmer observed it, and concluding I soon must die, resolved to make as good a hand of me as he could. While he was thus reasoning and resolving with himself, a *Slardral*, or Gentlemen Usher, came from court, commanding my master to carry me immediately thither for the diversion of the Queen and her ladies. Some of the latter had already been to see me, and reported strange things of my beauty, behaviour, and good sense. Her Majesty and those who attended her were beyond measure delighted with my demeanour. I fell on my knees, and begged the honour of kissing her Imperial foot; but this gracious princess held out her little finger towards me (after I was set on a table) which I embraced in both my arms, and put the tip of it with the utmost respect to my lip. She made me some general questions about my country and my travels, which I answered as distinctly and in as few words as I could. She asked whether I would be content to live at court. I bowed down to the board of the table, and humbly answered that I was my master's slave, but if I were at my own disposal, I should be proud to devote my life to her Majesty's service. She then asked my master whether he were willing to sell me at a good price. He, who apprehended I could not live a month, was ready enough to part with me, and demanded a thousand pieces of gold, which were ordered him on the spot, each piece being about the size of eight hundred moidores; but, allowing for the proportion of all things between that country and Europe, and the high price of gold among them, was hardly so great a sum as a thousand guineas would be in England. I then said to the Queen, since I was now her Majesty's most humble creature and vassal, I must beg the favour, that Glumdalclitch, who had always tended me with so much care and kindness, and understood to do it so well, might be admitted into her service, and continue to be my nurse and instructor. Her Majesty agreed to my petition, and easily got the farmer's consent, who was glad enough to have his daughter preferred at court: and the poor girl herself was not able to hide her joy. My late master withdrew, bidding me farewell, and saying he had left me in a good service; to which I replied not a word, only making him a slight bow.

The Queen observed my coldness, and when the farmer was gone out of the apartment, asked me the reason. I made bold to tell her Majesty that I owed no other obligation to my late master, than his not dashing out the brains of a poor harmless creature found by chance in his field; which obligation was amply recompensed by the gain he had made in showing me through half the kingdom, and the price he had now sold me for. That the life I had since led was laborious enough to kill an animal of ten times my strength. That my health was much impaired by the continual drudgery of entertaining the rabble every hour of the day, and that if my master had not thought my life in danger, her Majesty perhaps would not have got so cheap a bargain. But as I was out of all fear of being ill treated under the protection of so great and good an Empress, the Ornament of Nature, the Darling of the World, the Delight of her Subjects, the Phoenix of the Creation; so I hoped my late master's apprehensions would appear to be groundless, for I lately already found my spirits to revive by the influence of her most august presence.

This was the sum of my speech, delivered with great improprieties and hesitation; the latter part was altogether framed in the style peculiar to that people, whereof I learned some phrases from Glumdalclitch, while she was carrying me to court.

The Queen giving allowance for my defectiveness in speaking, was however surprised as so much wit and good sense in so diminutive an animal. She took me in her own hand, and carried me to the King, who was then retired to his cabinet. His Majesty, a prince of much gravity, and austere countenance, not well observing my shape at first view, asked the Queen after a cold manner, how long it was since she grew fond of a *splacknuck*; for such it seems he took me to be, as I lay upon my breast in her Majesty's right hand. But this princess, who hath an infinite deal of wit and humour, set me gently on my feet upon the scrutore, and commanded me to give his Majesty an account of myself, which I did in a very few words; and Glumdalclitch, who attended at the cabinet door, and could not endure I should be out of her sight, being admitted, confirmed all that had passed from my arrival at her father's house.

The King, although he be as learned a person as any in his dominions, and had been educated in the study of philosophy, and particularly mathematics; yet when he observed my shape exactly, and saw me walk erect, before I began to speak, conceived I might be a piece of clock-work (which is in that country arrived to a very great perfection) contrived by some ingenious artist. But when he heard my voice, and found what I delivered to be regular and rational, he could not conceal his astonishment. He was by no means satisfied with the relation I gave him of the manner I came into his kingdom, but thought it a story concocted between Glumdalclitch and her father, who had taught me a set of words to make me sell at a higher price. Upon this imagination he put several other questions to me, and still received rational answers, no otherwise defective than by a foreign accent, and an imperfect knowledge in the language, with some rustic phrases which I had learned at the farmer's house, and did not suit the polite style of a court.

His Majesty sent for three great scholars who were then in their weekly waiting, according to the custom in that country. These gentlemen, after they had a while examined my shape with much nicety, were of different opinions concerning me. They all agreed that I could not be produced according to the regular laws of nature, because I was not framed with a capacity of preserving my life, either by softness, or climbing of trees, or digging holes in the earth. They observed by my teeth, which they viewed with great exactness, that I was a carnivorous animal; yet most quadrupeds being an overmatch for me, and field mice, with some others, too nimble, they could imagine how I should be able to support myself, unless i fed upon snails and other insects, which they offered, by many learned arguments, to evince that I could not possibly do. They would not allow me to be a dwarf, because my littleness was beyond all degrees of comparison; for the Queen's favourite dwarf, the smallest ever known in that kingdom, was near thirty foot high. After much debate, they concluded unanimously that I was only *relplum scalcath*, which is interpreted literally, *lusus naturæ*; a determination exactly agreeable to the modern philosophy of Europe, whose professors, disdaining the old evasion of *occult causes*, whereby the followers of Aristotle endeavour in vain to disguise their ignorance, have invented this wonderful solution of all difficulties, to the unspeakable advancement of human knowledge.

After this decisive conclusion, I entreated to be heard a word or two. I applied myself to the King, and assured his Majesty that I came from a country which abounded with several millions of both sexes, and of my own stature; where the animals, trees, and houses were all in proportion, and where by consequence I might be as able to defend myself, and to find sustenance, as any of his Majesty's subject could do here; which I took for a full answer to those gentlemen's arguments. To this they only replied with a smile of contempt, saying that the farmer had instructed my very well in my lesson. The King, who had a much better understanding, dismissing his learned men, sent for the farmer, who by good fortune was not yet gone out of town. Having therefore first examined him privately, and then confronted him with me and the young girl, his Majesty began to think that what we told him might possibly be true. He desired the Queen to order that a particular care should be taken of me, and was of the opinion that Glumdalclitch should still continue in her office of tending me, because he observed we had a great affection for each other. A convenient apartment was provided for her at court; she had a sort of governess appointed to take care of her education, a maid to dress her, and two other servants for menial offices; but the care of me was wholly appropriate to herself. The Queen commanded her own cabinet-maker to contrive a box that might serve me for a bed-chamber, after the model that Glumdalclitch and I should agree upon. This man was a most ingenious artist, and according to my direction, in three weeks finished for me a wooden chamber of sixteen foot square, and twelve high, with sash-windows, a door, and two closets, like a London bed-chamber. The board that made the ceiling was to be lifted up and down by two hinges, to put in a bed ready furnished by her Majesty's upholsterer, which Glumdalclitch took out every day to air, made it with her own hands, and letting it down at night, locked up the roof over me. A nice workman, who was famous for little curiosities, undertook to make me two chairs, with backs and frames, of a substance not unlike ivory, and two tables, with a cabinet to put my things in. The room was quilted on all sides, as well as the floor and the ceiling, to prevent any accident from the carelessness of those who carried me, and to break the force of a jolt when I went in a coach. I desired to lock my door, to prevent rats and mice from coming in: the smith, after several attempts, made the smallest that ever was seen among them, for I have known a larger at the gate of a gentlemen's house in England. I made a shift to keep the key in a pocket of my own, fearing Glumdalclitch night lose it. The Queen likewise ordered the thinnest silks that could be gotten, to make me clothes, not much thicker than an English blanket, very cumbersome till I was accustomed to them. They were after the fashion of the kingdom, partly resembling the Persian, and partly the Chinese, and are a very grave and decent habit.

The Queen became so fond of my company, that she could not dine without me. I had a table placed upon the same at which her Majesty ate, just at her left elbow, and a chair to sit on. Glumdalclitch stood upon a stool on the floor, near my table, to assist and take care of me. I had an entire set of silver dishes and plates, and other necessaries, which, in proportion to those of the Queen, were not much bigger than what I have seen of the same kind in a London toy-shop, for the furniture of a babyhouse: these my little nurse kept in her pocket in a silver box, and gave me at meals as I wanted them, always cleaning them herself. No person dined with the Queen but the two Princesses Royal, the elder sixteen years old, and the younger at that time thirteen and a month. Her Majesty used to put a bit of meat upon one of my dishes, out of which I carved for myself, and her diversion was to see me eat in miniature. For the Queen (who had indeed but a weak stomach) took up at one mouthful as much as a dozen English farmers could eat at a meal, which to me was for some time a very nauseous sight. She would crunch the wing of a lark, bones and all, between her teeth, although it were nine times as large as that of a full-grown turkey; and put a bit of bread into her mouth, as big as two twelve-penny loaves. She drank out of a golden cup, above a hogshead at a draught. Her knives were twice as long as a scythe set straight upon the handle. The spoons, forks, and other instruments were all in the same proportion. I remember when Glumdalclitch carried me out of curiosity to see some of the tables at court, where ten or a dozen of these enormous knives and forks were lifted up together, I thought I had never till then beheld so terrible a sight.

It is the custom that every Wednesday (which, as I have before observed, was their Sabbath) the King and Queen, with the royal issue of both sexes, dine together in the apartment of his Majesty, to whom I was now become a great favourite; and at these times my little chair and table were placed at his left hand, before one of the saltcellars. This prince took a pleasure in conversing with me, enquiring into the manners, religion, laws, government, and learning of Europe; wherein I gave him the best account I was able. His apprehension was so clear, and his judgment so exact, that he made very wise reflections and observations upon all I said. But, I confess, that after I had been a little too copious in taking of my own beloved country, of our trade, and wars by sea and land, of our schisms in religion, and parties in the state, the prejudices of his education prevailed so far, that he could not forbear taking me up in his right hand, and stroking me gently with the other, after an hearty fit of laughing, asked me whether I were a Whig or a Tory. Then turning to his first minister, who waited behind him with a white staff, near as tall as the mainmast of the *Royal Sovereign*, he observed how contemptible a thing was human grandeur, which could be mimicked by such diminutive insects as I: and yet, said he, I dare engage that these creatures have their titles and distinctions of honour, they contrive little nests and burrows that they call houses and cities; they make a figure in dress and equipage; they love, they fight, they dispute, they cheat, they betray. And thus he continued on, while my colour came and went several times with indignation to hear our noble country, the mistress of arts and arms, the scourage of France, the arbitress of Europe, the seat of virtue, piety, honour and truth, the pride and envy of the world, so contemptuously treated.

But as I was not in a condition to resent injuries, so, upon mature thoughts, I began to doubt whether I were injured or no. For, after having been accustomed several months to the sight and converse of this people, and observed every object upon which I cast my eyes to be of proportionable magnitude, the horror I had first conceived from their bulk and aspect was so far worn off, that if I had then beheld a company of English lords and ladies in their finery and birthday clothes, acting their several parts in the most courtly manner, of strutting, and bowing, and prating, to say the truth, I should have been strongly tempted to laugh as much at them as the King and his grandees did at me. Neither indeed could I forbear smiling at myself, when the Queen used to place me upon her hand towards a looking-glass, by which both our persons appeared before me in full view together; and there could be nothing more ridiculous than the comparison; so that I really began to imagine myself dwindled many degrees below my usual size.

Nothing angered and mortified me so much as the Queen's dwarf, who being of the lowest stature that was ever in that country (for I verily think he was not full thirty foot high) became insolent at seeing a creature so much beneath him, that he would always affect to swagger and look big as he passed by me in the Queen's antechamber, while I was standing on some table talking with the lords or ladies of the court, and he seldom failed of a smart word or two upon my littleness; against which I could only revenge myself by calling him brother, challenging him to wrestle, and such repartees as are usual in the mouths of court pages. One day at dinner this malicious little cub was so nettled with something I had said to him, that raising himself upon the frame of her Majesty's chair, he took me up by the middle, as I was sitting down, not thinking any harm, and let me drop into a large silver bowl of cream, and then ran away as fast he could. I fell over head and ears, and if I had not been a good swimmer, it might have gone very hard with me; for Glumdalclitch in that instant happened to be at the other end of the room, and the Queen was in such a fright that she lacked presence of mind to assist me. But my little nurse ran to my relief, and took me out, after I had swallowed above a quart of cream. I was put to bed; however I received no other damage than the loss of a suit of clothes, which was utterly spoiled. The dwarf was soundly whipped, and as a further punishment, forced to drink up the bowl of cream, into which he had thrown me; neither was he ever restored to favour: for soon after the Queen bestowed him to a lady of high quality, so that I saw him no more, to my very great satisfaction; for I could not tell to what extremity such a malicious urchin might have carried his resentment.

He had before served me a scurvy trick, which set the Queen a laughing, although at the same time she were heartily vexed, and would have immediately cashiered him, if I had not been so generous as to intercede. Her Majesty had taken a marrow-bone upon her plate, and after knocking out the marrow, placed the bone again in the dish erect as it stood before; the dwarf watching his opportunity, while Glumdalclitch was gone to the sideboard, mounted upon the stool she stood on to take care of me at meals, took me up in both hands, and squeezing my legs together, wedged them into the marrow-bone above my waist, where I stuck for some time, and made a very ridiculous figure. I believe it was near a minute before any one knew what was become of me, for I thought it below me to cry out. But, as princes seldom get their meat hot, my legs were not scalded, only my stockings and breeches in a sad condition. The dwarf at my entreaty had no other punishment than a sound whipping.

I was frequently railed by the Queen upon account of my fearfulness, and she used to ask me whether the people of my country were as great cowards as myself. The occasion was this. The kingdom is much pestered with flies in summer; and these odious insects, each of them as big as a Dunstable lark, hardly gave me any rest while I sat at dinner, with their continual humming and buzzing about my ears. They would sometimes alight upon my victuals;

sometimes they would fix upon my nose or forehead, where they stung me to the quick, smelling very offensively, and I could easily trace that viscous matter, which our naturalists tell us enables those creatures to walk with their feet upwards upon a ceiling. I had much ado to defend myself against these detestable animals, and could not forbear starting when they came on my face. It was the common practice of the dwarf to catch a number of these insects in his hand, as schoolboys do among us, and let them out suddenly under my nose, on purpose to frighten me, and divert the Queen. My remedy was to cut them in pieces with my knife as they flew in the air, wherein my dexterity was much admired.

I remember one morning when Glumdalclitch had set me in my box upon a window, as she usually did in fair days to give me air (for I durst not venture to let the box be hung on a nail out of the window, as we do with cages in England) after I had lifted up one of my sashes, and sat down at my table to eat a piece of sweet cake for my breakfast, above twenty wasps, allured by the smell, came flying into the room, humming louder than the drones of as many bagpipes. Some of them seized my cake, and carried it piecemeal away, others flew about my head and face, confounding me with the noise, and putting me in the utmost terror of their stings. However I had the courage to rise and draw my short sword, and attack them in the air. I dispatched four of them, but the rest got away, and I presently shut my window. These insects were as large as as partridges: I took out their stings, found them an inch and a half long, and as sharp as needles. I carefully preserved them all, and having since shown them with some other curiosities in several parts of Europe, upon my return to England I gave three of them to Gresham College, and kept the fourth for myself.

CHAPTER 4

I now intend to give the reader a short description of this country, as far as I have travelled in it, which was not above two hundred miles round Lorbrulgrud the metropolis. For the Queen, whom I always attended, never went further when she accompanied the King in his progresses, and there stayed till his Majesty returned from reviewing his frontiers. The whole extent of this prince's dominions reacheth about six thousand miles in length, and from three to five breadths. From whence I cannot but conclude that our geographers of Europe are in a great error, by supposing nothing but sea between Japan and California; for it was ever my opinion, that there must be a balance of earth to counterpoise the great continent of Tartary; and therefore they ought to correct their maps and charts, by joining this vast tract of land to the north-west parts of America, wherein I shall be ready to lend them my assistance.

The kingdom is a peninsula, terminated to the north-east by a ridge of mountains thirty miles high, which are altogether impassable by reason of the volcanoes upon the tops. Neither do the most learned know what sort of mortals inhabit beyond those mountains, or whether they are inhabited at all. On the three other sides it is bounded by the ocean. There is not one sea-port in the whole kingdom, and those parts of the coasts into which the rivers issue are so full of pointed rocks, and the sea generally so rough, that there is no venturing with the smallest of their boats, so that these people are wholly excluded from any commerce with the rest of the world. But the large rivers are full of vessels, and abound with excellent fish, for they seldom get any from the sea, because the sea-fish are of the same size with those in Europe, and consequently not worth catching; whereby it is manifest, that nature, in the production of plants and animals of so extraordinary a bulk, is wholly confined to this continent, of which I leave the reasons to be determined by philosophers. However, now and then they take a whale that happens to be dashed against the rocks, which the common people feed on heartily. These whales I have known so large that a man could hardly carry one upon his shoulders; and sometimes for curiosity they are brought in hampers to Lorbrulgrud: I saw one of them in a dish at the King's table, which passed for a rarity, but I did not observe he was fond of it; for I think indeed the size disgusted him, although I have seen one somewhat larger in Greenland.

The country is well inhabited, for it contains fifty-one cities, near an hundred walled towns, and a great number of villages. To satisfy my curious reader, it may be sufficient to describe Lorbrulgrud. This city stands upon almost two equal parts on each side the river that passes through. It contains above eighty thousand houses, and about six hundred thousand inhabitants. It is in length three *glongluns* (which make about fifty-four English miles) and two and a half in breadth, as I measured it myself in the royal map made by the King's order, which was laid on the ground on purpose for me, and extended an hundred feet: I paced the diameter and circumference several times barefoot, and computing by the scale, measured it pretty exactly.

The King's palace is no regular edifice, but a heap of buildings about seven miles round: the chief rooms are generally two hundred and forty foot high, and broad and long in proportion. A coach was allowed to Glumdalclitch and me, wherein her governess frequently took her out to see the town, or go among the shops; and I was always of the party, carried in my box; although the girl at my own desire would often take me out, and hold me in her hand, that I might more conveniently view the houses and the people, as we passed along the streets. I reckoned our coach to be about a square of Westminster Hall, but not altogether so high; however, I cannot be very exact. One day the governess ordered our coachman to stop at several shops, where the beggars, watching their opportunity, crowded to the sides of the coach, and gave me the most horrible spectacles that ever an English eye beheld.

Besides the large box in which I was usually carried, the Queen ordered a smaller one to be made for me, of about twelve foot square, and ten high, for the convenience of travelling, because the other was somewhat too large for Glumdalclitch's lap, and cumbersome in the coach; it was made by the same artist, whom I directed in the whole contrivance. This travelling closet was an exact square with a window in the middle of three of the squares, and each window was latticed with iron wire on the outside, to prevent accidents in long journeys. On the fourth side, which had no window, two strong staples were fixed, through which the person that carried me, when I had a mind to be on horseback put in a leathern belt, and buckled it about his waist. This was always the office of some grave trusty servant in whom I could confide, whether I attended the King and Queen in their progresses, or were disposed to see the gardens, or pay a visit to some great lady or minister of state in the court, when Glumdalclitch happened to be out of order: for I soon began to be known and esteemed among the greatest officers, I suppose more upon account of their Majesties' favour, than any merit of my own. In journeys, when I was weary of the coach, a servant on horseback would buckle my box, and place it on a cushion before him; and there I had a full prospect of the country on three sides from my three windows. I had in this closet a field-bed and a hammock hung from the ceiling, two chairs and a table, neatly screwed to the floor, to prevent being tossed about by the agitation of the horse or the coach. And having been long used to sea-voyages, those motions, although sometimes very violent, did not much discompose me.

Whenever I had a mind to see the town, it was always in my travelling-closet, which Glumdalclitch held in her lap in a kind of open sedan, after the fashion of the country, borne by four men, and attended by two others in the Queen's livery. The people who had often heard of me, were very curious to crowd about the sedan, and the girl was complaisant enough to make the bearers stop, and to take me in her hand that I might be more conveniently seen.

I was very desirous to see the chief temple, and particularly the tower belonging to it, which is reckoned the highest in the kingdom. Accordingly one day my nurse carried me thither, but I may truly say I came back disappointed; for the height is not above three thousand foot, reckoning from the ground to the highest pinnacle top; which allowing for the difference between the size of those people and us in Europe, is no great matter for admiration, nor at all equal in proportion (if I rightly remember) to Salisbury steeple. But, not to detract from a nation to which during my life I shall acknowledge myself extremely obliged, it must be allowed that whatever this famous tower lacks in height is amply made up in beauty and strength. For the walls are near an hundred foot thick, built of hewn stone, whereof each is about forty foot square, and adorned on all sides with statues of gods and emperors cut in marble larger then life, placed in their several niches. I measured a little finger which had fallen down from one of these statues, and lay unperceived among some rubbish, and found it exactly four foot and an inch in length. Glumdalclitch wrapped it up in an handkerchief, and carried it home in her pocket to keep among other trinkets, of which the girl was very fond, as children at her age usually are.

The King's kitchen is indeed a noble building, vaulted at top, and about six hundred foot high. The great oven is not so wide by ten paces as the cupola at St. Paul's: for I measure the latter on purpose after my return. But if I should describe the kitchen-grate, the prodigious pots and kettles, the joints of meat turning on the spits, with many other particulars, perhaps I should hardly believed; at least a severe critic would be apt to think I enlarged a little, as travellers are often suspected to do. To avoid which censure, I fear I have run too much into the other extreme; and that if this treatise should happen to be translated into the language of Brobdingnag (which is the general name of that kingdom) and transmitted thither, the King and his people would have reason to complain that I had done them an injury by a false diminutive representation.

His Majesty seldom keeps above six hundred horses in his stables: they are generally from fifty-four to sixty foot high. But when he goes abroad on solemn days, he is attended for state by a militia guard of five hundred horse, which indeed I thought was the most splendid sight that could be ever beheld, till I saw part of his army in battalia, whereof I shall find another occasion to speak.

CHAPTER 5

I should have lived happy enough in that country, if my littleness had not exposed me to several ridiculous and troublesome accidents, some of which I shall venture to relate. Glumdalclitch often carried me into the gardens of the court in my smaller box, and would sometimes take me out of it and hold me in her hand, or set me down to walk. I remember, before the dwarf left the Queen, he followed us one day into those gardens, and my nurse having set me down, he and I being close together, near some dwarf apple-trees, I must needs show my wit by a silly allusion between him and the trees, which happens to hold in their language as it doth in ours. Whereupon, the malicious rogue watching his opportunity, when I was walking under one of them, shook it directly over my head, by which a dozen apples, each of them near as large as a Bristol barrel, came tumbling about my ears; one of them hit me on the back as I chanced to stoop, and knocked me down flat on my face, but I received no other hurt, and the dwarf was pardoned at my desire, because I had given the provocation.

Another day Glumdalclitch left me on a smooth grass-plot to divert myself while she walked at some distance with her governess. In the meantime there suddenly fell such a violent shower of hail, that I was immediately by the force of it struck to the ground: and when I was down, the hailstones gave me such cruel bangs all over the body, as I had been pelted with tennis-balls; however I made a shift to creep on all fours, and shelter myself by lying on my face on the leeside of a border of lemon thyme, but so bruised from head to foot that I could not go abroad in ten days. Neither is this at all to be wondered at, because nature in that country observing the same proportion through all her operations, a hailstone is near eighteen hundred times as large as one in Europe, which I can assert upon experience, having been so curious to weigh and measure them.

But a more dangerous accident happened to me in the same garden, when my little nurse believing she had put me in a secure place, which I often entreated her to do, that I might enjoy my own thoughts, and having left my box at home to avoid the trouble of carrying it, went to another part of the garden with her governess and some ladies of her acquaintance. While she was absent and out of hearing, a small white spaniel belonging to one of the chief gardeners, having got by accident into the garden, happened to range near the place where I lay. The dog following the scent, came directly up, and taking me in his mouth, ran straight to his master, wagging his tail, and set me gently on the ground. By good fortune he had been well taught, that I was carried between his teeth without the least hurt, or even tearing my clothes. But the poor gardener, who knew me well, and had a great kindness for me, was in a terrible fright. He gently took me up in both his hands, and asked me how I did; but I was so amazed and out of breath, that I could not speak a word. In a few minutes I came to myself, and he carried me safe to my little nurse, who by this time had returned to the place where she left me, and was in cruel agonies when I did not appear, nor answer when she called: she severely reprimanded the gardener on account of his dog. But the thing was hushed up, and never known at court; for the girl was afraid of the Queen's anger, and truly as to myself, I thought it would not be for my reputation that such a story should go about.

This accident absolutely determined Glumdalclitch never to trust me abroad for the future out of her sight. I had been long afraid of this resolution, and therefore concealed from her some little unlucky adventures that happened in those times when I was left by myself. Once a kite hovering over the garden made a swoop at me, and if I had not resolutely drawn my short sword, and run under a thick espalier, he would have certainly carried me away in his talons. Another time walking to the top of a fresh mole-hill, I fell to my neck in the hole through which that animal had cast up the earth, and coined some lie, not worth remembering, to excuse myself for spoiling my clothes. I likewise broke my right shin against the shell of a snail, which I happened to stumble over, as I was walking alone, and thinking on poor England.

I cannot tell whether I was more pleased or mortified, to observe in those solitary walks that the smaller birds did not appear to be at all afraid of me, but would hop about within a yard distance, looking for worms and other food with as much indifference and security as if no creature at all were near them. I remember a thrush had the confidence to snatch out of my hand with his bill a piece of cake that Glumdalclitch had just given me for my breakfast. When I attempted to catch any of these birds, they would boldly turn against me, endeavouring to pick my fingers, which I durst not venture within their reach; and then they would hop back unconcerned to hunt for worms or snails, as they did before. But one day I took a thick cudgel, and threw it with all my strength so luckily at a linnet that I knocked him down, and seizing him by the neck with both my hands, ran with him in triumph to my nurse. However, the bird, who had only been stunned, recovering himself, gave me so many boxes with his wings on both sides of my head and body, though I held him at arm's length, and was out of reach of his claws, that I was twenty times thinking to let him go. But I was soon relieved by one of our servants, who wrung the bird's neck, and I had him next day for dinner, by the Queen's command. This linnet, as near as I can remember, seemed to be somewhat larger than an English swan.

The Maids of Honour often invited Glumdalclitch to their apartments, and desired she would bring me along with her, on purpose to have the pleasure of seeing and touching me.

One day a young gentleman, who was nephew to my nurse's governess, came and pressed them both to see an execution. It was of a man who had murdered one of that gentleman's intimate acquaintance. Glumdalclitch was prevailed on to be of the company, very much against her inclination, for she was naturally tender-hearted; and as for myself, although I abhorred such kind of spectacles, yet my curiosity tempted me to seeing something that I thought must be extraordinary. The malefactor was fixed in a chair upon a scaffold erected for the purpose, and his head cut off at a blow with a sword of about forty foot long. The veins and arteries spouted up such a prodigious quantity of blood, and so high in the air, that the great *jet d'eau* at Versailles was not equal for the time it lasted; and the head, when it fell on the scaffold floor, gave such a bounce, as made me start, although I were at least half an English mile distant.

The Queen, who often used to hear me talk of my sea-voyages, and took all occasions to divert me when I was melancholy, asked me whether I understood how to handle a sail or an oar, and whether a little exercise of rowing might not be convenient for my health. I answered that I understood both very well. For although my proper employment had been to be surgeon or doctor to the ship, yet often, upon a pinch, I was forced to work like a common mariner. But I could not see how this could be done in their country, where the smallest wherry was equal to a first-rate man of war among us, and such a boat as I could manage would never live in any of their rivers. Her Majesty said, if I would contrive a boat, her own joiner should make it, and she would provide a place for me to sail in. The fellow was an ingenious workman, and by my instructions in ten days finished a pleasure-boat with all its tackling, able conveniently to hold eight Europeans. When it was finished, the Queen was so delighted, that she ran with it in her lap to the King, who ordered it to be put in a cistern full of water, with me in it, by way of trial; where I could not manage my two sculls, or little oars, for want of room. But the Queen had before contrived another project. She ordered the joiner to make a wooden trough of three hundred foot long, fifty broad, and eight deep; which being well pitched to prevent leaking, was placed on the floor along the wall, in an outer room of the palace. It had a cock near the bottom to let out the water when it began to grow stale, and two servants could easily fill it in half an hour. Here I often used to row for my own diversion, as well as that of the Queen and her ladies, who thought themselves well entertained with my skill and agility. Sometimes I would put up my sail, and then my business was only to steer, while the ladies gave me a gale with their fans; and when they were weary, some of the pages would blow my sail forward with their breath, while I showed my art by steering starboard or larboard as I pleased. When I had done, Glumdalclitch always carried my boat into her closet, and hung it on a nail to dry.

In this exercise I once met an accident which had like to have cost me my life. For one of the pages having put my boat into the trough, the governess who attended Glumdalclitch very officiously lifted me up to place me in the boat, but I happened to slip through her fingers, and should have infallibly fallen down forty feet upon the floor, if by the luckiest chance in the world, I had not been stopped by a corking-pin that stuck in the good gentlewoman's stomacher; the head of the pin passed between my shirt and the waistband of my breeches, and thus I was held by the middle in the air till Glumdalclitch ran to my relief.

Another time, one of the servants, whose office it was to fill my trough every third day with fresh water, was so careless to let a huge frog (not perceiving it) slip out of his pail. The frog lay concealed till I was put into my boat, but then seeing a resting-place, climb up, and made it lean so much on one side, that I was forced to balance it with all my weight on the other, to prevent overturning. When the frog was got in, it hopped at once half the length of the boat, and then over my head, backwards and forwards, daubing my face and clothes with its odious slime. The largeness of its features made it appear the most deformed animal that can be conceived. However, I desired Glumdalclitch to let me deal with it alone. I banged it a good while with one of my sculls, and at last forced it to leap out of the boat.

But the greatest danger I ever underwent in that kingdom was from a monkey, who belonged to one of the clerks of the kitchen. Glumdalclitch had locked me up in her closet, while she went somewhere upon business or a visit. The weather being very warm, the closet window was left open, as well as the windows, and the door of my bigger box, in which I usually lived, because of its large size and conveniency. As I sat quietly meditating at my table, I heard something bounce in at the closet window, and skip about from one side to the other; whereat, although I was much alarmed, yet I ventured to look out, but stirred not from my seat; and then I saw this frolicsome animal, frisking and leaping up and down, till at last he came to my box, which he seemed to view with great pleasure and curiosity, peeping in at the door and every window. I retreated to the farther corner of my room, or box, but the monkey looking in at every side, put me in such a fright, that I did not think to conceal myself under the bed, as I might easily have done. After some time spent in peeping, grinning, and chattering, he at last espied me, and reaching one of his paws in at the door, as a cat does when she plays with a mouse, although I often shifted place to avoid him, he at length seized the lapel of my coat (which being made of that country cloth, was very thick and strong) and dragged me out. He took me up in his right fore-foot, and held me as a nurse does a child she is going to suckle, just as I have seen the same sort of creature do with a kitten in Europe: and when I offered to struggle, he squeezed me so hard, that I thought it more prudent to submit. I have good reason to believe that he took me for a young one of his own species, by his often stroking my face very gently with his other paw. In these diversions he was interrupted by a noise at the closet door, as if somebody were opening it; whereupon he suddenly leaped up to the window at which he had come in, and thence upon the leads and gutters, walking upon three legs, and holding me in the fourth, till he clambered up to a roof that was next to ours. I heard Glumdalclitch give a shriek at the moment he was carrying me out. The poor girl was almost distracted: that quarter of the palace was all in an uproar; the servants ran for ladders; the monkey was seen by hundred in the court, sitting upon the ridge of a building, holding me like a baby in one of his fore-paws, and feeding me with the other, by cramming into my mouth some victuals he had squeezed out of the bag on one side of his chaps, and patting me when I would not eat; whereat many of the rabble below could not forbear laughing; neither do I think they justly ought to be blamed, for without question the sight was ridiculous enough to everybody by myself. Some of the people threw up stones, hoping to drive the monkey down; but this was strictly forbidden, or else very probably my brains had been dashed out.

The ladders were now applied, and mounted by several men, which the monkey observing, and finding himself almost encompassed, not being able to make speed enough with his three legs, let me drop on a ridge tile, and made his escape. Here I sat for some time three hundred yards from the ground, expecting every moment to be blown down by the wind, or to fall by my own giddiness, and come tumbling over and over from the ridge to the eaves; but an honest lad, one of my nurse's footmen, climbed up, and putting me into his breeches pocket, brought me down safe.

I was almost choked with the filthy stuff the monkey had crammed down my throat: but my dear little nurse picked it out of my mouth with a small needle, and then I fell a vomiting, which gave me great relief. Yet I was so weak and bruised in the sides with the squeezes given me by this odious animal, that I was forced to keep my bed a fortnight. The King, Queen, and all the court, sent every day to enquire after my health, and her Majesty made me several visits during my sickness. The monkey was killed, and an order made that no such animal should be kept about the palace.

When I attended the King after my recovery, to return him thanks for his favours, he was pleased to rally me a good deal upon this adventure. He asked me what my thoughts and speculations were while I lay in the monkey's paw, how I liked the victuals he gave me, his manner of feeding, and whether the fresh air on the roof had sharpened my stomach. He desired to know what I would have done upon such an occasion in my own country. I told his Majesty that in Europe we had no monkeys, except such as were brought for curiosities from other places, and so small that I could deal with a dozen of them together, if they presumed to attack me. And as for that monstrous animal with whom I was so lately engaged, (it was indeed as large as an elephant) if my fears had suffered me to think so far as to make use of my short sword (looking fiercely and clapping my hand upon the hilt as I spoke) when he poked his paw into my chamber, perhaps I should have given him such a wound, as would have made him glad to withdraw it with more haste than he put it in. This I delivered in a firm tone, like a person who was jealous lest his courage should be called in question. However, my speech produced nothing else besides a loud laughter, which all the respect due to his Majesty from those about him could not make them contain. This made me reflect how vain an attempt it is for a man to endeavour doing himself honour among those who are out of all degree of equality or comparison with him. And yet I have seen the moral of my own behaviour very frequent in England since my return, where a little contemptible varlet, without the least title to birth, person, wit, or common sense, shall presume to look with importance, and put himself upon a foot with the greatest persons of the kingdom.

CHAPTER 6

I used to attend the King's levee once or twice a week, and had often seen him under the barber's hand, which indeed was at first very terrible to behold; for the razor was almost twice as long as an ordinary scythe. His Majesty, according to the custom of the country, was only shaved twice a week. I once prevailed on the barber to give me some of the suds or lather, out of which I picked forty or fifty of the strongest stumps of hair. I then took a piece of fine wood, and cut it like the back of a comb, making several holes in it at equal distance with as small a needle as I could get from Glumdalclitch. I fixed in the stumps so artificially, scraping and sloping them with my knife towards the points, that I made a very tolerable comb; which was a seasonable supply, my own being so much broken in the teeth, that it was almost useless: neither did I know any artist in that country so nice and exact, as would undertake to make me another.

And this puts me in mind of an amusement wherein I spent many of my leisure hours. I desired the Queen's woman to save for me the combings of her Majesty's hair, whereof in time I got a good quantity, and consulting with my friend the cabinet-maker, who had received general orders to do little jobs for me, I directed him to make two chair-frames, no larger than those I had in my box, and then to bore little holes with a fine awl round those parts where I designed the backs and seats; through these holes I wove the strongest hairs I could pick out, just after the manner of cane-chairs in England. When they were finished, I made a present of them to her Majesty, who kept them in her cabinet, and used to show them for curiosities, as indeed they were the wonder of every one that beheld them. The Queen would have had me sit upon one of these chairs, but I absolutely refused to obey her, protesting I would rather die a thousand deaths than place my body on those precious hairs that once adorned her Majesty's head. Of these hairs (as I had always a mechanical genius) I likewise made a neat little purse about five foot long, with her Majesty's name deciphered in gold letters, which I gave to Glumdalclitch, by the Queen's consent. To say the truth, it was more for show than for use, being not of strength to bear the weight of the larger coins, and therefore she kept nothing in it but some little toys that girls are fond of.

The King, who delighted in music, had frequent concerts at court, to which I was sometimes carried, and set in my box on a table to hear them; but the noise was so great, that I could hardly distinguish the tunes. I am confident that all the drums and trumpets of a royal army, beating and sounding together just at your ears, could not equal it. My practice was to have my box removed from the places where the performers sat, as far as I could, then to shut the doors and windows of it, and draw the window curtains; after which I found their music not disagreeable.

I had learned in my youth to play a little upon the spinet. Glumdalclitch kept one in her chamber, and a master attended twice a week to teach her: I call it a spinet, because it somewhat resembled that instrument, and was played upon in the same manner. A fancy came into my head that I would entertain the King and Queen with an English tune upon this instrument. But this appeared extremely difficult; for the spinet was near sixty foot long, each key being almost a foot wide, so that, with my arms extended, I could not reach to above five keys, and to press them down required a good smart stroke with my fist, which would be too great a labour, and to no purpose. The method I contrived was this. I prepared two round sticks about the bigness of common cudgels; they were thicker at one end than the other, and I covered the thicker ends with a piece of a mouse's skin, that by rapping on them I might neither damage the tops of the keys, nor interrupt the sound. Before the spinet a bench was placed, about four foot below the keys, and I was put upon the bench. I ran sideling upon it that way and this, as fast as I could, banging the proper keys with my two sticks, and made a shift to play a jig, to the great satisfaction of both their Majesties: but it was the most violent exercise I ever underwent, and yet I could not strike above sixteen keys, nor, consequently, play the bass and treble together, as other artists do; which was a great disadvantage to my performance.

The King, who, as I before observed, was a prince of excellent understanding, would frequently order that I should be brought in my box, and set upon the table in his closet. He would then command me to bring one of my chairs out of the box, and sit down within three yards distance upon the top of the cabinet, which brought me almost to a level with his face. In this manner I had several conversations with him, I one day took the freedom to tell his Majesty, that the contempt he discovered towards Europe, and the rest of the world, did not seem answerable to those excellent qualities of the mind he was master of. That reason did not extend itself with the bulk of the body: on the contrary, we observed in our country that the tallest persons were usually least provided with it. That among other animals, bees and ants had the reputation of more industry, art and sagacity, than many of the larger kinds. And that, as inconsiderable as he took me to be, I hoped I might live to do his Majesty some signal service. The King heard me with attention, and began to conceive a much better opinion of me than he had ever before. He desired I would give him as exact an account of the government of England as I possibly could; because, as fond as princes commonly are of their own customs (for so he conjectured of other monarchs, by my former discourse), he should be glad to hear of anything that might deserve imitation.

Imagine with thyself, courteous reader, how often I then wished for the tongue of Demosthenes or Cicero, that might have enabled me to celebrate the praise of my own dear native country in a style equal to its merits and felicity.

I began my discourse by informing his Majesty that our dominions consisted of two islands, which composed three mighty kingdoms under one sovereign, beside our plantations in America. I dwelt long upon the fertility of our soil, and the temperature of our climate. I then spoke at large upon the constitution of an English Parliament, partly made up of an illustrious body called the House of Peers, persons of the noblest blood, and of the most ancient and ample patrimonies. I described that extraordinary care always taken of their education in arts and arms, to qualify them for being counsellors born to the king and kingdom, to have a share in the legislature, to be members of the highest Court of Judicature, from whence there could be no appeal, and to be champions always ready for the defence of their prince and country, by their valour, conduct, and fidelity. That these were the ornament and bulwark of the kingdom, worthy followers of their most renowned ancestors, whose honour had been the reward of their virtue, from which their posterity were never once known to degenerate. To these were joined several holy persons, as part of that assembly, under the title of Bishops, whose peculiar business it is to take care of religion, and of those who instruct the people therein. These were searched and sought out through the whole nation, by the prince and his wisest counsellors, among such of the priesthood as were most deservedly distinguished by the sancity of their lives, and the depth of their erudition; who were indeed the spiritual fathers of the clergy and the people.

That the other part of the Parliament consisted of an assembly called the House of Commons, who were all principal gentlemen, freely picked and culled out by the people themselves, for their great abilities and love of their country, to represent the wisdom of the whole nation. And these two bodies make up the most august assembly in Europe, to whom, in conjunction with the prince, the whole legislature is committed.

I then descended to the Courts of Justice, over which the Judges, those venerable sages and interpreters of the law, presided, for determining the disputed rights and properties of men, as well as for the punishment of vice, and protection of innocence. I mentioned the prudent management of our treasury; the valour and achievements of our forces by sea and land. I computed the number of our people, by reckoning how many million there might be of each religious sect, or political party among us. I did not omit even our sports and pastimes, or any other particular which I thought might add to the honour of my country. And I finished all with a brief historical account of affairs and events in England for about an hundred years past.

This conversation was not ended under five audiences, each of several hours, and the King heard the whole with great attention, frequently taking notes of what I spoke, as well as memorandums of several questions he intended to ask me.

When I had put an end to these long discourses, his Majesty in a sixth audience, consulting his notes, proposed many doubts, queries, and objections, upon every article. He asked what methods were used to cultivate the minds and bodies of our young nobility, and in what kind of business they commonly spent the first and teachable parts of their lives. What course was taken to supply that assembly when any noble family became extinct. What qualifications were necessary in those who were to be created new lords. Whether the humour of the prince, a sum of money to a court lady, or a prime minister, or a design of strengthening a party opposite to the public interest, ever happened to be motives in those advancements. What share of knowledge these lords had in the laws of their country, and how they came by it, so as to enable them to decide the properties of their fellow-subjects in the last resort. Whether they were always so free from avarice, partialities, or want, that a bribe, or some other sinister view, could have no place among them. Whether those holy lords I spoke of were always promoted to that rank upon account of their knowledge in religious matters, and the sancity of their lives, had never been compliers with the times while they were common priests, or slavish prostitute chaplains to some nobleman, whose opinions they continued servilely to follow after they were admitted into that assembly.

He then desired to know what arts were practised in electing those whom I called commoners: whether a stranger with a strong purse might not influence the vulgar voters to choose him before their own landlord, or the most considerable gentleman in the neighbourhood. How it came to pass, that people were so violently bent upon getting into this assembly, which I allowed to be a great trouble and expense, often to the ruin of their families, without any salary or pension: because this appeared such an exalted strain of virtue and public spirit, that his Majesty seemed to doubt it might possibly not be always sincere: and he desired to know whether such zealous gentlemen could have any views of refunding themselves for the charges and trouble they were at, by sacrificing the public good to the designs of a weak and vicious prince in conjunction with a corrupted ministry. He multiplied his questions, and sifted me thoroughly upon every part of this head, proposing numberless enquiries and objections, which I think it not prudent or convenient to repeat.

Upon what I said in relation to our Court of Justice, his Majesty desired to be satisfied in several points: and this I was the better able to do, having been formerly almost ruined by a long suit in chancery, which was decreed for me with costs. He asked, what time was usually spent in determining between right and wrong, and what degree of expense. Whether advocates and orators had liberty to plead in causes manifestly known to be unjust, vexations, or oppressive. Whether party religion or politics was observed to be of any weight in the scale of justice. Whether those pleading orators were persons educated in the general knowledge of equity, or only in provincial, national, and other local customs. Whether they or their judges had any part in penning those laws which they assumed the liberty of interpreting and glossing upon at their pleasure. Whether they had ever at different times pleaded for and against the same cause, and cited precedents to prove contrary opinions. Whether they were a rich or a poor corporation. Whether they received any pecuniary reward for pleading or delivering their opinions. And particularly whether they were ever admitted as members in the lower senate.

He fell next upon the management of our treasury; and said he thought my memory had failed me, because I computed our taxes at about five or six millions a year, and when I came to mention the issues, he found they sometimes amounted to more than double; for the notes he had taken were very particular in this point, because he hoped, as he told me, that the knowledge of our conduct might be useful to him, and he could not be deceived in his calculations. But, if what I had told him were true, he was still at a loss how a kingdom could run out of its estate like a private person. He asked me who were our creditors; and where we should find money to pay them. He wondered to hear me talk of such chargeable and extensive wars; that certainly we must be a quarrelsome people, or living among very bad neighbours, and that our generals must needs be richer than our kings. He asked what business we had out of our own islands, unless upon the score of trade or treaty, or to defend the coasts with our fleet. Above all, he was amazed to hear me talk of a mercenary standing army in the midst of peace, and among a free people. He said, if we were governed by our own consent in the persons of our representatives, he could not imagine of whom we were afraid, or against whom we were to fight; and would hear my opinion, whether a private man's house might not better be defended by himself, his children, and family, than by half a dozen rascals picked up at a venture in the streets, for small wages, who might get an hundred times more by cutting their throats.

He laughed at my odd kind of arithmetic (as he was pleased to call it) in reckoning the numbers of our people by a computation drawn from the several sects among us in religion and politics. He said, he knew no reason, why those who entertain opinions prejudicial to the public, should be obliged to change, or should not be obliged to conceal them. And it was a tyranny in any government to require the first, so it was weakness not to enforce the second: for a man may be allowed to keep poisons in his closet, but not to vend them about for cordials.

He observed that among the diversions of our nobility and gentry I had mentioned gaming. He desired to know at what age this entertainment was usually taken up, and when it was laid down; how much of their time it employed; whether it ever went so high as to affect their fortunes; whether mean vicious people, by their dexterity in that art, might not arrive at great riches, and sometimes keep our very nobles in dependence, as well as habituate them to vile companions, wholly take them from the improvement of their minds, and force them, by the losses they have received, to learn and practise that infamous dexterity upon others.

He was perfectly astonished with the historical account I gave him of our affairs during the last century, protesting it was only an heap of conspiracies, rebellions, murders, massacres, revolutions, banishments, the very worst effects that avarice, faction, hypocrisy, perfidiousness, cruelty, rage, madness, hatred, envy, lust, malice, or ambition could produce.

His Majesty in another audience was at the pains to recapitulate the sum of all I had given, compared the questions he made with the answers I had given, then taking me into his hands, and stroking me gently, delivered himself in these words, which I shall never forget nor the manner he spoke them in: My little friend Grildrig, you have made a most admirable panegyric upon your country; you have clearly proved that ignorance, idleness, and vice may be sometimes the only ingredients for qualifying a legislator; that laws are best explained, interpreted, and applied by those whose interest and abilities lie in perverting, confounding, and eluding them. I observe among you some lines of an institution, which in its original might have been tolerable, but these half erased, and the rest wholly blurred and blotted by corruptions. It does not appear from all you have said, how any one virtue is required towards the procurement of any one station among you; much less that men are ennobled on account of their virtue, that priests are advanced for their piety or learning, soldiers for their conduct or valour, judges for their integrity, senators for the love of their country, or counsellors for their wisdom. As for yourself (continued the King) who have spent the greatest part of your life in ätravelling, I am well disposed to hope you may hitherto have escaped many vices of your country. But by what I have gathered from your own relation, and the answers I have with much pains wringed and extorted from you, I cannot but conclude the bulk of your natives to be the most pernicious race of little odious vermin that nature ever suffered to crawl upon the surface of the earth.

CHAPTER 7

Nothing but an extreme love of truth could have hindered me from concealing this part of my story. It was in vain to discover my resentments, which were always turned into ridicule; and I was forced to rest with patience while my noble and most beloved country was so injuriously treated. I am heartily sorry as any of my readers can possibly be, that such an occasion was given: but this prince happened to be so curious and inquisitive upon every particular, that it could not consist either with gratitude or good manners to refuse giving him what satisfaction I was able. Yet thus much I may allowed to say in my own vindication, that I artfully eluded many of his questions, and gave to every point a more favourable turn by many degrees than the strictness of truth would allow. For I have always borne that laudable partiality to my own country, which Dionysius Halicarnassensis with so much justice recommends to an historian. I would hide the frailties and deformities of my political mother, and place her virtues and beauties in the most advantageous light. This was my sincere endeavour in those many discourses I had with that mighty monarch, although it unfortunately failed of success.

But great allowances should be given to a King who lives wholly secluded from the rest of the world, and must therefore be altogether unacquainted with the manners and customs that most prevail in other nations; the want of which knowledge will ever produce many prejudices, and a certain narrowness of thinking, from which we and the politer countries of Europe are wholly exempted. And it would be hard indeed, if so remote a prince's notions of virtue and vice were to be offered as a standard for all mankind.

To confirm what I have now said, and further, to show the miserable effects of a confined education, I shall here insert a passage which will hardly obtain belief. In hopes to ingratiate myself farther into his Majesty's favour, I told him of an invention discovered between three and four hundred years ago, to make a certain powder, into an heap of which the smallest spark of fire falling, would kindle the whole in a moment, although it were as big as a mountain, and make it fly up in the air together, with a noise and agitation greater than thunder. That a proper quantity of this powder rammed into an hollow tube of brass or iron, according to its bigness, would drive a ball of iron or lead with such violence and speed, as nothing was able to sustain its force. That the largest balls thus discharged, would not only destroy whole ranks of an army at once, but batter the strongest walls to the ground, sink down ships, with a thousand men in each, to the bottom of the sea; and, when linked together by a chain, would cut through masts and rigging, divide hundred of bodies in the middle, and lay all waste before them. That we often out this powder into large hollow balls of iron, and discharged them by an engine into some city we were besieging, which would rip up the pavements, tear the houses to pieces, burst and throw splinters on every side, dashing out the brains of all who came near. That I knew the ingredients very well, which were cheap, and common; I understood the manner of compounding them, and could direct his workmen how to make those tubes of a size proportionate to all other things in his Majesty's kingdom, and the largest need not be above an hundred foot long; twenty or thirty of which tubes, charged with the proper quantity of powder and balls, would batter down the walls of the strongest town in his dominions in a few hours, or destroy the whole metropolis, if ever it should pretend to dispute his absolute commands. This I humbly offered to his Majesty, as a small tribute of acknowledgement in return of so many marks that I had received of his royal favour and protection.

The King was struck with horror at the description I had given of those terrible engines, and the proposal I had made. He was amazed how so impotent and grovelling an insect as I (these were his expressions) could entertain such inhuman ideas, and in so familiar a manner as to appear wholly unmoved at all the scenes of blood and desolation, which I painted as the common effects of those destructive machines, whereof he said some evil genius, enemy to mankind, must have been the first contriver. As for himself, he protested that although few things delighted him so much as new discoveries in art or in nature, yet he would rather lose half his kingdom than be privy to such a secret, which he commanded me, as I valued my life, never to mention any more.

A strange effect of narrow principles and short views: that a prince possessed of every quality which procures veneration, love, and esteem; off strong parts, great wisdom, and profound learning, endued with admirable talents for government, and almost adored by his subjects, should from a nice unnecessary scruple, whereof in Europe we can have no conception, let slip an opportunity put into his hands, that would have made him absolute master of the lives, the liberties, and the fortunes of his people. Neither do I say this with the least intention to detract from the many virtues of that excellent King, whose character I am sensible will on this account be very much lessened in the opinions of an English reader: but I take this defect among them to have risen from their ignorance, they not having hitherto reduced politics into a science, as the more acute wits of Europe have done. For I remember very well, in a discourse one day with the King, when I happened to say there were several thousand books among us written upon the art of government, it gave him (directly contrary to my intention) a very mean opinion of our understandings. He professed both to abominate and despise all mystery, refinement, and intrigue, either in a prince or a minister. He could not tell what I meant by secrets of state, where an enemy or some rival nation were not in the case. He confined the knowledge of governing within very narrow bounds; to common sense and reason, to justice and lenity, to the speedy determination of civil and criminal causes; with some other obvious topics, which are not worth considering. And he gave it for his opinion, that whoever could make two ears of corn or two blades of grass to grow upon a spot of ground where only one grew before, would deserve better of mankind, and do more essential service to his country than the whole race of politicians put together.

The learning of this people is very defective, consisting only in morality, history, poetry, and mathematics, wherein they must be allowed to excel. But the last of these is wholly applied to what may be useful in life, to the improvement of agriculture, and all mechanical arts; so that among us it would be little esteemed. And as to ideas, entities, abstractions, and transcendentals, I could never drive the least conception into their heads.

No law of that country must exceed in words the number of letters in their alphabet, which consists only in two and twenty. But indeed few of them extend even to that length. They are expressed in the most plain and simple terms, wherein those people are not mercurial enough to discover above one interpretation; and to write a comment upon any law is a capital crime. As to the decision of civil causes, or proceedings against criminals, their precedents are so few, that they have little reason to boast of any extraordinary skill in either.

They have had the art of printing, as well as the Chinese, time out of mind. But their libraries are not very large; for that of the King, which is reckoned the biggest, does not amount to above a thousand volumes, placed in a gallery of twelve hundred foot long, from whence I had liberty to borrow what books I pleased. The Queen's joiner had contrived in one of Glumdalclitch's rooms a kind of wooden machine five and twenty foot high, formed like a standing ladder; the steps were each fifty foot long. It was indeed a moveable pair of stairs, the lowest end placed at ten foot distance from the wall of the chamber. The book I had mind to read was put up leaning against the wall. I first mounted to the upper step of the ladder, and turning my face towards the book, began at the top of the page, and so walking to the right and left about eight or ten paces, according to the length of the lines, till I had gotten a little below the level of my eyes, and then descending gradually till I came to the bottom; after which I mounted again, and began the other page in the same manner, and so turned over the leaf, which I could easily do with both my hands, for it was thick and stiff as a pasteboard, and in the largest folios not above eighteen or twenty foot long.

Their style is clear, masculine, and smooth, but not florid, for they avoid nothing more than multiplying unnecessary words, or using various expressions. I have persued many of their books, especially those in history and morality. Among the rest, I was much diverted with a little old treatise, which always lay in Glumdalclitch's bedchamber, and belonged to her governess, a grave elderly gentlewoman, who dealt in writings of morality and devotion. The book treats of the weakness of human kind, and is in little esteem, except among the women and the vulgar. However, I was curious to see what an author of that country could say upon such an subject. This writer went through all the usual topics of European moralists, showing how diminutive, contemptible, and helpless an animal was man in his own nature; how unable to defend himself from the inclemencies of the air, or the fury of wild beasts; how much he was excelled by one creature in strength, by another in speed, by a third in foresight, by a fourth in industry. He added that nature was degenerated in these latter declining ages of the world, and could now produce only small abortive births in comparison of those in ancient times. He said, it was very reasonable to think, not only that the species of men were originally much larger, but also, that there must have been giants in former ages, which, as it it asserted by history and tradition, so it has been confirmed by huge bones and skulls casually dug up in several parts of the kingdom, far exceeding the common dwindled race of man in our days. He argued that the very laws of nature absolutely required we should have been made in the beginning, of a size more large and robust, not so liable to destruction from every little accident of a tile falling from a house, or a stone cast from the hand of a boy, or of being drowned in a little brook. from this way of reasoning the author drew several moral applications useful in the conduct of life, but needless here to repeat. For my own part, I could not avoid reflecting how universally this talent was spread, of drawing lectures in morality, or indeed rather matter of discontent and repining from the quarrels we raise with nature. And I believe, upon a strict enquiry, those quarrels might be shown as ill grounded among us as they are among that people.

As to their military affairs, they boast that the King's army consists of an hundred and seventy-six thousand foot, and thirty-two thousand horse: if that may be called an army which is made up of tradesmen in the several cities, and farmers in the country, whose commanders are only the nobility and gentry, without pay or reward. They are indeed perfect enough in their exercises, and under very good discipline, wherein I saw no great merit; for how should it be otherwise, where every farmer is under the command of his own landlord, and every citizen under that of the principal men in his own city, chosen after the manner of Venice by ballot?

I have often seen the militia of Lorbrulgrud drawn out to exercise in a great field near the city of twenty miles square. They were in all not above twenty-five thousand foot, and six thousand horse; but it was impossible for me to compute their number, considering the space of ground they took up. A cavalier mounted on a large steed, might be about an hundred foot high. I have seen this whole body of horse, upon a word of command, draw their swords at once, and brandish them in the air. Imagination can figure nothing so grand, so surprising, and so astonishing. It looked as if ten thousand flashes of lightning were darting at the same time from every quarter of the sky.

I was curious to know how this prince, to whose dominions there is no access from any other country, come to think of armies, or to teach his people the practice of military discipline. But I was soon informed, both by conversation and reading their histories. For in the course of many ages they have been troubled with the same disease to which the whole race of mankind is subject; the nobility often contending for power, the people for liberty, and the King for absolute dominion. All which, however happily tempered by the laws of the kingdom, have been sometimes violated by each of the three parties, and have once or more occasioned civil wars, the last whereof was happily put an end to by this prince's grandfather by a general composition; and the militia, then settled with common, consent, hath been ever since kept in the strictest duty.

CHAPTER 8

I had always a strong impulse that I should some time recover my liberty, though it was impossible to conjecture by what means, or to form any project with the least hope of succeeding. This ship in which I sailed was the first ever known to be driven within sight of that coast, and the King had given strict orders, that if at any time another appeared, it should be taken ashore, and with all its crew and passengers brought in a tumbril to Lorbrulgrud. He was strongly bent to get me a woman of my own size, by whom I might propagate the breed: but I think I should rather have died than undergone the disgrace of leaving a posterity to be kept in cages like tame canary birds, and perhaps, in time, sold about the kingdom to persons of quality for curiosities. I was, indeed, treated with much kindness; I was the favourite of a great King and Queen, and the delight of the whole court, but it was upon such a foot as ill became the dignity of human kind. I could never forget those domestic pledges I had left behind me. I wanted to be among people whom I could converse upon even terms, and walk about the streets and fields without fear of being trod to death like a frog or a young puppy. But my deliverance came sooner than I expected, and in a manner not very common; the whole story and circumstances of which I shall faithfully relate.

I had now been two years in this country; and about the beginning of the third, Glumdalclitch and I attended the King and Queen in a progress to the south coast of the kingdom. I was carried, as usual, in my travelling-box, which, as I have already described, was a very convenient closet of twelve foot wide. And I had ordered a hammock to be fixed by silken ropes from the four corners at the top, to break the jolts, when a servant carried me before him on horseback, as I sometimes desired, and would often sleep in my hammock while we were upon the road. On the roof of my closet, just over the middle of the hammock, I ordered the joiner to cut out a hole of a foot square, to give me air in hot weather as I slept, which hole I shut at pleasure with a board that drew backwards and forwards through a groove.

When we came to our journey's end, the King thought proper to pass a few days at a palace he hath near Flanflasnic, a city within eighteen English miles of the seaside. Glumdalclitch and I were much fatigued; I had gotten a small cold, but the poor girl was so ill as to be confined to her chamber. I longed to see the ocean, which must be the only scene of my escape, if ever it should happen. I pretended to be worse than I really was, and desired leave to take the fresh air of the sea, with a page of whom I was very fond, and who had sometimes been trusted with me. I shall never forget with what unwillingness Glumdalclitch consented, nor the strict charge she gave the page to be careful of me, bursting at the same time into a flood of tears, as if she had forebodding of what was to happen. The boy took me out in my box about half an hour's walk from the palace, towards the rocks on the seashore. I ordered him to set me down, and lifting up one of my sashes, cast many a wistful melancholy look towards the sea. I found myself not very well, and told the page that I had a mind to take a nap in my hammock, which I hoped would do me good. I got in, and the boy shut the window close down to keep out the cold. I soon fell asleep, and all I can conjecture is, that while I slept, the page, thinking no danger could happen, went among the rocks to look for bird's eggs, having before observed him from my window searching about, and picking up one or two in the clefts. Be that as it will, I found myself suddenly awaked with a violent pull upon the ring which was fastened at the top of my box for the conveniency of carriage. I felt my box raised very high in the air, and then borne forward with prodigious speed. The first jolt had like to have shaken me out of my hammock, but afterwards the motion was easy enough. I called out several times as loud as I could raise my voice, but all to no purpose. I looked towards my windows, and could see nothing but the clouds and sky. I heard a noise just over me head like the clapping of wings, and then began to perceive the woeful condition I was in; that some eagle had got the ring of my box in his beak, with an intent to let it fall on a rock like a tortoise in a shell, and then pick out my body, and devour it. For the sagacity and smell of this bird enable him to discover his quarry at a great distance, though better concealed than I could be within a two-inch board.

In a little time I observed the noise and flutter of wings to increase very fast, and my box was tossed up and down, like a sign-post in a windy day. I heard several bangs or buffets, as I thought, given to the eagle (for such I am certain it must have been that held the ring of my box in his beak), and then all on a sudden felt myself falling perpendicularly down for above a minute, but with such incredible swiftness that I almost lost my breath. My fall was stopped by a terrible crash, that sounded louder to my ears than the cataract of Niagara; after which I was quite in the dark for another minute, and then my box began to rise so high that I could see light from the tops of my windows. I now perceived that I was fallen into the sea. My box, by the weight of my body, the goods that were in, and the broad plates of iron fixed for strength at the four corners of the top and bottom, floated about five foot deep in water. I did then, and do now suppose that the eagle which flew away with my box was pursued by two or three others, and forced to let me drop while he was defending himself against the rest, who hoped to share in the prey. The plates of iron fastened at the bottom of the box (for those were the strongest) preserved the balance while it fell, and hindered it from being broken on the surface of the water. Every joint of it was well grooved, and the door did not move on hinges, but up and down like a sash, which kept my closet so tight that very little water came in. I got with much difficulty out of my hammock, having first ventured to draw back the slip-board on the roof already mentioned, contrived on purpose to let in air, for want of which I found myself almost stifled.

How often did I then wish myself with my dear Glumdalclitch, from whom one single hour had so far divided me! And I may say with truth, that in the midst of my own misfortunes I could not forbear lamenting my poor nurse, the grief she would suffer for my loss, the displeasure of the Queen, and the ruin of her fortune. Perhaps many travellers have not been under greater difficulties and distress than I was in at this juncture, expecting every moment to see my box dashed in pieces, or at least overset by the first violent blast, or a rising wave. A breach in one single pane of glass would have been immediate death: nor could any thing have preserved the windows, but the strong lattice wires placed on the outside against accidents in travelling. I saw the water ooze in at several crannies, although the leaks were not considerable, and I endeavoured to stop them as well as I could. I was not able to lift up the roof of my closet, which otherwise I certainly should have done, and sat on the top of it, where I might at least preserve myself some hours longer than by being shut up, as I may call it, in the hold. Or, if I escaped these dangers for a day or two, what could I expect but a miserable death of cold and hunger! I was four hours under these circumstances, expecting and indeed wishing every moment to be my last.

I have already told the reader that there were two strong staples fixed upon that side of my box which had no window, and into which the servant who used to carry me on horseback would put a leathern belt, and buckle it about his waist. Being in this disconsolate state, I heard or at least thought I heard some kind of grating noise on that side of my box where the staples were fixed, and soon after I began to fancy that the box was pulled or towed along in the sea; for I now and then felt a sort of tugging, which made the waves rise near the tops of my windows, leaving me almost in the dark. This gave me some faint hopes of relief, although I was not able to imagine how it could be brought about. I ventured to unscrew one of my chairs, which were always fastened to the floor; and having made a hard shift to screw it down again directly under the slipping-board that I had lately opened, I mounted on the chair, and putting my mouth as near as I could to the hole, I called for help in a loud voice, and in all the languages I understood. I then fastened my handkerchief to a stick I usually carried, and thrusting it up the hole, waved it several times in the air, that if any boat or ship were near, the seamen might conjecture some unhappy mortal to be shut up in the box.

I found no effect from all I could do, but plainly perceived my closet to be moved along; and in the space of an hour, or better, that side of the box where the staples were, had no window, struck against something that was hard. I apprehended it to be a rock, and found myself tossed more than ever. I plainly heard a noise upon the cover of my closet, like that of a cable, and the grating of it as it passed through the ring. I then found myself hoisted up by degrees at least three foot higher than I was before. Whereupon I again thrust up my stick and handkerchief, calling for help till I was almost hoarse. In return to which, I heard a great shout repeated three times, giving me such transports of joy, as are not to be conceived but by those who feel them. I now heard a trampling over my head, and somebody calling through the hole with a loud voice in the English tongue: If there be anybody below, let them speak. I answered, I was an Englishman, drawn by ill fortune into the greatest calamity that ever any creature underwent, and begged, by all that is moving, to be delivered out of the dungeon I was in. The voice replied, I was safe, for my box was fastened to their ship; and the carpenter should immediately come and saw an hole in the cover, large enough to pull me out. I answered, that was needless and would take up too much time, for there was no more to be done, but let one of the crew out his finger into the ring, and take the box out of the sea into the ship, and so into the captain's cabin. Some of them upon hearing me talk so wildly thought I was mad; others laughed; for indeed it never came into my head that I was now got among people of my own stature and strength. The carpenter came, and in a few minutes sawed a passage about four foot square, then let down a small ladder, upon which I mounted, and from thence was taken into the ship in a very weak condition.

The sailors were all in amazement, and asked me a thousand questions, which I had no inclination to answer.

I was equally confounded at the sight of so many pigmies, for such I took them to be, after having so long accustomed my eyes to the monstrous objects I had left. But the Captain, Mr. Thomas Wilcocks, an honest worthy Shropshire man, observing I ready to faint, took me into his cabin, gave me a cordial to comfort me, and made me turn in upon his own bed, advising me to take a little rest, of which I had great need. Before I went to sleep I gave him to understand that I had some valuable furniture in my box, too good to be lost, a fine hammock, an handsome field-bed, two chairs, a table, and a cabinet; that my closet was hung on all sides, or rather quilted, with silk and cotton; that if he would let one of the crew bring my closet into his cabin, I would open it there before him, and show him my goods. The Captain hearing me utter these absurdities, concluded I was raving: however, (I suppose to pacify me) he promised to give order as I desired, and going upon deck sent some of his men down into my closet, from whence (as I afterwards found) they drew up all my goods, and stripped off the quilting; but the chairs, cabinet, and bedstead, being screwed to the floor, were much damaged by the ignorance of seamen, who tore them up by force. Then they knocked off some of the boards for the use of the ship, and when they had got all they had a mind for, let the hull drop into the sea, which by reason of many breaches made in the bottom and sides, sunk to rights. And indeed I was glad not to have been a spectator of the havoc they made; because I am confident it would have sensibly touched me, by bringing former passages into my mind, which I had rather forget.

I slept some hours, but perpetually disturbed with dreams of the place I had left, and the dangers I had escaped. However, upon waking I found myself much recovered. It was now about eight o'clock at night, and the Captain ordered supper immediately, thinking I had already fasted too long. He entertained me with great kindness, observing me not to look wildly, or talk inconsistently: and when we were left alone, desired I would give him a relation of my travels, and by what accident I came to be set adrift in that monstrous wooden chest. He said, that about twelve o'clock at noon, as he was looking through his glass, he spied it at a distance, and thought it was a sail, which he had a mind to make, being not much out of his course, in hopes of buying some biscuits, his own beginning to fall short. That upon coming nearer, and finding his error, he sent out his long-boat to discover what I was; that his men came back in a fright, swearing they had seen a swimming house. That he laughed at their folly, and went himself in the boat, ordering his men to take a strong cable along with them. That the weather being calm, he rowed round me several times, observed my windows, and the wire lattices that defended them. That he discovered two staples upon one side, which was all of boards, without any passage for light. He then commanded his men to row up to that side, and fastening a cable to one of the staples, ordered them to tow my chest (as he called it) towards the ship. When it was there, he gave directions to fasten another cable to the ring fixed in the cover, and to raise up my chest with pulleys, which all the sailors were not able to do above two or three foot. He said he saw my stick and handkerchief thrust out of the hole, and concluded that some unhappy men must be shut up in the cavity. I asked whether he or the crew had seen any prodigious birds in the air about the time he first discovered me. To which he answered, that discoursing this matter with the sailors while I was asleep, one of them said he had observed three eagles flying towards the north, but remarked nothing of their being larger than the usual size, which I suppose must be imputed to the great height they were at; and he could not guess the reason of my question. I then asked the Captain how far he reckoned we might be from land; he said, by the best computation he could make, we were at least an hundred leagues. I assured him, that he must be mistaken by almost half, for I had left the country from whence I came above two hours before I dropt into the sea. Whereupon he began again to think that my brain was disturbed, of which he gave me a hint, and advised me to go to bed in a cabin he had provided. I assured him I was well refreshed with his good entertainment and company, and as much in my senses as ever I was in my life. He then grew serious, and desired to ask me freely whether I were not troubled in mind by the consciousness off some enormous crime, for which I was punished at the command of some prince, by exposing me in that chest, as great criminals in other countries have been forced to sea in a leaky vessel without provisions; for although he should be sorry to have taken so ill a man into his ship, yet he would engage his word to set me safe on shore in the first port where we arrived. He added, that his suspicions were much increased by some very absurd speeches I had delivered at first to the sailors, and afterwards to himself, in relation to my closet or chest, as well as by my odd looks and behaviour while I was at supper.

I begged his patience to hear me tell my story, which I faithfully did from the last time I left England to the moment he first discovered me. And as truth always forceth its way into rational minds, so this honest worthy gentleman, who had some tincture of learning, and very good sense, was immediately convinced of my candour and veracity. But further to confirm all I had said, I entreated him to give order that my cabinet should be brought, of which I had the key in my pocket (for he had already informed me how the seamen disposed of my closet), I opened it in his presence and showed him the small collection of rarities I made in the country from whence I had been so strangely delivered. There was the comb I had contrived out of the stumps of the King's beard, and another of the same materials, but fixed into a paring of her Majesty's thumb-nail, which served for the back. There was a collection of needles and pins from a foot to half a yard long; four wasp-stings, like joiner's tacks; some combings of the Queen's hair; a gold ring which one day she made me a present of in a most obliging manner, taking it from her little finger, and throwing it over my head like a collar. I desired the Captain would please to accept this ring in return of his civilities, which he absolutely refused. I showed him a corn that I had cut off with my own hand, from a maid of honour's toe; it was about the bigness of a äKentish pippin, and grown so hard that when I returned to England, I got it hollowed into a cup, and set in silver. Lastly, I desired him to see the breeches I had then on, which were made of a mouse's skin.

I could force nothing on him but a footman's tooth, which I observed him to examine with great curiosity, and found he had a fancy for it. He received it with abundance of thanks, more than such a trifle could deserve. It was drawn by an unskilful surgeon, in a mistake, from one of Glumdalclitch's men, who was afflicted with the toothache, but it was as sound as any in his head. I got it cleaned, and put it into my cabinet. It was about a foot long, and four inches in diameter.

The Captain was very well satisfied with this plain relation I had given him, and said he hoped when we returned to England I would oblige the world by putting it in paper and making it public. My answer was that I thought we were already overstocked with books of travels; that nothing could now pass which was not extraordinary; wherein I doubted some authors less consulted truth than their own vanity, or interest, or the diversion of ignorant readers. That my story could contain little besides common events, without those ornamental descriptions of strange plants, trees, birds, and other animals, or of the barbarous customs and idolatry of savage people, with which most writers abound. However, I thanked him for his good opinion, and promised to take the matter into my thoughts.

He said he wondered at one thing very much, which was, to hear me speak so loud, asking me whether the King or Queen of that country were thick of hearing. I told him it was what I had been used to for above two years past, and that I admired as much at the voices of him and his men, who seemed to me only to whisper, and yet I could hear them well enough. But when I spoke in that country, it was like a man talking in the street to another looking out from the top of a steeple, unless when I was placed on a table, or held in any person's hand. I told him, I had likewise observed another thing, that when I first got into the ship, and the sailors stood all about me, I thought they were the most little contemptible creatures I had ever beheld. For indeed while I was in that prince's country, I could never endure to look in a glass after my eyes had been accustomed to such prodigious objects, because the comparison gave me so despicable a conceit of myself. The Captain said that while we were at supper he observed me to look at every thing with a sort of wonder, and that I often seemed hardly able to contain my laughter, which he knew not well how to take, but imputed it to some disorder in my brain. I answered, it was very true; and I wondered how I could forbear, when I saw his dishes the size of a silver three-pence, a leg of pork hardly a mouthful, a cup not so big as a nut-shell; and so I went on, describing the rest of his household-stuff and provisions after the same manner. For, although the Queen had ordered a little equipage of all things necessary for me while I was in her service, yet my ideas were wholly taken up with what I saw on every side of me, and I winked at my own littleness as people do at their own faults. The Captain understood my raillery very well, and merrily replied with the old English proverb, that he doubted my eyes were bigger than my belly, for he did not observe my stomach so good, although I had fasted all day; and continuing in his mirth, protested he would have gladly given an hundred pounds to have seen my closet in the eagle's bill, and afterwards in its fall from so great an height into the sea; which would certainly have been a most astonishing object, worthy to have the description of it transmitted to future ages: and the comparison of Phaeton was so obvious, that he could not forbear applying it, although I did not much admire the conceit.

The Captain having been at Tonquin, was in his return to England driven north-eastwards to the latitude of 44 degrees, and of longitude 143. But meeting a trade-wind two days after I came on board him, we sailed southward a long time, and coasting New Holland kept our course west-south-west, and then south-south-west till we doubled the Cape of Good Hope. Our voyage was very prosperous, but I shall not trouble the reader with a journal of it. The Captain called in at one or two ports, and sent in his long-boat for provisions and fresh water, but I never went out of the ship till we came into the Downs, which was on the third day of June, 1706, about nine months after my escape. I offered to leave my goods in security for payment of my freight; but the Captain protested he would not receive one farthing. We took kind leave of each other, and I made him promise he would come to see me at my house in Redriff. I hired a horse and guide for five shillings, which I borrowed of the Captain.

As I was on the road, observing the littleness of the houses, the trees, the cattle, and the people, I began to think myself in Lilliput. I was afraid of trampling on every traveller I met, and often called aloud to have them stand out of the way, so that I had like to have gotten one or two broken heads for my impertinence.

When I came to my house, for which I was forced to enquire, one of the servants opening the door, I bent down to go in (like a goose under a gate) for fear of striking my head. My wife ran out to embrace me, but I stopped lower than her knees, thinking she could otherwise never be able to reach my mouth. My daughter kneeled to ask my blessing, but I could not see her till she arose, having been so long used to stand with my head and eyes erect to above sixty foot; and then I went to take up her up with one hand, by the waist. I looked down upon the servants and one or two friends who were in the house, as if they had been pigmies, and I a giant. I told my wife, she had been to thrifty, for I found she had starved herself and her daughter to nothing. In short, I behaved myself so unaccountably, that they were all of the Captain's opinion when he first saw me, and concluded I had lost my wits. This I mention as an instance of the great power of habit and prejudice.

In a little time I and my family and friends came to a right understanding: but my wife protested I should never go to sea any more; although my evil destiny so ordered that she had not power to hinder me, as the reader may know hereafter. In the mean time I here conclude the second part of my unfortunate voyages.

CHILDREN'S CLASSICS

Rip Van Winkle
and other stories

Washington Irving

Rip Van Winkle

and other stories

PARRAGON

Rip Van Winkle
A Parragon Classic

This is a Siena Book
Siena is an imprint of Parragon

First published in 1905

This edition published in 1999 by
Parragon
13 Whiteladies Road
Clifton
Bristol BS8 1PB

Printed and bound in the UK

CONTENTS

RIP VAN WINKLE

A POSTHUMOUS WRITING OF
DIEDRICH KNICKERBOCKER

By Woden, God of Saxons,
From whence comes Wensday, that is Wodensday,
Truth is a thing that ever I will keep
Unto thylke day in which I creep into
My sepulchre—

CARTWRIGHT

[The following Tale was found among the papers of the late Diedrich Knickerbocker, an old gentleman of New York, who was very curious in the Dutch history of the province and the manners of the descendants from its primitive settlers. His historical researches, however, did not lie so much among books as among men, for the former are lamentably scanty on his favourite topics, whereas he found the old burghers, and still more their wives, rich in that legendary lore so invaluable to true history. Whenever, therefore, he happened upon a genuine Dutch family, snugly shut up in its low-roofed farmhouse, under a spreading sycamore, he looked upon it as a little clasped volume of black letter and studied it with the zeal of a bookworm.

The result of all these researches was a history of the province during the reign of the Dutch governors, which he published some years since. There have been various opinions as to the literary character of his work, and, to tell the truth, it is not a whit better than it should be. Its chief merit is its scrupulous accuracy, which indeed was a little questioned on its first appearance, but has since been completely established, and it is now admitted into all historical collections as a book of unquestionable authority.

The old gentleman died shortly after the publication of his work, and now that he is dead and gone, it cannot do much harm to his memory to say that his time might have been much better employed in weightier labours. He, however, was apt to ride his hobby his own way; and though it did now and then kick up the dust a little in the eyes of his neighbours and grieve the spirit of some friends, for whom he felt the truest deference and affection, yet his errors and follies are remembered "more in sorrow than in anger", and it begins to be suspected that he never intended to injure or offend. But however his memory may be appreciated by critics, it is still held dear by many folks, whose good opinion is well worth having; particularly by certain biscuit bakers, who have gone so far as to imprint his likeness on their new-year cakes, and have thus given him a chance for immortality, almost equal to being stamped on a Waterloo Medal, or a Queen Anne's Farthing.]

Whoever has made a voyage up the Hudson must remember the Kaatskill Mountains. They are a dismembered branch of the great Appalachian family, and are seen away to the west of the river, swelling up to a noble height and lording it over the surrounding country. Every change of season, every change of weather, indeed, every hour of the day produces some change in the magical hues and shapes of these mountains, and they are regarded by all the good wives, far and near, as perfect barometers. When the weather is fair and settled, they are clothed in blue and purple, and print their bold outlines on the clear evening sky; but, sometimes, when the rest of the landscape is cloudless, they will gather a hood of grey vapours about their summits, which, in the last rays of the setting sun, will glow and light up like a crown of glory.

At the foot of these fairy mountains, the voyager may have described the light smoke curling up from a village, whose shingle roofs gleam among the trees, just where the blue tints of the upland melt away into the fresh green of the nearer landscape. It is a little village of great antiquity, having been founded by some of the Dutch colonists in the early times of the province, just about the beginning of the government of the good Peter Stuyvesant (may he rest in peace!), and there were some of the houses of the original settlers standing within a few years, built of small yellow bricks brought from Holland, having latticed windows and gable fronts, surmounted with weathercocks.

In that same village, and in one of these very houses (which, to tell the precise truth, was sadly time-worn and weather-beaten), there lived many years since, while the country was yet a province of Great Britain, a simple, good-natured fellow of the name of Rip Van Winkle. He was a descendant of the Van Winkles who figured so gallantly in the chivalrous days of Peter Stuyvesant, and accompanied him to the siege of Fort Christina. He inherited, however, but little of the martial character of his ancestors. I have observed that he was a simple, good-natured man; he was, moreover, a kind neighbour, and an obedient, henpecked husband. Indeed, to the latter circumstance might be owing that meekness of spirit which gained him such universal popularity, for those men are most apt to be obsequious and conciliating abroad who are under the discipline of shrews at home. Their tempers, doubtless, are rendered pliant and malleable in the fiery furnace of domestic tribulation, and a curtain lecture is worth all the sermons in the world for teaching the virtues of patience and long-suffering. A termagant wife may, therefore, in some respects, be considered a tolerable blessing; and if so, Rip Van Winkle was thrice blessed.

Certain it is that he was a great favourite among all the good wives of the village, who, as usual with the amiable sex, took his part in all family squabbles and never failed, whenever they talked those matters over in their evening gossipings, to lay all the blame on Dame Van Winkle. The children of the village, too, would shout with joy whenever he approached. He assisted at their sports, made their playthings, taught them to fly kites and shoot marbles, and told them long stories of ghosts, witches, and Indians. Whenever he went dodging about the village, he was surrounded by a troop of them, hanging on his skirts, clambering on his back, and playing a thousand tricks on him with impunity; and not a dog would bark at him throughout the neighbourhood.

The great error in Rip's composition was an insuperable aversion to all kinds of profitable labour. It could not be from the want of assiduity or perseverance, for he would sit on a wet rock, with a rod as long and heavy as a Tartar's lance, and fish all day without a murmur, even though he should not be encouraged by a single nibble. He would carry a fowling piece on his shoulder for hours together, trudging through woods and swamps and up hill and down dale to shoot a few squirrels or wild pigeons. He would never refuse to assist a neighbour even in the roughest toil, and was a foremost man at all country frolics for husking Indian corn or building stone fences; the women of the village, too, used to employ him to run their errands and to do such little odd jobs as their less obliging husbands would not do for them. In a word, Rip was ready to attend to anybody's business but his own; but as to doing family duty and keeping his farm in order, he found it impossible.

In fact, he declared it was of no use to work on his farm; it was the most pestilent little piece of ground in the whole country; everything about it went wrong, and would go wrong, in spite of him. His fences were continually falling to pieces; his cow would either go astray or get among the cabbages; weeds were sure to grow quicker in his fields than anywhere else; the rain always made a point of setting in just as he had some outdoor work to do; so that though his patrimonial estate had dwindled away under his management, acre by acre, until there was little more left than a mere patch of Indian corn and potatoes, yet it was the worst-conditioned farm in the neighbourhood.

His children, too, were as ragged and wild as if they belonged to nobody. His son Rip, an urchin begotten in his own likeness, promised to inherit the habits, with the old clothes, of his father. He was generally seen trooping like a colt at his mother's heels, equipped in a pair of his father's cast-off galligaskins, which he had much ado to hold up with one hand as a fine lady does her train in bad weather.

Rip Van Winkle, however, was one of those happy mortals of foolish, well-oiled dispositions who like the world easy, eat white bread or brown, whichever can be got with least thought or trouble, and would rather starve on a penny than work for a pound. If left to himself, he would have whistled life away in perfect contentment; but his wife kept continually dinning in his ears about his idleness, his carelessness, and the ruin he was bringing on his family. Morning, noon, and night, her tongue was incessantly going, and everything he said or did was sure to produce a torrent of household eloquence. Rip had but one way of replying to all lectures of the kind, and that, by frequent use, had grown into a habit. He shrugged his shoulders, shook his head, cast up his eyes, but said nothing. This, however, always provoked a fresh volley from his wife, so that he was fain to draw off his forces and take to the outside of the house—the only side which, in truth, belongs to a henpecked husband.

Rip's sole domestic adherent was his dog, Wolf, who was as much henpecked as his master, for Dame Van Winkle regarded them as companions in idleness, and even looked upon Wolf with an evil eye as the cause of his master's going so often astray. True it is, in all points of spirit befitting an honourable dog, he was as courageous an animal as ever scoured the woods—but what courage can withstand the ever-during and all-besetting terrors of a woman's tongue? The moment Wolf entered the house his crest fell, his tail drooped to the ground, or curled between his legs, he sneaked about with a gallows air, casting many a sidelong glance at Dame Van Winkle, and at the least flourish of a broomstick or ladle he would fly to the door with yelping precipitation.

Times grew worse and worse with Rip Van Winkle as years of matrimony rolled on; a tart temper never mellows with age, and a sharp tongue is the only edged tool that grows keener with constant use. For a long while he used to console himself, when driven from home, by frequenting a kind of perpetual club of the sages, philosophers, and other idle personages of the village, which held its sessions on a bench before a small inn, designated by a rubicund portrait of His

Majesty George the Third. Here they used to sit in the shade through a long, lazy summer's day, talking listlessly over village gossip or telling endless sleepy stories about nothing. But it would have been worth any statesman's money to have heard the profound discussions that sometimes took place when by chance an old newspaper fell into their hands from some passing traveller. How solemnly they would listen to the contents, as drawled out by Derrick Van Bummel, the schoolmaster, a dapper, learned little man who was not to be daunted by the most gigantic word in the dictionary; and how sagely they would deliberate upon public events some months after they had taken place.

The opinions of this junto were completely controlled by Nicholas Vedder, a patriarch of the village and landlord of the inn, at the door of which he took his seat from morning till night, just moving sufficiently to avoid the sun and keep in the shade of a large tree, so that the neighbours could tell the hour by his movements as accurately as by a sundial. It is true he was rarely heard to speak, but smoked his pipe incessantly. His adherents, however (for every great man has his adherents), perfectly understood him, and knew how to gather his opinions. When anything that was read or related displeased him, he was observed to smoke his pipe vehemently and to send forth short, frequent, and angry puffs; but when pleased, he would inhale the smoke slowly and tranquilly and emit it in light and placid clouds, and sometimes, taking the pipe from his mouth and letting the fragrant vapour curl about his nose, would gravely nod his head in token of perfect approbation.

From even this stronghold the unlucky Rip was at length routed by his termagant wife, who would suddenly break in upon the tranquillity of the assemblage and call the members all to naught; nor was that august personage, Nicholas Vedder himself, sacred from the daring tongue of this terrible virago, who charged him outright with encouraging her husband in habits of idleness.

Poor Rip was at last reduced almost to despair, and his only alternative, to escape from the labour of the farm and clamour of his wife, was to take gun in hand and stroll away into the woods. Here he would sometimes seat himself at the foot of a tree and share the contents of his wallet with Wolf, with whom he sympathized as a fellow sufferer in persecution. "Poor Wolf," he would say, "thy mistress leads thee a dog's life of it; but never mind, my lad, whilst I live thou shalt never want a friend to stand by thee!" Wolf would wag his tail, look wistfully in his master's face, and if dogs can feel pity, I verily believe he reciprocated the sentiment with all his heart.

In a long ramble of the kind of a fine autumnal day, Rip had unconsciously scrambled to one of the highest parts of the Kaatskill Mountains. He was after his favourite sport of squirrel shooting, and the still solitudes had echoed and re-echoed with the reports of his gun. Panting and fatigued, he threw himself, late in the afternoon, on a green knoll, covered with mountain herbage, that crowned the brow of a precipice. From an opening between the trees he could overlook all the lower country for many a mile of rich woodland. He saw at a distance the lordly Hudson, far, far below him, moving on its silent but majestic course, with the reflection of a purple cloud or the sail of a lagging bark here and there sleeping on its glassy bosom, and at last losing itself in the blue highlands.

On the other side he looked down into a deep mountain glen, wild, lonely, and shagged, the bottom filled with fragments from the impending cliffs, and scarcely lighted by the reflected rays of the setting sun. For some time Rip lay musing on this scene. Evening was gradually advancing; the mountains began to throw their long blue shadows over the valleys. He saw that it would be dark long before he could reach the village, and he heaved a heavy sigh when he thought of encountering the terrors of Dame Van Winkle.

As he was about to descend, he heard a voice from a distance, hallooing, "Rip Van Winkle! Rip Van Winkle!" He looked around, but could see nothing but a crow winging its solitary flight across the mountain. He thought his fancy must have deceived him, and turned again to descend, when he heard the same cry ring through the still evening air, "Rip Van Winkle! Rip Van Winkle!" At the same time Wolf bristled up his back and, giving a low growl, skulked to his master's side, looking fearfully down into the glen. Rip now felt a vague apprehension stealing over him; he looked anxiously in the same direction and perceived a strange figure slowly toiling up the rocks, and bending under the weight of something he carried on his back. He was surprised to see any human being in this lonely and unfrequented place, but supposing it to be some one of the neighbourhood in need of his assistance, he hastened down to yield it.

On nearer approach he was still more surprised at the singularity of the stranger's appearance. He was a short, square-built old fellow, with thick, bushy hair and a grizzled beard. His dress was of the antique Dutch fashion—a cloth jerkin strapped around the waist and several pairs of breeches, the outer one of ample volume, decorated with rows of buttons down the sides and bunches at the knees. He bore on his shoulder a stout keg that seemed full of liquor, and made signs for Rip to approach and assist him with the load. Though rather shy and distrustful of this new acquaintance, Rip complied with his usual alacrity, and mutually relieving one another, they clambered up a narrow gully, apparently the dry bed of a mountain torrent. As they ascended, Rip every now and then heard long rolling peals, like distant thunder, that seemed to issue out of a deep ravine, or rather cleft, between lofty rocks, toward which their rugged path conducted. He paused for an instant, but supposing it to be the muttering of one of those transient thunder showers which often take place in mountain heights, he proceeded. Passing through the ravine, they came to a hollow, like a small amphitheatre, surrounded by perpendicular precipices, over the brinks of which impending trees shot their branches, so that you only caught glimpses of the azure sky and the bright evening cloud. During the whole time, Rip and his companion had laboured on in silence, for though the former marvelled greatly what could be the object of carrying a keg of liquor up this wild mountain, yet there was something strange and incomprehensible about the unknown that inspired awe and checked familiarity.

On entering the amphitheatre, new objects of wonder were to be seen. On a level spot in the centre was a company of odd-looking personages playing at ninepins. They were dressed in a quaint, outlandish fashion; some wore short doublets, others jerkins, with long knives in their belts, and most of them had enormous breeches, of similar style with that of the guide's. Their visages, too, were peculiar; one had a large beard, broad face, and small piggish eyes, the face of another seemed to consist entirely of nose and was surmounted by a white sugarloaf hat set off with a little red cock's tail. They all had beards, of various shapes and colours. There was one who seemed to be the commander. He was a stout old gentleman, with a weather-beaten countenance; he wore a laced doublet, broad belt and hanger, high-crowned hat and feather, red stockings, and high-heeled shoes, with roses in them. The whole group reminded Rip of the figures in an old Flemish painting, in the parlour of Dominie Van Shaick, the village parson, and which had been brought over from Holland at the time of the settlement.

What seemed particularly odd to Rip was that though these folks were evidently amusing themselves, yet they maintained the gravest faces, the most mysterious silence, and were, withal, the most melancholy party of pleasure he had ever witnessed. Nothing interrupted the stillness of the scene but the noise of the balls, which, whenever they were rolled, echoed along the mountains like rumbling peals of thunder.

As Rip and his companion approached them, they suddenly desisted from their play and stared at him with such fixed, statuelike gaze and such strange, uncouth, lacklustre countenances that his heart turned within him and his knees smote together. His companion now emptied the contents of the keg into large flagons and made signs to him to wait upon the company. He obeyed with fear and trembling; they quaffed the liquor in profound silence and then returned to their game.

By degrees Rip's awe and apprehension subsided. He even ventured, when no eye was fixed upon him, to taste the beverage, which he found had much of the flavour of excellent Hollands. He was naturally a thirsty soul and was soon tempted to repeat the draught. One taste provoked another; and he reiterated his visits to the flagon so often that at length his senses were overpowered, his eyes swam in his head, his head gradually declined, and he fell into a deep sleep.

On waking, he found himself on the green knoll whence he had first seen the old man of the glen. He rubbed his eyes—it was a bright, sunny morning. The birds were hopping and twittering among the bushes, and the eagle was wheeling aloft and breasting the pure mountain breeze. "Surely," thought Rip, "I have not slept here all night." He recalled the occurrences before he fell asleep. The strange man with a keg of liquor—the mountain ravine—the wild retreat among the rocks—the woebegone party at ninepins—the flagon—"Oh! That flagon! That wicked flagon!" thought Rip. "What excuse shall I make to Dame Van Winkle?"

He looked around for his gun, but in place of the clean, well-oiled fowling piece he found an old firelock lying by him, the barrel encrusted with rust, the lock falling off, and the stock worm-eaten. He now suspected that the grave roysters of the mountain had put a trick upon him, and, having dosed him with liquor, had robbed him of his gun. Wolf, too, had disappeared, but he might have strayed away after a squirrel or partridge. He whistled after him and shouted his name, but all in vain; the echoes repeated his whistle and shout, but no dog was to be seen.

He determined to revisit the scene of the last evening's gambol, and if he met with any of the party, to demand his dog and gun. As he rose to walk, he found himself stiff in the joints and wanting in his usual activity. "These mountain beds do not agree with me," thought Rip, "and if this frolic should lay me up with a fit of the rheumatism, I shall have a blessed time with Dame Van Winkle." With some difficulty he got down into the glen; he found the gully up which he and his companion had ascended the preceding evening, but to his astonishment a mountain stream was now foaming down it, leaping from rock to rock and filling the glen with babbling murmurs. He, however, made shift to scramble up its sides, working his toilsome way through thickets of birch, sassafras, and witch hazel, and sometimes tripped up or entangled by the wild grapevines that twisted their coils or tendrils from tree to tree and spread a kind of network in his path.

At length he reached to where the ravine had opened through the cliffs to the amphitheatre, but no traces of such opening remained. The rocks presented a high, impenetrable wall over which the torrent came tumbling in a sheet of feathery foam and fell into a broad, deep basin, black from the shadows of the surrounding forest. Here, then, poor Rip was brought to a stand. He again called and whistled after his dog; he was only answered by the cawing of a flock of idle crows, sporting high in air about a dry tree that overhung a sunny precipice, and who, secure in their elevation, seemed to look down and scoff at the poor man's perplexities. What was to be done? The morning was passing away, and Rip felt famished for want of his breakfast. He grieved to give up his dog and gun; he dreaded to meet his wife, but it would not do to starve among the mountains. He shook his head, shouldered the rusty firelock, and, with a heart full of trouble and anxiety, turned his steps homeward.

As he approached the village he met a number of

people, but none whom he knew, which somewhat surprised him, for he had thought himself acquainted with every one in the country around. Their dress, too, was of a different fashion from that to which he was accustomed. They all stared at him with equal marks of surprise, and whenever they cast their eyes upon him invariably stroked their chins. The constant recurrence of this gesture induced Rip, involuntarily, to do the same, when, to his astonishment, he found his beard had grown a foot long!

He had now entered the skirts of the village. A troop of strange children ran at his heels, hooting after him and pointing at his grey beard. The dogs, too, not one of which he recognized for an old acquaintance, barked at him as he passed. The very village was altered; it was larger and more populous. There were rows of houses which he had never seen before, and those which had been his familiar haunts had disappeared. Strange names were over the doors—strange faces at the windows—everything was strange. His mind now misgave him; he began to doubt whether both he and the world around him were not bewitched. Surely this was his native village, which he had left but the day before. There stood the Kaatskill Mountains—there ran the silver Hudson at a distance—there was every hill and dale precisely as it had always been. Rip was sorely perplexed. "That flagon last night," thought he, "has addled my poor head sadly!"

It was with some difficulty that he found the way to his own house, which he approached with silent awe, expecting every moment to hear the shrill voice of Dame Van Winkle. He found the house gone to decay—the roof fallen in, the windows shattered, and the doors off the hinges. A half-starved dog that looked like Wolf was skulking about it. Rip called him by name, but the cur snarled, showed his teeth, and passed on. This was an unkind cut indeed. "My very dog," sighed poor Rip, "has forgotten me!"

He entered the house, which, to tell the truth, Dame Van Winkle had always kept in neat order. It was empty, forlorn, and apparently abandoned. This desolateness overcame all his connubial fears—he called loudly for his wife and children; the lonely chambers rang for a moment with his voice, and then all again was silence.

He now hurried forth and hastened to his old resort, the village inn—but it too was gone. A large, rickety, wooden building stood in its place, with great gaping windows, some of them broken and mended with old hats and petticoats, and over the door was painted, "the Union Hotel, by Jonathan Doolittle". Instead of the great tree that used to shelter the quiet little Dutch inn of yore, there now was reared a tall, naked pole, with something on the top that looked like a red nightcap, and from it was fluttering a flag, on which was a singular assemblage of stars and stripes—all this was strange and incomprehensible. He recognized on the sign, however, the ruby face of King George, under which he had smoked so many a peaceful pipe; but even this was singularly metamorphosed. The red coat was changed for one of blue and buff, a sword was held in the hand instead of a sceptre, the head was decorated with a cocked hat, and underneath was painted in large characters, GENERAL WASHINGTON.

There was, as usual, a crowd of folk about the door, but none that Rip recollected. The very character of the people seemed changed. There was a busy, bustling, disputatious tone about it, instead of the accustomed phlegm and drowsy tranquillity. He looked in vain for the sage Nicholas Vedder, with his broad face, double chin, and fair long pipe, uttering clouds of tobacco smoke instead of idle speeches; or Van Bummel, the schoolmaster, doling forth the contents of an ancient newspaper. In place of these, a lean, bilious-looking fellow, with his pockets full of handbills, was haranguing vehemently about rights of citizens—elections—members of congress—liberty—Bunker's Hill—heroes of seventy-six—and other words, which were a perfect Babylonish jargon to the bewildered Van Winkle.

The appearance of Rip, with his long, grizzled beard, his rusty fowling piece, his uncouth dress, and an army of women and children at his heels, soon attracted the attention of the tavern politicians. They crowded around him, eyeing him from head to foot with great curiosity. The orator bustled up to him and, drawing him partly aside, inquired "on which side he voted?" Rip stared in vacant stupidity. Another short but busy little fellow pulled him by the arm, and, rising on tiptoe, inquired in his ear, "whether he was Federal or Democrat?" Rip was equally at a loss to comprehend the question; when a knowing, self-important old gentleman in a sharp cocked hat made his way through the crowd, putting them to the right and left with his elbows as he passed, and, planting himself before Van Winkle, with one arm akimbo, the other resting on his cane, his keen eyes and sharp hat penetrating, as it were, into his very soul, demanded in an austere tone, "what brought him to the election with a gun on his shoulder, and a mob at his heels, and whether he meant to breed a riot in the village?" "Alas! Gentlemen," cried Rip, somewhat dismayed, "I am a poor, quiet man, a native of the place, and a loyal subject of the king, God bless him!"

Here a general shout burst from the bystanders. "A tory! A tory! A spy! A refugee! Hustle him! Away with him!" It was with great difficulty that the self-important man in the cocked hat restored order; and, having assumed a tenfold austerity of brow, demanded again of the unknown culprit what he came there for and whom he was seeking. The poor man humbly assured him that he meant no harm, but merely came there in search of some of his neighbours, who used to keep about the tavern.

"Well—who are they? Name them."

Rip bethought himself a moment, and inquired, "Where's Nicholas Vedder?"

There was a silence for a little while, when an old man replied, in a thin, piping voice, "Nicholas Vedder! Why, he is dead and gone these eighteen years! There was a wooden tombstone in the churchyard that used to tell about him, but that's rotten and gone too."

"Where's Brom Dutcher?"

"Oh, he went off to the army in the beginning of the war; some say he was killed at the storming of Stony Point—others say he was drowned in a squall at the foot of Antony's Nose. I don't know—he never came back again."

"Where's Van Bummel, the schoolmaster?"

"He went off to the wars, too, was a great militia general, and is now in congress."

Rip's heart died away at hearing of these sad changes in his home and friends, and finding himself thus alone in the world. Every answer puzzled him, too, by treating of such enormous lapses of time and of matters which he could not understand: war—congress—Stony

Point. He had no courage to ask after any more friends, but cried out in despair, "Does nobody here know Rip Van Winkle?"

"Oh, Rip Van Winkle!" exclaimed two or three. "Oh, to be sure! That's Rip Van Winkle yonder, leaning against the tree."

Rip looked, and beheld a precise counterpart of himself as he went up the mountain: apparently as lazy, and certainly as ragged. The poor fellow was now completely confounded. He doubted his own identity, and whether he was himself or another man. In the midst of his bewilderment, the man in the cocked hat demanded who he was, and what was his name?

"God knows," exclaimed he, at his wit's end. "I'm not myself—I'm somebody else—that's me yonder—no that's somebody else got into my shoes—I was myself last night, but I fell asleep on the mountain, and they've changed my gun, and everything's changed, and I'm changed, and I can't tell what's my name, or who I am!"

The bystanders began now to look at each other, nod, wink significantly, and tap their fingers against their foreheads. There was a whisper also about securing the gun and keeping the old fellow from doing mischief, at the very suggestion of which the self-important man in the cocked hat retired with some precipitation. At this critical moment a fresh, comely woman pressed through the throng to get a peep at the grey-bearded man. She had a chubby child in her arms, which, frightened at his looks, began to cry. "Hush, Rip," cried she, "hush, you little fool; the old man won't hurt you." The name of the child, the air of the mother, the tone of her voice, all awakened a train of recollections in his mind. "What is your name, my good woman?" asked he.

"Judith Gardenier."

"And your father's name?"

"Ah, poor man, Rip Van Winkle was his name, but it's twenty years since he went away from home with his gun, and never has been heard of since—his dog came home without him; but whether he shot himself, or was carried away by the Indians, nobody can tell. I was then but a little girl."

Rip had but one question more to ask; but he put it with a faltering voice:

"Where's your mother?"

"Oh, she too had died but a short time since; she broke a blood vessel in a fit of passion, at a New England pedlar."

There was a drop of comfort, at least, in this intelligence. The honest man could contain himself no longer. He caught his daughter and her child in his arms. "I am your father!" cried he. "Young Rip Van Winkle once—old Rip Van Winkle now! Does nobody know poor Rip Van Winkle?"

All stood amazed, until an old woman, tottering out from among the crowd, put her hand to her brow and, peering under it in his face for a moment, exclaimed, "Sure enough! It is Rip Van Winkle—it is himself! Welcome home again, old neighbour. Why, where have you been these twenty long years?"

Rip's story was soon told, for the whole twenty years had been to him but as one night. The neighbours stared when they heard it; some were seen to wink at each other and put their tongues in their cheeks, and the self-important man in the cocked hat, who, when the alarm was over, had returned to the field, screwed down the corners of his mouth and shook his head—upon which there was a general shaking of the head throughout the assemblage.

It was determined, however, to take the opinion of old Peter Vanderdonk, who was seen slowly advancing up the road. He was a descendant of the historian of that name, who wrote one of the earliest accounts of the province. Peter was the most ancient inhabitant of the village, and well versed in all the wonderful events and traditions of the neighbourhood. He recollected Rip at once and corroborated his story in the most satisfactory manner. He assured the company that it was a fact, handed down from his ancestor the historian, that the Kaatskill Mountains had always been haunted by strange beings. That it was affirmed that the great Hendrick Hudson, the first discoverer of the river and country, kept a kind of vigil there every twenty years, with his crew of the *Half Moon,* being permitted in this way to revisit the scenes of his enterprise and keep a guardian eye upon the river and the great city called by his name. That his father had once seen them in their old Dutch dresses playing at ninepins in a hollow of the mountain, and that he himself had heard, one summer afternoon, the sound of their balls, like distant peals of thunder.

To make a long story short, the company broke up and returned to the more important concerns of the election. Rip's daughter took him home to live with her; she had a snug, well-furnished house, and a stout, cheery farmer for a husband, whom Rip recollected for one of the urchins that used to climb upon his back. As to Rip's son, and heir, who was the ditto of himself, seen leaning against the tree, he was employed to work on the farm, but evinced a hereditary disposition to attend to anything else but his business.

Rip now resumed his old walk and habits; he soon found many of his former cronies, though all rather the worse for the wear and tear of time, and preferred making friends among the rising generation, with whom he soon grew into great favour.

Having nothing to do at home, and being arrived at that happy age when a man can be idle with impunity, he took his place once more on the bench at the inn door and was reverenced as one of the patriarchs of the village, and a chronicle of the old times "before the war". It was some time before he could get into the regular track of gossip, or could be made to comprehend the strange events that had taken place during his torpor. How that there had been a revolutionary war—that the country had thrown off the yoke of old England—and that, instead of being a subject of his Majesty George the Third, he was now a free citizen of the United States. Rip, in fact, was no politician—the changes of states and empires made but little impression on him; but there was one species of despotism under which he had long groaned, and that was—petticoat government. Happily that was at an end; he had got his neck out of the yoke of matrimony and could go in and out whenever he pleased, without dreading the tyranny of Dame Van Winkle. Whenever her name was mentioned, however, he shook his head, shrugged his shoulders, and cast up his eyes, which might pass either for an expression of resignation to his fate or joy at his deliverance.

He used to tell his story to every stranger that arrived at Mr Doolittle's hotel. He was observed, at first, to vary on some points every time he told it, which was, doubtless, owing to his having so recently awaked. It at last settled down precisely to the tale I have related, and not a man, woman, or child in the neighbourhood but knew it by heart. Some always pretended to doubt the reality of it, and insisted that Rip had been out of his head, and that this was one point on which he always remained flighty. The old Dutch inhabitants, however, almost universally gave it full credit. Even to this day they never hear a thunderstorm of a summer afternoon about the Kaatskill but they say Hendrick Hudson and his crew are at their game of ninepins; and it is a common wish of all henpecked husbands in the neighbourhood, when life hangs heavy on their hands, that they might have a quieting draught out of Rip Van Winkle's flagon.

NOTE

The foregoing Tale, one would suspect, had been suggested to Mr Knickerbocker by a little German superstition about the Emperor Frederick *der Rothbart* and the Kypphaüser mountain. The subjoined note, however, which he had appended to the tale, shows that it is an absolute fact, narrated with his usual fidelity:

"The story of Rip Van Winkle may seem incredible to many, but nevertheless I give it my full belief, for I know the vicinity of our old Dutch settlements to have been very subject to marvellous events and appearances. Indeed, I have heard many stranger stories than this, in the villages along the Hudson, all of which were too well authenticated to admit of a doubt. I have even talked with Rip Van Winkle myself, who, when last I saw him, was a very venerable old man and so perfectly rational and consistent on every other point that I think no conscientious person could refuse to take this into the bargain; nay, I have seen a certificate on the subject taken before a country justice and signed with a cross, in the justice's own handwriting. The story, therefore, is beyond the possibility of doubt.

D.K."

POSTSCRIPT

The following are travelling notes from a memorandum book of Mr Knickerbocker:

The Kaatsberg, or Catskill Mountains, have always been a region full of fable. The Indians considered them the abode of spirits, who influenced the weather, spreading sunshine or clouds over the landscape, and sending good or bad hunting seasons. They were ruled by an old squaw spirit, said to be their mother. She dwelt on the highest peak of the Catskills and had charge of the doors of day and night, to open and shut them at the proper hour. She hung up the new moons in the skies and cut up the old ones into stars. In times of drought, if properly propitiated, she would spin light summer clouds out of cobwebs and morning dew and send them off from the crest of the mountain, flake after flake, like flakes of carded cotton, to float in the air; until, dissolved by the heat of the sun, they would fall in gentle showers, causing the grass to spring, the fruits to ripen, and the corn to grow an inch an hour. If displeased, however, she would brew up clouds black as ink, sitting in the midst of them like a bottle-bellied spider in the midst of its web; and when these clouds broke, woe betide the valleys!

In old times, say the Indian traditions, there was a kind of Manitou or Spirit, who kept about the wildest recesses of the Catskill Mountains, and took a mischievous pleasure in wreaking all kinds of evils and vexations upon the red men. Sometimes he would assume the form of a bear, a panther, or a deer, lead the bewildered hunter a weary chase through tangled forests and among ragged rocks, and then spring off with a loud ho! ho! leaving him aghast on the brink of a beetling precipice or raging torrent.

The favourite abode of this Manitou is still shown. It is a great rock or cliff on the loneliest part of the mountains, and, from the flowering vines which clamber about it and the wild flowers which abound in its neighbourhood, is known by the name of the Garden Rock. Near the foot of it is a small lake, the haunt of the solitary bittern, with water snakes basking in the sun on the leaves of the pond lilies which lie on the surface. This place was held in great awe by the Indians, insomuch that the boldest hunter would not pursue his game within its precincts. Once upon a time, however, a hunter who had lost his way penetrated to the Garden Rock, where he beheld a number of gourds placed in the crotches of trees. One of these he seized and made off with, but in the hurry of his retreat he let it fall among the rocks, when a great stream gushed forth, which washed him away and swept him down precipices, where he was dashed to pieces, and the stream made its way to the Hudson and continues to flow to the present day; being the identical stream known by the name of the Kaaters-kill.

THE SPECTRE BRIDEGROOM

A TRAVELLER'S TALE

He that supper for is dight,
He lyes full cold, I trow, this night!
Yestreen to chamber I him led,
This night Gray-Steel has made his bed.

SIR EGER, SIR GRAHAME,
AND SIR GRAY-STEEL

On the summit of one of the heights of the Odenwald, a wild and romantic tract of Upper Germany that lies not far from the confluence of the Main and the Rhine, there stood, many, many years since, the Castle of the Baron Von Landshort. It is now quite fallen to decay and almost buried among beech trees and dark firs, above which, however, its old watchtower may still be seen, struggling, like the former possessor I have mentioned, to carry a high head and look down upon the neighbouring country.

The baron was a dry branch of the great family of Katzenellenbogen,* and inherited the relics of the property and all the pride of his ancestors. Though the warlike disposition of his predecessors had much impaired the family possessions, yet the baron still

* i.e. Cat's-elbow. The name of a family of those parts very powerful in former times. The appellation, we are told, was given in compliment to a peerless dame of the family, celebrated for her fine arm.

endeavoured to keep up some show of former state. The times were peaceable, and the German nobles, in general, had abandoned their inconvenient old castles, perched like eagles' nests among the mountains, and had built more convenient residences in the valleys; still the baron remained proudly drawn up in his little fortress, cherishing, with hereditary inveteracy, all the old family feuds, so that he was on ill terms with some of his nearest neighbours on account of disputes that had happened between their great-great-grandfathers.

The baron had but one child, a daughter; but nature, when she grants but one child, always compensates by making it a prodigy, and so it was with the daughter of the baron. All the nurses, gossips, and country cousins assured her father that she had not her equal for beauty in all Germany; and who should know better than they? She had, moreover, been brought up with great care under the superintendence of two maiden aunts, who had spent some years of their early life at one of the little German courts and were skilled in all the branches of knowledge necessary to the education of a fine lady. Under their instructions she became a miracle of accomplishments. By the time she was eighteen she could embroider to admiration and had worked whole histories of the saints in tapestry with such strength of expression in their countenances that they looked like so many souls in purgatory. She could read without great difficulty, and had spelled her way through several church legends and almost all the chivalric wonders of the Heldenbuch. She had even made considerable proficiency in writing, could sign her own name without missing a letter, and so legibly that her aunts could read it without spectacles. She excelled in making little elegant good-for-nothing ladylike knickknacks of all kinds; was versed in the most abstruse dancing of the day; played a number of airs on the harp and guitar; and knew all the tender ballads of the Minnelieders by heart.

Her aunts, too, having been great flirts and coquettes in their younger days, were admirably calculated to be vigilant guardians and strict censors of the conduct of their niece, for there is no chaperone so rigidly prudent and decorous as a superannuated coquette. She was rarely suffered out of their sight; never went beyond the domains of the castle, unless well attended, or rather well watched; had continual lectures read to her about strict decorum and implicit obedience; and, as to the men—pah!—she was taught to hold them at such a distance, and in such absolute distrust, that, unless properly authorized, she would not have cast a glance upon the handsomest cavalier in the world—no, not if he were even dying at her feet.

The good effects of this system were wonderfully apparent. The young lady was a pattern of docility and correctness. While others were wasting their sweetness in the glare of the world and liable to be plucked and thrown aside by every hand, she was coyly blooming into fresh and lovely womanhood under the protection of those immaculate spinsters, like a rosebud blushing forth among guardian thorns. Her aunts looked upon her with pride and exultation, and vaunted that though all the other young ladies in the world might go astray, yet, thank Heaven, nothing of the kind could happen to the heiress of Katzenellenbogen.

But, however scantily the Baron Von Landshort might be provided with children, his household was by no means a small one, for Providence had enriched him with abundance of poor relations. They, one and all, possessed the affectionate disposition common to humble relatives, were wonderfully attached to the baron, and took every possible occasion to come in swarms and enliven the castle. All family festivals were commemorated by these good people at the baron's expense; and when they were filled with good cheer they would declare that there was nothing on earth so delightful as these family meetings, these jubilees of the heart.

The baron, though a small man, had a large soul, and it swelled with satisfaction at the consciousness of being the greatest man in the little world about him. He loved to tell long stories about the dark old warriors whose portraits looked grimly down from the walls around, and he found no listeners equal to those that fed at his expense. He was much given to the marvellous, and a firm believer in all those supernatural tales with which every mountain and valley in Germany abounds. The faith of his guests exceeded even his own; they listened to every tale of wonder with open eyes and mouth, and never failed to be astonished, even though repeated for the hundredth time. Thus lived the Baron Von Landshort, the oracle of his table, the absolute monarch of his little territory, and happy, above all things, in the persuasion that he was the wisest man of the age.

At the time of which my story treats there was a great family gathering at the castle, on an affair of the utmost importance: it was to receive the destined bridegroom of the baron's daughter. A negotiation had been carried on between the father and an old nobleman of Bavaria to unite the dignity of their houses by the marriage of their children. The preliminaries had been conducted with proper punctilio. The young people were betrothed without seeing each other, and the time was appointed for the marriage ceremony. The young Count Von Altenburg had been recalled from the army for the purpose, and was actually on his way to the baron's to receive his bride. Missives had even been received from him, from Würzburg, where he was accidentally detained, mentioning the day and hour when he might be expected to arrive.

The castle was in a tumult of preparation to give him a suitable welcome. The fair bride had been decked out with uncommon care. The two aunts had superintended her toilet and quarrelled the whole morning about every article of her dress. The young lady had taken advantage of their contest to follow the bent of her own taste, and fortunately it was a good one. She looked as lovely as youthful bridegroom could desire, and the flutter of expectation heightened the lustre of her charms.

The suffusions that mantled her face and neck, the gentle heaving of the bosom, the eye now and then lost in reverie, all betrayed the soft tumult that was going on in her little heart. The aunts were continually hovering around her, for maiden aunts are apt to take great interest in affairs of this nature. They were giving her a world of staid counsel how to deport herself, what to say, and in what manner to receive the expected lover.

The baron was no less busied in preparations. He had, in truth, nothing exactly to do, but he was naturally a fuming bustling little man, and could not remain passive when all the world was in a hurry. He worried from top to bottom of the castle with an air of infinite anxiety; he continually called the servants from their work to exhort them to be diligent; and buzzed about every hall and chamber, as idly restless and importunate as a bluebottle fly on a warm summer's day.

In the meantime the fatted calf had been killed; the forests had rung with the clamour of the huntsmen; the kitchen was crowded with good cheer; the cellars had yielded up whole oceans of *Rhein-wein* and *Ferne-wein;* and even the great Heidelberg tun had been laid under contribution. Everything was ready to receive the distinguished guest with *Saus und Braus* in the true spirit of German hospitality—but the guest delayed to make his appearance. Hour rolled after hour. The sun that had poured his downward rays upon the rich forest of the Odenwald now just gleamed along the summits of the mountains. The baron mounted the highest tower, and strained his eyes in hope of catching a distant sight of the count and his attendants. Once he thought he beheld them; the sound of horns came floating from the valley, prolonged by the mountain echoes. A number of horsemen were seen far below, slowly advancing along the road; but when they had nearly reached the foot of the mountain they suddenly struck off in a different direction. The last ray of sunshine departed—the bats began to flit by in the twilight—the road grew dimmer and dimmer to the view; and nothing appeared stirring in it but now and then a peasant lagging homeward from his labour.

While the old castle of Landshort was in this state of perplexity a very interesting scene was transacting in a different part of the Odenwald.

The young Count Von Altenburg was tranquilly pursuing his route in that sober jog-trot way, in which a man travels toward matrimony when his friends have taken all the trouble and uncertainty of courtship off his hands, and a bride is waiting for him as certainly as a dinner at the end of his journey. He had encountered at Würzburg a youthful companion in arms with whom he had seen some service on the frontiers, Herman Von Starkenfaust, one of the stoutest hands and worthiest hearts of German chivalry, who was now returning from the army. His father's castle was not far distant from the old fortress of Landshort, although an hereditary feud rendered the families hostile and strangers to each other.

In the warmhearted moment of recognition the young friends related all their past adventures and fortunes, and the count gave the whole history of his intended nuptials with a young lady whom he had never seen but of whose charms he had received the most enrapturing descriptions.

As the route of the friends lay in the same direction, they agreed to perform the rest of their journey together; and, that they might do it the more leisurely, set off from Würzburg at an early hour, the count having given directions for his retinue to follow and overtake him.

They beguiled their wayfaring with recollections of their military scenes and adventures; but the count was apt to be a little tedious, now and then, about the reputed charms of his bride, and the felicity that awaited him.

In this way they had entered among the mountains of the Odenwald, and were traversing one of its most lonely and thickly wooded passes. It is well known that the forests of Germany have always been as much infested by robbers as its castles by spectres; and at this time the former were particularly numerous, from the hordes of disbanded soldiers wandering about the country. It will not appear extraordinary, therefore, that the cavaliers were attacked by a gang of these stragglers in the midst of the forest. They defended themselves with bravery, but were nearly overpowered, when the count's retinue arrived to their assistance. At sight of them the robbers fled, but not until the count had received a mortal wound. He was slowly and carefully conveyed back to the city of Würzburg, and a friar summoned from a neighbouring convent, who was famous for his skill in administering to both soul and body; but half of his skill was superfluous; the moments of the unfortunate count were numbered.

With his dying breath he entreated his friend to repair instantly to the castle of Landshort and explain the fatal cause of his not keeping his appointment with his bride. Though not the most ardent of lovers, he was one of the most punctilious of men, and appeared earnestly solicitous that his mission should be speedily and courteously executed. "Unless this is done," said he, "I shall not sleep quietly in my grave!" He repeated these last words with peculiar solemnity. A request, at a moment so impressive, admitted no hesitation. Starkenfaust endeavoured to soothe him to calmness, promised faithfully to execute his wish, and gave him his hand in solemn pledge. The dying man pressed it in acknowledgement, but soon lapsed into delirium—raved about his bride—his engagements—his plighted word; ordered his horse that he might ride to the castle of Landshort; and expired in the fancied act of vaulting into the saddle.

Starkenfaust bestowed a sigh and a soldier's tear on the untimely fate of his comrade, and then pondered on the awkward mission he had undertaken. His heart was heavy and his head perplexed, for he was to present himself an unbidden guest among hostile people, and to damp their festivity with tidings fatal to their hopes. Still there were certain whisperings of curiosity in his bosom to see this far-famed beauty of Katzenellenbogen, so cautiously shut up from the world, for he was a passionate admirer of the sex, and there was a dash of eccentricity and enterprise in his character that made him fond of all singular adventure.

Previous to his departure he made all due arrangements with the holy fraternity of the convent for the funeral solemnities of his friend, who was to be buried in the cathedral of Würzburg, near some of his illustrious relatives; and the mourning retinue of the count took charge of his remains.

It is now high time that we should return to the ancient family of Katzenellenbogen, who were impatient for their guest, and still more for their dinner; and to the worthy little baron, whom we left airing himself on the watchtower.

Night closed in, but still no guest arrived. The baron descended from the tower in despair. The banquet, which had been delayed from hour to hour, could no longer be postponed. The meats were already overdone; the cook in an agony; and the whole household had the look of a garrison that had been reduced by famine. The baron was obliged reluctantly to give orders for the feast without the presence of the guest. All were seated at table, and just on the point of commencing when the sound of a horn from without the gate gave notice of the approach of a stranger. Another long blast filled the old courts of the castle with its echoes, and was answered by the warder from the walls. The baron hastened to receive his future son-in-law.

The drawbridge had been let down, and the stranger was before the gate. He was a tall, gallant cavalier, mounted on a black steed. His countenance was pale, but he had a beaming, romantic eye, and an air of stately melancholy. The baron was a little mortified that he should have come in this simple, solitary style. His dignity for a moment was ruffled, and he felt disposed to consider it a want of proper respect for the important occasion and the important family with which he was to be connected. He pacified himself, however, with the conclusion that it must have been youthful impatience which had induced him thus to spur on sooner than his attendants.

"I am sorry," said the stranger, "to break in upon you thus unseasonably—"

Here the baron interrupted him with a world of compliments and greetings, for, to tell the truth, he prided himself upon his courtesy and eloquence. The stranger attempted, once or twice, to stem the torrent of words, but in vain, so he bowed his head and suffered it to flow on. By the time the baron had come to a pause, they had reached the inner court of the castle, and the stranger was again about to speak when he was once more interrupted by the appearance of the female part of the family, leading forth the shrinking and blushing bride. He gazed on her for a moment as one entranced; it seemed as if his whole soul beamed forth in the gaze, and rested upon that lovely form. One of the maiden aunts whispered something in her ear; she made an effort to speak; her moist blue eye was timidly raised, gave a shy glance of inquiry on the stranger, and was cast again to the ground. The words died away, but there was a sweet smile playing about her lips and a soft dimpling of the cheek that showed her glance had not been unsatisfactory. It was impossible for a girl of the fond age of eighteen, highly predisposed for love and matrimony, not to be pleased with so gallant a cavalier.

The late hour at which the guest had arrived left no time for parley. The baron was peremptory, and deferred all particular conversation until the morning, and led the way to the untasted banquet.

It was served up in the great hall of the castle. Around the walls hung the hard-favoured portraits of the heroes of the house of Katzenellenbogen and the trophies which they had gained in the field and the chase. Hacked corslets, splintered jousting spears, and tattered banners were mingled with the spoils of sylvan warfare; the jaws of the wolf and the tusks of the boar grinned horribly among cross-bows and battle-axes, and a huge pair of antlers branched immediately over the head of the youthful bridegroom.

The cavalier took but little notice of the company or the entertainment. He scarcely tasted the banquet, but seemed absorbed in admiration of his bride. He conversed in a low tone that could not be overheard—for the language of love is never loud; but where is the female ear so dull that it cannot catch the softest whisper of the lover? There was a mingled tenderness and gravity in his manner that appeared to have a powerful effect upon the young lady. Her colour came and went as she listened with deep attention. Now and then she made some blushing reply, and when his eye was turned away, she would steal a sidelong glance at his romantic countenance and heave a gentle sigh of tender happiness. It was evident that the young couple were completely enamoured. The aunts, who were deeply versed in the mysteries of the heart, declared that they had fallen in love with each other at first sight.

The feast went on merrily, or at least noisily, for the guests were all blessed with those keen appetites that attend upon light purses and mountain air. The baron told his best and longest stories, and never had he told them so well or with such great effect. If there was anything marvellous, his auditors were lost in astonishment; and if anything facetious, they were sure to laugh exactly in the right place. The baron, it is true, like most great men, was too dignified to utter any joke but a dull one; it was always enforced, however, by a bumper of excellent Hockheimer, and even a dull joke, at one's own table, served up with jolly old wine, is irresistible. Many good things were said by poorer and keener wits that would not bear repeating, except on similar occasions; many sly speeches whispered in ladies' ears that almost convulsed them with suppressed laughter; and a song or two roared out by a poor but merry and broad-faced cousin of the baron that absolutely made the maiden aunts hold up their fans.

Amidst all this revelry, the stranger guest maintained a most singular and unseasonable gravity. His countenance assumed a deeper cast of dejection as the evening advanced; and, strange as it may appear, even the baron's jokes seemed only to render him the more melancholy. At times he was lost in thought, and at times there was a perturbed and restless wandering of the eye that bespoke a mind but ill at ease. His conversations with the bride became more and more earnest and mysterious. Lowering clouds began to steal over the fair serenity of her brow, and tremors to run through her tender frame.

All this could not escape the notice of the company. Their gaiety was chilled by the unaccountable gloom of the bridegroom; their spirits were infected; whispers and glances were interchanged, accompanied by shrugs and dubious shakes of the head. The song and the laugh grew less and less frequent; there were dreary pauses in the conversation, which were at length succeeded by wild tales and supernatural legends. One dismal story produced another still more dismal, and the baron nearly frightened some of the ladies into hysterics with the history of the goblin horseman that carried away the fair Leonora; a dreadful story, which has since been put into excellent verse, and is read and believed by all the world.

The bridegroom listened to this tale with profound attention. He kept his eyes steadily fixed on the baron, and, as the story drew to a close, began gradually to rise from his seat, growing taller and taller, until, in the baron's entranced eye, he seemed almost to tower into a giant. The moment the tale was finished, he heaved a deep sigh, and took a solemn farewell of the company. They were all amazement. The baron was perfectly thunderstruck.

"What! Going to leave the castle at midnight? Why, everything was prepared for his reception; a chamber was ready for him if he wished to retire."

The stranger shook his head mournfully and mysteriously. "I must lay my head in a different chamber tonight!"

There was something in this reply and the tone in which it was uttered that made the baron's heart misgive him, but he rallied his forces and repeated his hospitable entreaties.

The stranger shook his head silently, but positively, at every offer; and, waving his farewell to the company, stalked slowly out of the hall. The maiden aunts were absolutely petrified—the bride hung her head, and a tear stole to her eye.

The baron followed the stranger to the great court of the castle, where the black charger stood pawing the earth, and snorting with impatience. When they had reached the portal, whose deep archway was dimly lighted by a cresset, the stranger paused, and addressed the baron in a hollow tone of voice, which the vaulted roof rendered still more sepulchral.

"Now that we are alone," said he, "I will impart to you the reason of my going. I have a solemn, an indispensable engagement—"

"Why," said the baron, "cannot you send someone in your place?"

"It admits of no substitute—I must attend it in person—I must away to Würzburg cathedral—"

"Ay," said the baron, plucking up spirit, "but not until tomorrow—tomorrow you shall take your bride there."

"No! no!" replied the stranger, with tenfold solemnity, "my engagement is with no bride—the worms! The worms expect me! I am a dead man—I have been slain by robbers—my body lies at Würzburg—at midnight I am to be buried—the grave is waiting for me—I must keep my appointment!"

He sprang on his black charger, dashed over the drawbridge, and the clattering of his horse's hoofs was lost in the whistling of the night blast.

The baron returned to the hall in the utmost consternation and related what had passed. Two ladies fainted outright, others sickened at the idea of having banqueted with a spectre. It was the opinion of some that this might be the wild huntsman, famous in German legend. Some talked of mountain sprites, of wood demons, and of other supernatural beings, with which the good people of Germany have been so grievously harassed since time immemorial. One of the poor relations ventured to suggest that it might be some sportive evasion of the young cavalier, and that the very gloominess of the caprice seemed to accord with so melancholy a personage. This, however, drew on him the indignation of the whole company, and especially of the baron, who looked upon him as little better than an infidel, so that he was fain to abjure his heresy as speedily as possible and come into the faith of the true believers.

But whatever may have been the doubts entertained, they were completely put to an end by the arrival, next day, of regular missives, confirming the intelligence of the young count's murder, and his interment in Würzburg cathedral.

The dismay at the castle may well be imagined. The baron shut himself up in his chamber. The guests, who had come to rejoice with him, could not think of abandoning him in his distress. They wandered about the courts, or collected in groups in the hall, shaking their heads and shrugging their shoulders at the troubles of so good a man; and sat longer than ever at table, and ate and drank more stoutly than ever, by way of keeping up their spirits. But the situation of the widowed bride was the most pitiable. To have lost a husband before she had even embraced him—and such a husband! If the very spectre could be so gracious and noble, what must have been the living man? She filled the house with lamentations.

On the night of the second day of her widowhood, she had retired to her chamber, accompanied by one of her aunts, who insisted on sleeping with her. The aunt, who was one of the best tellers of ghost stories in all Germany, had just been recounting one of her longest, and had fallen asleep in the very midst of it. The chamber was remote, and overlooked a small garden. The niece lay pensively gazing at the beams of the rising moon, as they trembled on the leaves of an aspen tree before the lattice. The castle clock had just tolled midnight when a soft strain of music stole up from the garden. She rose hastily from her bed, and stepped lightly to the window. A tall figure stood among the shadows of the trees. As it raised its head, a beam of moonlight fell upon the countenance. Heaven and earth! She beheld ! A loud shriek at that moment burst upon her ear, and her aunt, who had been awakened by the music and had followed her silently to the window, fell into her arms. When she looked again, the spectre had disappeared.

Of the two females, the aunt now required the more soothing, for she was perfectly beside herself with terror. As to the young lady, there was something, even in the spectre of her lover, that seemed endearing. There was still the semblance of manly beauty; and though the shadow of a man is but little calculated to satisfy the affections of a lovesick girl, yet, where the substance is not to be had, even that is consoling. The aunt declared she would never sleep in that chamber again; the niece, for once, was refractory, and declared as strongly that she would sleep in no other in the castle. The consequence was that she had to sleep in it alone; but she drew a promise from her aunt not to relate the story of the spectre, lest she should be denied the only melancholy pleasure left her on earth—that of inhabiting the chamber over which the guardian shade of her lover kept its nightly vigils.

How long the good old lady would have observed this promise is uncertain, for she dearly loved to talk of the marvellous, and there is a triumph in being the first to tell a frightful story; it is, however, still quoted in the neighbourhood, as a memorable instance of female secrecy, that she kept it to herself for a whole week, when she was suddenly absolved from all further restraint by intelligence brought to the breakfast table one morning that the young lady was not to be found. Her room was empty—the bed had not been slept in—the window was open, and the bird had flown!

The astonishment and concern with which the intelligence was received can only be imagined by those who have witnessed the agitation which the mishaps of a great man cause among his friends. Even the poor relations paused for a moment from the indefatigable labours of the trencher, when the aunt, who had at first been struck speechless, wrung her hands, and shrieked out, "The goblin! The goblin! She's carried away by the goblin."

In a few words she related the fearful scene of the garden, and concluded that the spectre must have carried off his bride. Two of the domestics corroborated the opinion, for they had heard the clattering of a horse's hoofs down the mountain about midnight, and had no doubt that it was the spectre on his black charger, bearing her away to the tomb. All present were struck with the direful probability, for events of the kind are extremely common in Germany, as many well-authenticated histories bear witness.

What a lamentable situation was that of the poor baron! What a heart-rending dilemma for a fond father, and a member of the great family of Katzenellenbogen! His only daughter had either been rapt away to the grave, or he was to have some wood demon for a son-in-law, and, perchance, a troop of goblin grand-children. As usual, he was completely bewildered, and all the castle in an uproar. The men were ordered to take horse and scour every road and path and glen of the Odenwald. The baron himself had just drawn on his jackboots, girded on his sword, and was about to mount his steed to sally forth on the doubtful quest when he was brought to a pause by a new apparition. A lady was seen approaching the castle, mounted on a palfrey, attended by a cavalier on horseback. She galloped up to the gate, sprang from her horse, and, falling at the baron's feet, embraced his knees. It was his lost daughter and her companion—! The baron was astounded. He looked at his daughter, then at the spectre, and almost doubted the evidence of his senses. The latter, too, was wonderfully improved in his appearance since his visit to the world of spirits. His dress was splendid, and set off a noble figure of manly symmetry. He was no longer pale and melancholy. His fine countenance was flushed with the glow of youth, and joy rioted in his large dark eye.

The mystery was soon deared up. The cavalier (for, in truth, as you must have known all the while, he was no goblin) announced himself as Sir Herman Von Starkenfaust. He related his adventure with the young count. He told how he had hastened to the castle to deliver the unwelcome tidings, but that the eloquence of the baron had interrupted him in every attempt to tell his tale. How the sight of the bride had completely captivated him, and that to pass a few hours near her he had tacitly suffered the mistake to continue. How he had been sorely perplexed in what way to make a decent retreat, until the baron's goblin stories had suggested his eccentric exit. How, fearing the feudal hostility of the family, he had repeated his visits by stealth—had haunted the garden beneath the young lady's window—had wooed—had won—had borne away in triumph—and, in a word, had wedded the fair.

Under any other circumstances the baron would have been inflexible, for he was tenacious of paternal authority and devoutly obstinate in all family feuds; but he loved his daughter; he had lamented her as lost; he rejoiced to find her still alive; and, though her husband was of a hostile house, yet, thank Heaven, he was not a goblin. There was something, it must be acknowledged, that did not exactly accord with his notions of strict veracity, in the joke the knight had passed upon him of his being a dead man; but several old friends present, who had served in the wars, assured him that every stratagem was excusable in love, and that the cavalier was entitled to especial privilege, having lately served as a trooper.

Matters, therefore, were happily arranged. The baron pardoned the young couple on the spot. The revels at the castle were resumed. The poor relations overwhelmed this new member of the family with loving kindness; he was so gallant, so generous—and so rich. The aunts, it is true, were somewhat scandalized that their system of strict seclusion and passive obedience should be so badly exemplified, but attributed it all to their negligence in not having the windows grated.

One of them was particularly mortified at having her marvellous story marred, and that the only spectre she had ever seen should turn out a counterfeit; but the niece seemed perfectly happy at having found him substantial flesh and blood—and so the story ends.

MOUNTJOY

OR SOME PASSAGES OUT OF THE LIFE OF A CASTLE-BUILDER

I was born among romantic scenery, in one of the wildest parts of the Hudson, which at that time was not so thickly settled as at present. My father was descended from one of the old Huguenot families, that came over to this country on the revocation of the edict of Nantes. He lived in a style of easy, rural independence, on a patrimonial estate that had been for two or three generations in the family. He was an indolent, good-natured man, who took the world as it went, and had a kind of laughing philosophy, that parried all rubs and mishaps, and served him in the place of wisdom. This was the part of his character least to my taste; for I was of an enthusiastic, excitable temperament, prone to kindle up with new schemes and projects, and he was apt to dash my sallying enthusiasm by some unlucky joke; so that whenever I was in a glow with any sudden excitement, I stood in mortal dread of his good-humour.

Yet he indulged me in every vagary; for I was an only son, and of course a personage of importance in the household. I had two sisters older than myself, and one younger. The former were educated at New York, under the eye of a maiden aunt; the latter remained at home, and was my cherished playmate, the companion of my thoughts. We were two imaginative little beings, of quick susceptibility, and prone to see wonders and mysteries in everything around us. Scarce had we learned to read, when our mother made us holiday presents of all the nursery literature of the day; which at that time consisted of little books covered with gilt paper, adorned with "cuts", and filled with tales of fairies, giants, and enchanters. What draughts of delightful fiction did we then inhale! My sister Sophy was of a soft and tender nature. She would weep over the woes of the Children in the Wood, or quake at the dark romance of Blue-Beard, and the terrible mysteries of the blue chamber. But I was all for enterprise and adventure. I burned to emulate the deeds of that heroic prince who delivered the white cat from her enchantment; or he of no less royal blood, and doughty emprise, who broke the charmed slumber of the Beauty in the Wood!

The house in which we lived was just the kind of place to foster such propensities. It was a venerable mansion, half villa, half farmhouse. The oldest part was of stone, with loop-holes for musketry, having served as a family fortress in the time of the Indians. To this there had been made various additions, some of brick, some of wood, according to the exigencies of the moment; so that it was full of nooks and crooks, and chambers of all sorts and sizes. It was buried among willows, elms, and cherry trees, and surrounded with roses and hollyhocks with honeysuckle and sweet-briar clambering about every window. A brood of hereditary pigeons sunned themselves upon the roof; hereditary swallows and martins built about the eaves and chimneys; and hereditary bees hummed about the flower-beds.

Under the influence of our story-books every object around us now assumed a new character, and a charmed interest. The wild flowers were no longer the mere ornaments of the fields, or the resorts of the toilful bee; they were the lurking places of fairies. We would watch the humming-bird, as it hovered around the trumpet creeper at our porch, and the butterfly as it flitted up into the blue air, above the sunny tree tops, and fancy them some of the tiny beings from fairyland. I would call to mind all that I had read of Robin Goodfellow and his power of transformation. Oh, how I envied him that power! How I longed to be able to compress my form into utter littleness; to ride the bold dragon-fly; swing on the tall bearded grass; follow the ant into his subterraneous habitation, or dive into the cavernous depths of the honeysuckle!

While I was yet a mere child I was sent to a daily school, about two miles distant. The schoolhouse was on the edge of wood, close by a brook overhung with birches, alders, and dwarf willows. We of the school who lived at some distance came with our dinners put up in little baskets. In the intervals of school hours we would gather round a spring, under a tuft of hazel-bushes, and have a kind of picnic; interchanging the rustic dainties with which our provident mothers had fitted us out. Then when our joyous repast was over, and my companions were disposed for play, I would draw forth one of my cherished story-books, stretch myself on the greensward, and soon lose myself in its bewitching contents.

I became an oracle among my schoolmates on account of my superior erudition, and soon imparted to them the contagion of my infected fancy. Often in the evening, after school hours, we would sit on the trunk of some fallen tree in the woods, and vie with each other in telling extravagant stories, until the whip-poor will began his nightly moaning, and the fire-flies sparkled in the gloom. Then came the perilous journey homeward. What delight we would take in getting up wanton panics in some dusky part of the wood; scampering like frightened deer; pausing to take breath; renewing the panic, and scampering off again, wild with fictitious terror!

Our greatest trial was to pass a dark, lonely pool, covered with pond-lilies, peopled with bull-frogs and water snakes, and haunted by two white cranes. Oh! the terrors of that pond! How our little hearts would beat as we approached it; what fearful glances we would throw around! And if by chance a plash of a wild duck, or the guttural twang of a bull-frog, struck our ears, as we stole quietly by—away we sped, nor paused until completely out of the woods. Then, when I reached home, what a world of adventures and imaginary terrors would I have to relate to my sister Sophy!

As I advanced in years, this turn of mind increased upon me, and became more confirmed. I abandoned myself to the impulses of a romantic imagination, which controlled my studies, and gave a bias to all my habits. My father observed me continually with a book in my hand, and satisfied himself that I was a profound student; but what were my studies? Works of fiction; tales of chivalry; voyages of discovery; travels in the East; everything, in short, that partook of adventure and romance. I well remember with what zest I entered upon that part of my studies which treated of the heathen mythology, and particularly of the sylvan deities. Then indeed my school books became dear to me. The neighbourhood was well calculated to foster the reveries of a mind like mine. It abounded with solitary retreats, wild streams, solemn forests, and silent valleys. I would ramble about for a whole day with a volume of Ovid's *Metamorphoses* in my pocket, and work myself into a kind of self-delusion, so as to identify the surrounding scenes with those of which I had just been reading. I would loiter about a brook that glided through the shadowy depths of the forest, picturing it to myself the haunt of Naiads. I would steal round some bushy copse that opened upon a glade, as if I expected to come suddenly upon Diana and her nymphs, or to behold Pan and his satyrs bounding, with whoop and halloo, through the woodland. I would throw myself, during the panting heats of a summer noon, under the shade of some wide-spreading tree, and muse and dream away the hours, in a state of mental intoxication. I drank in the very light of day, as nectar, and my soul seemed to bathe with ecstasy in the deep blue of a summer sky.

In these wanderings, nothing occurred to jar my feelings, or bring me back to the realities of life. There is a repose in our mighty forests that gives full scope to the imagination. Now and then I would hear the distant sound of the wood-cutter's axe, or the crash of some tree which he had laid low; but these noises, echoing along the quiet landscape, could easily be wrought by fancy into harmony with its illusions. In general, however, the woody recesses of the neighbourhood were peculiarly wild and unfrequented. I could ramble for a whole day, without coming upon any traces of cultivation. The partridge of the wood scarcely seemed to shun my path, and the squirrel, from his nut-tree, would gaze at me for an instant, with sparkling eye, as if wondering at the unwonted intrusion.

I cannot help dwelling on this delicious period of my life; when as yet I had known no sorrow, nor experienced any worldly care. I have since studied much, both of books and men, and of course have grown too wise to be so easily pleased; yet with all my wisdom, I must confess I look back with a secret feeling of regret to the days of happy ignorance, before I had begun to be a philosopher.

It must be evident that I was in a hopeful training for one who was to descend into the arena of life, and wrestle with the world. The tutor, also, who superintended my studies in the more advanced stage of my education was just fitted to complete the *fata morgana* which was forming in my mind. His name was Glencoe. He was a pale, melancholy-looking man, about forty years of age; a native of Scotland, liberally educated, and who had devoted himself to the instruction of youth from taste rather than necessity; for, as he said, he loved the human heart, and delighted to study it in its earlier impulses. My two elder sisters, having returned home from a city boarding-school, were likewise placed under his care, to direct their reading in history and belles-lettres.

We all soon became attached to Glencoe. It is true, we were at first somewhat prepossessed against him. His meagre, pallid countenance, his broad pronunciation, his inattention to the little forms of society, and an awkward and embarrassed manner, on first acquaintance, were much against him; but we soon discovered that under this unpromising exterior existed the kindest urbanity of temper; the warmest sympathies; the most enthusiastic benevolence. His mind was ingenious and acute. His reading had been various, but more abstruse than profound; his memory was stored, on all subjects, with facts, theories, and quotations, and crowded with crude materials for thinking. These, in a moment of excitement, would be, as it were, melted down, and poured forth in the lava of a heated imagination. At such moments, the change in the whole man was wonderful. His meagre form would acquire a dignity and grace; his long, pale visage would flash with a hectic glow; his eyes would beam with intense speculation; and there would be pathetic tones and deep modulations in his voice, that delighted the ear, and spoke movingly to the heart.

But what most endeared him to us was the kindness and sympathy with which he entered into all our interests and wishes. Instead of curbing and checking our young imaginations with the reins of sober reason, he was a little too apt to catch the impulse and be hurried away with us. He could not withstand the excitement of any sally of feeling or fancy, and was prone to lend heightening tints to the illusive colouring of youthful anticipations.

Under his guidance my sisters and myself soon entered upon a more extended range of studies; but while they wandered, with delighted minds, through the wide field of history and belles-lettres, a nobler walk was opened to my superior intellect.

The mind of Glencoe presented a singular mixture of philosophy and poetry. He was fond of metaphysics and prone to indulge in abstract speculations, though his metaphysics were somewhat fine spun and fanciful, and his speculations were apt to partake of what my father most irreverently termed "humbug". For my part, I delighted in them, and the more especially because they set my father to sleep and completely confounded my sisters. I entered with my accustomed eagerness into this new branch of study. Metaphysics were now my passion. My sisters attempted to accompany me, but they soon faltered, and gave out before they had got halfway through Smith's *Theory of the Moral Sentiments*. I, however, went on, exulting in my strength. Glencoe supplied me with books, and I devoured them with appetite, if not digestion. We walked and talked together under the trees before the house, or sat apart, like Milton's angels, and held high converse upon themes beyond the grasp of ordinary intellects. Glencoe possessed a kind of philosophic chivalry, in imitation of the old peripatetic sages, and was continually dreaming of romantic enterprises in morals, and splendid systems for the improvement of society. He had a fanciful mode of illustrating abstract subjects, peculiarly to my taste; clothing them with the language of poetry, and throwing round them almost the magic hues of fiction. "How charming," thought I, "is divine philosophy"; not harsh and crabbed, as dull fools suppose,

But a perpetual feast of nectar'd sweets,
Where no crude surfeit reigns.

I felt a wonderful self-complacency at being on such excellent terms with a man whom I considered on a parallel with sages of antiquity, and looked down with a sentiment of pity on the feebler intellects of my sisters, who could comprehend nothing of metaphysics. It is true, when I attempted to study them by myself, I was apt to get in a fog; but when Glencoe came to my aid, everything was soon as clear to me as day. My ear drank in the beauty of his words; my imagination was dazzled with the splendour of his illustrations. It caught up the sparkling sands of poetry that glittered through his speculations, and mistook them for the golden ore of wisdom. Struck with the facility with which I seemed to imbibe and relish the most abstract doctrines, I conceived a still higher opinion of my mental powers, and was convinced that I also was a philosopher.

I was now verging toward man's estate, and though my education had been extremely irregular—following the caprices of my humour, which I mistook for the impulses of my genius—yet I was regarded with wonder and delight by my mother and sisters, who considered me almost as wise and infallible as I consider myself. This high opinion of me was strengthened by a declamatory habit, which made me an oracle and orator at the domestic board. The time was now at hand, however, that was to put my philosophy to the test.

We had passed through a long winter, and the spring at length opened upon us with unusual sweetness. The soft serenity of the weather; the beauty of the surrounding country; the joyous notes of the birds; the balmy breath of flower and blossom, all combined to fill my bosom with indistinct sensations, and nameless wishes. Amid the soft seductions of the season, I lapsed into a state of utter indolence, both of body and mind.

Philosophy had lost its charms for me. Metaphysics—faugh! I tried to study; took down volume after volume, ran my eye vacantly over a few pages, and threw them by with distaste. I loitered about the house, with my hands in my pockets, and an air of complete vacancy. Something was necessary to make me happy; but what was that something? I sauntered to the apartments of my sisters, hoping their conversation might amuse me. They had walked out, and the room was vacant. On the table lay a volume which they had been reading. It was a novel. I had never read a novel, having conceived a contempt for works of the kind, from hearing them universally condemned. It is true, I had remarked they were universally read; but I considered them beneath the attention of a philosopher, and never would venture to read them, lest I should lessen my mental superiority in the eyes of my sisters. Nay, I had taken up a work of the kind now and then, when I knew my sisters were observing me, looked into it for a moment, and then laid it down, with a slight supercilious smile. On the present occasion, out of mere listlessness, I took up the volume and turned over a few of the first pages. I thought I heard someone coming, and laid it down. I was mistaken; no one was near, and what I had read tempted my curiosity to read a little further. I leaned against a window-frame, and in a few minutes was completely lost in the story. How long I stood there reading I know not, but I believe for nearly two hours. Suddenly I heard my sisters on the stairs, when I thrust the book into my bosom, and the two other volumes which lay near into my pockets, and hurried out of the house to my beloved woods. Here I remained all day beneath the trees, bewildered, bewitched, devouring the contents of these delicious volumes, and only returned to the house when it was too dark to peruse their pages.

This novel finished, I replaced it in my sisters' apartment, and looked for others. Their stock was ample, for they had brought home all that were current in the city; but my appetite demanded an immense supply. All this course of reading was carried on clandestinely, for I was a little ashamed of it, and fearful that my wisdom might be called in question; but this very privacy gave it additional zest. It was "bread eaten in secret"; it had the charm of a private amour.

But think what must have been the effect of such a course of reading on a youth of my temperament and turn of mind; indulged, too, amid romantic scenery and in the romantic season of the year. It seemed as if I had entered upon a new scene of existence. A train of combustible feelings were lighted up in me, and my soul was all tenderness and passion. Never was youth more completely love-sick, though as yet it was a mere general sentiment, and wanted a definite object. Unfortunately, our neighbourhood was particularly deficient in female society, and I languished in vain for some divinity to whom I might offer up this most uneasy burden of affections. I was at one time seriously enamoured of a lady whom I saw occasionally in my rides, reading at the window of a country-seat; and actually serenaded her with my flute; when, to my confusion, I discovered that she was old enough to be my mother. It was a sad damper to my romance; especially as my father heard of it, and made it the subject of one of those household jokes which he was apt to serve up at every meal-time.

I soon recovered from this check, however, but it was only to relapse into a state of amorous excitement. I passed whole days in the fields, and along the brooks; for there is something in the tender passion that makes us alive to the beauties of nature. A soft sunshiny morning infused a sort of rapture into my breast. The song of the birds melted me to tenderness. I would lie by the side of some rivulet for hours, and form garlands of the flowers on its banks, and muse on ideal beauties, and sigh from the crowd of undefined emotions that swelled my bosom.

In this state of amorous delirium, I was strolling one morning along a beautiful wild brook, which I had discovered in a glen. There was one place where a small waterfall, leaping from among rocks into a natural basin, made a scene such as a poet might have chosen as the haunt of some shy Naiad. It was here I usually retired to banquet on my novels. In visiting the place this morning I traced distinctly, on the margin of the basin, which was of fine clear sand, the prints of a female foot of the most slender and delicate proportions. This was sufficient for an imagination like mine. Robinson Crusoe himself, when he discovered the print of a savage foot on the beach of his lonely island, could not have been more suddenly assailed with thick-coming fancies.

I endeavoured to track the steps, but they only passed for a few paces along the fine sand, and then were lost among the herbage. I remained gazing in reverie upon this passing trace of loveliness. It evidently was not made by any of my sisters, for they knew nothing of this haunt; beside, the foot was smaller than theirs; it was remarkable for its beautiful delicacy.

My eye accidentally caught two or three half-withered wild flowers lying on the ground. The unknown nymph had doubtless dropped them from her bosom! Here was a new document of taste and sentiment. I treasured them up as invaluable relics. The place, too, where I found them, was remarkably picturesque, and the most beautiful part of the brook. It was overhung with a fine elm, intwined with grapevines. She who could select such a spot, who could delight in wild brooks, and wild flowers, and silent solitudes, must have fancy, and feeling,and tenderness; and with all these qualities, she must be beautiful!

But who could be this Unknown that had thus passed by, as in a morning dream, leaving merely flowers and fairy footsteps to tell of her loveliness? There was a mystery in it that bewildered me. It was so vague and disembodied, like those "airy tongues that syllable men's names" in solitude. Every attempt to solve the mystery was vain. I could hear of no being in the neighbourhood to whom this trace could be ascribed. I haunted the spot, and became daily more and more enamoured. Never, surely, was passion more pure and spiritual, and never lover in more dubious situation. My case could be compared only to that of the amorous prince in the fairy tale of Cinderella; but he had a glass slipper on which to lavish his tenderness. I, alas! was in love with a footstep!

The imagination is alternately a cheat and a dupe; nay, more, it is the most subtle of cheats, for it cheats itself and becomes the dupe of its own delusions. It conjures up "airy nothings", gives to them a "local habihtion and a name", and then bows to their control as implicitly as though they were realities. Such was now my case. The good Numa could not more thoroughly have persuaded himself that the nymph Egeria hovered about her sacred fountain and communed with him in spirit, than I had deceived myself into a kind of visionary intercourse with the airy phantom fabricated in my brain. I constructed a rustic seat at the foot of the tree where I had discovered the footsteps. I made a kind of bower there, where I used to pass my mornings reading poetry and romances. I carved hearts and darts on the tree, and hung it with garlands. My heart was full to overflowing, and wanted some faithful bosom into which it might relieve itself. What is a lover without a confidante? I thought at once of my sister Sophy, my early playmate, the sister of my affections. She was so reasonable, too, and of such correct feelings, always listening to my words as oracular sayings, and admiring my scraps of poetry as the very inspirations of the muse. From such a devoted, such a rational being, what secrets could I have?

I accordingly took her one morning to my favourite retreat. She looked around, with delighted surprise, upon the rustic seat, the bower, the tree carved with emblems of the tender passion. She turned her eyes upon me to inquire the meaning.

"Oh, Sophy," exclaimed I, clasping both her hands in mine, and looking earnestly in her face, "I am in love."

She started with surprise.

"Sit down," said I, "and I will tell you all."

She seated herself upon the rustic bench, and I went into a full history of the footstep, with all the associations of idea that had been conjured up by my imagination.

Sophy was enchanted; it was like a fairy tale; she had read of such mysterious visitations in books, and the loves thus conceived were always for beings of superior order, and were always happy. She caught the illusion in all its force; her cheek glowed; her eye brightened.

"I dare say she's pretty," said Sophy.

"Pretty!" echoed I, "she is beautiful!" I went through all the reasoning by which I had logically proved the fact to my own satisfaction. I dwelt upon the evidences of her taste, her sensibility to the beauties of nature;

her soft meditative habit, that delighted in solitude. "Oh," said I, clasping my hands, "to have such a companion to wander through these scenes; to sit with her by this murmuring stream; to wreathe garlands round her brows; to hear the music of her voice mingling with the whisperings of these groves;—"

"Delightful! delightful!" cried Sophy; "what a sweet creature she must be! She is just the friend I want. How I shall dote upon her! Oh, my dear brother! you must not keep her all to yourself. You must let me have some share of her!"

I caught her to my bosom: "You shall—you shall!" cried I, "my dear Sophy; we will all live for each other!"

The conversation with Sophy heightened the illusions of my mind; and the manner in which she had treated my day-dream identified it with facts and persons and gave it still more the stamp of reality. I walked about as one in a trance, heedless of the world around, and lapped in an elysium of the fancy.

In this mood I met one morning with Glencoe. He accosted me with his usual smile, and was proceeding with some general observations, but paused and fixed on me an inquiring eye.

"What is the matter with you?" said he, "you seem agitated; has anything in particular happened?"

"Nothing," said I, hesitating; "at least nothing worth communicating to you."

"Nay, my dear young friend," said he, "whatever is of sufficient importance to agitate you is worthy of being communicated to me."

"Well; but my thoughts are running on what you would think a frivolous subject."

"No subject is frivolous that has the power to awaken strong feelings."

"What think you," said I, hesitating, "what think you of love?"

Glencoe almost started at the question. "Do you call that a frivolous subject?" replied he. "Believe me, there is none fraught with such deep, such vital interest. If you talk, indeed, of the capricious inclination awakened by the mere charm of perishable beauty, I grant it to be idle in the extreme; but that love which springs from the concordant sympathies of virtuous hearts; that love which is awakened by the perception of moral excellence, and fed by meditation on intellectual as well as personal beauty; that is a passion which refines and ennobles the human heart. Oh, where is there a sight more nearly approaching to the intercourse of angels, than that of two young beings, free from the sins and follies of the world, mingling pure thoughts, and looks, and feelings, and becoming as it were soul of one soul and heart of one heart! How exquisite the silent converse that they hold; the soft devotion of the eye, that needs no words to make it eloquent! Yes, my friend, if there be anything in this weary world worthy of heaven, it is the pure bliss of such a mutual affection!"

The words of my worthy tutor overcame all further reserve. "Mr Glencoe," cried I, blushing still deeper, "I am in love."

"And is that what you were ashamed to tell me? Oh, never seek to conceal from your friend so important a secret. If your passion be unworthy, it is for the steady hand of friendship to pluck it forth; if honourable, none but an enemy would seek to stifle it. On nothing does the character and happiness so much depend as on the first affection of the heart. Were you caught by some fleeting and superficial charm—a bright eye, a blooming cheek, a soft voice, or a voluptuous form—I would warn you to beware; I would tell you that beauty is but a passing gleam of the morning, a perishable flower; that accident may becloud and blight it, and that at best it must soon pass away. But were you in love with such a one as I could describe; young in years, but still younger in feelings; lovely in person, but as a type of the mind's beauty; soft in voice, in token of gentleness of spirit; blooming in countenance, like the rosy tints of morning kindling with the promise of a genial day; an eye beaming with the benignity of a happy heart; a cheerful temper, alive to all kind of impulses, and frankly diffusing its own felicity; a self-poised mind, that needs not lean on others for support; an elegant taste, that can embellish solitude, and furnish out its own enjoyments—"

"My dear sir," cried I, for I could contain myself no longer, "you have described the very person!"

"Why, then, my dear young friend," said he, affectionately pressing my hand, "in God's name, love on!"

For the remainder of the day I was in some such state of dreamy beatitude as a Turk is said to enjoy when under the influence of opium. It must be already manifest how prone I was to bewilder myself with picturings of the fancy, so as to confound them with existing realities. In the present instance, Sophy and Glencoe had contributed to promote the transient delusion. Sophy, dear girl, had as usual joined with me in my castle-building, and indulged in the same train of imaginings, while Glencoe, duped by my enthusiasm, firmly believed that I spoke of a being I had seen and known. By their sympathy with my feelings they in a manner became associated with the Unknown in my mind, and thus linked her with the circle of my intimacy.

In the evening, our family party was assembled in the hall, to enjoy the refreshing breeze. Sophy was playing some favourite Scotch airs on the piano, while Glencoe, seated apart, with his forehead resting on his hand, was buried in one of those pensive reveries that made him so interesting to me.

"What a fortunate being I am!" thought I, "blessed with such a sister and such a friend! I have only to find out this amiable Unknown, to wed her, and be happy! What a paradise will be my home, graced with a partner of such exquisite refinement! It will be a perfect fairy bower, buried among sweets and roses. Sophy shall live with us, and be the companion of all our enjoyments. Glencoe, too, shall no more be the solitary being that he now appears. He shall have a home with us. He shall have his study, where, when he pleases, he may shut himself up from the world, and bury himself in his own reflections. His retreat shall be sacred; no one shall intrude there; no one but myself, who will visit him now and then, in his seclusion, where we will devise grand schemes together for the improvement of mankind. How delightfully our days will pass, in a round of rational pleasures and elegant employments! Sometimes we will have music; sometimes we will read; sometimes we will wander through the flower garden, when I will smile with complacency on every flower my wife has planted; while in the long winter evenings the ladies will sit at their work, and listen with hushed attention to Glencoe and myself, as we discuss the abstruse doctrines of metaphysics."

From this delectable reverie, I was startled by my

father's slapping me on the shoulder: "What possesses the lad?" cried he; "here have I been speaking to you half a dozen times, without receiving an answer."

"Pardon me, sir," replied I; "I was so completely lost in thought, that I did not hear you."

"Lost in thought! And pray what were you thinking of? Some of your philosophy, I suppose."

"Upon my word," said my sister Charlotte, with an arch laugh, "I suspect Harry's in love again."

"And if I were in love, Charlotte," said I, somewhat nettled, and recollecting Glencoe's enthusiastic eulogy of the passion, "if I were in love, is that a matter of jest and laughter? Is the tenderest and most fervid affection that can animate the human breast, to be made a matter of cold-hearted ridicule?"

My sister coloured. "Certainly not, brother!—nor did I mean to make it so, nor to say anything that should wound your feelings. Had I really suspected you had formed some genuine attachment, it would have been sacred in my eyes; but—but," said she, smiling, as if at some whimsical recollection, "I thought that you you might be indulging in another little freak of the imagination."

"I'll wager any money," cried my father, "he has fallen in love again with some old lady at a window!"

"Oh no!" cried my dear sister Sophy, with the most gracious warmth; "she is young and beautiful."

"From what I understand," said Glencoe, rousing himself, "she must be lovely in mind as in person."

I found my friends were getting me into a fine scrape. I began to perspire at every pore, and felt my ears tingle.

"Well, but," cried my father, "who is she?—what is she? Let us hear something about her."

This was no time to explain so delicate a matter. I caught up my hat, and vanished out of the house.

The moment I was in the open air, and alone, my heart upbraided me. Was this respectful treatment to my father—to *such* a father, too—who had always regarded me as the pride of his age—the staff of his hopes? It is true, he was apt sometimes to laugh at my enthusiastic flights, and did not treat my philosophy with due respect; but when had he ever thwarted a wish of my heart? Was I then to act with reserve toward him, in a matter which might affect the whole current of my future life? "I have done wrong," thought I; "but it is not too late to remedy it. I will hasten back and open my whole heart to my father!"

I returned accordingly, and was just on the point of entering the house, with my heart full of filial piety, and a contrite speech upon my lips, when I heard a burst of obstreperous laughter from my father, and a loud titter from my two elder sisters.

"A footstep!" shouted he, as soon as he could recover himself, "in love with a footstep! Why, this beats the old lady at the window!" And then there was another appalling burst of laughter. Had it been a clap of thunder, it could hardly have astounded me more completely. Sophy, in the simplicity of her heart, had told all, and had set my father's risible propensities in full action.

Never was poor mortal so thoroughly crestfallen as myself. The whole delusion was at an end. I drew off silently from the house, shrinking smaller and smaller at every fresh peal of laughter; and wandering about until the family had retired, stole quietly to my bed. Scarce any sleep, however, visited my eyes that night! I lay overwhelmed with mortification, and meditating how I might meet the family in the morning. The idea of ridicule was always intolerable to me; but to endure it on a subject by which my feelings had been so much excited, seemed worse than death. I almost determined, at one time, to get up, saddle my horse, and ride off, I knew not whither.

At length I came to a resolution. Before going down to breakfast, I sent for Sophy, and employed her as ambassador to treat formally in the matter. I insisted that the subject should be buried in oblivion; otherwise I would not show my face at table. It was readily agreed to; for not one of the family would have given me pain for the world. They faithfully kept their promise. Not a word was said of the matter; but there were wry faces, and suppressed titters, that went to my soul; and whenever my father looked me in the face, it was with such a tragic-comical leer—such an attempt to pull down a serious brow upon a whimsical mouth—that I had a thousand times rather he had laughed outright.

For a day or two after the mortifying occurrence just related, I kept as much as possible out of the way of the family, and wandered about the fields and woods by myself. I was sadly out of tune; my feelings were all jarred and unstrung. The birds sang from every grove, but I took no pleasure in their melody; and the flowers of the field bloomed unheeded around me. To be crossed in love is bad enough; but then one can fly to poetry for relief, and turn one's woes to account in soul-subduing stanzas. But to have one's whole passion, object and all, annihilated, dispelled, proved to be such stuff as dreams are made of—or, worse than all, to be turned into a proverb and a jest—what consolation is there in such a case?

I avoided the fatal brook where I had seen the footstep. My favourite resort was now the banks of the Hudson, where I sat upon the rocks and mused upon the current that dimpled by, or the waves that laved the shore; or watched the bright mutations of the clouds, and the shifting lights and shadows of the distant mountain. By degrees a returning serenity stole over my feelings; and a sigh now and then, gentle and easy, and unattended by pain, showed that my heart was recovering its susceptibility.

As I was sitting in this musing mood my eye became gradually fixed upon an object that was bome along by the tide. It proved to be a little pinnace, beautifully modelled, and gaily painted and decorated. It was an unusual sight in this neighbourhood, which was rather lonely; indeed, it was rare to see any pleasure-barks in this part of the river. As it drew nearer, I perceived that there was no one on board; it had apparently drifted from its anchorage. There was not a breath of air; the little bark came floating along on the glassy stream, wheeling about with the eddies. At length it ran aground, almost at the foot of the rock on which I was seated. I descended to the margin of the river, and drawing the bark to shore, admired its light and elegant proportions and the taste with which it was fitted up. The benches were covered with cushions, and its long streamer was of silk. On one of the cushions lay a lady's glove, of delicate size and shape, with beautifully tapered fingers. I instantly seized it and thrust it in my bosom; it seemed a match for the fairy footstep that had so fascinated me.

In a moment all the romance of my bosom was again in a glow. Here was one of the very incidents of fairy tale; a bark sent by some invisible power, some good genius, or benevolent fairy, to waft me to some delectable adventure. I recollected something of an enchanted bark, drawn by white swans, that conveyed a knight down the current of the Rhine, on some enterprise connected with love and beauty. The glove, too, showed that there was a lady fair concerned in the present adventure. It might be a gauntlet of defiance, to dare me to the enterprise.

In the spirit of romance and the whim of the moment, I sprang on board, hoisted the light sail, and pushed from shore. As if breathed by some presiding power, a light breeze at that moment sprang up, swelled out the sail, and dallied with the silken streamer. For a time I glided along under steep umbrageous banks, or across deep sequestered bays; and then stood out over a wide expansion of the river toward a high rocky promontory. It was a lovely evening; the sun was setting in a congregation of clouds that threw the whole heavens in a glow, and were reflected in the river. I delighted myself with all kinds of fantastic fancies, as to what enchanted island, or mystic bower, or necromantic palace, I was to be conveyed by the fairy bark.

In the revel of my fancy I had not noticed that the gorgeous congregation of clouds which had so much delighted me was in fact a gathering thunder-gust. I perceived the truth too late. The clouds came hurrying on, darkening as they advanced. The whole face of nature was suddenly changed, and assumed that baleful and livid tint predictive of a storm. I tried to gain the shore, but before I could reach it a blast of wind struck the water and lashed it at once into foam. The next moment it overtook the boat. Alas! I was nothing of a sailor; and my protecting fairy forsook me in the moment of peril. I endeavoured to lower the sail; but in so doing I had to quit the helm; the bark was overturned in an instant, and I was thrown into the water. I endeavoured to cling to the wreck, but missed my hold; being a poor swimmer, I soon found myself sinking, but grasped a light oar that was floating by me. It was not sufficient for my support; I again sank beneath the surface; there was a rushing and bubbling sound in my ears, and all sense forsook me.

How long I remained insensible, I know not. I had a confused notion of being moved and tossed about, and of hearing strange beings and strange voices around me; but all was like a hideous dream. When I at length recovered full consciousness and perception, I found myself in bed in a spacious chamber, furnished with more taste than I had been accustomed to. The bright rays of a morning sun were intercepted by curtains of a delicate rose colour, that gave a soft, voluptuous tinge to every object. Not far from my bed, on a classic tripod, was a basket of beautiful exotic flowers, breathing the sweetest fragrance.

"Where am I? How came I here?"

I tasked my mind to catch at some previous event, from which I might trace up the thread of existence to the present moment. By degrees I called to mind the fairy pinnace, my daring embarkation, my adventurous voyage, and my disastrous shipwreck. Beyond that, all was chaos. How came I here? What unknown region had I landed upon? The people that inhabited it must be gentle and amiable, and of elegant tastes, for they loved downy beds, fragrant flowers, and rose-coloured curtains.

While I lay thus musing, the tones of a harp reached my ear. Presently they were accompanied by a female voice. It came from the room below; but in the profound stillness of my chamber not a modulation was lost. My sisters were all considered good musicians, and sang very tolerably; but I had never heard a voice like this. There was no attempt at difficult execution, or striking effect; but there were exquisite inflections, and tender turns, which art could not reach. Nothing but feeling and sentiment could produce them. It was soul breathed forth in sound. I was always alive to the influence of music; indeed, I was susceptible of voluptuous influences of every kind—sounds, colours, shapes, and fragrant odours. I was the very slave of sensation.

I lay mute and breathless, and drank in every note of this siren strain. It thrilled through my whole frame, and filled my soul with melody and love. I pictured to myself, with curious logic, the form of the unseen musician. Such melodious sounds and exquisite inflections could only be produced by organs of the most delicate flexibility. Such organs do not belong to coarse, vulgar forms; they are the harmonious results of fair proportions and admirable symmetry. A being so organized must be lovely.

Again my busy imagination was at work. I called to mind the Arabian story of a prince, borne away during sleep by a good genius, to the distant abode of a princess of ravishing beauty. I do not pretend to say that I believed in having experienced a similar transportation; but it was my inveterate habit to cheat myself with fancies of the kind, and to give the tinge of illusion to surrounding realities.

The witching sound had ceased, but its vibrations still played round my heart, and filled it with a tumult of soft emotions. At this moment, a self-upbraiding pang shot through my bosom. "Ah, recreant!" a voice seemed to exclaim, "is this the stability of thine affections? What! hast thou so soon forgotten the nymph of the fountain? Has one song, idly piped in thine ear, been sufficient to charm away the cherished tenderness of a whole summer?"

The wise may smile—but I am in a confiding mood, and must confess my weakness. I felt a degree of compunction at this sudden infidelity, yet I could not resist the power of present fascination. My peace of mind was destroyed by conflicting claims. The nymph of the fountain came over my memory, with all the associations of fairy footsteps, shady groves, soft echoes, and wild streamlets; but this new passion was produced by a strain of soul-subduing melody, still lingering in my ear, aided by a downy bed, fragrant flowers, and rose-coloured curtains. "Unhappy youth!" sighed I to myself, "distracted by such rival passions, and the empire of thy heart thus violently contested by the sound of a voice, and the print of a footstep!"

I had not remained long in this mood, when I heard the door of the room gently opened. I turned my head to see what inhabitant of this enchanted palace should appear; whether page in green, hideous dwarf, or haggard fairy. It was my own man Scipio. He advanced with cautious step, and was delighted, as he said, to find me so much myself again. My first questions were as to where I was and how I came there? Scipio told me a long story of his having been fishing in a canoe at the time of my harebrained cruise; of his noticing the gathering squall, and my impending danger; of his hastening to join me, but arriving just in time to snatch me from a watery grave; of the great difficulty in restoring me to animation; and of my being subsequently conveyed, in a state of insensibility, to this mansion.

"But where am I?" was the reiterated demand.

"In the house of Mr Somerville."

"Somerville—Somerville!" I recollected to have heard that a gentleman of that name had recently taken up his residence at some distance from my father's abode, on the opposite side of the Hudson. He was commonly known by the name of "French Somerville", from having passed part of his early life in France, and from his exhibiting traces of French taste in his mode of living, and the arrangements of his house. In fact, it was in his pleasure-boat, which had got adrift, that I had made my fanciful and disastrous cruise. All this was simple, straightforward matter of fact, and threatened to demolish all the cobweb romance I had been spinning, when fortunately I again heard the tinkling of a harp. I raised myself in bed, and listened.

"Scipio," said I, with some little hesitation, "I heard someone singing just now. Who was it?"

"Oh, that was Miss Julia."

"Julia! Julia! Delightful! what a name! And, Scipio—is she—is she pretty?"

Scipio grinned from ear to ear. "Except Miss Sophy, she was the most beautiful young lady he had ever seen."

I should observe, that my sister Sophia was considered by all the servants a paragon of perfection.

Scipio now offered to remove the basket of flowers; he was afraid their odour might be too powerful; but Miss Julia had given them that morning to be placed in my room.

These flowers, then, had been gathered by the fairy

fingers of my unseen beauty; that sweet breath which had filled my ear with melody had passed over them. I made Scipio hand them to me, culled several of the most delicate, and laid them on my bosom.

Mr Somerville paid me a visit not long afterward. He was an interesting study for me, for he was the father of my unseen beauty, and probably resembled her. I scanned him closely. He was a tall and elegant man, with an open, affable manner, and an erect and graceful carriage. His eyes were bluish-grey, and though not dark, yet at times were sparkling and expressive. His hair was dressed and powdered, and being lightly combed up from his forehead, added to the loftiness of his aspect. He was fluent in discourse, but his conversation had the quiet tone of polished society, without any of those bold flights of thought, and picturings of fancy, which I so much admired.

My imagination was a little puzzled, at first, to make out of this assemblage of personal and mental qualities, a picture that should harmonize with my previous idea of the fair unseen. By dint, however, of selecting what it liked, and giving a touch here and a touch there, it soon finished out a satisfactory portrait.

"Julia must be tall," thought I, "and of exquisite grace and dignity. She is not quite so courtly as her father, for she has been brought up in the retirement of the country. Neither is she of such vivacious deportment; for the tones of her voice are soft and plaintive, and she loves pathetic music. She is rather pensive—yet not too pensive; just what is called interesting. Her eyes are like her father's except that they are of a purer blue, and more tender and languishing. She has light hair—not exactly flaxen, for I do not like flaxen hair, but between that and auburn. In a word, she is a tall, elegant, imposing, languishing, blue-eyed, romantic-looking beauty." And having thus finished her picture, I felt ten times more in love with her than ever.

I felt so much recovered that I would at once have left my room, but Mr Somerville objected to it. He had sent early word to my family of my safety; and my father arrived in the course of the morning. He was shocked at learning the risk I had run, but rejoiced to find me so much restored, and was warm in his thanks to Mr Somerville for his kindness. The other only required, in return, that I might remain two or three days as his guest, to give time for my recovery, and for our forming a closer acquaintance; a request which my father readily granted. Scipio accordingly accompanied my father home, and returned with a supply of clothes, and with affectionate letters from my mother and sisters.

The next morning, aided by Scipio, I made my toilet with rather more care than usual, and descended the stairs with some trepidation, eager to see the original of the portrait which had been so completely pictured in my imagination.

On entering the parlour, I found it deserted. Like the rest of the house, it was furnished in a foreign style. The curtains were of French silk; there were Grecian couches, marble tables, pier-glasses, and chandeliers. What chiefly attracted my eye, were documents of female taste that I saw around me; a piano, with an ample stock of Italian music; a book of poetry lying on the sofa; a vase of fresh flowers on a table, and a portfolio open with a skilful and half-finished sketch of them. In the window was a canary bird, in a gilt cage, and near by, the harp that had been in Julia's arms. Happy harp! But where was the being that reigned in this little empire of delicacies?—that breathed poetry and song, and dwelt among birds and flowers, and rose-coloured curtains?

Suddenly I heard the hall door fly open, the quick pattering of light steps, a wild, capricious strain of music, and the shrill barking of a dog. A light, frolic nymph of fifteen came tripping into the room, playing on a flageolet, with a little spaniel romping after her. Her gypsy hat had fallen back upon her shoulders; a profusion of glossy brown hair was blown in rich ringlets about her face, which beamed through them with the brightness of smiles and dimples.

At sight of me she stopped short, in the most beautiful confusion, stammered out a word or two about looking for her father, glided out of the door, and I heard her bounding up the staircase, like a frightened fawn, with the little dog barking after her.

When Miss Somerville returned to the parlour, she was quite a different being. She entered, stealing along by her mother's side with noiseless step, and sweet timidity: her hair was prettily adjusted, and a soft blush mantled on her damask cheek. Mr Somerville accompanied the ladies, and introduced me regularly to them. There were many kind inquiries and much sympathy expressed, on the subject of my nautical accident, and some remarks upon the wild scenery of the neighbourhood, with which the ladies seemed perfectly acquainted.

"You must know," said Mr Somerville, "that we are great navigators, and delight in exploring every nook and corner of the river. My daughter, too, is a great hunter of the picturesque, and transfers every rock and glen to her portfolio. By the way, my dear, show Mr Mountjoy that pretty scene you have lately sketched."

Julia complied blushing, and drew from her portfolio a coloured sketch. I almost started at the sight. It was my favourite brook. A sudden thought darted across my mind. I glanced down my eye, and beheld the divinest little foot in the world. Oh, blissful conviction! The struggle of my affections was at an end. The voice and the footstep were no longer at variance. Julia Somerville was the nymph of the fountain!

What conversation passed during breakfast I do not recollect, and hardly was conscious of at the time, for my thoughts were in complete confusion. I wished to gaze on Miss Somerville, but did not dare. Once, indeed, I ventured a glance. She was at that moment darting a similar one from under a covert of ringlets. Our eyes seemed shocked by the rencontre, and fell; hers through the natural modesty of her sex, mine through a bashfulness produced by the previous workings of my imagination. That glance, however, went like a sunbeam to my heart.

A convenient mirror favoured my diffidence, and gave me the reflection of Miss Somerville's form. It is true it only presented the back of her head, but she had the merit of an ancient statue; contemplate her from any point of view, she was beautiful. And yet she was totally different from everything I had before conceived of beauty. She was not the serene, meditative maid that I had pictured the nymph of the fountain; nor the tall, soft, languishing, blue-eyed, dignified being that I had fancied the minstrel of the harp. There was nothing of dignity about her: she was girlish in her appearance, and scarcely of the middle size; but then there was the tenderness of budding youth; the sweetness of the halfblown rose, when not a tint or perfume has been withered or exhaled; there were smiles and dimples, and all the soft witcheries of ever-varying expression. I wondered that I could ever have admired any other style of beauty.

After breakfast, Mr Somerville departed to attend to the concerns of his estate, and gave me in charge of the ladies. Mrs Somerville also was called away by household cares, and I was left alone with Julia! Here, then, was the situation which of all others I had most coveted. I was in the presence of the lovely being that had so long been the desire of my heart. We were alone; propitious opportunity for a lover! Did I seize upon it? Did I break out in one of my accustomed rhapsodies? No such thing! Never was being more awkwardly embarrassed.

"What can be the cause of this?" thought I. "Surely, I cannot stand in awe of this young girl. I am of course her superior in intellect, and am never embarrassed in company with my tutor, notwithstanding all his wisdom."

It was passing strange. I felt that if she were an old woman, I should be quite at my ease; if she were even an ugly woman, I should make out very well: it was her beauty that overpowered me. How little do lovely women know what awful beings they are, in the eyes of inexperienced youth! Young men brought up in the fashionable circles of our cities will smile at all this. Accustomed to mingle incessantly in female society, and to have the romance of the heart deadened by a thousand frivolous flirtations, women are nothing but women in their eyes; but to a susceptible youth like myself, brought up in the country, they are perfect divinities.

Miss Somerville was at first a little embarrassed

herself; but, somehow or other, women have a natural adroitness in recovering their self-possession; they are more alert in their minds, and graceful in their manners. Beside, I was but an ordinary personage in Miss Somerville's eyes; she was not under the influence of such a singular course of imaginings as had surrounded her, in my eyes, with the illusions of romance. Perhaps, too, she saw the confusion in the opposite camp and gained courage from the discovery. At any rate she was the first to take the field.

Her conversation, however, was only on commonplace topics, and in an easy, well-bred style. I endeavoured to respond in the same manner; but I was strangely incompetent to the task. My ideas were frozen up; even words seemed to fail me. I was excessively vexed at myself, for I wished to be uncommonly elegant. I tried two or three times to turn a pretty thought, or to utter a fine sentiment; but it would come forth so trite, so forced, so mawkish, that I was ashamed of it. My very voice sounded discordantly, though I sought to modulate it into the softest tones. "The truth is," thought I to myself, "I cannot bring my mind down to the small talk necessary for young girls; it is too masculine and robust for the mincing measure of parlour gossip. I am a philosopher—and that accounts for it."

The entrance of Mrs Somerville at length gave me relief. I at once breathed freely, and felt a vast deal of confidence come over me. "This is strange," thought I, "that the appearance of another woman should revive my courage; that I should be a better match for two women than one. However, since it is so, I will take advantage of the circumstance, and let this young lady see that I am not so great a simpleton as she probably thinks me."

I accordingly took up the book of poetry which lay upon the sofa. It was Milton's *Paradise Lost*. Nothing could have been more fortunate; it afforded a fine scope for my favourite vein of grandiloquence. I went largely into a discussion of its merits, or rather an enthusiastic eulogy of them. My observations were addressed to Mrs Somerville, for I found I could talk to her with more ease than to her daughter. She appeared alive to the beauties of the poet, and disposed to meet me in the discussion; but it was not my object to hear her talk; it was to talk myself. I anticipated all she had to say, overpowered her with the copiousness of my ideas, and supported and illustrated them by long citations from the author.

While thus holding forth, I cast a side glance to see how Miss Somerville was affected. She had some embroidery stretched on a frame before her, but had paused in her labour, and was looking down as if lost in mute attention. I felt a glow of self-satisfaction, but I recollected, at the same time, with a kind of pique, the advantage she had enjoyed over me in our tête-à-tête. I determined to push my triumph, and accordingly kept on with redoubled ardour, until I had fairly exhausted my subject, or rather my thoughts.

I had scarce come to a full stop, when Miss Somerville raised her eyes from the work on which they had been fixed, and turning to her mother, observed: "I have been considering, mamma, whether to work these flowers plain, or in colours."

Had an ice-bolt shot to my heart, it could not have chilled me more effectually. "What a fool," thought I, "have I been making myself—squandering away fine thoughts, and fine language, upon a light mind, and an ignorant ear! This girl knows nothing of poetry. She has no soul, I fear, for its beauties. Can any one have real sensibility of heart, and not be alive to poetry! However, she is young; this part of her education has been neglected: there is time enough to remedy it. I will be her preceptor. I will kindle in her mind the sacred flame, and lead her through the fairy land of song. But after all, it is rather unfortunate that I should have fallen in love with a woman who knows nothing of poetry."

I passed a day not altogether satisfactory. I was a little disappointed that Miss Somerville did not show any poetical feeling. "I am afraid, after all," said I to myself, "she is light and girlish, and more fitted to pluck wild flowers, play on the flageolet, and romp with little dogs, than to converse with a man of my turn."

I believe, however, to tell the truth, I was more out of humour with myself. I thought I had made the worst first appearance that ever hero made, either in novel or fairy tale. I was out of all patience, when I called to mind my awkward attempts at ease and elegance in the tête-à-tête. And then my intolerable long lecture about poetry to catch the applause of a heedless auditor! But there I was not to blame. I had certainly been eloquent: it was her fault that the eloquence was wasted. To meditate upon the embroidery of a flower, when I was expatiating on the beauties of Milton! She might at least have admired the poetry, if she did not relish the manner in which it was delivered: though that was not despicable, for I had recited passages in my best style, which my mother and sisters had always considered equal to a play. "Oh, it is evident," thought I, "Miss

Somerville has very little soul!"

Such were my fancies and cogitations during the day, the greater part of which was spent in my chamber, for I was still languid. My evening was passed in the drawingroom, where I overlooked Miss Somerville's portfolio of sketches.

They were executed with great taste, and showed a nice observation of the peculiarities of nature. They were all her own, and free from those cunning tints and touches of the drawing-master, by which young ladies' drawings, like their heads, are dressed up for company. There was no garish and vulgar trick of colours, either; all was executed with singular truth and simplicity.

"And yet," thought I, "this little being, who has so pure an eye to take in, as in a limpid brook, all the graceful forms and magic tints of nature, has no soul for poetry!"

Mr Somerville, toward the latter part of the evening, observing my eye to wander occasionally to the harp, interpreted and met my wishes with his accustomed civility.

"Julia, my dear," said he, "Mr Mountjoy would like to hear a little music from your harp; let us hear, too, the sound of your voice."

Julia immediately complied, without any of that hesitation and difficulty, by which young ladies are apt to make company pay dear for bad music. She sang a sprightly strain, in a brilliant style, that came trilling playfully over the ear; and the bright eye and dimpling smile showed that her little heart danced with the song. Her pet canary bird, who hung close by, was wakened by the music, and burst forth into an emulating strain.

Julia smiled with a pretty air of defiance, and played louder.

After some time, the music changed, and ran into a plaintive strain, in a minor key. Then it was, that all the former witchery of her voice came over me; then it was that she seemed to sing from the heart and to the heart. Her fingers moved about the chords as if they scarcely touched them. Her whole manner and appearance changed; her eyes beamed with the softest expression; her countenance, her frame, all seemed subdued into tenderness. She rose from the harp, leaving it still vibrating with sweet sounds, and moved toward her father to bid him good night.

His eyes had been fixed on her intently, during her performance. As she came before him he parted her shining ringlets with both his hands, and looked down with the fondness of a father on her innocent face. The music seemed still lingering in its lineaments, and the action of her father brought a moist gleam in her eye. He kissed her fair forehead, after the French mode of parental caressing: "Good night, and God bless you," said he, "my good little girl!"

Julia tripped away, with a tear in her eye, a dimple in her cheek, and a light heart in her bosom. I thought it the prettiest picture of paternal and filial affection I had ever seen.

When I retired to bed, a new train of thoughts crowded into my brain. "After all," said I to myself, "it is clear this girl has a soul, though she was not moved by my eloquence. She has all the outward signs and evidences of poetic feeling. She paints well, and has an eye for nature. She is a fine musician, and enters into the very soul of song. What a pity that she knows nothing of poetry! But we will see what is to be done. I am irretrievably in love with her; what then am I to do? Come down to the level of her mind, or endeavour to raise her to some kind of intellectual equality with myself? That is the most generous course. She will look up to me as a benefactor. I shall become associated in her mind with the lofty thoughts and harmonious graces of poetry. She is apparently docile: beside, the difference of our ages will give me an ascendancy over her. She cannot be over sixteen years of age, and I am full turned of twenty." So, having built this most delectable of air-castles, I fell asleep.

The next morning I was quite a different being. I no longer felt fearful of stealing a glance at Julia; on the contrary, I contemplated her steadily, with the benignant eye of a benefactor. Shortly after breakfast I found myself alone with her, as I had on the preceding morning; but I felt nothing of the awkwardness of our previous tête-à-tête. I was elevated by the consciousness of my intellectual superiority, and should almost have felt a sentiment of pity for the ignorance of the lovely little being, if I had not felt also the assurance that I should be able to dispel it. "But it is time," thought I, "to open school."

Julia was occupied in arranging some music on her piano. I looked over two or three songs; they were Moore's Irish melodies.

"These are pretty things!" said I, flirting the leaves over lightly, and giving a slight shrug, by way of qualifying the opinion.

"Oh, I love them of all things," said Julia, "they're so touching!"

"Then you like them for the poetry," said I with an encouraging smile.

"Oh yes; she thought them charmingly written."

Now was my time. "Poetry," said I, assuming a didactic attitude and air, "poetry is one of the most pleasing studies that can occupy a youthful mind. It renders us susceptible of the gentle impulses of humanity, and cherishes a delicate perception of all that is virtuous and elevated in morals, and graceful and beautiful in physics. It—"

I was going on in a style that would have graced a professor of rhetoric, when I saw a light smile playing about Miss Somerville's mouth, and that she began to turn over the leaves of a music-book. I recollected her inattention to my discourse of the preceding morning. "There is no fixing her light mind," thought I, "by abstract theory; we will proceed practically." As it happened, the identical volume of Milton's *Paradise Lost* was lying at hand.

"Let me recommend to you, my young friend," said I, in one of those tones of persuasive admonition, which I had so often loved in Glencoe, "let me recommend to you this admirable poem; you will find in it sources of intellectual enjoyment far superior to those songs which have delighted you." Julia looked at the book, and then at me, with a whimsically dubious air. "Milton's *Paradise Lost*?" said she; "oh, I know the greater part of that by heart."

I had not expected to find my pupil so far advanced; however, the *Paradise Lost* is a kind of school-book, and its finest passages are given to young ladies as tasks.

"I find," said I to myself, "I must not treat her as so complete a novice; her inattention yesterday could not have proceeded from absolute ignorance, but merely from a want of poetic feeling. I'll try her again."

I now determined to dazzle her with my own erudition, and launched into a harangue that would have done honour to an institute. Pope, Spenser, Chaucer, and the old dramatic writers were all dipped into, with the excursive flight of a swallow. I did not confine myself to English poets, but gave a glance at the French and Italian schools; I passed over Ariosto in full wing, but paused on Tasso's *Jerusalem Delivered*. I dwelt on the character of Clorinda: "There's a character," said I, "that you will find well worthy a woman's study. It shows to what exalted heights of heroism the sex can rise, how gloriously they may share even in the stern concerns of men."

"For my part," said Julia, gently taking advantage of a pause, "for my part, I prefer the character of Sophronia."

I was thunderstruck. She then had read Tasso! This girl that I had been treating as an ignoramus in poetry! She proceeded with a slight glow of the cheek, summoned up perhaps by a casual glow of feeling:

"I do not admire those masculine heroines," said she, "who aim at the bold qualities of the opposite sex. Now Sophronia only exhibits the real qualities of a woman, wrought up to their highest excitement. She is modest, gentle, and retiring, as it becomes a woman to be; but she has all the strength of affection proper to a woman. She cannot fight for her people as Clorinda does, but she can offer herself up, and die to serve them. You may admire Clorinda, but you surely would be more apt to love Sophronia; at least," added she, suddenly appearing to recollect herself, and blushing at having launched into such a discussion, "at least that is what papa observed when we read the poem together."

"Indeed," said I, dryly, for I felt disconcerted and nettled at being unexpectedly lectured by my pupil;

"indeed, I do not exactly recollect the passage."

"Oh," said Julia, "I can repeat it to you;" and she immediately gave it in Italian.

Heavens and earth!—here was a situation! I knew no more of Italian than I did of the language of Psalmanazar. What a dilemma for a would-be-wise man to be placed in! I saw Julia waited for my opinion.

"In fact," said I, hesitating, "I—I do not exactly understand Italian."

"Oh," said Julia, with the utmost naïveté, "I have no doubt it is very beautiful in the translation."

I was glad to break up school, and get back to my chamber, full of the mortification which a wise man in love experiences on finding his mistress wiser than himself. "Translation! translation!" muttered I to myself, as I jerked the door shut behind me: "I am surprised my father has never had me instructed in the modern languages. They are all important. What is the use of Latin and Greek? No one speaks them; but here, the moment I make my appearance in the world, a little girl slaps Italian in my face. However, thank heaven, a language is easily learned. The moment I return home, I'll set about studying Italian; and to prevent future surprise, I will study Spanish and German at the same time; and if any young lady attempts to quote Italian upon me again, I'll bury her under a heap of High Dutch poetry!"

I felt now like some mighty chieftain, who has carried the war into a weak country, with full confidence of success, and been repulsed and obliged to draw off his forces from before some inconsiderable fortress.

"However," thought I, "I have as yet brought only my light artillery into action; we shall see what is to be done with my heavy ordnance. Julia is evidently well versed in poetry; but it is natural she should be so; it is allied to painting and music, and is congenial to the light graces of the female character. We will try her on graver themes."

I felt all my pride awakened; it even for a time swelled higher than my love. I was determined completely to establish my mental superiority, and subdue the intellect of this little being; it would then be time to sway the sceptre of gentle empire, and win the affections of her heart.

Accordingly, at dinner I again took the field, *en potence*. I now addressed myself to Mr Somerville, for I was about to enter upon topics in which a young girl like her could not be well versed. I led, or rather forced, the conversation into a vein of historical erudition, discussing several of the most prominent facts of ancient history, and accompanying them with sound, indisputable apothegms.

Mr Somerville listened to me with the air of a man receiving information. I was encouraged, and went on gloriously from theme to theme of school declamation. I sat with Marius on the ruins of Carthage; I defended the bridge with Horatius Cocles; thrust my hand into the flame with Marius Scaevola, and plunged with Curtius into the yawning gulf; I fought side by side with Leonidas, at the straits of Thermopylae; and was going full drive into the battle of Plataea, when my memory, which is the worst in the world, failed me, just as I wanted the name of the Lacedaemonian commander.

"Julia, my dear," said Mr Somerville, "perhaps you may recollect the name of which Mr Mountjoy is in quest?"

Julia coloured slightly. "I believe," said she, in a low

voice, "I believe it was Pausanias."

This unexpected sally, instead of re-enforcing me, threw my whole scheme of battle into confusion, and the Athenians remained unmolested in the field.

I am half inclined, since, to think Mr Somerville meant this as a sly hit at my schoolboy pedantry; but he was too well bred not to seek to relieve me from my mortification. "Oh!" said he, "Julia is our family book of reference for names, dates, and distances, and has an excellent memory for history and geography."

I now became desperate; as a last resource I turned to metaphysics. "If she is a philosopher in petticoats," thought I, "it is all over with me." Here, however, I had the field to myself. I gave chapter and verse of my tutor's lectures, heightened by all his poetical illustrations; I even went further than he had ever ventured, and plunged into such depths of metaphysics, that I was in danger of sticking in the mire at the bottom. Fortunately, I had auditors who apparently could not detect my flounderings. Neither Mr Somerville nor his daughter offered the least interruption.

When the ladies had retired, Mr Somerville sat some time with me; and as I was no longer anxious to astonish, I permitted myself to listen, and found that he was really agreeable. He was quite communicative, and from his conversation I was enabled to form a juster idea of his daughter's character, and the mode in which she had been brought up. Mr Somerville had mingled much with the world, and with what is termed fashionable society. He had experienced its cold elegancies and gay insincerities; its dissipation of the spirits and squanderings of the heart. Like many men of the world, though he had wandered too far from nature ever to return to it, yet he had the good taste and good feeling to look back fondly to its simple delights, and to determine that his child, if possible, should never leave them. He had superintended her education with scrupulous care, storing her mind with the graces of polite literature, and with such knowledge as would enable it to furnish its own amusement and occupation, and giving her all the accomplishments that sweeten and enliven the circle of domestic life. He had been particularly sedulous to exclude all fashionable affectations; all false sentiment, false sensibility, and false romance. "Whatever advantages she may possess," said he, "she is quite unconscious of them. She is a capricious little being, in everything but her affections; she is, however, free from art; simple, ingenuous, amiable, and, I thank God! happy."

Such was the eulogy of a fond father, delivered with a tenderness that touched me. I could not help making a casual inquiry, whether, among the graces of polite literature, he had included a slight tincture of metaphysics. He smiled, and told me he had not.

On the whole, when, as usual, that night, I summed up the day's observations on my pillow, I was not altogether dissatisfied. "Miss Somerville," said I, "loves poetry, and I like her the better for it. She has the advantage of me in Italian: agreed; what is it to know a variety of languages, but merely to have a variety of sounds to express the same idea? Original thought is the ore of the mind; language is but the accidental stamp and coinage by which it is put into circulation. If I can furnish an original idea, what care I how many languages she can translate it into? She may be able also to quote names, and dates, and latitudes better than I; but that is a mere effort of the memory. I admit she is more accurate in history and geography than I;

but then she knows nothing of metaphysics."

I had now sufficiently recovered to return home; yet I could not think of leaving Mr Somerville's without having a little further conversation with him on the subject of his daughter's education.

"This Mr Somerville," thought I, "is a very accomplished, elegant man; he has seen a good deal of the world, and, upon the whole, has profited by what he has seen. He is not without information, and, as far as he thinks, appears to think correctly; but after all, he is rather superficial, and does not think profoundly. He seems to take no delight in those metaphysical abstractions that are the proper aliment of masculine minds." I called to mind various occasions in which I had indulged largely in metaphysical discussions, but could recollect no instance where I had been able to draw him out. He had listened, it is true, with attention, and smiled as if in acquiescence, but had always appeared to avoid reply. Beside, I had made several sad blunders in the glow of eloquent declamation; but he had never interrupted me, to notice and correct them, as he would have done had he been versed in the theme.

"Now, it is really a great pity," resumed I, "that he should have the entire management of Miss Somerville's education. What a vast advantage it would be, if she could be put for a little time under the superintendence of Glencoe. He would throw some deeper shades of thought into her mind, which at present is all sunshine; not but that Mr Somerville has done very well, as far as he has gone; but then he has merely prepared the soil for the strong plants of useful knowledge. She is well versed in the leading facts of history, and the general course of belles-lettres," said I; "a little more philosophy would do wonders."

I accordingly took occasion to ask Mr Somerville for a few moments' conversation in his study, the morning I was to depart. When we were alone I opened the matter fully to him. I commenced with the warmest eulogium of Glencoe's powers of mind, and vast acquirements, and ascribed to him all my proficiency in the higher branches of knowledge. I begged, therefore, to recommend him as a friend calculated to direct the studies of Miss Somerville; to lead her mind, by degrees, to the contemplation of abstract principles, and to produce habits of philosophical analysis; "which," added I, gently smiling, "are not often cultivated by young ladies." I ventured to hint, in addition, that he would find Mr Glencoe a most valuable and interesting acquaintance for himself; one who would stimulate and evolve the powers of his mind; and who might open to him tracts of inquiry and speculation, to which perhaps he had hitherto been a stranger.

Mr Somerville listened with grave attention. When I had finished, he thanked me in the politest manner for the interest I took in the welfare of his daughter and himself. He observed that, as regarded himself, he was afraid he was too old to benefit by the instruction of Mr Glencoe, and that as to his daughter, he was afraid her mind was but little fitted for the study of metaphysics. "I do not wish," continued he, "to strain her intellects with subjects they cannot grasp, but to make her familiarly acquainted with those that are within the limits of her capacity. I do not pretend to prescribe the boundaries of female genius, and am far from indulging the vulgar opinion that women are unfitted by nature for the highest intellectual pursuits. I speak only with reference to my daughter's tastes and talents. She will never make a learned woman; nor, in truth, do I desire it; for such is the jealousy of our sex, as to mental as well as physical ascendancy, that a learned woman is not always the happiest. I do not wish my daughter to excite envy, nor to battle with the prejudices of the world; but to glide peaceably through life, on the good will and kind opinion of her friends. She has ample employment for her little head, in the course I have marked out for her; and is busy at present with some branches of natural history, calculated to awaken her perceptions to the beauties and wonders of nature, and to the inexhaustible volume of wisdom constantly spread open before her eyes. I consider that woman most likely to make an agreeable companion, who can draw topics of pleasing remark from every natural object; and most likely to be cheerful and contented, who is continually sensible of the order, the harmony, and the invariable beneficence, that reign throughout the beautiful world we inhabit."

"But," added he, smiling, "I am betraying myself into a lecture, instead of merely giving a reply to your kind offer. Permit me to take the liberty, in return, of inquiring a little about your own pursuits. You speak of having finished your education; but of course you have a line of private study and mental occupation marked out; for you must know the importance, both in point of interest and happiness, of keeping the mind employed. May I ask what system you observe in your intellectual exercises?"

"Oh, as to system," I observed, "I could never bring myself into any thing of the kind. I thought it best to let my genius take its own course, as it always acted the most vigorously when stimulated by inclination."

Mr Somerville shook his head. "This same genius," said he, "is a wild quality, that runs away with our most promising young men. It has become so much the fashion, too, to give it the reins, that it is now thought an animal of too noble and generous a nature to be brought to harness. But it is all a mistake. Nature never designed these high endowments to run riot through society, and throw the whole system into confusion. No, my dear sir, genius, unless it acts upon system, is very apt to be a useless quality to society; sometimes an injurious, and certainly a very uncomfortable one, to its possessor. I have had many opportunities of seeing the progress through life of young men who were accounted geniuses, and have found it too often end in early exhaustion and bitter disappointment; and have as often noticed that these effects might be traced to a total want of system. There were no habits of business, of steady purpose, and regular application, superinduced upon the mind; everything was left to chance and impulse, and native luxuriance, and everything of course ran to waste and wild entanglement. Excuse me if I am tedious on this point, for I feel solicitous to impress it upon you, being an error extremely prevalent in our country and one into which too many of our youth have fallen. I am happy, however, to observe the zeal which still appears to actuate you for the acquisition of knowledge, and augur every good from the elevated bent of your ambition. May I ask what has been your course of study for the last six months?"

Never was question more unluckily timed. For the last six months I had been absolutely buried in novels and romances.

Mr Somerville perceived that the question was embarrassing, and with his invariable good breeding, immediately resumed the conversation, without waiting for a reply. He took care, however, to turn it in such a way as to draw from me an account of the whole manner in which I had been educated, and the various currents of reading into which my mind had run. He then went on to discuss, briefly but impressively, the different branches of knowledge, most important to a young man in my situation; and to my surprise I found him a complete master of those studies on which I had supposed him ignorant, and on which I had been descanting so confidently.

He complimented me, however, very graciously, upon the progress I had made, but advised me for the present to turn my attention to the physical rather than the moral sciences. "These studies," said he, "store a man's mind with valuable facts, and at the same time repress selfconfidence, by letting him know how boundless are the realms of knowledge, and how little we can possibly know. Whereas metaphysical studies, though of an ingenious order of intellectual employment, are apt to bewilder some minds with vague speculations. They never know how far they have advanced, or what may be the correctness of their favourite theory. They render many of our young men verbose and declamatory, and prone to mislike the aberrations of their fancy for the inspirations of divine philosophy."

I could not but interrupt him, to assent to the truth of these remarks, and to say that it had been my lot, in the course of my limited experience, to encounter young men of the kind, who had overwhelmed me by their verbosity.

Mr Somerville smiled. "I trust," said he, kindly, "that you will guard against these errors. Avoid the eagerness with which a young man is apt to hurry into conversation, and to utter the crude and ill-digested notions which he has picked up in his recent studies. Be assured that extensive and accurate knowledge is the slow acquisition of a studious lifetime; that a young man, however pregnant his wit, and prompt his talent, can have mastered but the rudiments of learning, and, in a manner, attained the implements of study. Whatever may have been your past assiduity, you must be sensible that as yet you have but reached the threshold of true knowledge; but at the same time, you have the advantage that you are still very young, and have amply time to learn."

Here our conference ended. I walked out of the study, a very different being from what I was on entering it. I had gone in with the air of a professor about to deliver a lecture; I came out like a student who had failed in his examination, and been degraded in his class.

"Very young," and "on the threshold of knowledge"! This was extremely flattering, to one who had considered himself an accomplished scholar, and profound philosopher.

"It is singular," thought I; "there seems to have been a spell upon my faculties, ever since I have been in this house. I cerhinly have not been able to do myself justice. Whenever I have undertaken to advise, I have had the tables turned upon me. It must be that I am strange and diffident among people I am not accustomed to. I wish they could hear me talk at home!"

"After all," added I, on further reflection, "after all, there is a great deal of force in what Mr Somerville has said. Somehow or other, these men of the world do now and then hit upon remarks that would do credit to a philosopher. Some of his general observations came so home, that I almost thought they were meant for myself. His advice about adopting a system of study is very judicious. I will immediately put it in practice. My mind shall operate henceforward with the regularity of clockwork."

How far I succeeded in adopting this plan, how I fared in the further pursuit of knowledge, and how I succeeded in my suit to Julia Somerville, may afford matter for a further communication to the public, if this simple record of my early life is fortunate enough to excite any curiosity.

THE LEGEND OF SLEEPY HOLLOW

FOUND AMONG THE PAPERS OF
THE LATE DIEDRICH KNICKERBOCKER

A pleasing land of drowsy head it was,
Of dreams that wave before the half-shut eye;
And of gay castles in the clouds that pass,
For ever flushing round a summer sky.
CASTLE OF INDOLENCE

In the bosom of one of those spacious coves which indent the eastern shore of the Hudson, at that broad expansion of the river denominated by the ancient Dutch navigators the Tappan Zee, and where they always prudently shortened sail, and implored the protection of St Nicholas when they crossed, there lies a small market town or rural port, which by some is called Greensburgh, but which is more generally and properly known by the name of Tarry Town. This name was given, we are told, in former days, by the good housewives of the adjacent country, from the inveterate propensity of their husbands to linger about the village tavern on market days. Be that as it may, I do not vouch for the fact, but merely advert to it, for the sake of being precise and authentic. Not far from this village, perhaps about two miles, there is a little valley, or rather lap of land, among high hills, which is one of the quietest places in the whole world. A small brook glides through it, with just murmur enough to lull one to repose; and the occasional whistle of a quail or tapping of a woodpecker is almost the only sound that ever breaks in upon the uniform tranquillity.

I recollect that, when a stripling, my first exploit in squirrel shooting was in a grove of tall walnut trees that shades one side of the valley. I had wandered into it at noontime, when all nature is peculiarly quiet, and was startled by the roar of my own gun, as it broke the Sabbath stillness around, and was prolonged and reverberated by the angry echoes. If ever I should wish for a retreat, whither I might steal from the world and its distractions and dream quietly away the remnant of a troubled life, I know of none more promising than this little valley.

From the listless repose of the place, and the peculiar character of its inhabitants, who are descendants from the original Dutch settlers, this sequestered glen has long been known by the name of SLEEPY HOLLOW, and its rustic lads are called the Sleepy Hollow Boys throughout all the neighbouring country. A drowsy, dreamy influence seems to hang over the land, and to pervade the very atmosphere. Some say that the place was bewitched by a high German doctor during the early days of the settlement; others, that an old Indian chief, the prophet or wizard of his tribe, held his powwows there before the country was discovered by Master Hendrick Hudson. Certain it is, the place still continues under the sway of some witching power that holds a spell over the minds of the good people, causing them to walk in a continual reverie. They are given to all kinds of marvellous beliefs, are subject to trances and visions, and frequently see strange sights, and hear music and voices in the air. The whole neighbourhood abounds with local tales, haunted spots, and twilight superstitions; stars shoot and meteors glare oftener across the valley than in any other part of the country, and the nightmare, with her whole ninefold, seems to make it the favourite scene of her gambols.

The dominant spirit, however, that haunts this enchanted region and seems to be commander-in-chief of all the powers of the air is the apparition of a figure on horseback without a head. It is said by some to be the ghost of a Hessian trooper, whose head had been carried away by a cannon ball, in some nameless battle during the Revolutionary War, and who is ever and anon seen by the country folk, hurrying along in the gloom of night, as if on the wings of the wind. His haunts are not confined to the valley, but extend at times to the adjacent roads, and especially to the vicinity of a church at no great distance. Indeed, certain of the most authentic historians of those parts, who have been careful in collecting and collating the floating facts concerning this spectre, allege that the body of the trooper, having been buried in the churchyard, the ghost rides forth to the scene of battle in nightly quest of his head; and that the rushing speed with which he sometimes passes along the Hollow, like a midnight blast, is owing to his being belated, and in a hurry to get back to the churchyard before daybreak.

Such is the general purport of this legendary superstition, which has furnished materials for many a wild story in that region of shadows; and the spectre is known, at all the country firesides, by the name of the Headless Horseman of Sleepy Hollow.

It is remarkable that the visionary propensity I have mentioned is not confined to the native inhabitants of the valley, but is unconsciously imbibed by everyone who resides there for a time. However wide awake they may have been before they entered that sleepy region, they are sure, in a little time, to inhale the witching influence of the air, and begin to grow imaginative—to dream dreams and see apparitions.

I mention this peaceful spot with all possible laud; for it is in such little retired Dutch valleys, found here and there embosomed in the great State of New York, that population, manners, and customs remain fixed; while the great torrent of migration and improvement, which is making such incessant changes in other parts of this restless country, sweeps by them unobserved. They are like those little nooks of still water which border a rapid stream, where we may see the straw and bubble riding quietly at anchor, or slowly revolving in their mimic harbour, undisturbed by the rush of the passing current. Though many years have elapsed since I trod the drowsy shades of Sleepy Hollow, yet I question whether I should not still find the same trees and the same families vegetating in its sheltered bosom.

In this by-place of nature there abode, in a remote period of American history, that is to say, some thirty years since, a worthy wight of the name of Ichabod Crane, who sojoumed, or, as he expressed it, "tarried", in Sleepy Hollow, for the purpose of instructing the children of the vicinity. He was a native of Connecticut, a State which supplies the Union with pioneers for the mind as well as for the forest, and sends forth yearly its legions of frontier woodsmen and country schoolmasters. The cognomen of Crane was not inapplicable to his person. He was tall, but exceedingly lank, with narrow shoulders, long arms and legs, hands that dangled a mile out of his sleeves, feet that might have served for shovels, and his whole frame most loosely hung together. His head was small, and flat at top, with huge ears, large green glassy eyes, and a long snipe nose, so that it looked like a weathercock, perched upon his spindle neck, to tell which way the wind blew. To see him striding along the profile of a hill on a windy day, with his clothes bagging and fluttering about him, one might have mistaken him for the genius of famine descending upon the earth, or some scarecrow eloped from a cornfield.

His schoolhouse was a low building of one large room, rudely constructed of logs, the windows partly glazed, and partly patched with leaves of old copy-books. It was most ingeniously secured at vacant hours by a withe twisted in the handle of the door and stakes set against the window shutters, so that, though a thief might get in with perfect ease, he would find some embarrassment in getting out; an idea most probably borrowed by the architect, Yost Van Houten, from the mystery of an eel pot. The schoolhouse stood in a rather lonely but pleasant situation, just at the foot of a woody hill, with a brook running close by, and a formidable birch tree growing at one end of it. From hence the low murmur of his pupils' voices, conning over their lessons, might be heard in a drowsy summer's day, like the hum of a beehive, interrupted now and then by the authoritative voice of the master, in the tone of menace or command, or, peradventure, by the appalling sound of the birch, as he urged some tardy loiterer along the flowery path of knowledge. Truth to say, he was a conscientious man, and ever bore in mind the golden maxim, "Spare the rod and spoil the child." Ichabod Crane's scholars certainly were not spoiled.

I would not have it imagined, however, that he was

one of those cruel potentates of the school who joy in the smart of their subjects; on the contrary, he administered justice with discrimination rather than severity, taking the burthen off the backs of the weak, and laying it on those of the strong. Your mere puny stripling that winced at the least flourish of the rod was passed by with indulgence; but the claims of justice were satisfied by inflicting a double portion on some little, tough, wrongheaded, broad-skirted Dutch urchin, who sulked and swelled and grew dogged and sullen beneath the birch. All this he called "doing his duty by their parents"; and he never inflicted a chastisement without following it by the assurance, so consolatory to the smarting urchin, that "he would remember it, and thank him for it the longest day he had to live".

When school hours were over, he was even the companion and playmate of the larger boys; and on holiday afternoons would convoy some of the smaller ones home, who happened to have pretty sisters, or good housewives for mothers, noted for the comforts of the cupboard. Indeed it behooved him to keep on good terms with his pupils. The revenue arising from his school was small, and would have been scarcely sufficient to furnish him with daily bread, for he was a huge feeder, and though lank, had the dilating powers of an anaconda; but to help out his maintenance, he was, according to country custom in those parts, boarded and lodged at the houses of the farmers whose children he instructed. With these he lived successively a week at a time; thus going the rounds of the neighbourhood, with all his worldly effects tied up in a cotton handkerchief.

That all this might not be too onerous on the purses of his rustic patrons, who are apt to consider the costs of schooling a grievous burden and schoolmasters as mere drones, he had various ways of rendering himself born useful and agreeable. He assisted the farmers occasionally in the lighter labours of their farms, helped to make hay, mended the fences, took the horses to water, drove the cows from pasture, and cut wood for the winter fire. He laid aside, too, all the dominant dignity and absolute sway with which he lorded it in his little empire, the school, and became wonderfully gentle and ingratiating. He found favour in the eyes of the mothers by petting the children, particularly the youngest, and would sit with a child on one knee, and rock a cradle with his foot for whole hours together.

In addition to his other vocations, he was the singing master of the neighbourhood, and picked up many bright shillings by instructing the young folks in psalmody. It was a matter of no little vanity to him, on Sundays, to take his station in front of the church gallery, with a band of chosen singers; where, in his own mind, he completely carried away the palm from the parson. Certain it is, his voice resounded far above all the rest of the congregation; and there are peculiar quavers still to be heard in that church, and which may even be heard half a mile off, quite to the opposite side of the millpond, on a still Sunday morning, which are said to be legitimately descended from the nose of Ichabod Crane. Thus, by diverse little makeshifts in that ingenious way which is commonly denominated "by hook and by crook", the worthy pedagogue got on tolerably enough, and was thought, by all who understood nothing of the labour of headwork, to have a wonderfully easy life of it.

The schoolmaster is generally a man of some importance in the female circle of a rural neighbourhood, being considered a kind of idle gentlemanlike personage, of vastly superior taste and accomplishments to the rough country swains, and, indeed, inferior in learning only to the parson. His appearance, therefore, is apt to occasion some little stir at the tea table of a farmhouse, and the addition of a supernumerary dish of cakes or sweetmeats, or, peradventure, the parade of a silver teapot. Our man of letters, therefore, was peculiarly happy in the smiles of all the country damsels. How he would figure among them in the churchyard, between services on Sundays! gathering grapes for them from the wild vines that overrun the surrounding trees, reciting for their amusement all the epitaphs on the tombstones, or sauntering, with a whole bevy of them, along the banks of the adjacent millpond, while the more bashful country bumpkins hung sheepishly back, envying his superior elegance and address.

From his half-itinerant life, also, he was a kind of travelling gazette, carrying the whole budget of local gossip from house to house, so that his appearance was always greeted with satisfaction. He was, moreover, esteemed by the women as a man of great erudition, for he had read several books quite through, and was a perfect master of Cotton Mather's *History of New England Witchcraft*, in which, by the way, he most firmly and potently believed.

He was, in fact, an odd mixture of small shrewdness and simple credulity. His appetite for the marvellous, and his powers of digesting it, were equally extraordinary; and both had been increased by his residence in this spellbound region. No tale was too gross or monstrous for his capacious swallow. It was often his delight, after his school was dismissed in the afternoon, to stretch himself on the rich bed of clover, bordering the little brook that whimpered by his schoolhouse, and there con over old Mather's direful tales, until the gathering dusk of the evening made the printed page a mere mist before his eyes. Then, as he wended his way, by swamp and stream and awful woodland, to the farmhouse where he happened to be quartered, every sound of nature, at that witching hour, fluttered his excited imagination: the moan of the whippoorwill* from the hillside; the boding cry of the tree toad, that harbinger of storm; the dreary hooting of the screech owl, or the sudden rustling in the thicket of birds frightened from their roost. The fireflies, too, which sparkled most vividly in the darkest places, now and then startled him, as one of uncommon brightness would stream across his path; and if, by chance, a huge blockhead of a beetle came winging his blundering flight against him, the poor varlet was ready to give up the ghost, with the idea that he was struck with a witch's token. His only resource on such occasions, either to drown thought or drive away evil spirits, was to sing psalm tunes; and the good people of Sleepy Hollow, as they sat by their doors of an evening, were often filled with awe, at hearing his nasal melody, "in linked sweetness long drawn out", floating from the distant hill or along the dusky road.

Another of his sources of fearful pleasure was to pass long winter evenings with the old Dutch wives as they sat spinning by the fire, with a row of apples roasting and spluttering along the hearth, and listen to their

* The whippoorwill is a bird which is only heard at night. It receives its name from its note, which is thought to resemble those words.

marvellous tales of ghosts and goblins, and haunted fields, and haunted brooks, and haunted bridges, and haunted houses, and particularly of the headless horseman, or galloping Hessian of the Hollow, as they sometimes called him. He would delight them equally by his anecdotes of witchcraft, and of the direful omens and portentous sights and sounds in the air, which prevailed in the earlier times of Connecticut; and would frighten them woefully with speculations upon comets and shooting stars, and with the alarming fact that the world did absolutely turn around, and that they were half the time topsy-turvy!

But if there was a pleasure in all this, while snugly cuddling in the chimney corner of a chamber that was all a ruddy glow from the crackling wood fire, and where, of course, no spectre dared to show his face, it was dearly purchased by the terrors of his subsequent walk homewards. What fearful shapes and shadows beset his path amidst the dim and ghastly glare of a snowy night! With what wistful look did he eye every trembling ray of light streaming across the waste fields from some distant window! How often was he appalled by some shrub covered with snow, which, like a sheeted spectre, beset his very path! How often did he shrink with curdling awe at the sound of his own steps on the frosty crust beneath his feet; and dread to look over his shoulder, lest he should behold some uncouth being tramping close behind him! And how often was he thrown into complete dismay by some rushing blast, howling among the trees, in the idea that it was the Galloping Hessian on one of his nightly scourings!

All these, however, were mere terrors of the night, phantoms of the mind that walk in darkness; and though he had seen many spectres in his time, and been more than once beset by Satan in diverse shapes, in his lonely perambulations, yet daylight put an end to all these evils; and he would have passed a pleasant life of it, in despite of the devil and all his works, if his path had not been crossed by a being that causes more perplexity to mortal man than ghosts, goblins, and the whole race of witches put together, and that was—a woman.

Among the musical disciples who assembled, one evening in each week, to receive his instructions in psalmody, was Katrina Van Tassel, the daughter and only child of a substantial Dutch farmer. She was a blooming lass of fresh eighteen, plump as a partridge, ripe and melting and rosy-cheeked as one of her father's peaches, and universally famed, not merely for her beauty, but her vast expectations. She was withal a little of a coquette, as might be perceived even in her dress, which was a mixture of ancient and modern fashions, as most suited to set off her charms. She wore the ornaments of pure yellow gold, which her great-great-grandmother had brought over from Saardam; the tempting stomacher of the olden time; and withal a provokingly short petticoat, to display the prettiest foot and ankle in the country around.

Ichabod Crane had a soft and foolish heart toward the sex; and it is not to be wondered at that so tempting a morsel soon found favour in his eyes, more especially after he had visited her in her paternal mansion. Old Baltus Van Tassel was a perfect picture of a thriving, contented, liberal-hearted farmer. He seldom, it is true, sent either his eyes or his thoughts beyond the boundaries of his own farm; but within those everything was snug, happy, and well-conditioned. He was satisfied with his wealth, but not proud of it; and piqued himself upon the hearty abundance, rather than the style in which he lived. His stronghold was situated on the banks of the Hudson, in one of those green, sheltered, fertile nooks, in which the Dutch farmers are so fond of nestling. A great elm tree spread its broad branches over it, at the foot of which bubbled up a spring of the softest and sweetest water, in a little well, formed of a barrel, and then stole sparkling away through the grass, to a neighbouring brook that bubbled along among alders and dwarf willows. Hard by the farmhouse was a vast barn that might have served for a church; every window and crevice of which seemed bursting forth with the treasures of the farm; the flail was busily resounding within it from morning to night; swallows and martins skimmed twittering about the eaves; and rows of pigeons, some with one eye turned up, as if watching the weather, some with their heads under their wings, or buried in their bosoms, and others swelling, and cooing, and bowing about their dames, were enjoying the sunshine on the roof. Sleek unwieldy porkers were grunting in the repose and abundance of their pens; whence sallied forth, now and then, troops of sucking pigs, as if to snuff the air. A stately squadron of snowy geese were riding in an adjoining pond, convoying whole fleets of ducks; regiments of turkeys were gobbling through the farmyard, and guinea fowls fretting about it with their peevish discontented cry. Before the barn door strutted the gallant cock, that pattern of a husband, a warrior, and a fine gentleman, clapping his burnished wings and crowing in the pride and gladness of his heart—sometimes tearing up the earth with his feet, and then generously calling his ever-hungry family of wives and children to enjoy the rich morsel which he had discovered.

The pedagogue's mouth watered as he looked upon this sumptuous promise of luxurious winter fare. In his devouring mind's eye he pictured to himself every roasting pig running about with a pudding in his belly and an apple in his mouth; the pigeons were snugly put to bed in a comfortable pie, and tucked in with a coverlet of crust; the geese were swimming in their own gravy; and the ducks pairing cosily in dishes, like snug married couples, with a decent competency of onion sauce. In the porkers he saw carved out the future sleek side of bacon, and juicy relishing ham; not a turkey but he beheld daintily trussed up, with its gizzard under its wing, and, peradventure, a necklace of savoury sausages; and even bright chanticleer himself lay sprawling on his back, in a sidedish, with uplifted claws, as if craving that quarter which his chivalrous spirit disdained to ask while living.

As the enraptured Ichabod fancied all this, and as he rolled his great green eyes over the fat meadow lands, the rich fields of wheat, of rye, of buckwheat, and Indian corn, and the orchards burthened with ruddy fruit, which surrounded the warm tenement of Van Tassel, his heart yearned after the damsel who was to inherit these domains, and his imagination expanded with the idea how they might be readily turned into cash, and the money invested in immense tracts of wild land, and shingle palaces in the wilderness. Nay, his busy fancy already realized his hopes, and presented to him the blooming Katrina, with a whole family of children, mounted on the top of a wagon loaded with household trumpery, with pots and kettles dangling beneath; and he beheld himself bestriding a pacing mare, with a colt at her heels, setting out for Kentucky, Tennessee, or the Lord knows where.

When he entered the house the conquest of his heart was complete. It was one of those spacious farmhouses, with high-ridged, but lowly sloping roofs, built in the style handed down from the first Dutch settlers, the low projecting eaves forming a piazza along the front, capable of being closed up in bad weather. Under this were hung flails, harness, various utensils of husbandry, and nets for fishing in the neighbouring river. Benches were built along the sides for summer use; and a great spinning wheel at one end, and a churn at the other, showed the various uses to which this important porch might be devoted. From this piazza the wondering Ichabod entered the hall, which formed the centre of the mansion and the place of usual residence. Here, rows of resplendent pewter, ranged on a long dresser, dazzled his eyes. In one corner stood a huge bag of wool ready to be spun; in another a quantity of linsey-woolsey just from the loom; ears of Indian corn and strings of dried apples and peaches hung in gay festoons along the walls, mingled with the gaud of red peppers; and a door left ajar gave him a peep into the best parlour, where the claw-footed chairs and dark mahogany tables shone like mirrors; and irons, with their accompanying shovel and tongs, glistened from their covert of asparagus tops; mock oranges and conch shells decorated the mantelpiece; strings of various coloured birds' eggs were suspended above it; a great ostrich egg was hung from the centre of the room, and a corner cupboard, knowingly left open, displayed immense treasures of old silver and well-mended china.

From the moment Ichabod laid his eyes upon these regions of delight, the peace of his mind was at an end, and his only study was how to gain the affections of the peerless daughter of Van Tassel. In this enterprise, however, he had more real difficulties than generally fell to the lot of a knight-errant of yore, who seldom had anything but giants, enchanters, fiery dragons, and such like easily conquered adversaries to contend with; and had to make his way merely through gates of iron and brass, and walls of adamant, to the castle keep, where the lady of his heart was confined; all which he achieved as easily as a man would carve his way to the centre of a Christmas pie; and then the lady gave him her hand as a matter of course. Ichabod, on the contrary, had to win his way to the heart of a country coquette, beset with a labyrinth of whims and caprices, which were forever presenting new difficulties and impediments; and he had to encounter a host of fearful adversaries of real flesh and blood, the numerous rustic admirers, who beset every portal to her heart, keeping a watchful and angry eye upon each other, but ready to fly out in the common cause against any new competitor.

Among these the most formidable was a burly, roaring, roystering blade, of the name of Abraham, or, according to the Dutch abbreviation, Brom Van Brunt, the hero of the country round, which rang with his feats of strength and hardihood. He was broad-shouldered and double jointed, with short curly black hair, and a bluff but not unpleasant countenance, having a mingled air of fun and arrogance. From his Herculean frame and great powers of limb, he had received the nickname of BROM BONES, by which he was universally known. He was famed for great knowledge and skill in horsemanship, being as dexterous on horseback as a Tartar. He was foremost at all races and cockfights; and, with the ascendency which bodily strength acquires in rustic life, was the umpire in all disputes, setting his hat on one side and giving his decisions with an air and tone admitting of no gainsay or appeal. He was always ready for either a fight or a frolic; but had more mischief than ill will in his composition, and, with all his overbearing roughness, there was a strong dash of waggish good humour at bottom. He had three or four boon companions, who regarded him as their model and at the head of whom he scoured the country, attending every scene of feud or merriment for miles around. In cold weather he was distinguished by a fur cap, surmounted with a flaunting fox's tail; and when the folks at a country gathering descried this well-known crest at a distance, whisking about among a squad of hard riders, they always stood by for a squall. Sometimes his crew would be heard dashing along past the farmhouses at midnight, with whoop and halloo, like a troop of Don Cossacks; and the old dames, startled out of their sleep, would listen for a moment till the hurry-scurry had clattered by, and then exclaim, "Ay, there goes Brom Bones and his gang!" The neighbours looked upon him with a mixture of awe, admiration, and good will and when any madcap prank or rustic brawl occurred in the vicinity, always shook their heads and warranted Brom Bones was at the bottom of it.

This rantipole hero had for some time singled out the blooming Katrina for the object of his uncouth gallantries, and though his amorous toyings were something like the gentle caresses and endearments of a bear, yet it was whispered that she did not altogether discourage his hopes. Certain it is, his advances were signals for rival candidates to retire, who felt no inclination to cross a lion in his amours; insomuch, that when his horse was seen tied to Van Tassel's paling, on a Sunday night, a sure sign that his master was courting, or, as it is termed, "sparking", within, all other suitors passed by in despair, and carried the war into other quarters.

Such was the formidable rival with whom Ichabod Crane had to contend, and, considering all things, a stouter man than he would have shrunk from the competition, and a wiser man would have despaired. He had, however, a happy mixture of pliability and perseverance in his nature; he was in form and spirit like a supple jack—yielding, but tough; though he bent, he never broke; and though he bowed beneath the slightest pressure, yet, the moment it was away—jerk! he was as erect, and carried his head as high as ever.

To have taken the field openly against his rival would have been madness, for he was not a man to be thwarted in his amours. Ichabod, therefore, made his advances in a quiet and gently insinuating manner. Under cover of his character of singing master, he made frequent visits to the farmhouse; not that he had anything to apprehend from the meddlesome interference of parents, which is so often a stumbling block in the path of lovers. Balt Van Tassel was an easy indulgent soul; he loved his daughter better even than his pipe, and, like a reasonable man and an excellent father, let her have her way in everything. His notable wife, too, had enough to do to attend to her housekeeping and manage her poultry; for, as she sagely observed, ducks and geese are foolish things, and must be looked after, but girls can take care of themselves. Thus while the busy dame bustled about the house, or plied her spinning wheel at one end of the piazza, honest Balt would sit smoking his evening pipe at the other, watching the achievements of a little wooden warrior, who, armed with a sword in each hand, was most valiantly fighting the wind on the pinnacle of the barn. In the meantime, Ichabod would carry on his suit with the daughter by the side of the spring under the great elm, or sauntering along in the twilight, that hour so favourable to the lover's eloquence.

I profess not to know how women's hearts are wooed and won. To me they have always been matters of riddle and admiration. Some seem to have but one vulnerable point, or door of access, while others have a thousand avenues, and may be captured in a thousand different ways. It is a great triumph of skill to gain the former, but a still greater proof of generalship to maintain possession of the latter, for the man must battle for his fortress at every door and window. He who wins a thousand common hearts is therefore entitled to some renown; but he who keeps undisputed sway over the heart of a coquette is indeed a hero. Certain it is, this was not the case with the redoubtable Brom Bones; and from the moment Ichabod Crane made his advances, the interests of the former evidently declined; his horse was no longer seen tied at the palings on Sunday nights, and a deadly feud gradually arose between him and the preceptor of Sleepy Hollow.

Brom, who had a degree of rough chivalry in his nature, would fain have carried matters to open warfare, and have settled their pretensions to the lady according to the mode of those most concise and simple reasoners, the knights-errant of yore—by single combat; but Ichabod was too conscious of the superior might of his adversary to enter the lists against him. He had overheard a boast of Bones that he would "double the schoolmaster up, and lay him on a shelf of his own schoolhouse", and he was too wary to give him an opportunity. There was something extremely provoking in this obstinately pacific system; it left Brom no alternative but to draw upon the funds of rustic-waggery in his disposition, and to play off boorish practical jokes upon his rival. Ichabod became the object of whimsical persecution to Bones and his gang of rough riders. They harried his hitherto peaceful domains; smoked out his singing school by stopping up the chimney; broke into the schoolhouse at night, in spite of its formidable fastenings of withe and window stakes, and turned everything topsy-turvy, so that the poor schoolmaster began to think all the witches in the country held their meetings there. But what was still more annoying, Brom took all opportunities of turning him into ridicule in presence of his mistress, and had a scoundrel dog whom he taught to whine in the most ludicrous manner, and introduced as a rival of Ichabod's to instruct her in psalmody.

In this way matters went on for some time, without producing any material effect on the relative situation of the contending powers. On a fine autumnal afternoon, Ichabod, in pensive mood, sat enthroned on the lofty stool whence he usually watched all the concerns of his little literary realm. In his hand he swayed a ferule, that sceptre of despotic power; the birch of justice reposed on three nails, behind the throne, a constant terror to evildoers; while on the desk before him might be seen sundry contraband articles and prohibited weapons, detected upon the persons of idle urchins, such as halfmunched apples, popguns, whirligigs, fly cages, and whole legions of rampant little paper gamecocks. Apparently there had been some appalling act of justice recently inflicted, for his scholars were all busily intent upon their books, or slyly whispering behind them with one eye kept upon the master; and a kind of buzzing stillness reigned throughout the schoolroom. It was suddenly interrupted by the appearance of a Negro, in tow-cloth jacket and trousers, a round-crowned fragment of a hat, like the cap of Mercury, and mounted on the back of a ragged, wild, half-broken colt, which he managed with a rope by way of halter. He came clattering up to the school door with an invitation to Ichabod to attend a merrymaking or "quilting frolic" to be held that evening at Mynheer Van Tassel's; and having delivered his message he dashed over the brook and was seen scampering away up the hollow, full of the importance and hurry of his mission.

All was now bustle and hubbub in the late quiet schoolroom. The scholars were hurried through their lessons, without stopping at trifles; those who were nimble skipped over half with impunity, and those who were tardy had a smart application now and then in the rear to quicken their speed or help them over a tall word. Books were flung aside without being put away on the shelves, inkstands were overturned, benches thrown down, and the whole school was turned loose an hour before the usual time, bursting forth like a legion of young imps, yelping and racketing about the green, in joy at their early emancipation.

The gallant Ichabod now spent at least an extra half hour at his toilet, brushing and furbishing up his best and indeed only suit of rusty black, and arranging his looks by a bit of broken looking glass that hung up in the schoolhouse. That he might make his appearance before his mistress in the true style of a cavalier he borrowed a horse from the farmer with whom he was domiciliated, a choleric old Dutchman of the name of

Hans Van Ripper, and, thus gallantly mounted, issued forth, like a knight-errant in quest of adventures. But it is meet I should, in the true spirit of romantic story, give some account of the looks and equipments of my hero and his steed. The animal he bestrode was a broken-down plough horse that had outlived almost everything but his viciousness. He was gaunt and shagged, with a ewe neck and a head like a hammer; his rusty mane and tail were tangled and knotted with burrs; one eye had lost its pupil and was glaring and spectral, but the other had the gleam of a genuine devil in it. Still he must have had fire and mettle in his day, if we may judge from the name he bore of Gunpowder. He had, in fact, been a favourite steed of his master's, the choleric Van Ripper, who was a furious rider, and had infused, very probably, some of his own spirit into the animal, for, old and broken-down as he looked, there was more of the lurking evil in him than in any young filly in the country.

Ichabod was a suitable figure for such a steed. He rode with short stirrups, which brought his knees nearly up to the pommel of the saddle; his sharp elbows stuck out like grasshoppers'; he carried his whip perpendicularly in his hand, like a sceptre, and, as his horse jogged on, the motion of his arms was not unlike the flapping of a pair of wings. A small wool hat rested on the top of his nose, for so his scanty strip of forehead might be called; and the skirts of his black coat fluttered out almost to the horse's tail. Such was the appearance of Ichabod and his steed, as they shambled out of the gate of Hans Van Ripper, and it was altogether such an apparition as is seldom to be met with in broad daylight.

It was, as I have said, a fine autumnal day, the sky

was clear and serene, and nature wore that rich and golden livery which we always associate with the idea of abundance. The forests had put on their sober brown and yellow, while some trees of the tenderer kind had been nipped by the frosts into brilliant dyes of orange, purple, and scarlet. Streaming files of wild ducks began to make their appearance high in the air; the bark of the squirrel might be heard from the groves of beech and hickory nuts, and the pensive whistle of the quail at intervals from the neighbouring stubble field.

The small birds were taking their farewell banquets. In the fullness of their revelry, they fluttered, chirping and frolicking, from bush to bush, and tree to tree, capricious from the very profusion and variety around them. There was the honest cock robin, the favourite game of stripling sportsmen, with its loud querulous note; and the twittering blackbirds flying in sable clouds; and the golden-winged woodpecker, with his crimson crest, his broad black gorget, and splendid plumage; and the cedar bird, with its red-tipped wings and yellow-tipped tail, and its little monteiro cap of feathers; and the blue jay, that noisy coxcomb, in his gay light-blue coat and white underclothes; screaming and chattering, nodding and bobbing and bowing, and pretending to be on good terms with every songster of the grove.

As Ichabod jogged slowly on his way, his eye, ever open to every symptom of culinary abundance, ranged with delight over the treasures of jolly autumn. On all sides he beheld vast store of apples, some hanging in oppressive opulence on the trees, some gathered into baskets and barrels for the market, others heaped up in rich piles for the cider press. Farther on he beheld great fields of Indian corn, with its golden ears peeping from their leafy coverts and holding out the promise of cakes and hasty pudding; and the yellow pumpkins lying beneath them, turning up their fair round bellies to the sun, and giving ample prospects of the most luxurious of pies; and anon he passed the fragrant buckwheat fields, breathing the odour of the beehive, and as he beheld them, soft anticipations stole over his mind of dainty slapjacks, well buttered and garnished with honey or treacle, by the delicate little dimpled hand of Katrina Van Tassel.

Thus feeding his mind with many sweet thoughts and "sugared suppositions", he journeyed along the sides of a range of hills which look out upon some of the goodliest scenes of the mighty Hudson. The sun gradually wheeled his broad disc down into the west. The wide bosom of the Tappan Zee lay motionless and glassy, excepting that here and there a gentle undulation waved and prolonged the blue shadow of the distant mountain. A few amber clouds floated in the sky, without a breath of air to move them. The horizon was of a fine golden tint, changing gradually into a pure apple green, and from that into the deep blue of the mid-heaven. A slanting ray lingered on the woody crests of the precipices that overhung some parts of the river, giving greater depth to the dark-grey and purple of their rocky sides. A sloop was loitering in the distance, dropping slowly down with the tide, her sail hanging uselessly against the mast; and as the reflection of the sky gleamed along the still water, it seemed as if the vessel was suspended in the air.

It was toward evening that Ichabod arrived at the castle of the Heer Van Tassel, which he found thronged with the pride and flower of the adjacent country. Old farmers, a spare leathern-faced race, in homespun coats and breeches, blue stockings, huge shoes, and magnificent pewter buckles. Their brisk withered little dames, in close-crimped caps, long-waisted short gowns, homespun petticoats, with scissors and pincushions and gay calico pockets hanging on the outside. Buxom lasses, almost as antiquated as their mothers, excepting where a straw hat, a fine ribbon, or perhaps a white frock gave symptoms of city innovation. The sons, in short square-skirted coats with rows of stupendous brass buttons, and their hair generally queued in the fashion of the times, especially if they could procure an eel skin for the purpose, it being esteemed throughout the country as a potent nourisher and strengthener of the hair.

Brom Bones, however, was the hero of the scene, having come to the gathering on his favourite steed Daredevil, creature, like himself, full of mettle and mischief, and which no one but himself could manage. He was, in fact, noted for preferring vicious animals, given to all kinds of tricks, which kept the rider in constant risk of his neck, for he held a tractable well-broken horse as unworthy of a lad of spirit.

Fain would I pause to dwell upon the world of charms that burst upon the enraptured gaze of my hero as he entered the state parlour of Van Tassel's mansion. Not those of the bevy of buxom lasses, with their luxurious display of red and white, but the ample charms of a genuine Dutch country tea table, in the sumptuous time of autumn. Such heaped-up platters of cakes of various and almost indescribable kinds, known only to experienced Dutch housewives! There was the doughty doughnut, the tenderer oly koek, and the crisp and crumbling cruller; sweet cakes and short-cakes, ginger cakes and honey cakes, and the whole family of cakes. And then there were apple pies and peach pies and pumpkin pies; besides slices of ham and smoked beef; and moreover delectable dishes of preserved plums, and peaches, and pears, and quinces; not to mention broiled shad and roasted chickens; together with bowls of milk and cream, all mingled higgledy-piggledy, pretty much as I have enumerated them, with the motherly teapot sending up its clouds of vapour from the midst—Heaven bless the mark! I want breath and time to discuss this banquet as it deserves, and am too eager to get on with my story. Happily, Ichabod Crane was not in so great a hurry as his historian, but did ample justice to every dainty.

He was a kind and thankful creature whose heart dilated in proportion as his skin was filled with good cheer, and whose spirits rose with eating as some men's do with drink. He could not help, too, rolling his large eyes around him as he ate, and chuckling with the possibility that he might one day be lord of all this scene of almost unimaginable luxury and splendour. Then, he thought, how soon he'd turn his back upon the old schoolhouse; snap his fingers in the face of Hans Van Ripper, and every other niggardly patron, and kick any itinerant pedagogue out of doors that should dare to call him comrade!

Old Baltus Van Tassel moved about among his guests with a face dilated with content and good humour, round and jolly as the harvest moon. His hospitable attentions were brief, but expressive, being confined to a shake of the hand, a slap on the shoulder, a loud laugh, and a pressing invitation to "fall to, and help themselves".

And now the sound of the music from the common room, or hall, summoned to the dance. The musician was an old grey-headed Negro, who had been the itinerant orchestra of the neighbourhood for more than half a century. His instrument was as old and battered as himself. The greater part of the time he scraped on two or three strings, accompanying every movement of the bow with a motion of the head; bowing almost to the ground and stamping with his foot whenever a fresh couple were to start.

Ichabod prided himself upon his dancing as much as upon his vocal powers. Not a limb, not a fibre about him was idle; and to have seen his loosely hung frame in full motion, and clattering about the room, you would have thought Saint Vitus himself, that blessed patron of the dance, was figuring before you in person. He was the admiration of all the Negroes, who, having gathered, of all ages and sizes, from the farm and the neighbourhood, stood forming a pyramid of faces at every door and window, gazing with delight at the scene. How could the flogger of urchins be otherwise than animated and joyous? The lady of his heart was his partner in the dance, and smiling graciously in reply to all his amorous oglings, while Brom Bones, sorely smitten with love and jealousy, sat brooding by himself in one corner.

When the dance was at an end, Ichabod was attracted to a knot of the sager folks, who, with old Van Tassel, sat smoking at one end of the piazza, gossiping over former times, and drawing out long stories about the war.

This neighbourhood, at the time of which I am speaking, was one of those highly favoured places which abound with chronicle and great men. The British and American line had run near it during the war; it had, therefore, been the scene of marauding, and infested with refugees, cowboys, and all kinds of border chivalry. Just sufficient time had elapsed to enable each storyteller to dress up his tale with a little becoming fiction, and, in the indistinctness of his recollection, to make himself the hero of every exploit.

There was the story of Doffue Martling, a large bluebearded Dutchman, who had nearly taken a British frigate with an old iron nine-pounder from a mud breastwork, only that his gun burst at the sixth discharge. And there was an old gentleman who shall be nameless, being too rich a mynheer to be lightly mentioned, who, in the Battle of White Plains, being an excellent master of defence, parried a musket ball with a small sword, insomuch that he absolutely felt it whizz around the blade and glance off at the hilt, in proof of which he was ready at any time to show the sword, with the hilt a little bent. There were several more that had been equally great in the field, not one of whom but was persuaded that he had a considerable hand in bringing the war to a happy termination.

But all these were nothing to the tales of ghosts and apparitions that succeeded. The neighbourhood is rich in legendary treasures of the kind. Local tales and superstitions thrive best in these sheltered long-settled retreats, but are trampled under foot by the shifting throng that forms the population of most of our country places. Besides, there is no encouragement for ghosts in most of our villages, for they have scarcely had time to finish their first nap and turn themselves in their graves before their surviving friends have travelled away from the neighbourhood; so that when they turn out at night to walk their rounds they have no acquaintance left to call upon. This is perhaps the reason why we so seldom hear of ghosts except in our long-established Dutch communities.

The immediate cause, however, of the prevalence of supernatural stories in these parts was doubtless, owing to the vicinity of Sleepy Hollow. There was a contagion in the very air that blew from that haunted region; it breathed forth an atmosphere of dreams and fancies infecting all the land. Several of the Sleepy Hollow people were present at Van Tassel's, and, as usual, were doling out their wild and wonderful legends. Many dismal tales were told about funeral trains, and mourning cries and wailings heard and seen about the great tree where the unfortunate Major André was taken, and which stood in the neighbourhood. Some mention was made also of the woman in white that haunted the dark glen at Raven Rock, and was often heard to shriek on winter nights before a storm, having perished there in the snow. The chief part of the stories, however, turned upon the favourite spectre of Sleepy Hollow, the headless horseman, who had been heard several times of late, patrolling the country, and, it was said, tethered his horse nightly among the graves in the churchyard.

The sequestered situation of this church seems always to have made it a favourite haunt of troubled spirits. It stands on a knoll, surrounded by locust trees and lofty elms, from among which its decent white-washed walls shine modestly forth, like Christian purity beaming through the shades of retirement. A gentle slope descends from it to a silver sheet of water, bordered by high trees, between which peeps may be caught at the blue hills of the Hudson. To look upon its grass-grown yard, where the sunbeams seem to sleep so quietly, one would think that there at least the dead might rest in peace. On one side of the church extends a wide woody dell, along which raves a large brook among broken rocks and trunks of fallen trees. Over a deep black part of the stream, not far from the church, was formerly thrown a wooden bridge; the road that led to it, and the bridge itself, were thickly shaded by overhanging trees, which cast a gloom about it, even in the daytime, but occasioned a fearful darkness at night. This was one of the favourite haunts of the headless horseman, and the place where he was most frequently encountered. The tale was told of old Brouwer, a most heretical disbeliever in ghosts, how he met the horseman returning from his foray into Sleepy Hollow, and was obliged to get up behind him; how they galloped over bush and brake, over hill and swamp, until they reached the bridge, when the horseman suddenly turned into a skeleton, threw old Brouwer into the brook, and sprang away over the treetops with a clap of thunder.

This story was immediately matched by a thrice marvellous adventure of Brom Bones, who made light of the galloping Hessian as an arrant jockey. He affirmed that, on returning one night from the neighbouring village of Sing Sing, he had been overtaken by this midnight trooper; that he had offered to race with him for a bowl of punch, and should have won it too, for Daredevil beat the goblin horse all hollow, but, just as they came to the church bridge, the Hessian bolted and vanished in a flash of fire.

All these tales, told in that drowsy undertone with which men talk in the dark, the countenances of the listeners only now and then receiving a casual gleam from the glare of a pipe, sank deep in the mind of Ichabod. He repaid them in kind with large extracts from his invaluable author, Cotton Mather, and added many marvellous events that had taken place in his native State of Connecticut, and fearful sights which he had seen in his nightly walks about Sleepy Hollow.

The revel now gradually broke up. The old farmers gathered together their families in their wagons, and were heard for some time rattling along the hollow roads and over the distant hills. Some of the damsels mounted on pillions behind their favourite swains, and their lighthearted laughter, mingling with the clatter of hoofs, echoed along the silent woodlands, sounding fainter and fainter until they gradually died away—and the late scene of noise and frolic was all silent and deserted. Ichabod only lingered behind, according to the custom of country lovers, to have a tête-à-tête with the heiress, fully convinced that he was now on the high road to success. What passed at this interview I will not pretend to say, for in fact I do not know. Something, however, I fear me, must have gone wrong, for he certainly sallied forth, after no very great interval, with an air quite desolate and chopfallen. Oh these women! these women! Could that girl have been playing off any of her coquettish tricks? Was her encouragement of the poor pedagogue all a mere sham to secure her conquest of his rival? Heaven only knows, not I! Let it suffice to say, Ichabod stole forth with the air of one who had been sacking a hen roost rather than a fair lady's heart. Without looking to the right or left to notice the scene of rural wealth, on which he had so often gloated, he went straight to the stable, and with several hearty cuffs and kicks roused his steed most uncourteously from the comfortable quarters in which he was soundly sleeping, dreaming of mountains of corn and oats, and whole valleys of timothy and clover.

It was the very witching time of night that Ichabod,

heavyhearted and crestfallen, pursued his travel homeward, along the sides of the lofty hills which rise above Tarry Town, and which he had traversed so cheerily in the afternoon. The hour was as dismal as himself. Far below him, the Tappan Zee spread its dusky and indistinct waste of waters, with here and there the tall mast of a sloop, riding quietly at anchor under the land. In the dead hush of midnight he could even hear the barking of the watchdog from the opposite shore of the Hudson, but it was so vague and faint as only to give an idea of his distance from this faithful companion of man. Now and then, too, the long-drawn crowing of a cock, accidentally awakened, would sound far, far off, from some farmhouse away among the hills—but it was like a dreaming sound in his ear. No signs of life occurred near him, but occasionally the melancholy chirp of a cricket, or perhaps the guttural twang of a bullfrog, from a neighbouring marsh, as if sleeping uncomfortably and turning suddenly in his bed.

All the stories of ghosts and goblins that he had heard in the afternoon now came crowding upon his recollection. The night grew darker and darker; the stars seemed to sink deeper in the sky, and driving clouds occasionally hid them from his sight. He had never felt so lonely and dismal. He was, moreover, approaching the very place where many of the scenes of the ghost stories had been laid. In the centre of the road stood an enormous tulip tree, which towered like a giant above all the other trees of the neighbourhood and formed a kind of landmark. Its limbs were gnarled and fantastic, large enough to form trunks for ordinary trees, twisting down almost to the earth and rising again into the air. It was connected with the tragical story of the unfortunate André, who had been taken prisoner hard by; and was universally known by the name of Major André's tree. The common people regarded it with a mixture of respect and superstition, partly out of sympathy for the fate of its ill-starred namesake, and partly from the tales of strange sights and doleful lamentations told concerning it.

As Ichabod approached this fearful tree, he began to whistle; he thought his whistle was answered—it was but a blast sweeping sharply through the dry branches. As he approached a little nearer, he thought he saw something white hanging in the midst of the tree—he paused and ceased whistling; but on looking more narrowly, perceived that it was a place where the tree had been scathed by lightning and the white wood laid bare. Suddenly he heard a groan—his teeth chattered and his knees smote against the saddle; it was but the rubbing of one huge bough upon another as they were swayed about by the breeze. He passed the tree in safety, but new perils lay before him.

About two hundred yards from the tree a small brook crossed the road and ran into a marshy and thickly wooded glen, known by the name of Wiley's swamp. A few rough logs, laid side by side, served for a bridge over this stream. On that side of the road where the brook entered the wood, a group of oaks and chestnuts, matted thick with wild grapevines, threw a cavernous gloom over it. To pass this bridge was the severest trial. It was at this identical spot that the unfortunate André was captured, and under the covert of those chestnuts and vines were the sturdy yeomen concealed who surprised him. This has ever since been considered a haunted stream, and fearful are the feelings of the schoolboy who has to pass it alone after dark.

As he approached the stream his heart began to

thump; he summoned up, however, all his resolution, gave his horse half a score of kicks in the ribs, and attempted to dash briskly across the bridge; but instead of starting forward, the perverse old animal made a lateral movement and ran broadside against the fence. Ichabod, whose fears increased with the delay, jerked the reins on the other side, and kicked lustily with the contrary foot; it was all in vain; his steed started, it is true, but it was only to plunge to the opposite side of the road into a thicket of brambles and alder bushes. The schoolmaster now bestowed both whip and heel upon the starveling ribs of old Gunpowder, who dashed forward, snuffling and snorting, but came to a stand just by the bridge with a suddenness that had nearly sent his rider sprawling over his head. Just at this moment a plashy tramp by the side of the bridge caught the sensitive ear of Ichabod. In the dark shadow of the grove, on the margin of the brook, he beheld something huge, misshapen, black and towering. It stirred not, but seemed gathered up in the gloom, like some gigantic monster ready to spring upon the traveller.

The hair of the affrighted pedagogue rose upon his head with terror. What was to be done? To turn and fly was now too late; and besides, what chance was there of escaping ghost or goblin, if such it was, which could ride upon the wings of the wind? Summoning up, therefore, a show of courage, he demanded in stammering accents—"Who are you?" He received no reply. He repeated his demand in a still more agitated voice. Still there was no answer. Once more he cudgelled the sides of the inflexible Gunpowder, and, shutting his eyes, broke forth with involuntary fervour into a psalm tune. Just then the shadowy object of alarm put itself in motion, and, with a scramble and a bound, stood at once in the middle of the road. Though the night was dark and dismal, yet the form of the unknown might now in some degree be ascertained. He appeared to be a horseman of large dimensions, and mounted on a black horse of powerful frame. He made no offer of molestation or sociability, but kept aloof on one side of the road, jogging along on the blind side of old Gunpowder, who had now got over his fright and waywardness.

Ichabod, who had no relish for this strange midnight companion, and bethought himself of the adventure of Brom Bones with the Galloping Hessian, now quickened his steed, in hopes of leaving him behind. The stranger, however, quickened his horse to an equal pace. Ichabod pulled up, and fell into a walk, thinking to lag behind the other did the same. His heart began to sink within him; he endeavoured to resume his psalm tune, but his parched tongue clove to the roof of his mouth, and he could not utter a stave. There was something in the moody and dogged silence of this pertinacious companion that was mysterious and appalling. It was soon fearfully accounted for. On mounting a rising ground, which brought the figure of his fellow-traveller in relief against the sky, gigantic in height, and muffled in a cloak, Ichabod was horror-struck on perceiving that he was headless! But his horror was still more increased on observing that the head, which should have rested on his shoulders, was carried before him on the pommel of the saddle. His terror rose to desperation; he rained a shower of kicks and blows upon Gunpowder, hoping, by a sudden movement, to give his companion the slip—but the spectre started full jump with him. Away then they dashed, through thick and thin, stones flying and sparks flashing at every bound. Ichabod's flimsy garments fluttered in the air as he stretched his long lank body away over his horse's head, in the eagerness of his flight.

They had now reached the road which turns off to Sleepy Hollow; but Gunpowder, who seemed possessed with a demon, instead of keeping up it, made an opposite turn, and plunged headlong downhill to the left. This road leads through a sandy hollow, shaded by trees for about a quarter of a mile, where it crosses the bridge famous in goblin story, and just beyond swells the green knoll on which stands the whitewashed church.

As yet the panic of the steed had given his unskilful rider an apparent advantage in the chase; but just as he had got halfway through the hollow, the girths of the saddle gave way, and he felt it slipping from under him. He seized it by the pommel and endeavoured to hold it firm, but in vain; and had just time to save himself by clasping old Gunpowder around the neck when the saddle fell to the earth, and he heard it trampled under foot by his pursuer. For a moment the terror of Hans Van Ripper's wrath passed across his mind—for it was his Sunday saddle; but this was no time for petty fears; the goblin was hard on his haunches, and (unskilful rider that he was!) he had much ado to maintain his seat, sometimes slipping on one side, sometimes on the other, and sometimes jolted on the high ridge of his horse's backbone with a violence that he verily feared would cleave him asunder.

An opening in the trees now cheered him with the hopes that the church bridge was at hand. The wavering reflection of a silver star in the bosom of the brook told him that he was not mistaken. He saw the walls of the church dimly glaring under the trees beyond. He recollected the place where Brom Bones's ghostly competitor had disappeared. "If I can but reach that bridge," thought Ichabod, "I am safe." Just then he heard the black steed panting and blowing close behind him; he even fancied that he felt his hot breath. Another convulsive kick in the ribs and old Gunpowder sprang upon the bridge; he thundered over the resounding planks; he gained the opposite side; and now Ichabod cast a look behind to see if his pursuer should vanish, according to rule, in a flash of fire and brimstone. Just then he saw the goblin rising in his stirrups, and in the very act of hurling his head at him. Ichabod endeavoured to dodge the horrible missile, but too late. It encountered his cranium with a tremendous crash—he was tumbled headlong into the dust, and Gunpowder, the black steed, and the goblin rider, passed by like a whirlwind.

The next morning the old horse was found without his saddle, and with the bridle under his feet, soberly cropping the grass at his master's gate. Ichabod did not make his appearance at breakfast—dinner hour came, but no Ichabod. The boys assembled at the schoolhouse, and strolled idly about the banks of the brook; but no schoolmaster. Hans Van Ripper now began to feel some uneasiness about the fate of poor Ichabod, and his saddle. An inquiry was set on foot, and after diligent investigation they came upon his traces. In one part of the road leading to the church was found the saddle trampled in the dirt; the tracks of horses' hoofs deeply dented in the road, and evidently at furious speed, were traced to the bridge, beyond which, on the bank of a broad part of the brook, where the water ran deep and black, was found the hat of the unfortunate Ichabod, and close beside it a shattered pumpkin.

The brook was searched, but the body of the schoolmaster was not to be discovered. Hans Van Ripper, as executor of his estate, examined the bundle which contained all his worldly effects. They consisted of two shirts and a half, two stocks for the neck, a pair or two of worsted stockings, an old pair of corduroy small clothes, a rusty razor, a book of psalm tunes full of dogs' ears, and a broken pitchpipe. As to the books and furniture of the schoolhouse, they belonged to the community, excepting Cotton Mather's *History of Witchcraft, a New England Almanac,* and a book of dreams and fortune-telling; in which last was a sheet of foolscap much scribbled and blotted in several fruitless attempts to make a copy of verses in honour of the heiress of Van Tassel. These magic books and the poetic scrawl were forthwith consigned to the flames by Hans Van Ripper, who from that time forward determined to send his children no more to school, observing that he never knew any good come of this same reading and writing. Whatever money the schoolmaster possessed, and he had received his quarter's pay but a day or two before, he must have had about his person at the time of his disappearance.

The mysterious event caused much speculation at the church on the following Sunday. Knots of gazers and gossips were collected in the churchyard, at the bridge, and at the spot where the hat and pumpkin had been found. The stories of Brouwer, of Bones, and a whole budget of others were called to mind; and when they had diligently considered them all and compared them with the symptoms of the present case, they shook their heads and came to the conclusion that Ichabod had been carried off by the galloping Hessian. As he was a bachelor and in nobody's debt, nobody troubled his head any more about him. The school was removed to a different quarter of the hollow, and another pedagogue reigned in his stead.

It is true an old farmer, who had been down to New York on a visit several years after, and from whom this account of the ghostly adventure was received, brought home the intelligence that Ichabod Crane was still alive; that he had left the neighbourhood, partly through fear of the goblin and Hans Van Ripper, and partly in mortification at having been suddenly dismissed by the heiress; that he had changed his quarters to a distant part of the country, had kept school and studied law at the same time, had been admitted to the bar, turned politician, electioneered, written for the newspapers, and finally had been made a justice of the Ten Pound Court. Brom Bones too, who shortly after his rival's disappearance conducted the blooming Katrina in triumph to the altar, was observed to look exceedingly knowing whenever the story of Ichabod was related, and always burst into a hearty laugh at the mention of the pumpkin, which led some to suspect that he knew more about the matter than he chose to tell.

The old country wives, however, who are the best judges of these matters, maintain to this day that Ichabod was spirited away by supernatural means; and it is a favourite story often told about the neighbourhood around the winter evening fire. The bridge became more than ever an object of superstitious awe, and that may be the reason why the road has been altered of late years, so as to approach the church by the border of the millpond. The schoolhouse, being deserted, soon fell to decay, and was reported to be haunted by the ghost of the unfortunate pedagogue; and the ploughboy, loitering homeward of a still summer evening, has often fancied his voice at a distance, chanting a melancholy psalm tune among the tranquil solitudes of Sleepy Hollow.

POSTSCRIPT

FOUND IN THE HANDWRITING OF MR KNICKERBOCKER

The preceding Tale is given, almost in the precise words in which I heard it related at a Corporation meeting of the ancient city of Manhattoes, at which were present many of its sagest and most illustrious burghers. The narrator was a pleasant, shabby, gentlemanly old fellow, in pepper-and-salt clothes, with a sadly humorous face, and one whom I strongly suspected of being poor—he made such efforts to be entertaining. When his story was concluded, there was much laughter and approbation, particularly from two or three deputy aldermen, who had been asleep a greater part of the time. There was, however, one tall, dry-looking old gentleman with beetling eyebrows, who maintained a grave and rather severe face throughout, now and then folding his arms, inclining his head, and looking down upon the floor, as if turning a doubt over in his mind. He was one of your wary men, who never laugh but upon good grounds—when they have reason and the law on their side. When the mirth of the rest of the company had subsided and silence was restored, he leaned one arm on the elbow of his chair, and, sticking the other akimbo, demanded, with a slight but exceedingly sage motion of the head, and contraction of the brow, what was the moral of the story, and what it went to prove?

The storyteller, who was just putting a glass of wine to his lips as a refreshment after his toils, paused for a moment, looked at his inquirer with an air of infinite deference, and, lowering the glass slowly to the table, observed that the story was intended most logically to prove:

"That there is no situation in life but has its advantages and pleasures—provided we will but take a joke as we find it.

"That, therefore, he that runs races with goblin troopers is likely to have rough riding of it.

"Ergo, for a country schoolmaster to be refused the hand of a Dutch heiress is a certain step to high preferment in the state."

The cautious old gentleman knit his brows tenfold closer after this explanation, being sorely puzzled by the ratiocination of the syllogism; while, methought, the one in pepper-and-salt eyed him with something of a triumphant leer. At length, he observed, that all this was very well, but still he thought the story a little on the extravagant—there were one or two points on which he had his doubts.

"Faith, sir," replied the storyteller, "as to that matter, I don't believe one-half of it myself."

D.K.

THE PRIDE OF THE VILLAGE

May no wolfe howle; no screech owle stir
A wing about thy sepulchre!
No boysterous winds or stormes come hither,
To starve or wither
Thy soft sweet earth! but, like a spring,
Love kept it ever flourishing.

HERRICK

In the course of an excursion through one of the remote counties of England, I had struck into one of those crossroads that lead through the more secluded parts of the country, and stopped one afternoon at a village, the situation of which was beautifully rural and retired. There was an air of primitive simplicity about its inhabitants, not to be found in the villages which lie on the great coach roads. I determined to pass the night there, and, having taken an early dinner, strolled out to enjoy the neighbouring scenery.

My ramble, as is usually the case with travellers, soon led me to the church, which stood at a little distance from the village. Indeed, it was an object of some curiosity, its old tower being completely overrun with ivy, so that only here and there a jutting buttress, an angle of grey wall, or a fantastically carved ornament peered through the verdant covering. It was a lovely evening. The early part of the day had been dark and showery, but in the afternoon it had cleared up; and though sullen clouds still hung overhead, yet there was a broad tract of golden sky in the west from which the setting sun gleamed through the dripping leaves, and lit up all nature with a melancholy smile. It seemed like the parting hour of a good Christian, smiling on the sins and sorrows of the world, and giving, in the serenity of his decline, an assurance that he will rise again in glory.

I had seated myself on a half-sunken tombstone, and was musing, as one is apt to do at this sober-thoughted hour, on past scenes and early friends—on those who were distant and those who were dead—and indulging in that kind of melancholy fancying which has in it something sweeter even than pleasure. Every now and then the stroke of a bell from the neighbouring tower fell on my ear; its tones were in unison with the scene, and, instead of jarring, chimed in with my feelings, and it was some time before I recollected that it must be tolling the knell of some new tenant of the tomb.

Presently I saw a funeral train moving across the village green; it wound slowly along a lane, was lost, and reappeared through the breaks of the hedges, until it passed the place where I was sitting. The pall was supported by young girls, dressed in white; and another, about the age of seventeen, walked before, bearing a chaplet of white flowers, a token that the deceased was a young and unmarried female. The corpse was followed by the parents. They were a venerable couple of the better order of peasantry. The father seemed to repress his feelings, but his fixed eye, contracted brow, and deeply-furrowed face showed the struggle that was passing within. His wife hung on his arm, and wept aloud with the convulsive bursts of a mother's sorrow.

I'followed the funeral into the church. The bier was placed in the centre aisle, and the chaplet of white flowers, with a pair of white gloves, were hung over the seat which the deceased had occupied.

Everyone knows the soul-subduing pathos of the funeral service, for who is so fortunate as never to have followed someone he has loved to the tomb? But when performed over the remains of innocence and beauty, thus laid low in the bloom of existence—what can be more affecting? At that simple but most solemn consignment of the body to the grave—"Earth to earth—ashes to ashes—dust to dust!"—the tears of the youthful companions of the deceased flowed unrestrained. The father still seemed to struggle with his feelings, and to comfort himself with the assurance that the dead are blessed which die in the Lord; but the mother only thought of her child as a flower of the field cut down and withered in the midst of its sweetness; she was like Rachel, "mourning over her children, and would not be comforted".

On returning to the inn, I learned the whole story of the deceased. It was a simple one, and such as has often been told. She had been the beauty and pride of the village. Her father had once been an opulent farmer, but was reduced in circumstances. This was an only child, and brought up entirely at home, in the simplicity of rural life. She had been the pupil of the village pastor, the favourite lamb of his little flock. The good man watched over her education with paternal care; it was limited, and suitable to the sphere in which she was to move, for he only sought to make her an ornament to her station in life, not to raise her above it. The tenderness and indulgence of her parents and the exemption from all ordinary occupations had fostered a natural grace and delicacy of character that accorded with the fragile loveliness of her form. She appeared like some tender plant of the garden, blooming accidentally amid the hardier natives of the fields.

The superiority of her charms was felt and acknowledged by her companions, but without envy, for it was surpassed by the unassuming gentleness and winning kindness of her manners. It might be truly said of her:

This is the prettiest low-born lass, that ever
Ran on the green-sward; nothing she does or seems,
But smacks of something greater than herself;
Too noble for this place.

The village was one of those sequestered spots which still retain some vestiges of old English customs. It had its rural festivals and holiday pastimes, and still kept up some faint observance of the once-popular rites of May. These, indeed, had been promoted by its present pastor, who was a lover of old customs and one of those simple Christians that think their mission fulfilled by promoting joy on earth and good will among mankind. Under his auspices the Maypole stood from year to year in the centre of the village green; on May Day it was decorated with garlands and streamers, and a queen or lady of the May was appointed, as in former times, to preside at the sports and distribute the prizes and rewards. The picturesque situation of the village and the fancifulness of its rustic fetes would often attract the notice of casual visitors. Among these, on one May Day, was a young officer whose regiment had been recently quartered in the neighbourhood. He was charmed with the native taste that pervaded this village pageant, but, above all, with the dawning loveliness of the queen of May. It was the village favourite, who was crowned with flowers, and blushing and smiling in all the beautiful confusion of girlish diffidence and delight. The artlessness of rural habits enabled him readily to make her acquaintance; he gradually won his way into her intimacy; and paid his court to her in that unthinking way in which young officers are too apt to trifle with rustic simplicity.

There was nothing in his advances to startle or alarm. He never even talked of love; but there are modes of making it more eloquent than language, and which convey it subtilely and irresistibly to the heart. The beam of the eye, the tone of voice, the thousand tendernesses which emanate from every word and look and action—these form the true eloquence of love, and can always be felt and understood, but never described. Can we wonder that they should readily win a heart, young, guileless, and susceptible? As to her, she loved almost unconsciously; she scarcely inquired what was the growing passion that was absorbing every thought and feeling, or what were to be its consequences. She, indeed, looked not to the future. When present, his looks and words occupied her whole attention; when absent, she thought but of what had passed at their recent interview. She would wander with him through the green lanes and rural scenes of the vicinity. He taught her to see new beauties in nature; he talked in the language of polite and cultivated life, and breathed into her ear the witcheries of romance and poetry.

Perhaps there could not have been a passion between the sexes more pure than this innocent girl's. The gallant figure of her youthful admirer and the splendour of his military attire might at first have charmed her eye; but it was not these that had captivated her heart. Her attachment had something in it of idolatry.

She looked up to him as to a being of a superior order. She felt in his society the enthusiasm of a mind naturally delicate and poetical, and now first awakened to a keen perception of the beautiful and grand. Of the sordid distinctions of rank and fortune she thought nothing; it was the difference of intellect, of demeanour, of manners from those of the rustic society to which she had been accustomed that elevated him in her opinion. She would listen to him with charmed ear and downcast look of mute delight, and her cheek would mantle with enthusiasm; or if ever she ventured a shy glance of timid admiration, it was as quickly withdrawn, and she would sigh and blush at the idea of her comparative unworthiness.

Her lover was equally impassioned; but his passion was mingled with feelings of a coarser nature. He had begun the connection in levity, for he had often heard his brother officers boast of their village conquests, and thought some triumph of the kind necessary to his reputation as a man of spirit. But he was too full of youthful fervour. His heart had not yet been rendered sufficiently cold and selfish by a wandering and a dissipated life; it caught fire from the very flame it sought to kindle, and before he was aware of the nature of his situation he became really in love.

What was he to do? There were the old obstacles which so incessantly occur in these heedless attachments. His rank in life—the prejudices of titled connections—his dependence upon a proud and unyielding father—all forbade him to think of matrimony: but when he looked down upon this innocent being, so tender and confiding, there was a purity in her manners, a blamelessness in her life, and a beseeching modesty in her looks that awed down every licentious feeling. In vain did he try to fortify himself by a thousand heartless examples of men of fashion, and to chill the glow of generous sentiment with that cold derisive levity with which he had heard them talk of female virtue; whenever he came into her presence, she was still surrounded by that mysterious but impassive charm of virgin purity in whose hallowed sphere no guilty thought can live.

The sudden arrival of orders for the regiment to repair to the continent completed the confusion of his mind. He remained for a short time in a state of the most painful irresolution; he hesitated to communicate the tidings until the day for marching was at hand, when he gave her the intelligence in the course of an evening ramble.

The idea of parting had never before occurred to her. It broke in at once upon her dream of felicity; she looked upon it as a sudden and insurmountable evil, and wept with the guileless simplicity of a child. He drew her to his bosom, and kissed the tears from her soft cheek; nor did he meet with a repulse, for there are moments of mingled sorrow and tenderness which hallow the caresses of affection. He was naturally impetuous; and the sight of beauty, apparently yielding in his arms, the confidence of his power over her, and the dread of losing her for ever, all conspired to overwhelm his better feelings—he ventured to propose that she should leave her home and be the companion of his fortunes.

He was quite a novice in seduction, and blushed and faltered at his own baseness; but so innocent of mind was his intended victim that she was at first at a loss to comprehend his meaning; and why she should leave her native village, and the humble roof of her parents.

When at last the nature of his proposal flashed upon her pure mind, the effect was withering. She did not weep—she did not break forth into reproach—she said not a word but she shrunk back aghast as from a viper; gave him a look of anguish that pierced to his very soul; and, clasping her hands in agony, fled, as if for refuge, to her father's cottage.

The officer retired, confounded, humiliated, and repentant. It is uncertain what might have been the result of the conflict of his feelings had not his thoughts been diverted by the bustle of departure. New scenes, new pleasures, and new companions soon dissipated his self-reproach and stifled his tenderness; yet, amidst the stir of camps, the revelries of garrisons, the array of armies, and even the din of battles, his thoughts would sometimes steal back to the scenes of rural quiet and village simplicity—the white cottage—the footpath along the silver brook and up the hawthorn hedge, and the little village maid loitering along it, leaning on his arm, and listening to him with eyes beaming with unconscious affection.

The shock which the poor girl had received, in the destruction of all her ideal world, had indeed been cruel. Faintings and hysterics had at first shaken her tender frame, and were succeeded by a settled and pining melancholy. She had beheld from her window the march of the departing troops. She had seen her faithless lover borne off, as if in triumph, amidst the sound of drum and trumpet and the pomp of arms. She strained a last aching gaze after him, as the morning sun glittered about his figure, and his plume waved in the breeze; he passed away like a bright vision from her sight, and left her all in darkness.

It would be trite to dwell on the particulars of her

after story. It was, like other tales of love, melancholy. She avoided society, and wandered out alone in the walks she had most frequented with her lover. She sought, like the stricken deer, to weep in silence and loneliness, and brood over the barbed sorrow that rankled in her soul. Sometimes she would be seen late of an evening sitting in the porch of the village church; and the milkmaids, returning from the fields, would now and then overhear her singing some plaintive ditty in the hawthorn walk. She became fervent in her devotions at church; and as the old people saw her approach, so wasted away, yet with a hectic bloom, and that hallowed air which melancholy diffuses around the form, they would make way for her, as for something spiritual, and, looking after her, would shake their heads in gloomy foreboding.

She felt a conviction that she was hastening to the tomb, but looked forward to it as a place of rest. The silver cord that had bound her to existence was loosed, and there seemed to be no more pleasure under the sun. If ever her gentle bosom had entertained resentment against her lover, it was extinguished. She was incapable of angry passions; and in a moment of saddened tenderness, she penned him a farewell letter. It was couched in the simplest language, but touching from its very simplicity. She told him that she was dying, and did not conceal from him that his conduct was the cause. She even depicted the sufferings which she had experienced, but concluded with saying that she could not die in peace until she had sent him her forgiveness and her blessing.

By degrees her strength declined, that she could no longer leave the cottage. She could only totter to the window, where, propped up in her chair, it was her enjoyment to sit all day and look out upon the landscape. Still she uttered no complaint, nor imparted to anyone the malady that was preying on her heart. She never even mentioned her lover's name, but would lay her head on her mother's bosom and weep in silence. Her poor parents hung, in mute anxiety, over this fading blossom of their hopes, still flattering themselves that it might again revive to freshness, and that the bright unearthly bloom which sometimes flushed her cheek might be the promise of returning health.

In this way she was seated between them one Sunday afternoon; her hands were clasped in theirs, the lattice was thrown open, and the soft air that stole in brought with it the fragrance of the clustering honeysuckle which her own hands had trained around the window.

Her father had just been reading a chapter in the Bible; it spoke of the vanity of worldly things, and of the joys of heaven; it seemed to have diffused comfort and serenity through her bosom. Her eye was fixed on the distant village church; the bell had tolled for the evening service; the last villager was lagging into the porch; and everything had sunk into that hallowed stillness peculiar to the day of rest. Her parents were gazing on her with yearning hearts. Sickness and sorrow, which pass so roughly over some faces, had given to hers the expression of a seraph's. A tear trembled in her soft blue eye. Was she thinking of her faithless lover? Or were her thoughts wandering to that distant churchyard, into whose bosom she might soon be gathered?

Suddenly the clang of hoofs was heard—a horseman galloped to the cottage—he dismounted before the window—the poor girl gave a faint exclamation, and sank back in her chair: it was her repentant lover! He rushed into the house and flew to clasp her to his bosom; but her wasted form—her deathlike countenance—so wan, yet so lovely in its desolation—smote him to the soul, and he threw himself in agony at her feet. She was too faint to rise—she attempted to extend her trembling hand—her lips moved as if she spoke, but no word was articulated—she looked down upon him with a smile of unutterable tenderness—and closed her eyes for ever!

Such are the particulars which I gathered of this village story. They are but scanty, and I am conscious have little novelty to recommend them. In the present rage also for strange incident and high-seasoned narrative they may appear trite and insignificant, but they interested me strongly at the time; and, taken in connection with the affecting ceremony which I had just witnessed, left a deeper impression on my mind than many circumstances of a more striking nature. I have passed through the place since, and visited the church again, from a better motive than mere curiosity. It was a wintry evening; the trees were stripped of their foliage; the churchyard looked naked and mournful, and the wind rustled coldly through the dry grass. Evergreens, however, had been planted about the grave of the village favourite, and osiers were bent over it to keep the turf uninjured.

The church door was open, and I stepped in. There hung the chaplet of flowers and the gloves, as on the day of the funeral; the flowers were withered, it is true, but care seemed to have been taken that no dust should soil their whiteness. I have seen many monuments where art has exhausted its powers to awaken the sympathy of the spectator, but I have met with none that spoke more touchingly to my heart than this simple but delicate memento of departed innocence.